TEMPTATION'S TRAP

"What are you trying to do?" he snarled, raking her with his eyes as he pushed her away from him.

"Nothing a wife wouldn't do with her husband," she answered without shame.

"Or a whore with any man," he returned cruelly.

"I am not a whore. And if you'd give me half a chance, I'd prove it to you."

"You may not have taken money for it, but that doesn't change what you are. And don't think I have any intention of becoming another one of your long list of conquests!"

"I'd never think of you like that," Libby said, trying not to laugh.

Cordell's eyes became mere slits. "And just how do you think of me?"

"I think of you as my husband. And all I want is to please you . . . dear."

"Please me? *Please* me? If you think you're going to trap me with this little act of yours, it isn't going to work! So I suggest, my dear wife, that from now on you just stay out of my way. If I need a woman, I know where to find one."

ECSTASY'S MASQUERADE

GWEN CLEARY

ZEBRA BOOKS
KENSINGTON PUBLISHING CORP.

ZEBRA BOOKS

are published by

Kensington Publishing Corp.
475 Park Avenue South
New York, NY 10016

First printing: August, 1989

Printed in the United States of America

For Abigail—

You will always hold a very special place in my heart.

Chapter One

March 27, 1876
St. Louis, Missouri

Please don't let him find me, Libby silently prayed, her breath still coming in ragged gasps from her frantic flight. She was hidden behind huge freight containers soon to be loaded aboard the *Benton,* moored nearby, and she drew her knees up to her chest, circled them with her arms, and buried her forehead in the folds of her skirt. Tears flowed onto the worn gray fabric, threatening to weaken her resolve to leave her failing mother behind with the man she'd come to despise.

All night, despite a constant drizzle, Libby—Elizabeth Marie Hollis—remained on the docks, clutching her threadbare carpetbag to her chest. The fear assailed her that her stepfather would bring the law and force her to return to his home, where his abuse had been increasing over the last year, ever since her mother had taken to bed. How much her life had changed from the safe and secure world of music and culture she had known as a little girl living with her mother and grandparents!

Her father had been struck down by a runaway wagon before he and her mother could be married. Libby and her mother had remained with her grandparents until their deaths ten years ago. Then her mother had married Reverend Elijah Ardsworth, a dour and fanatical preacher, who her mother had said would provide them a home.

Although he had arrived from Ohio an unknown with few possessions, the reverend quickly became a powerful and respected member of the religious community, able to incite even the most passive to join in his causes. Elijah Ardsworth was a giant of a man whose darker side was kept well buried until Libby began to blossom into a raven-haired young woman. What should have been a special time in her life had turned into a nightmare as Ardsworth became increasingly convinced that she was the devil's personal agent, sent to recruit men's souls for hell.

"Mere females are not put on this earth with such dark beauty and tempting curves unless it is to lure a man to do Satan's bidding, as did your very own mother," he lectured, his thick, bushy brows slanting ominously. Then he'd put his hands on Libby, claiming it would cleanse the evil from her soul. During the last year, although Libby had tried her hardest to be a good girl, he had begun to take the basest of liberties.

On Sundays, after particularly fiery sermons heated his blood, his abuse grew worse, until one day Libby had been called into his spartan study. She was forced to kneel before the big man while he placed his hairy hands upon her bowed head. "Pray for your eternal soul, you serpent's daughter of hell! Only through the healing powers of my touch can your salvation be redeemed," he chanted.

Near hysteria when his fingers began to make their lurid, bold descent, Libby grabbed his heavy, prized brass crucifix from the desk near her and blindly struck at him. Blood gushed from his temple and he crumpled to the floor.

A scream erupted from Libby's lips at the grisly sight, and she dropped the cross as if it were the devil's scepter. Dear Lord, she had never raised a hand, even in her own defense, to anyone before. For what seemed like eternity she stood over the body, afraid to move until he issued a pain-ridden groan.

Her heart pounding wildly, she ran to her room and snatched the carpetbag she had hidden beneath her narrow bed. She had secretly prepared to leave for months, but had never expected to do it under such dire circumstances.

She paused before her mother's open door, still trembling. The pale woman, who looked far older than her thirty-three years, studied Libby with dull, knowing eyes before giving her only child a weak smile. Libby hesitated and took a step into the room. Her mother slowly nodded her understanding that Libby must leave.

"You think these handbills'll bring any women to Fort Benton?" the burly dockworker asked his companion. The man placed the small stack atop the container which shielded Libby and set about his chores.

"Can't say as I'd venture a guess," the shorter of the two replied. "But it'd sure be nice to have a few more white women to set eyes on instead of little but them Injun and nigger whores what lives there now."

"You're darn tootin' it would."

Their deep voices trailed off as they toted their loads toward the steamer. Fascinated by the prospect of leaving St. Louis behind, Libby reached out and grabbed one of the handbills. Once she was settled back in her corner, she pushed her sodden locks from her face and scanned the neatly printed page:

WANTED:
GIRLS OF HIGH MORAL FIBER
BECOME *BENTON GIRLS*.
EMPLOYMENT AS A LAUNDRESS GUARANTEED.
EARN $40 PER MONTH.
GOOD, CLEAN, HONEST WORK
APPLY AT BENTON WASH HOUSE.
FORT BENTON, MONTANA TERRITORY.

Libby could hardly believe her good fortune! Someone far from St. Louis and Ardsworth's influence was looking for girls to do washing for forty dollars a month. From the time she was seven years old, Libby had toiled over

9

hot washtubs, helping her mother do laundry for the town's well-to-do citizens to earn money to send her to school. Ardsworth had refused to contribute a cent to Libby's schooling, warning that education fostered the growth of evil thoughts in the weaker sex; it was a frivolous expenditure he would never condone. Libby sighed: that was the only time she could remember her mother ever standing up against the man.

She chewed on her nails. The advertisement read "girls of high moral fiber." Could she apply for such a job after what Ardsworth had done to her? She felt a heavy burden of guilt . . . somehow she had to put it all behind her, although she wondered: if she'd been a better daughter, would he have touched her the way he had?

Carefully folding the sheet, Libby placed it in her skirt pocket and waited for an opportunity to sneak aboard the steamer. It was her best chance to escape what she was certain would be an unspeakable punishment if Ardsworth ever caught her. She made a silent vow: the Reverend Elijah Ardsworth was never going to put his vile hands on Elizabeth Marie Hollis again, no matter what she had to do!

Chapter Two

As the sun climbed above the skyline, Libby bunched her skirts and crept among the many barrels and crates until she was as close to the steamer's gangplank as she could get without risking discovery. Careful to remain hidden, she sat back on her heels and nibbled at her cuticles, watching, waiting.

When the men knocked off for a break, Libby saw her chance. With as much nerve as she could muster she straightened her back, smoothed her hair, and proudly walked on board as if she were one of the first-class passengers, despite her wet, bedraggled appearance. She quickly made her way past noisy livestock and the containers piled high along the main deck and sprinted up the stairs. Undetected, she selected a cabin on the upper deck and slipped inside to wait until the steamer was under way.

The cabin was decorated in a delicate rose brocade, designed for the utmost comfort in a confined space. Libby stepped around the room. She fingered the furnishings and delighted in the pleasing woods and fabrics. She hadn't been in the cabin long when outside the door she heard angry, hushed voices.

Katherine Rutcliff followed her father to her cabin door, dreading the argument she knew was coming.

"Papa, *please,*" Katherine beseeched him, her big brown

11

eyes narrowed in silent fury.

Addison Rutcliff ran his fingers through his graying hair, determination in each syllable. "Now *don't* try to sway me with that innocent little-girl ploy of yours, daughter. You are going to Fort Benton to marry Cordell Chandler and *that's final*."

Katherine screwed up her face. "But—"

"*No*. You can wipe that expression off your face. I'm sick and tired of your excuses. Not even that whiney little voice you use to get your way is going to help this time! Not after the biggest gossip in the whole town caught you bareass naked in Martin Sheraton's bed, and the boy engaged to that nice Morley girl, too."

"Papa, I can explain—"

"Hush up! I'm not finished," he said through tight lips. "You have explained for the last time." He shook his head. "Sometimes I can hardly believe you are of my blood. If I hadn't made a promise to your dear departed mother, God rest her soul, I'd disown you for all the grief you've caused. But I'm telling you, this is the last time I'll lift a finger on your behalf. You should consider yourself lucky that I was able to find anyone to take you to wife."

Her ample bosom heaving, Katherine took a deep breath and clenched her teeth. "I'll get off this boat before I'll marry some hick rancher who lives out in the middle of nowhere with no one for company but a bunch of dirty old cows."

"At least a bunch of *dirty old cows* shouldn't spark any amorous notions on your part."

"Papa!"

"Those cows provide quite a sizable income for the man, I'm told. You could do a lot worse than a wealthy rancher. He doesn't know about your past, or I never could have arranged with his Aunt Matilde for you two to be wed."

"I don't want to be a rancher's wife. And particularly not some *auntie's boy* who would let an old maiden aunt arrange a marriage for him," she said with distaste. "It will be a hell living there!"

12

"Maybe I should have let you dig your own grave into hell," he said, exasperated. "It would have been the best thing for Cordell Chandler, poor unsuspecting bastard. I pray he has more strength to deal with you than I've had."

"No one has to 'deal with me.' I'll take care of myself," she said coldly.

"You'll do as I say this time, or I swear, I'll disinherit you. *Then* how will you care for yourself? By spreading your legs for a living?" Katherine's face turned a murderous red. "Don't worry, I'll never have people say Addison Rutcliff couldn't find a suitable husband to take his daughter in hand and make a decent wife out of her. Is that clear?" His voice was menacing.

Her lips pursed, her eyes flashing in anger, Katherine swallowed a sarcastic retort. "Yes, Papa. You've made yourself perfectly clear."

"Then can I assume I am safe in sending a wire to Chandler and letting him know that his bride-to-be will be arriving on the *Benton?*"

"Yes," she said sharply. "Send the damned telegram."

"From now on you also are to watch your tongue. After all, Chandler thinks he is marrying a lady, not a slut."

"I am not a slut!" she retorted with fierce conviction.

He expelled a weary breath. "No . . . I'm afraid you are quite free with your favors. For the life of me, I wish it weren't true."

She pouted. "I can't help it if men find me attractive. Besides, your precious Cordell Chandler and his aunt probably only want the dowry you promised, anyway."

"We'll not debate the merits of your attributes further, much less those of Cordell Chandler and his aunt," he said tiredly, the remembrance of Matilde Chandler bringing a flicker of longing to his heart. He blocked her from his mind—many years ago he'd made the mistake of letting her go. He put his hand on the doorknob to Katherine's cabin. "Now that that's settled, let's have a look at where you'll be spending the next two months."

Libby shrank back, certain she was about to be discovered by the man and his petulant daughter. "Oh, please, not yet," Libby whispered behind her hand. The boat hadn't left the dock yet, and if she were found out, she'd be put ashore for certain.

"Before I go inside that dreary little cubicle, why don't I see you ashore? Your business interests are more important than accompanying your only daughter to make sure she doesn't somehow disgrace you between St. Louis and Fort Benton." Katherine colored every word with sarcasm.

The old man heaved an exhausted sigh. "You may see me ashore, but I'm waiting until I see the ship depart." In a conciliatory gesture he added, "I told you I'd visit you as soon as I've completed the business deal I'm working on." He took his hand from the knob. "Shall we have a look around?"

Katherine expelled a sigh of boredom. "If we must."

When the footfalls grew distant, Libby carefully peeked out the door to catch sight of a tall, dark-haired young woman who appeared to be about the same age as Libby, seventeen—except that she was exquisitely dressed.

When the couple turned the corner, Libby breathed a sigh of relief and shut the door. She had some time before the young woman would be back. Hesitating only a fraction of a second, Libby opened the trunk in the middle of the floor and selected a simple blue striped muslin day dress which matched her eyes.

She stripped off her worn cotton. With water from the pitcher on the stand she dampened a plush washcloth and began to scrub the grime from her body. All the while she washed, she imagined what it would be like if she were the one traveling to meet Cordell Chandler, the wealthy rancher she had overheard the man and his daughter talking about. At the thought of marriage and all it implied, Libby's skin tingled. She rubbed the goosebumps which had risen along her arms. "Cordell Chandler," she sang the name. "Cordell Chandler." It had a nice ring to it, even if the rancher was said to let some maiden aunt rule his life.

* * *

Katherine hurried through a tiresome tour of the ship with her father, and at the first opportunity trundled the old man down the gangplank. "Just remember what I said," he advised. "I'll disown you if you don't marry Chandler."

"I love you too, Papa." She pulled a guileless face.

As she made her way back up the gangplank, Katherine, livid over her defeat and intent on leaving her father's sight immediately, bumped into some luggage being carried by a seedy-looking man sporting a red moustache.

"Pardon me, miss . . . I hope your collision with my bag won't cause a bruise on such beautiful skin," Sheldon Sharpe said silkenly. His eyes darted keenly from the older gentleman on the dock to the beauty's voluptuous, curving body as she tried to squeeze past him.

Katherine frowned, then her expression changed when she noticed her father's scowl. She gazed coyly into the face of her newfound shipmate. Normally Katherine wouldn't lower herself to acknowledge the presence of a man with such obvious intentions; she had always preferred a challenge. A calculating gleam sparked into her eyes, and she sent her father a vindictive nod before taking the man's arm. "Why, Mister—"

"Sharpe. Sheldon Sharpe. But you, my sweet thing, may call me Shelley."

"And you may call me Katherine . . . Shelley."

"It would be my delight, dear lady." He stroked his moustache, leading her the rest of the way up the gangplank.

"Why, Shelley, I know a man such as yourself would never allow a lady to come to harm purposely," she said with a wicked giggle, thinking about the comment he'd made concerning a bruise to her skin. "Why don't we take a stroll around the ship and learn a little bit about each other before we go to my cabin and check for bruises?"

The floor began to vibrate beneath Libby's feet. The

steamer gave a jerk and she almost lost her footing. She rushed to the window and looked out. They were under way; the docks were slowly receding to be replaced by the lapping, muddy waters of the Missouri River. She let out a sigh and allowed her shoulders to relax. Now all she had to do was stay out of the captain's way. That shouldn't be too difficult, since a steamer this size could easily accommodate two hundred passengers as well as all the freight, live cargo, and firewood.

Merrily humming a tune and thinking about the new life she was going to make for herself, Libby was so absorbed in her fantasies that she did not hear the door squeak open or notice the man and woman step inside.

"Who are you and what the devil are you doing in here?" the woman shrilled.

Chapter Three

Taken by surprise at the couple's unexpected intrusion, Libby grabbed a blanket to cover herself.

"I asked, what you are doing in here?" the dark-haired woman demanded. It was the girl Libby had seen earlier. Her arm was linked with a tall, sauve-looking man dressed in a striking scarlet brocade vest and black suit coat. He was not the same man Libby had seen before, though.

A leering smile tweaked his curling lips. "It would be wise to answer the lady," he advised.

"Would you believe your father sent me to keep an eye on you?" Libby's attempt at levity died in the air.

"Hardly. Now, if you do not leave right this instant, I shall send Shelley here to call the captain and have you arrested!" she shrieked.

"May I at least dress first? You wouldn't want people to say that they saw a half-dressed young girl leaving your cabin." Right after the words were out, Libby was surprised at her own audacity. She'd never have dared to speak to Reverend Ardsworth in such a fearless manner. Although she knew she had no right to be in the cabin, much less acting so boldly, it felt good to assert herself.

"Be quick about it."

Her heart pounding in her certainty that the woman might indeed give her over to the captain, Libby turned her back as best she could and slipped on her worn gray cotton dress with the little modesty afforded her under the lewd gaze of the man. While Libby bent down to lace her shoes, she noticed the man and woman in the corner, whispering and every now and then sending her a speculative glance, as if they were measuring her. Uneasily, Libby stood up and started for the door.

Her eyes now shifty brown slits, the woman called out, "Wait! Let me introduce myself," taking Libby by complete surprise. "I am Miss Katherine Rutcliff, and this is Mr. Sheldon Sharpe. If you will sit down and explain to us why you are in my cabin, perhaps we might be able to come to an amicable agreement, one of benefit to us all. It is obvious you have not paid for the voyage. Miss?"

"Miss Elizabeth Hollis . . . Libby."

There was something about the pair which bothered Libby, so she told them about going to Fort Benton to work in the wash house, careful to leave out the reason for her flight.

"You mean to tell me you are a simple laundress?" Katherine laughed and placed a hand on Sharpe's sleeve. "Shelley, you are the sly one. Your idea is perfect. Libby, how would you like to wear pretty clothes and be treated like a lady?"

"I *am* a lady," Libby retorted lamely. She wondered if their whispers had been about this notion Katherine was talking about.

"Of course you are. What I meant was, since we *do* bear a slight resemblance to one another, how would you like to change places with me for the duration of the trip? You can wear some of my clothes, since it seems you intended to anyway." She picked up the striped dress Libby had gotten out of the trunk and tossed it at Libby. "And you won't have to worry about the captain discovering you stowed away on his steamer." When Libby hesitated, Katherine curtly added, "Oh, I guess I forgot to mention it, but if you refuse, I fully intend to turn you over to the captain."

"Why? I don't understand," Libby blurted out, now reeling from Katherine's proposal.

Katherine's eyes shot to her new companion and an illicit grin washed over her lips. Sharpe shrugged his

18

indifference.

"Go ahead and tell her if you want, my dear," Sharpe added to reinforce his apathy.

"You really are a no-good bastard, aren't you, Shelley?" Katherine laughed. "That's what I liked about you from the moment we met." Her face lost all amusement when her gaze drifted back to Libby. "Knowing why is none of your concern. Will you do it or not?"

The thought of being returned to the Reverend Ardsworth caused Libby's head to spin. What harm could it do to agree to this plan? The woman probably wasn't aware Libby had overheard her conversation with her father—Libby had some insight into Katherine's reasons for wanting to trade places. Libby looked at Sheldon Sharpe, standing there like a cocky rooster; he looked terribly slick to her, his chest puffed out, his thumbs hooked in his vest pockets. Katherine no doubt wanted to make another conquest before she was forced to marry the rancher.

Katherine crossed her arms over her chest and tapped her foot. "Well, Miss Hollis? We haven't got all day, you know."

Libby felt the icy fear of entrapment: she had no other choice. She tried to look on the lighter side: at least for the remainder of the journey she would be afforded the respect of a lady for once in her life. And after all, once they reached Fort Benton, they would go their separate ways and no one would be the wiser.

She took a deep breath to bolster her newfound courage. "All right, I'll do it. But what about paying for my, I mean *your*, passage as Elizabeth Marie Hollis?"

Katherine wore a self-satisfied grin, and a triumphant glitter danced in her sparkling brown eyes. "Don't you worry about a thing. Shelley and I'll take care of everything . . . Katherine." Arm in arm they turned from Libby, then stopped and Katherine threw back over her shoulder, "You are expected to dine with the captain this evening. I'll be back later to prepare you for your role. We wouldn't want you to let us down, or you'll suffer the

19

consequences." With that, the pair left Libby standing stunned in the middle of the room.

Libby slumped onto the bed, wondering if she had just freed herself from one nightmare only to embark upon another. For what seemed like hours, she stared at the floor, her fingers tented over her mouth until Katherine returned.

"Well, have you finished going through my things yet?" Katherine sneered.

"Of course not, I—"

"Don't bother trying to make excuses, I'm not interested." Katherine waved her off. Sorting through her dresses, she picked out a few of her favorites, which she would use during the trip. "All you have to do until we reach Fort Benton is play your part. Then you are welcome to disappear into your dreary wash house and scrub your little heart out, for all I care. Understand?" she asked sweetly, venom dripping from every syllable.

Libby bit her lip. "Quite."

"Good. Let's not waste any more time." Katherine opened the trunk and took out a painted box. She removed a handful of mementos and sat down next to Libby. Sorting through the stack of photographs, she began passing them to Libby one by one. "This is a picture of Papa and Mama before she died twelve years ago."

"I'm sorry," Libby said with an understanding that could come only from one who had shared a similar loss.

"Don't be. I don't even remember her. And as for my father, he's always been too busy away making money to warrant anyone's sympathy."

Katherine's remark revealed much more about her personality, the self-pity and inner rage, than she had probably intended. She had grown up without the comfort and love of either parent, which might explain why she now freely gave her favors to men, Libby surmised, thinking about the heated conversation at the door earlier. Maybe Katherine was so generous with her body because she was hoping to capture a father's love and nurturing through all ose men.

Slowly, methodically, Katherine described her sordid ast, leaving out very little, giving Libby all the shocking etails of her history she would need to become Katherine utcliff during the trip.

The next two months passed like a dreamy whirlwind or Libby. She was treated with respect and enjoyed all the menities of the upper classes. She dined regularly at the aptain's table on bacon, beans, salt pork, and a variety f dried fruits. She tasted antelope, deer, and buffalo.

She was introduced to the Conrad brothers, the largest erchants in the Territory of Montana. She became iends with Conrad Kohrs and his charming wife Au- usta, a splendid, tall woman of impressive bearing, with ounds of thick dark hair. Here was a woman who elieved in being direct. The Kohrses owned the ranch ext to Cordell Chandler's in the Deer Lodge Valley, and hen they learned from the captain that Libby was Chan- ler's intended, they invited her into their inner circle of iends who were traveling together.

Although at first Libby feared sharing a cabin with atherine, she was relieved not to have to suffer atherine's biting tongue. Since Katherine had moved into heldon Sharpe's cabin, she had made no attempt to see ibby or to cultivate any of the friendships Libby had ade.

Shortly after dinner one evening, while the two women at visiting, Augusta placed a gentle hand on Libby's arm. Dell didn't tell us he was planning to take a wife. It's bout time. Folks had begun to think Dell was never going o get married." At the apprehension in Libby's face, ugusta Kohrs smiled kindly. "Don't you worry, atherine. Cordell Chandler is a good man. He might ake a little taming, but he's well worth it."

"I do hope so," Libby said cryptically, fretting over how he awful muddle she was in would turn out once they eached Fort Benton. How were she and Katherine ever

21

going to resume their own identities now? When Augusta cast her a bemused look, Libby added shyly, "You see our marriage was arranged by his aunt. I've never met the man."

"It's just like Matilde Chandler to take charge." Augusta slipped a comforting arm around Libby's shoulders. "Don't you be worrying. Dell may howl like a rooster getting his tail feathers plucked, but he is really more of a mother hen underneath that hard exterior of his." She laughed. Then she bent her head toward Libby in the posture of a conspirator. "Just don't you tell him I compared him to a mother hen."

During the day they'd stroll the deck and marvel at the untamed shoreline bursting with wild game and cotton woods. They saw Indians practically every day. Sometimes Captain Massie would allow the heavily painted natives on board to trade. Around every bend was a new and fascinating sight, and Libby took to her new life with relish, almost forgetting it was a ruse.

She met Katherine accidentally a few times, and Katherine spoke to her once during a dance in the main salon. She had danced a square dance with Mr. Sharpe, who informed her how pleased they were with her performance. Afterward the captain warned Libby to stay away from the couple, stating that although there wasn't proof, he believed they were a pair of cardsharks who were cheating at Pedro, a popular card game.

Her dream world was complete until the day they were to dock. Early that morning she had wandered into the captain's office. Tacked to the wall was a "Wanted" poster accusing Elizabeth Marie Hollis of viciously attacking a man of God without cause. It gave a description and offered a liberal reward. Libby's face reddened and she dropped her head when the captain's smile took on a strange twist.

"Wrote that up myself after I received a telegraph message at Bismarck. Pretty good job, if I say so myself." He looked pointedly at her. "The girl thought she had a clever disguise. But I've already sent word to the sheriff. That's one crime which won't go unpunished, trying to harm a man of the cloth."

Libby swallowed hard and started to inch her way out of the man's office.

"Don't leave. I personally want to hand you over when we dock."

Chapter Four

The steamboat blasted its whistle and the customary cannon salute was returned by the people on the levee at Fort Benton. The bustling town was fringed with bluffs to the west and off in the distance mountains rose blue and abrupt from the wide expanse of prairie. As Libby watched all the activity on shore, she was reminded of the town's history, which Augusta Kohrs had proudly related to her one afternoon on their way upriver. Once called Fort Lewis, in homage to Meriwether Lewis of the Lewis and Clark expedition, the town's name was changed to Fort Benton on Christmas Eve, 1850. In a jubilant ceremony abounding with free-flowing alcoholic spirits, the settlement was renamed in honor of Senator Thomas Hart Benton of Missouri.

Fighting back tears, Libby kept her gaze directed out the window. All along the treeless shoreline were hundreds of people from the town, waving and shouting their welcome. Small children and dogs ran about the bull trains lined up near shore waiting to load the provisions brought upriver by the steamer. The sun mingled with dust to give the atmosphere a golden haze. If Libby hadn't felt so forlorn, it would have been easy to get caught up in all the gleeful excitement of their arrival.

A big man in a fringed leather jacket, white shirt, and string tie adjusted his wide-brimmed hat as he walked up the gangplank, his heavy boots thudding against the boards with the beat of authority. Libby put her hand to her throat: he had to be the sheriff; she could see his six-shooter strapped low on his hip. She studied his face: he was well tanned, with black hair curling over his collar, and dark eyes that could almost be considered black, if it weren't for the touch of gold in them. His features were strong. He didn't appear to be a man who could be swayed . . . even if she *was* telling the truth. After all, she had run away. Who would believe the word of a runaway girl against a respected minister?

Libby's heart all but burst as she waited to be arrested. When the door to the captain's office swung open she held her breath, too afraid to move, much less try to run past the man.

"Is this her, Captain Massie?" the tall, dark man asked in a deep baritone, emotionless.

Before the captain could answer, Libby blurted out, "Ah, no. *No!*" All the while she edged toward the door, her feet seeming to have developed a mind of their own . . . or maybe it was the instinct for survival which spurred her on and made her heart race. "Now I really must be going, Captain Massie. If you gentlemen will excuse me, I have packing to do." She gave them a cordial nod.

"Wait just a minute, young lady." Captain Massie grinned, blocking her flight. "I didn't detain you here just so someone else would have the pleasure of handing you over to this hard-hearted son-of-a-bitch." He chuckled.

Was the captain actually taking delight in turning in an innocent victim? That was too much. Libby's anger overtook her and she pinched her lips. "What type of man would take *pleasure* in a situation such as this?" she demanded.

"Well, Massie, she's got you this time." The stranger gave an amused frown and relaxed his stance. "Can't say as I'm totally thrilled with this whole situation myself."

"But I thought—" sputtered the captain, an embarrassing red beginning to blotch his throat.

"Well, you thought wrong." The man turned to Libby. "Come along, Miss. I have a lot to get done today." He headed for the door. When Libby didn't follow, he stopped. She thought she noticed the strangest of smiles when he asked, "You coming or not?"

Remembering her visit to a jail with Reverend Ardsworth while he made his calls, she asked, "You aren't going to put me in chains, are you?"

He laughed, although Libby saw nothing humorous in her question. My God! Was he some kind of pervert, like the reverend? "Never heard it quite expressed that way before, particularly by a woman. But the ball-and-chain will come soon enough, I guess."

"Please try to remember, I'm only a girl."

He let his gaze assess her openly, causing the heat to rise in Libby's cheeks. "That's not the way it was sold to me."

"How could you let anyone *sell* you something without first hearing from everyone concerned?" Libby questioned, still disbelieving. How *could* she have been caught after she'd come so close to making a successful escape?

"Meaning you?" He shoved his hat back on his head, then shrugged.

"Of course."

"I think your actions speak for themselves. Especially since receiving the report Massie here brought upriver. By the way, Massie, thanks for sending it ashore so promptly." The captain nodded before the man turned his attention back to Libby. "As I said before, you coming or not?"

"Do I have a choice?" she mumbled.

He gazed at her, his brows drawn together, and shook his head. "You made that choice when you boarded this steamer. Considering the size of the reception party called out on account of you, I'd say you don't." With that he walked down the gangplank and immediately was surrounded by a terribly serious crowd which included two huge, whiskered men wearing badges. Did they think her crime was so heinous that it would take more than one lawman to apprehend her?

Libby gazed skyward and swore to herself that she

wasn't going to let them see her cry. She smoothed back her dark hair, thrust out her chin, and strolled proudly down the gangplank to meet her sorry fate.

To her surprise, Augusta Kohrs intercepted her at the bottom of the gangplank and pulled her aside. "Well? What do you think of him?"

Libby glanced at the man. "He's awfully big and dark, and he has a cold, hard look about him," she answered, wondering why such a fine lady such as Augusta would even be speaking to her after finding out the charges leveled against her.

"You're dark-complexioned yourself, my dear," she laughed. "Nervous?"

Libby nodded silently, unable to speak for fear she would break down.

"You just take my hand and we'll face them together," Augusta advised, twining her fingers around Libby's.

"Thank you for all your kindness," Libby managed feebly.

They walked over to the crowd and Libby prepared for the worst. When Augusta opened her mouth to speak, Libby shut her eyes. "Gentlemen, I am proud to be the one to introduce Miss Katherine Rutcliff." She wrapped her arm around the man's and pushed him together with Libby. "Cordell Chandler's fiancée."

Libby's knees started to buckle. She wasn't being arrested for attacking the reverend . . . she was being introduced to the people at Fort Benton as Cordell Chandler's intended. She looked up at the big man, who was gallantly supporting her so she didn't make a complete spectacle out of herself by crumpling to the ground. Captain Massie must have thought they already knew each other; that's why he hadn't introduced them. She almost wanted to laugh out loud . . . she and Cordell Chandler had been discussing two entirely different topics as they disembarked.

The natty crowd converged on her and began offering their best wishes until an angry screech rent the air. The congratulations ceased and a heavy silence permeated the docks. All eyes turned to two bulky men. A woman wearing a green print dress was being dragged screaming from the steamer.

The violent scene before Libby brought the last threatening conversation she'd had with Katherine flashing before her mind. Libby had been dressing for dinner. Feeling secure in her enforced role and surrounded by supportive people, Libby had grown lax about locking the cabin door. When the door swung open and a very inebriated Katherine swaggered into the room, Libby felt her heart lurch.

Katherine fought to focus her eyes, hiccupping when she opened her mouth. She put an unsteady hand to her lips. "Aren't you going to greet me, or do you merely plan to stand there?" Her head jerked as another spasm grasped her. "Maybe you think you're too good for a simple laundress." She giggled before her lips hardened.

"What do you want?" Libby asked quietly, ignoring Katherine's attempts to poke fun at her.

"What do I want? What do I want," Katherine mocked. "I'll tell you what I want, *Miss Katherine Rutcliff.* I want to warn you that if you think you can run around playing your little role so well that I will let you get away with it once we dock at Fort Benton, you've got another thing coming!"

The gall of the woman! Despite her fears, Libby could not control the impulse to retort, "Let me get away with this? This charade was your idea, not mine. And if you expect me to continue, I think it is about time you tell me why."

Katherine settled a blurry gaze on the dark-haired girl. "If I expect? My, my, we've changed." She hiccupped again. "What happened to the scared little rodent who was so eager not to be discovered by our illustrious captain? Why, you didn't require much convincing at all!"

Katherine waited for Libby to concede defeat. When she didn't, Katherine snapped, "You'll continue as me, if for no other reason than to enjoy the pleasures you've become accustomed to. But what the hell . . . why not tell you why I needed a stand-in?" Katherine smiled at Libby's apparent shock over her tinted language. "Don't tell me you find swearing unbefitting a lady! You know, all my life I've had that drilled into me. 'Katherine, you're father is a very important man so you must always act *like a lady*,' my various governesses preached. But you see, when I acted like a good little lady, it was if I were just another one of my father's statues; he wasn't even aware I was in the room." Her face grew bitter. "But when I acted like the painted women my father used to sneak off to be with, I got his attention, all right."

Libby shook her head, her heart filled with both pity and sorrow for the unhappy little girl Katherine must have been.

"Don't look at me like that," Katherine spat, rubbing her bloodshot eyes. Her tongue shot out and licked her lips. "I like men. *And* I like the things they do to me: their hands all over my body, their bodies hot on mine." She hesitated to let Libby absorb her full implications. "I don't intend to give that up before I have to marry some rancher. That's what Papa is sending me to Montana for, you know . . . to marry some man who lives out in the middle of nowhere. So I can become the good little wife. Well, by changing places with you, Papa will still receive a good report card and I can be free to enjoy life a little longer." She crossed her arms over her chest. "Now you know." She put her hand on the doorknob. "Just remember when the ship docks: *I* am Katherine Rutcliff, and *I* will be the one walking down the gangplank in all *my* finery to greet Cordell Chandler."

"What will all the people I've met on board say?" Libby asked.

"That's my concern and I'll handle it." Katherine shrugged her indifference. "I always have."

"Then just *why* did you come in here?"

"To remind you not to get any grand ideas that you can continue to be me. Shelley and I've watched you, and I don't want you overplaying your role. Because at midnight, *Elizabeth Hollis,* you turn back into a pumpkin."

29

And with that she stumbled from the room.

Libby felt drained, the ghosts of her own childhood a pale imitation of those of Katherine's impressionable years. Would she ever be able to make her home in Fort Benton as a laundress after this trip? What would the Kohrses and Conrads think when they found out she was not Katherine Rutcliff?

All the commotion snapped her attention back to the present.

"Wait! Stop!" The woman being dragged from the ship jerked her arm loose and pointed directly at Libby, shrieking like a banshee, "She's an imposter! She's not Katherine Rutcliff!"

Chapter Five

A shiver went through Libby when she saw Katherine battling those two men. Cordell must have felt Libby's reaction, because he pulled her in closer to him in a protective gesture which nearly overwhelmed Libby. No man had tried to shield her from life's cold hard realities since her grandfather had died. The thought sent a warming sensation to her heart.

"Elizabeth Hollis, you rotten cheat! You tell them the truth!" Katherine bellowed as the two men lifted her off her feet. She kicked a trunk being unloaded, sending it cascading down the gangplank.

"Why, my dear, isn't that your trunk?" Augusta asked, concern edging her features. "Katherine?"

"Wh—what? Oh, yes, yes—that is the trunk I've been using," Libby answered once she regained her senses.

One of the men left the crowd to see about the chest at Cordell's instruction. The large case lay open, dresses, shoes, gloves and unmentionables scattered everywhere. An embarrassed blush staining the squat man's cheeks, he began to retrieve the articles and stuff them back inside.

Katherine gave a mighty push, sending one of her captors splashing into the Missouri, the other yelping headlong after him. Her freedom gained, Katherine lifted her skirts and dashed into the crowd.

"I'm Katherine Rutcliff! *She* is the one who attacked that minister. I caught her in my cabin! She's the one!

She's the one!" she managed to scream before being re-strained.

Libby put her hand to her throat. What was she going to do? She had been taught to do the right thing, to tell the truth; she wasn't a liar.

"I don't know who this Elizabeth Hollis is, but I certainly can vouch for Katherine," Augusta said, her eyes flashing in indignation. Who was the imposter trying to ruin this day for Cordell and Katherine? "Con and I were introduced to Katherine," she put her arm around Libby, "by Captain Massie shortly after we left St. Louis. And we have spent nearly two months in her company. If you are indeed who you are," Augusta turned to Katherine, "then why didn't you step forward before this, young woman?"

"I —"

Katherine hesitated too long; Augusta moved to finish her sentence for her. "Because you aren't Katherine Rutcliff, that's why. You are Elizabeth Hollis. And just why are you so desperate to deny your birth?"

" 'Cause she beat up some preacher, that she did. And now she's tryin' to escape what's comin' to her for her evil deed," answered one of the crowd.

In shock, Augusta clasped her palm to her cheek. "Oh, my."

Confused thoughts of what was happening whirled in Libby's mind until her attention caught at two of the nicely dressed women in the gathering.

"I felt sorry for the poor thing when my George first told me the sordid tale. Couldn't imagine a young girl attacking a man of God like that. Funny thing, though, I remember a story like that back in Toledo years ago, when things weren't quite what they seemed. But seeing this girl for myself, I can tell the poor child must be deranged."

"Yeah, deranged," answered a runty man nearby. "Think we oughta see ta some leather straps, tie her up right and get her committed ta an asylum which'll do her some good."

"No. No!" Libby gasped, horrified at the mention of such a solution. "Not that!"

"Why not? Looks like it might be the best thing for er," Cordell put in, studying Libby's face with a strange intensity which unsettled her even more.

"Look what we found on her." One of the men who had climbed out of the river approached Cordell, dripping. The man took a sheet of paper out of his pocket and presented it to Cordell. "Looks like she started out with it a her mind to work in the wash house and then fell in ith that Sharpe fella. We think them's been cheating olks at cards, but there's no proof. Looked for him when ll this commotion started, but seems he's slithered away. His kind don't hang 'round long when there's a ruckus."

"Yes. Yes," Libby said quickly. "That is all she wanted, job." When questioning eyes turned to her, she added, "I adn't mentioned it to anyone, but Elizabeth was in my abin at the beginning of the voyage and did mention eeding work. Of course, we didn't speak of her troubles ith the minister." All eyes held inquiring gazes, causing ibby to feel the need to elaborate. "It was a mistake. lizabeth had entered the wrong cabin. We spoke only riefly," she offered, careful to remain as close to the truth s possible. "Gentlemen, I'm certain she's merely just istraught right now, caught in such a disguise and all. he was really quite lucid on the ship. There's no need to end her to an asylum."

"Maybe not," grumbled one of the men holding the truggling Katherine. "But this one's sure gonna have t' alm down if she wants t' stay outa that place." He shot Catherine a disgusted look. "You should consider yourself ost lucky t' have Dell's intended speak up fer you like he done." Then he turned to Cordell. "We'll keep her in ustody and send for the preacher. Says here, right on this aper, that the man wants t' be notified of the girl's vhereabouts." He shook his head. "Probably thinks he an still save her soul."

Libby thought her heart was going to stop when she eard the man's comment about the reverend's intentions. Dear God—Reverend Ardsworth, coming here? The min- te he got here he would identify her and her nightmare

33

would begin all over again. She would be safe until he
arrived . . . they would keep Katherine locked up in her
place until he came. Libby looked at Katherine, who was
shooting darts of hatred at her. Libby firmed her own
resolve. She had made a promise to herself never to let the
Reverend Ardsworth near her again. Her survival instinct
came to the fore. Changing identities with Katherine
hadn't been Libby's idea in the first place. No real harm
would come to Katherine. After all, she hadn't wanted to
marry Cordell Chandler anyway. She could just continue
to play the part of Elizabeth Marie Hollis for a little while
longer.

Libby looked up at Cordell. His features were set and
unyielding, yet there was an inner kindness which radiated
through that hardened surface. How far was she actually
willing to carry this ruse in order to protect herself from
the reverend?

Reaching a hard decision, Libby swallowed her last
thoughts of putting an end to this masquerade and said to
Katherine, "Sometimes being deceptive and trying to dis-
guise who you are does not work out the way you plan.
I'm sure you have learned a lesson from that today . . .
Elizabeth."

Katherine hissed at Libby, bared her claws, and fought
to reach Libby, as if to gouge out her eyes. The men
dragged Katherine from the docks screaming and howling.
She cursed, "I'll get you for this if it's the last thing I do!
I'll get you! I swear I will!"

From behind a nearby wagon Sheldon Sharpe quietly
watched. He'd been waiting to see who would be the
victor, since he had no intention of letting Katherine drag
him into such a fracas. He considered himself a man
meant to savor life's pleasures. Katherine had been one of
those pleasures. Pity . . . he hadn't tired of her yet. He
rubbed his chin, a calculating awareness sparking his eyes.
Katherine was the daughter of a very wealthy business-
man; Cordell Chandler was a prominent man in Montana.
From what Katherine had told him of her reasons for
coming to Fort Benton, and with what had now tran-

pired, he might just be able to reap some benefit from it. With increased interest he remained in his position, listening, watching, waiting. . . .

"I'm glad that's over," Augusta said after the woman had been safely taken off to jail. "Cordell, you should gather Katherine's things and get started home as soon as possible. I know Matilde must be planning a simply grand wedding." She stopped and looked around. "By the way, where is Matilde? I thought we'd see her here by this time, surely."

"Matilde's in Helena. Her gout's acting up again and she thinks a change will do her some good. She won't be back until she's feeling better. You know Matilde when she gets a bee in her bonnet."

"You certainly can't take this young lady out to your ranch house unchaperoned with no one but a bunch of cowboys living out there," Augusta protested. "Katherine, you're welcome to stay with us—isn't she, Con?"

Conrad Kohrs, a man who used his good judgment in all he did, rubbed his full bush beard. "Dear, you know we won't be returning right away. I have business with the Conrads, and there's the cattle to see to on the Sun River before we return home."

"Oh." Augusta put her hands to her cheeks. "I completely forgot."

"It's quite all right." Libby breathed a silent sigh. It was the perfect excuse to get out of the situation gracefully. "I certainly can't impose upon you anyway," Libby said. "I'll remain in town and come out to the ranch at a later date. It'll give me a chance to adjust to my new surroundings." She would have the protection of Cordell Chandler's name while she stayed in Fort Benton, and then she'd disappear before the reverend came or Cordell Chandler could return to claim her.

"You'll do no such thing," Cordell said in a tone brooking no argument. This certainly didn't seem to be a man who could be controlled by anyone, much less an aunt,

35

Libby thought. "I came here to claim a bride. Hell, a lot of my friends and associates are in town. I suppose I can wait one more day to start back. We'll have the wedding right here in Fort Benton, tonight."

Chapter Six

For the second time in so few short months Libby felt trapped. But this time the snare was of her own making. Somehow she had to extricate herself from yet another major crisis in her young life. She looked over at Cordell Chandler. He was busy accepting congratulatory pats on the back from a half dozen men.

He was such a big man. Not an ounce of fat anywhere, she guessed from what she could see. He was powerfully built, and his muscles stretched at his trousers; his neck was thick and strong; his chest was broad between those immense shoulders.

While she studied him, she realized she was beginning to wonder why Katherine Rutcliff wouldn't want such a man. Cordell Chandler had displayed a dynamic disposition, and he was one of the most handsome men she had ever seen. He not only possessed a vast personal wealth, but had a host of friends who believed in him as well. The thought of having friends made Libby's arms tingle with an excited anticipation; the reverend had never allowed her friendships while she was growing up, insisting her wicked birth would contaminate the innocent. Despite the loneliness of a friendless childhood, Libby never gave up hope of someday surrounding herself with friends just like Cordell Chandler's.

"If you'll pardon us now," Cordell said with a charming smile that beamed the power of his alluring personality. "I should be getting Miss Rutcliff into the hotel so she can rest for the day."

Cordell moved back through the crowd to Libby's si[de] and took her arm. He quietly squeezed it and gave her [a] tug when she tried to remain planted in her spot. "Co[me] along, dear one," he said through strained lips that on[ly] she could see.

Sharpe waited as Cordell led his lovely intended awa[y] from the crowd. "Pity," he grumbled to himself, "yo[u] aren't the real Katherine Rutcliff. I think I could learn [to] like you real well . . . real well indeed. You sure do ha[ve] the looks! If only you had the money to go with it."

He shrugged. He had learned long ago that money w[as] the most important commodity life had to offer. Wi[th] enough money, he could buy anything he wanted, inclu[d]ing all the beautiful women he'd ever desired. He rubbe[d] his chin, smooth from his careful ministrations. Katheri[ne] Rutcliff had that kind of money.

The gathering of well-wishers thinned before Shar[pe] made his way toward the jail. He started around to t[he] front entrance, then swung back to the side of the buil[d]ing when the two deputies who had escorted Katherine [to] jail pushed open the door and stepped into the sun.

Morris Critter, a bulky man in a worn jacket, squinte[d] toward the steamer. "Quite a morning, don't you think[?] What with that crazy shecat, I've had me enough excit[e]ment for one day."

"Yeah," agreed Jake Sipson, a clean-cut looking man [of] about thirty. Can't say as I minded too much, though[.] He rubbed his hands. "That little swim was even worth t[he] chance I got me to feel up that woman."

"Have to admit," Morris stretched out his hands befo[re] him and traced the path of her luscious shape in the ai[r,] "she's got downright nice curves in all the right places[."] He caught a glimpse of Cordell and his fiancée. "But wh[at] about Dell's woman? Now *there's* a woman who cou[ld] boil my blood, real royal-like."

"I know what you mean. But she's a real lady; w[e]

shouldn't ought to be talking about her like that."

"You're right, but my pecker's sure speaking up loud enough." He scratched his stiffened crotch.

Morris chuckled. "Come on, let's go get us something to drink. That'll cool you off a bit."

Mulling over the conversation he'd just overheard, Sharpe hesitated along the edge of the boardwalk until the two men moved off toward the Eagle Bird Saloon. Quietly he slithered into the jail, unsure whether he would be met by some other law officer. The room was deserted. He looked about him. Rifles hung in a neat row from behind a glass case. Two six-shooters dangled from gunbelts slung over a hatrack next to a beat-up desk. A door with iron bars separated the holding area from the sheriff's office.

Sharpe stepped to the door and grabbed the bars. "Katherine?"

"Shelley, you've got to get me out of here," she shrilled. "Go tell those idiots the truth!"

He pivoted to rescue Katherine, planning to harvest the reward of her gratitude, then halted. The beginnings of a plot to reap a more substantial sum than he'd first anticipated rose like a mountain of gold before his eyes.

Sharpe had been listening to the men discuss the bright future Cordell Chandler had in politics. Politics was like a fickled mistress; regardless of the caliber of the man involved, his fate hung in the balance of public whim. "I wonder just how vulnerable you really are, Mr. Big Man," Sharpe said of Cordell Chandler.

Sharpe's boots made determined thuds back across the wooden floorboards until he was inside the barred door and standing face-to-face with Katherine.

"What the devil are you waiting for?" she demanded.

"I have an idea I think just might appeal to that vengeful little heart of yours, Sweetness. . . ."

Libby slipped into a self-enforced silence while Cordell took charge and got her settled in a room at the Overland Hotel on Front Street. It was a single-story wooden plank structure with rooms in back of a small lobby. Her room was tiny, but neatly appointed, with a narrow bed and washstand. A plain white cotton panel hung at the single window.

"Thank you for helping me settle in. I think I'll rest for a while, if you don't mind." Libby stood just inside the door.

"But I *do* mind," he said in a steady voice as cold as a Montana winter. He stepped inside and shut the door. "Sit down, *Miss Rutcliff*, and take off that infernal hat. It looks like you are wearing a fruitstand on your head."

"I think I'd rather not. And there's nothing wrong with my hat." She looked about the room again, fidgeting with her gloved fingers before fumbling with the ribbons to remove her headdress. There was nowhere to sit but on the bed. Surely he didn't expect her to settle herself *there* in his presence.

Cordell noticed her apprehension. "You needn't worry yourself that I'm going to try to take advantage of you. You'd have to be the last woman on earth, and then I'd have to give it some serious consideration. Now sit down before my patience is totally gone. We have some talking to do."

Oh, my goodness, from his tone and the way he said my name, he knows who I am, she trembled, backing over to perch gingerly on the bed. She was about to blurt out the truth and throw herself on his mercy when she remembered what Augusta Kohrs had advised. "Just remember my words, Dear. Cordell Chandler is not a man who'll take to some weak clinging vine of a woman afraid of her own shadow. He's a strong man and he'll need an equally strong woman who'll give him a run for his money. This untamed land won't forgive a weak spirit, and neither will Cordell Chandler. Think of the man like the land; he's as untamed as it is, but he'll respond to determination and a strong heart."

"I know about you, and if you think I have any intention of getting myself married to your kind, you're crazy." He stood towering above Libby, his hands staunchly on

40

his hips, his face a glowering mass of muscle.

"So you know." She threw her head back to meet his dark eyes with her own level stare. "And I suppose you have a spotless past yourself. Oh no, I suppose you don't. But then again, it *is* all right for a man to have a less-than-perfect past, whereas a woman is not to be forgiven her mistakes. And for your information, I am not at fault for what happened to me!" she spat. Her words seemed to take him aback. Augusta was right; strength was the only way to deal with this man.

"I'm in no mood for excuses. I'm going to talk and you're going to listen. If you try to interrupt me, I'll stuff a gag in your mouth. Do we understand each other, Miss Rutcliff?"

"Miss Rutcliff?"

"Yeah. And that's the way I intend to keep it."

Somehow he must also know about Katherine's past. Libby wasn't sure whether she should be more relieved because he didn't know about her own past, or that he said he'd never marry Katherine. The idea disturbed her. "Why did you suggest that we get married tonight if you had no intention of marrying me?"

"You don't listen well, either." He clenched his fists. The expression on his face warned Libby he truly would like to gag her. Why didn't he? The reverend would have struck her for such insubordination and would have felt that God had guided his hand. Cordell Chandler really was a gentleman underneath his tough veneer. It was cause for thought.

He ran his fingers through his thick black hair and rubbed his neck. "For your information, I couldn't let a fine woman like Augusta Kohrs rearrange her plans and take someone like you in. That's what she would have done, you know."

"Well, then, what do you suggest?" Libby asked, feeling more secure about the pose she was taking. "I have no desire to marry you either," Libby put in, then had to think about her words.

"I suggest I take you back to the docks and put you

41

aboard the *Benton* right now."

"That's impossible."

"Look, no one forced you to come here."

"Maybe my st . . . ah . . . father forced me."

"From what I read, there isn't a man alive who ever had to force you, Honey."

"Oh? Could it be you are already beginning to soften towards me by using such endearments?" Libby gave him a sugary smile.

He leaned over, one hand resting on each side of her on the bed. "Or could it be it is *you* who are warming to my charm?" he asked seductively.

Frightened by the sudden change in him, Libby scooted back to the headboard. "Hardly."

"Good," he said with steel in his voice. "Since neither one of us has any desire to be stuck with the other and you are not willing to return to the steamer right now, I just happen to have figured out a plan."

Chapter Seven

Libby scooted off the bed and stood in front of Cordell Chandler, coming a little past shoulder height as she stared up into those magical black eyes with the golden sparkle. Fighting the inclination to melt into a mass of trembling nerves before him, she took a bolstering breath of air. "What is your great plan?"

Cordell stared back at the woman, sparks of anger radiating from his every pore. "Women like you pull a tidy fainting routine. Did you know that a *chaise longue* was once designed to be put in every parlor and nicknamed the 'fainting couch' just to accommodate the weaker sex?"

"What does that have to do with us?" Libby asked, completely baffled by the direction of their conversation.

"You females use the couch to gain an unfair advantage over some poor man every time you turn around . . . women's delicate sensibilities being what they are, unable to handle a man's crudity, so it's been said," he scoffed.

"Why, I've *never* found it necessary to make use of a couch in that way," Libby responded proudly, not giving any thought to what she'd just said.

"Hah! Of course not. I've known lots of women like you. Your type has her own special way of making use of a couch."

She bristled. "That's an absurd accusation."

He cocked a brow. "It's no accusation, Miss Rutcliff."

Libby's eyes grew wild. "You . . . you mean to tell me that you and some . . . some *lady* have used one of those

43

couches for other purposes?" She stumbled over her words, shocked by the implication.

"Haven't you?" he shot back, nonplussed.

"I would *never* do such a thing!" she protested.

He looked unconvinced, despite the force of her objections. "Ah, but that's exactly what you are going to do. Tonight."

Libby slapped her hand over her heart. "I am not! And if you, Sir, think that—"

"Relax, Miss Rutcliff. I just want you to faint, nothing more." He sent her a telling grin. "With your many, shall we say, varied special talents, I'm certain you can handle it."

"What?" Libby sputtered in response to such an absurd notion. "Why go to all this trouble? Why not simply call off the wedding?"

"It would take too much explaining to call off this wedding—"

"Don't you mean *since* you wish to save face—"

"Your face as well as my face, Miss Rutcliff."

She bit her lip and stepped to the window. Pushing back the curtain, she stared out at the distant hills. Montana was to be a fresh beginning, a new start, a place where she could build a life for herself without fear. Why did everything have to be so complicated? All she'd wanted when she'd boarded the steamer back in St. Louis was to find a new life working in a wash house, not to be the center of attention for the entire town. Becoming involved in such a deceptive tangle was more than she'd ever bargained for. She could refuse, but events had already gone too far for that. She took a deep breath and let it out with a wistful sigh. She knew what she had to do.

"All right," she agreed, realizing she had no option but to tell the truth about herself. That she couldn't chance.

Cordell watched her closely as she stood proud before him. "Anyway, as I started to say, tonight after you make your big entrance, walk as far as the couch. I'll make sure there'll be one in the room tonight in case any of the ladies feels the urge—"

"But I'm the one who's going to *feel the urge*." Libby cast him an indignant frown. "Is that correct?"

"Smart girl . . . that's right. You'll get as far as the couch and then faint. When you come to, you'll plead sudden illness, so bad it won't allow you to continue with the ceremony, though you'll feel just terrible about inconveniencing all the good folks of Fort Benton who went to such a great deal of trouble for us."

"I don't like the idea of deceiving people," she said, attempting to cling to some remnant of her belief in honesty, despite the twists her life had taken lately.

"Do you think I like it? These people are my friends. But because you refuse to get back on the *Benton* and leave quietly, we simply do not have any other choice."

"That's all well and good . . . but what if they insist? Then what am I supposed to do, since you seem to have it all figured out?"

"They won't insist, since folks out here believe in taking care of their womenfolk. Besides, even if for some strange reason they do, I'll be there and make sure you're taken back to your room."

Libby was not convinced. "So? What happens the next morning? Won't we be forced to go through the same thing all over again?"

"No, because I'll pull out with the bull train before dawn. You can tell everyone we had a long discussion and decided it would be better to postpone the wedding until you're feeling stronger, and of course, until Aunt Matilde can attend. People should accept that readily enough. Then, before I'm forced to return for you and the wedding gossip dies down, you can quietly slip out of town." When Libby did not look as if she'd been persuaded, he added, "Don't worry, I'll pay your passage to anywhere you wish to go."

"It sounds all too easy. What if something goes wrong?"

"It *is* easy. That's what's going to make it work. It is so simple that with a little effort even *your* kind can't mess it up."

"Thank you for your vote of confidence. I'm deeply touched."

"I'm sure you have been touched—and from what I read in that report, quite often."

Libby's teeth sank into her lower lip before she asked "What report?"

"That's none of your concern. All I care is that you clearly understand what you're suppose to do. Do you?"

"Are you afraid you ended up with an addlepated bride-to-be?" She sent him her most quelling gaze, wishing the whole thing was just a bad dream, that she'd wake up before she was forced to put the man's plan into action and play yet another role. "Of course, I understand what's expected of me . . . you want me to play some withering violet who succumbs to the overwhelming pressures of a wedding ceremony to such a powerful, devastatingly handsome man."

Libby was immediately sorry. From the look of the man, he was well aware that he was devastatingly handsome, and now he knew that she thought so too. At her last comment Cordell's eyes narrowed and an unreadable gleam hovered in the black depths while they stared at each other in silence.

"Look, Honey," he cut through the tense stillness. "I came here looking for a wife to raise a family with, a woman to work alongside me to build a life. I hadn't bargained for a spoiled heiress who enjoys giving her favors away to anyone who's even remotely interested."

The lack of subtlety got her dander up, even though he wasn't, in actuality, referring to her. "Who said I was that type?"

"This marriage may have been arranged by my aunt but I'm no fool. I had you checked out by Pinkerton. Unfortunately, I only just got the report this morning right before I walked up the gangplank to claim my *sweet innocent, blushing bride*."

"Yes. Unfortunate," Libby mumbled, thinking that the type of relationship he'd described sounded like the final chapter from a splendid romance novel. To be a true partner and work alongside your husband in a marriage and not just be a drudge, worn out before your time, as her mother had been, would be more than a woman could ever hope for. Unable to quell her curiosity about a man who would openly set forth such a desire, she asked, "Why didn't you select your own bride, instead of letting your aunt make such an important decision for you?"

He cast her a decidedly annoyed expression. "That, Miss Rutcliff, is my business. If you have no further questions about what you're suppose to do tonight, I'll be going. I've got much more important things to do with my time than stand here talking to the likes of you."

"Then don't let our minor problem detain you from tending to more important matters," she said as smartly as she could, stinging from the force of his words.

"I'd no intention of it." He smiled wickedly. "Get some rest. I want you in top form for your performance tonight."

"You needn't worry, Mr. Chandler," she said through tight lips. "Tonight I'll give the performance of my life."

Chapter Eight

Once Cordell Chandler left, Libby sank down onto the bed, feeling physically drained, but emotionally refreshed, near the point of exhilaration. After her mother had married the reverend, Libby'd had the spark of independence exorcized from her as if it had belonged to the devil. But this morning she'd engaged in a verbal sparring match, and no bolt of lightning had come from the sky to strike her down. Nor had Cordell Chandler attempted to harm her physically, even though he was furious enough with her.

Thinking about it, Libby realized she was free, truly free. She'd spoken her mind without fear. That feeling of freedom had come from Cordell Chandler. Making every effort not to think about the big man, further than what she had to do tonight, Libby put her head on the pillow and soon was deep in sleep.

Libby's mind did a visualize replay of her life. Her mother's voice floated through her subconscious, sobbing, "Libby, I pray the fates will hold for you a good, strong man who will love and cherish you. Oh, Child, don't let yourself be trapped into a nightmare with someone like Elijah Ardsworth."

For hours Libby tossed and turned, voices and faces swirling about her, pleading, moralizing, and warning her of the future. She awoke with a start, trembling, perspiration trailing down her hairline. Somehow she had to ensure her protection against the reverend. . . .

48

* * *

Katherine paced back and forth inside her cell, wringing her hands. "I don't care how good you think your plan is. I am not going to stay in this cell while you go off after that Hollis woman! Do you hear me, Shelley?"

"I can't help but hear you, the way you're screeching. If you'll just be quiet long enough to let me finish before that caterwauling of yours brings those two deputies back, I think we both can benefit from this situation."

Her lips pinched, Katherine snarled, "No one is going to benefit from *anything* unless you get me out of here so I can put a stop to that wedding."

"Damn! I *never* should have told you what I overheard," Sharpe groaned, wiping his forehead.

"Well, you did. Now are you going to get me out of here or not?" she demanded.

Sharpe tweaked his moustache in contemplation, remembering how Katherine had skillfully maneuvered the Hollis girl into changing places with her on the ship so Katherine could be his constant companion. She'd warmed his bed well with her greedy little fingers and tongue. He certainly wouldn't mind poking her on a regular basis. That thought alone was almost enough to let her out. But Sheldon Sharpe was true to only one thing: his pursuit of riches.

If he used the keys he saw hanging from that big ring on the wall, Katherine would find a way to stop the wedding. If she did that, she would ruin all the plans he had for Cordell Chandler. Of course, maybe he could realize even more profit. If he released Katherine and somehow kept her from interfering with the wedding, he could blackmail her, since she would not have wed Chandler as her father had instructed; and he could still blackmail Chandler, who'd undoubtedly want the whole sorry situation kept quiet to save his reputation. Sharpe ran a finger along his moustache. He was a gambler, after all, a man used to taking chances. The prospects for even more money were too great to pass up the opportunity to milk

49

every angle.

"I'll get a room at the Etaphone Rest. I hear board's only six bucks a week there. If you promise to wait for me in the room before trying anything on your own, I'll get the keys."

Katherine had no intention of keeping any promises to the gambler, but she agreed just to get herself out of the jail cell. She slipped her arms between the bars and drew Sharpe's head to her. Licking her lips slowly, she angled her face and kissed him as she rubbed her body sensuously against the black iron separating them. "That's just a sample of my appreciation, Shelley, Honey." Sharpe eyed her suspiciously, but took the keys off the wall and returned to her chamber.

"After I unlock your cell, you wait until I make sure it's clear, then sneak over to the stand of trees out back. After I get a room at the boardhouse I'll step out where you can see me. It's up the street to the north. I'll hold up my fingers to let you know what the room number will be and leave the door ajar. Then you carefully sneak into the room and wait for me. You understand?"

"Yes," she hissed, anxious to be done with the cell.

Sharpe put the big iron key in the lock and clicked it open.

When Katherine pushed against the bars, Sharpe held them closed tight. "Stay here until I go outside and make sure it's all clear. Then, after I rent that room and get you set, I think I'll mosey on over to the telegraph office and send Reverend Ardsworth a telegram to let him know where to find his precious Miss Elizabeth Hollis," Sharpe said, thinking he could reap yet another reward—from the minister.

Katherine fought to control her impatience as Sharpe returned the keys to their resting place and left the jail. For five minutes she waited until she could no longer stand it. She creaked the bars open and stepped into the outer office. Just as she was about to turn the doorknob, two loud male voices boomed through the opening door. She cursed her bad luck and rushed back to the cell to wait.

"Have to admit that cool drink hit the spot, but Dell's still got himself a woman any man would like to bed, even if she *is* a lady," admitted Jake.

"I ain't arguing with you. Just don't let nobody else hear you talk like that. Now, let's get back inside. The sheriff'd have our hides if that crazy gal escaped while we was out wetting our whistles."

Now at the Choteau Hotel in the room Cordell had secured for her, and with the wedding only an hour away, Libby brushed her shiny black curls while she rehearsed in the mirror what she was going to say at the appropriate moment. She put the back of her hand to her forehead. "Oh, surely you can see I'm much too weak to marry you tonight, Cordell," she whined. She screwed up her face. "No. That sounds too much like a vapid imbecile." She took a breath and put some animation into her expression. "Oh, Cordell." She sighed. "You're so considerate to offer to postpone the wedding for little ol' me." She laughed. That was even worse. She pinched her lips and tried to look serious. "Oh, Cordell, I can't marry you tonight, because I'm not Katherine Rutcliff." She stared at her reflection. "That would work just fine, you silly girl. Then *you'll* be the one sitting in the jail while the real Katherine Rutcliff walks down the aisle with Cordell Chandler." No . . . she could not go to jail. She had to go through with his plan despite her feelings; she had no other option. She had to protect herself from her stepfather. With more determination she looked solemnly at herself and chided, "All right, Libby, get it right this time." She took a deep breath. "Cordell . . ."

The sweet, haunting strings of violin music drifted into the room where Libby was putting the finishing touches on her attire. Dressed in ivory satin, with yards of lace draped about the skirt and forming the long sleeves and trailing veil, Libby felt an inner warmth unlike anything she'd ever experienced. She smoothed an errant black curl

51

and fastened the pearl drop earrings. She picked up the bouquet of white roses and baby's breath, specially grown under Addison Rutcliff's direction and brought upriver by steamer. She held the fragrant petals to her nose. She inhaled deeply and wondered if all brides shared a common feeling at this special moment in their lives.

Sudden tears stood ready to mar the glow pinking her cheeks when she realized that this wasn't actually her own wedding day. Fingers trembling with emotion, she lightly brushed over the cool, smooth satin bodice. She had once dreamed of being married in flowing white. But here she stood in a special gown designed for someone else, a stand-in for another. Feeling the blow of remorse for what might have been, she felt a terrible anguish. She was not a completely innocent bride, and because of Reverend Ardsworth's probing hands, she never could be.

A knock at the door put an instant halt to her abstracted musings. "I see you're ready," Cordell said, coming into the room. Despite his tense stance and straight lips, his eyes exuded appreciation for what he saw and caused Libby's cheeks to burn.

Libby shrank behind the washstand and held up a shawl in front of her. Propping up her broken resolve, she said with a flippant air, "Don't you know it's bad luck to see the bride right before the wedding?"

The gleam left his eyes. "There isn't going to be a wedding, or have you forgotten?"

She lowered her head. "No, I haven't forgotten." Cordell Chandler stood before her decked out in black tie and gray pinstriped jacket, looking as if he'd just stepped out of a fancy Eastern fashion magazine she had once seen. His appearance would set any woman's heart fluttering, and Libby was no exception.

"Good. Just wanted to make sure you remember your lines."

Libby's flight of fancy crashed in flames. He hadn't really even noticed her. He was merely interested in making sure she, or rather Katherine, did not end the evening as his wife. She stiffened. "Don't worry, I've been practicing and know precisely what I'm supposed to do."

"Just see that you don't suddenly forget." He offered his arm. "Shall we?"

Libby took her place just the other side of the dining room door of the Choteau Hotel and waited for the wedding march to begin as Cordell left to join the other men in the wedding party. She peeked inside the room. Cordell stood near a flowered arch at the head of the crowded room, which he had hastily rented for the occasion. It looked like the town's flower gardens had been raided, for a riot of late spring blooms adorned the walls, chairs, and every conceivable surface.

She gazed around at the rows of guests who'd come to witness the wedding of their friend and associate. The Conrad brothers and the Kohrses were conversing with a man she heard them call Granville Stuart. Two matronly women laughed at something said by a stately gentleman they identified as Governor Benjamin Potts.

Surprisingly, the women were dressed in the latest fashions, not the plain calico that Libby had expected to see on the frontier. Other clusters of guests were busy whispering. Why, Cordell Chandler must know every influential individual in the territory, Libby surmised, counting at least a hundred and fifty people jammed into the room.

The wedding march began and all eyes turned expectantly to the door. This was it! Her debut and final performance, the finale of her new life, would happen in the next fifteen minutes!

Chapter Nine

Libby was about to make her grand entrance when the music stopped. Oh, no! Cordell Chandler had had a change of mind. He was going to tell everyone of her, or rather Katherine's, past. She would be shamed. The good people of the town would shun her. She swallowed and squeezed her eyes shut, waiting for the dreaded announcement.

"Katherine," Cordell said. He placed a hand on her arm. When she slowly opened her eyes, he was smiling. "Katherine, I want you to meet Governor Potts. He has most graciously requested that I allow him to give you away, since he just learned your father was detained in St. Louis and won't be here to do the honors."

"Of course, only with your permission, my dear," the kindly gentleman said in a voice which generated confidence. He extended his hand and placed it on Libby's arm in a comforting gesture.

The highly esteemed governor of the Territory of Montana had just asked her permission to give her away! Back home she would never have been allowed a glimpse at such a venerable man. The reverend had always forced her to leave the room while he entertained guests, saying that her very presence in his house was shame enough.

All the wondrous things happening to Libby demonstrated how wrong the reverend had been and brought tears to her eyes. She snuffled them back.

"I didn't mean for my suggestion to upset you, my dear.

know I can never take your father's place. I just thought—"

With a sob of emotion she cut in, "Governor, you would do me the greatest honor if you'd give me away this evening." After the words were out, Libby ventured a speculative look at Cordell; he was furiously frowning.

"The governor will be doing us both a great honor," Cordell said without cheer.

"Loosen up, Dell. This is your wedding day, man. One would think you were attending a funeral, with all the enthusiasm you're showing." The governor laughed, apparently pleased with the joke he'd made, and missed the dark exchange between the prospective groom and his bride. "Why don't you go back inside and take your place? We certainly don't want to keep your guests waiting, now do we?"

Cordell glared at Libby, his eyes shooting glacial sparks. Then he gave a curt nod and strode back into the room.

Again the wedding march began. Her hands shaking, Libby stepped inside on the governor's arm and stood still for a moment as the guests came to their feet. Oohs and ahs resounded from every row. Libby felt a swell of pride when she heard one man tell another how lucky Cordell was to get such a gorgeous bride. Hearing how attractive she was was something new for Libby. She smiled to herself: she'd found her feelings of self-worth growing at every turn since she landed at Fort Benton.

Libby's bright smile withered when her eyes settled on the lone figure standing off in a far corner. The thin red moustache was unmistakable: Sheldon Sharpe. Panic threatened to overtake her. What was he doing here? Besides Katherine, he was the only person who knew her identity. Did he intend to expose her? Would people believe him? Libby's thoughts raced with excuses to recant anything the man, a known gambler and cardsharp, might say about her.

Just as the inclination to flee was about to overwhelm her, Sharpe's lips gathered into a smirk and he mouthed the words, "Don't worry, Miss Hollis, this is your day.

Enjoy it." He leaned back against the wall and complaisantly folded his arms over his chest.

Sharpe had used her name. Was it his way of sending
her some subliminal message? Even if his intention was
merely to give her a temporary reprieve, Libby experienced
the prick of gratitude. At least she wasn't about to be
humiliated by a gambler in front of the townspeople. No
. . . she would mar her dignity all by herself if she didn't
give an award-winning performance.

A small measure of confidence returned and she drew
her eyes from Sharpe to sneak a glance at Cordell. He was
standing with his hands clasped in front of him, his
expression shuttered. He was such a darkly handsome
man. She felt a slicing disappointment that he didn't seem
to be so taken with her appearance as were the guests. Her
eyes wandered to his mouth: it was full and sensuous, a
mouth Libby knew had tasted a good many lips. Yet his
aunt had chosen his bride. Why? She scolded herself; it
was none of her business. She was there to play her role
and then leave town quietly.

As Libby and the governor started down the aisle, she
heard a smartly dressed woman proclaim, "How I wish
the governor had given me away at our wedding, Herbert."

"He probably would have if you'd been as beautiful,"
whispered her balding partner.

"Or important and lucky enough to marry Cordell
Chandler," she retorted.

Libby lifted her head. The pulse in her neck was hammering. This was every woman's dream, but her nightmare. She looked ahead at Cordell: he was signaling her
with expectant black eyes. She swung her gaze in the
direction he had been indicating.

There stood the fainting couch, her main prop in this
drama.

The sounds of music and an overwhelming fragrance of
flowers assaulted her senses as she and the governor
moved closer to the pink satin couch. Nearer and nearer
they stepped. Libby began to wonder if she was going to

make it to the couch before actually fainting, she was so nervous. She desperately rehearsed the lines she had learned earlier. *Cordell, I fear we must postpone the ceremony. Please do forgive me, but I'm afraid I am much too ill to continue this evening.*

Governor Potts looked over at the young woman next to him. She was the epitome of refinement and breeding; it showed in her graceful carriage and demure manner. He'd have to jot off a note to Addison Rutcliff as soon as he got back to his office, congratulating the man on the fine job he'd done raising the girl. Maybe he'd be the first to send along a photograph of himself with the bride and groom, let Addison know that people in Montana were watching after the man's only daughter. It didn't hurt to do a little politicking on his and Cordell's behalf, either. After all, despite their friendship, Addison Rutcliff was an extremely wealthy and powerful man.

"You'll be fine, Katherine," the governor whispered, feeling a shiver tremble through the girl. He rested his hand on hers. "All brides are a little nervous. Just remember, Cordell Chandler is considered quite a catch by women out here. And you are about to reel him in, my dear." He smiled indulgently. "He's a good man, and he'll make you a fine husband."

Cordell Chandler is a good man, and he'll make you a fine husband. The words echoed in Libby's head over and over, obliterating her memorized speech. She looked again at the flowered-bedecked couch. It might as well be a coffin. Could she go through with it? She looked up at Cordell, her temples violently throbbing. Could she not?

Chapter Ten

Libby was almost even with the pink satin chaise no more than two feet to her left. For an instant the thought of forgoing the couch and meeting Cordell Chandler at the altar seemed more desirable than this farce in which she was about to play a starring role. *No,* she screamed to the voice inside her. This was her chance to be utterly free of all others for the first time in her life.

She lifted the back of her hand to her forehead, gave a shrill sigh, and collapsed onto the couch, right on cue.

Governor Potts was there immediately, patting her hand while the guests gasped and rushed forward. Libby heard the murmurs and whispers from behind her lids as the startled women offered counsel. She forced herself to lie still, although being the center of attention with all this concern was another new experience for her.

"There's nothing to worry about," Cordell Chandler said, pushing his way through the tight cluster of people surrounding Libby. "I'm sure she'll be fine. No doubt it's nothing more than the overtiring journey . . . you know how hard traveling to the frontier can be on a woman used to the comforts of the big city."

Why, that pompous male specimen! Libby wanted to shout. He was playing his part to the hilt, while she was supposed to be the weak, helpless female unable to endure the rigors of a steamer trip. When he put his hand on her cheek and brushed back a stray ringlet of hair, a foreign tingling sensation followed the path of his fingertips. It unsettled Libby further and caused her to flutter her lashes.

"Look," a woman's scratchy voice cried, "she's comin' 'round."

Caught, Libby slowly opened her eyes to stare into Cordell Chandler's strong features. If she hadn't known better, Libby would've sworn there was true concern there. She put her hand up to her brow. "My goodness, what happened?"

"You had a fainting spell, my dearest one," Cordell said, gently stroking her hand.

"Here, give 'er this." A man handed Cordell a glass of water.

"Let me help you sit up, my angel," Cordell crooned, smiling between his teeth so that only Libby could see the insincerity of his words.

"Thank you . . . darling." Libby smiled sweetly back and let him cradle her head while she sipped from the glass.

"Do you feel well enough to continue now, dear heart?" He spoke in such terms of endearment that Libby almost began to wonder if she really was going to be ill. How could the women of the town believe such a sappy performance?

"Of course she don't," said a spindly matron in a stern voice. "A soft, city-bred gal like this one needs her rest. You should've known better than to expect such a pampered, frail young thing to step off the boat in the morning and rush right into marrying you the same night," she reproved.

With earnest anxiety oozing from every word, Cordell affected a deep remorse. "You know how it is, Mrs. Cornswell . . . I can remember when Bench won your hand. Why, he couldn't *wait* to put his brand on such a charming, attractive lady such as yourself." He flashed the matron an alluring smile.

Agatha Cornswell waved him off with a girlish blush. "Ah, Dell, that was a long time ago. You were no more than a boy then. Besides, I was a big, strapping girl, not

59

some delicate little ornament like Katherine here."

"Hmph. Pity she ain't stronger. My Caroline here," the pinched-faced woman linked her arm with a striking blonde's, "woulda made a much better choice. Made outa good, hardy pioneer stock, she is. And not at all bad to look on, neither," snipped the disgruntled mother, giving a superior sniff down the length of her nose at Libby.

Libby had made too many gains in her own sense of worth to allow the comparison of herself to the pale blonde beauty to shrink behind her old wall of self doubt now. But she secretly wondered what connection the girl had had with Cordell Chandler . . . had he once been interested in her? The light in the girl's eyes when she gazed at Cordell spoke for itself: she carried strong feelings for the big rancher. A stab of jealousy hit Libby.

"We all know you had your sights set on Caroline and Dell makin' a match," Bench Cornswell, a square man with thinning gray hair, interjected, "and you're still feelin' all fired up 'cause—"

Agatha shot her husband a quelling glare. "Hush up, Bench . . . this isn't no time to be dredging up the past."

Bench reddened and quickly tried to recover. "Ah, gosh, Aggie . . . I was just trying to say that Katherine here'll make a mighty fine politician's wife down there in Washington someday, her being such a fancy little filly."

"Don't let it bother you, Bench. My bride-to-be and I thank you for the compliment. Katherine's beauty and her many *talents* will undoubtedly be considered an invaluable asset in many circles," Cordell said warmly. He then settled icy eyes on Libby, who had not missed the double-edged meaning of his words. She tried to ignore the possibility that the word "talents" might actually mean sexual favors, although it was a stinging wound. She forced herself to focus on what Bench Cornswell had said.

Libby turned her attention to Caroline. So the girl had been part of Cordell Chandler's past, and he had plans to run for political office someday. No doubt he was already campaigning, the way he handled these people. Libby bit her tongue to keep from screaming . . . had the entire town of Fort Benton slipped so easily under his spell?

Libby looked into Cordell Chandler's triumphant face. The guests were doing his work for him. They had her nicely catagorized as a weak, vapid female who would have a difficult time withstanding the rigors of life out on the frontier. She wasn't weak; she was strong. She had proved it by taking charge of her life. That comment about her being a pampered, frail young thing was almost enough to make her leap off the couch and strut to the altar. But no . . . she certainly didn't want a man who thought worse than nothing of her, even though he was considered a prime catch.

She swallowed another unwelcome notion of going through with the ceremony. What was wrong with her? This was her big scene, the one for which she'd been rehearsing all afternoon. Her heart racing, her mouth dry and scratchy as burlap, she said weakly, "Oh, Cordell, I think it would be best if you helped me back to my room so I could rest."

"Yes, of course," Cordell said with just the right touch of self-sacrificing seriousness.

Murmurs of disbelief and disappointment echoed through the crowd as Cordell helped Libby to her feet and started back down the aisle.

Everything was going according to schedule. Cordell had planned well. He'd known exactly how the guests would react and had manipulated them into a position of sympathy and support. He'd even set the stage for her later departure from Fort Benton by having folks think she was too weak to survive out here. He would make a fine politician someday, with all the style and flare he'd exhibited.

"No guts?" mouthed Sheldon Sharpe, shaking his head when he caught Libby's eye.

That tendency toward rashness which had often gotten Libby into trouble with the reverend when she was little was now beginning to surface. She'd like to show them all she wasn't weak!

Her head began to throb and a pain shot up the back of

her neck from the tension. For a moment she thought she actually was going to faint. Her knees began to give way. Cordell caught her and swept her up into his arms to the delightful squeals of the guests.

"You two just remember to come right on back now, y' hear? There ain't goin' t' be no honeymoonin' without benefit of the preacher," a wiry young man gibed.

"Don't go giving me any ideas, Harvester," Cordell laughed good-naturedly.

Libby stared up into Cordell's face, her eyes wide that the guests would even think such a thing. What she saw in his expression gave her no comfort. He couldn't possibly think he was going to take advantage of her before he left tomorrow morning, could he?

They were almost to the door when Cordell said in a loud voice, "Are you absolutely sure, Katherine dear, that you aren't up to getting married this evening?" He swung around with Libby in his arms so she was the one directly facing the guests, on the center stage. "I really hate to disappoint all these fine people who went to so much trouble for us."

That was all it took. His self-enhancing comment at her expense cut the final thread encasing her composure. Libby's temper unraveled.

Before she stopped to think, she blurted, "Well, we shan't disappoint them, then. Governor Potts, if you're willing to take another chance and walk me down the aisle once more, we'll try this again."

Chapter Eleven

Libby was certain she saw a purple flush of hatred color the edges of Cordell's handsome face as he set her on her feet. His eyes had lost their golden sparkle and now were as two cold, hard, black stones.

In a threatening voice he asked, "Are you absolutely certain you're well enough, Katherine . . . dear?"

"Why Cordell Chandler, the way you talk," came the crisp voice of a richly clad older woman. "Folks might think you're a tryin' to keep from a-weddin' this fine young lady. And her travelin' all this way, too!"

Finely tuned echoes seconded the general consensus, proving just how capricious a crowd could be. Cordell didn't stand a chance, and from the look on his face, he knew it. While it should have given Libby the sweet taste of victory, the rashness of her tongue had succeeded only in immeasurably complicating both their lives. She had set in motion a wheel of fate which would only stop at the altar. She had not merely upstaged Cordell Chandler's performance in their little play, she had rewritten the ending.

Fear welled up inside her at being escorted down the aisle alongside Governor Potts. The guests had reclaimed their seats and sat expectantly as the fiddle player started up once again. Cordell had returned to his position, but she could not decode the secrets behind the bland expression he wore. With each step a voice inside her screamed that she was turning farce into tragedy.

They were once again even with the now infamous fainting couch. She gazed at it a trifle long, causing the governor to whisper in a soothing voice, "You won't have need of that this time, my dear."

Libby swallowed all self-recrimination for not following Cordell Chandler's plan and raised her head proudly. After all, she reminded herself, hadn't the man stated quite clearly that he wouldn't touch her? It wasn't as if it was going to be a real marriage. Cordell Chandler was here to marry Katherine Rutcliff, not Elizabeth Marie Hollis. The thought gave her a twinge. She found herself perplexed; was it fear or disappointment?

At the arch of flowers, Governor Potts solemnly placed Libby's hand in Cordell's and stepped aside. Libby was trembling, her resolve of a minute ago fading until Cordell's big, strong fingers closed over hers. Despite his scowling, rigid stance, he exuded a confident warmth which held her mesmerized as the young, hunched preacher began to speak.

"Dearly beloved, we are gathered here today in the sight of God and these witnesses to join together Cordell and Katherine . . ."

While the preacher droned on, Libby could only think of the preacher saying Cordell was being united with Katherine. *Katherine!* The name tore at Libby, leaving her senses gratefully numbed to the commotion which had erupted at the back of the room.

As the guests sat intently listening to the ceremony, Katherine walked boldly into the room. Her eyes glittered and a calculating smile twisted her lips at the scene before her. The little fool thought she was going to get away with marrying Cordell Chandler. At the thought Katherine stopped to take a good look at the big rancher. On the docks this morning she'd been too distraught to give the man any consideration. Now she noticed what an enticing fellow he was. Perhaps being married to Cordell Chandler would have its advantages after all. She let her eyes travel the length of him. He'd probably make a pretty interesting bed partner; a man that big had to have endowments lacking in men of lesser size.

Katherine took a step forward and pointed an accusing finger. "Stop—".

Sharpe moved with blazing swiftness, clamped a hand over Katherine's mouth, and circled her waist. "Shhh, sweetness."

Agatha Cornswell's head snapped around. "What do you two think you're doing?" she whispered in an annoyed voice.

Sharpe quickly managed to hide Katherine's face in the crook of his arm. "My wife feels faint."

"Help me to the couch," Katherine said in muffled tones.

Agatha glanced from the couch back to the strange couple. "My God, that couch has already had enough of a workout tonight!"

"Couch, dear, *please*," Katherine moaned, putting on what she was sure was a good act.

Agatha raised her brows. "Well, you can't go disturbing folks any more than you already have. Look at everybody who's already turned to see what's going on. What are you standing around for? Get her some fresh air. Can't you see there's a wedding going on?" When the couple did not depart immediately, she added, "Get out, before you ruin the ceremony."

"We wouldn't want to do that, would we, sweetness?"

Katherine slitted her eyes at the woman as Sharpe removed her from the room. Once outside, Katherine swung away from the gambler. "You bastard! Why did you stop me? I'm going back inside there and put a halt to that wedding right now!"

"No you're not. If you stopped to think before you acted, you'd realize there's more to gain by waiting."

Panic beginning to overtake her, she cried, "But Papa'll disown me!"

"Not if you follow my plan."

Still fuming, Katherine snipped, "Oh, yes—your precious little plan. All we have to do is let them get married and think they'll live happily ever after. Then, as soon as they can't live without each other, we blackmail them separately, is that correct?"

"You're doing so well, why don't you continue?"

She made a face. "Since Cordell Chandler is interested in going into politics, he won't dare chance a scandal. And our precious Elizabeth Hollis would do *anything* to keep her beloved from knowing that she attacked a man of God, not to mention the little twit's desire to protect her husband's career." Katherine inhaled impatiently. "But if they don't respond to our demands?"

"After I left you this afternoon at the boarding house, did some checking. Except, of course, counting the women Chandler's had in his past, he has a spotless reputation; there's no way he's going to let it be tarnished. He'll pay, and so will the Hollis girl, And after we've collected a good portion of the Chandler fortune, then—"

"Then we let Chandler and the rest of the community know the truth about Elizabeth Hollis, I step in to accept his apologies and console him, and of course, I marry him, right?"

"Right. See how easy it'll be." He puffed out his chest. "Just like holding a royal flush. We can't lose."

"Yes, that's what the South said at the beginning of the Civil War."

"Think of it this way, then: if you go back in there now and embarrass the man in front of all his friends, you may stop the wedding, but you'll be sure to lose your best chance at Chandler as well. He's not going to be any too eager to marry someone who made such a spectacle of herself this morning, not to mention one who did it again tonight. *Then* what will your Papa say?"

Katherine mulled over Shelley's plan. From what she'd seen of Cordell Chandler, Shelley might just be right. She couldn't chance losing Chandler. She didn't have any other ploys in mind. She'd go along with Shelley's scheme but with one little twist of her own.

". . . I now pronounce you man and wife. What God

hath joined together, let no man put asunder." There was an awkward pause before the preacher finally cleared his throat and suggested, "You'll have a lifetime to gawk at each other. Now kiss your bride, Dell, before some well-meaning young buck does it for you."

An amused murmur buzzed through the guests and Libby's cheeks colored. Cordell was just standing there, his countenance as glacial as his pose. He didn't intend to kiss her. For a moment she wasn't sure whether she was relieved or embarrassed. Reverend Ardsworth's groping hands had left Libby filled with dread at any man's intimate touch, whether it be the lips or . . .

Still, Cordell remained still as a statue. Libby glanced at the faces filled with bewildered amusement. She had to do something. She just couldn't let them become a laughing-stock. He could have exposed her, yet he hadn't. Cordell Chandler was much too important a man to suffer the ribbing which would surely be meted out . . . although someone of his ilk could certainly handle himself under *any* circumstances, from what Libby had seen.

Forcing aside her own dire apprehensions, and before giving thought to the full implications of what she was about to do, Libby folded back her veil, stood on tiptoe, and wrapped her arms around Cordell's strong neck. Her senses ignited when her skin came into contact with his, and she felt him tense as she drew his head down to join her lips with his.

Libby's movements were clumsy as she pressed her body closer to his. At first the contact brought back the horrors of Reverend Ardsworth and she started to shrink back, but Cordell held her. Realizing the powerful arms which had encircled her were not the hurting, probing hands of the reverend, Libby forced herself to relax and found the experience not unpleasing. She let her lips part in response to Cordell's deepening kiss and discovered that the sharing between a man and a woman could hold the promise of something beautiful and special.

"All right, Dell," an old-timer hooted, "you might a been a little slow gettin' out a the startin' gate, but we thinks you already made up fer it. You got the rest of the night t' *kiss* yore bride after we all get a chance t' celebrate this shindig," he howled with mirth.

Cordell immediately broke the kiss and glowered at Libby. She stood confused and dismayed by the changes in her generated by the unexpected magic of Cordell's touch and a few words spoken by a preacher.

"We was wonderin' when you was gonna come up fer a breather," roared a grizzled trapper.

To drumming applause and cheers, Cordell took Libby's arm to escort her among the guests. Before the first person reached them, he paused and growled, "Just because you managed to coerce me into marrying you, don't think you've won yet."

Chapter Twelve

Cordell and Libby stood stiffly together and accepted the town's boisterous congratulations while three ladies scurried about, removing layers of flowers from the long tables at the edge of the room and setting out a sumptuous spread. Not able to endure Cordell's hostility any longer, Libby excused herself.

"Mrs. Cornswell, you all went to too much trouble," Libby observed, joining the woman who was spearheading the table arrangements.

"Nonsense! We all kicked in and made it a potluck. Even Hattie Arthur broke down and baked that there pan of sticky buns," she pointed to the plump confections, "and her the sourest old biddy over her Caroline losing out and all."

Libby's attention was drawn immediately to the pale blonde standing near the arch, wistfully staring at Cordell. Curiosity got the better of her and she ventured to ask, "Were Cordell and Caroline once engaged?"

Agatha Cornswell squirmed inside her shawl and fidgeted, rearranging a plate of food. When Libby repeated her question, the platter of sticky buns slipped from Agatha's hands and shattered on the floor.

"Oh, dear!" Agatha swept shaking fingers to her lips.

Libby regarded the woman's nervousness closely but did not press her further, although a hundred puzzling questions about Cordell and Caroline danced in Libby's mind. "Here, Mrs. Cornswell, let me help you."

Libby bent down and had just begun collecting the broken pieces of china when a pleasant male voice called out, "Hold that pose."

A puff of smoke exploded into the air with a pop as Libby looked up, startled, to see an aging photographer emerge from a black cloth attached to a big box.

"Potter's the name. Cornelius Potter, Mrs. Chandler," he said warmly, extending his hand.

"Mr. Potter." Libby nodded, returning the greeting with the usual genial conversation.

"Potter, I didn't know you were in town. Glad you could make it," Cordell said.

"Sorry, Dell. I dropped a platter." Agatha bobbed, flustered, and scurried from the room with the remnants of the buns and china.

"Wonder what got into her," Cordell mused out loud. "Haven't seen her quite so shaken since Bench broke his leg."

Libby looked at him askance. "I don't know. I just asked her about Caroline Arthur."

Cordell shot Libby an unreadable glance and shifted his attention to Cornelius. "What brings you to these parts? Putting together another picture book?"

At Libby's blank expression, Cornelius chuckled. "You see, my dear, I gained a small measure of notoriety for photographing the westward movement back in 1859 when I traveled out here on a wagon train."

"A wagon train of camels, don't you mean?" Cordell laughed. "Katherine, Cornelius is quite famous for that candid book of frontier life which launched a long and illustrious career.

"Yes." Cornelius smiled wanly, remembering how he'd lost the only woman he'd ever truly loved to the captain of that wagon train. Forcing himself to brighten, he said, "And speaking of my career, why don't you put your arm around that beautiful bride of yours and let me get on with it." Cornelius moved back to his equipment while Cordell and Libby took their places.

Libby stiffened when Cordell pulled her close and whispered in her ear, "You might as well smile. This fiasco is your show."

"Hold that pose."

For what seemed an eternity, Libby did manage to smile as she endured the attention heaped upon them. Finally Cordell took her hand and announced amid cheers and hoopla that he and his bride were going to retire, since they had to get an early start tomorrow. Much to Libby's dismay, they were escorted by a rambunctious lot to the finest room in the hotel, secured earlier as a wedding gift from the Kohrses who had had Libby's and Cordell's clothes brought to the room as well. Secretly Libby had hoped to return to her own room at the Overland.

"Well, what ya' waiting fer, Dell? Ain't ya gonna tote the little woman over the threshold?" The bald man hiccupped and stood blurry-eyed, his mouth set in a sly angle. Cordell turned to Libby, his eyes glittering with mischief, promptly tossed her over his shoulder, and strode into the room. He slammed the door shut before any of the astounded guests, who had insisted on observing an old tradition by accompanying the couple to their door, could comment on his unorthodox behavior.

"You beast! How could you? Put me down!"

"Gladly." Cordell unceremoniously dumped her on the beige fainting couch in the corner, lushly decorated in heavy walnut and brass, with delicate lace curtains.

"Ohh!" Libby squealed, hitting the cushion with a thud. "What do you think you're doing?"

"I put you on your wedding bed. If you'd had half a brain, you'd have stayed put on that damned couch earlier and we wouldn't be in this fix right now. But since we are, consider this your bed for the night." Cordell walked over to the big featherbed and sat down.

"If you hadn't overplayed your part, we wouldn't be here right now, don't you mean?" she sputtered, still stinging from his tirade.

He narrowed his eyes. "If I hadn't *overplayed* my part!"

He shook his head, rubbing the back of his neck. "Well, we're here, and I, for one, intend to be comfortable."

"You're not planning to sleep in here with me tonight, are you?" Libby croaked, visibly shaken.

"Sleep?" Cordell's lips drew into a wry grin. At Libby's sudden pose for flight, he added, "You can quit looking like the scared little virgin. I know better, remember?"

His bitter words caused Libby to garner her courage and recount the advice Augusta Kohrs had offered: Cordell admired strength. No matter how she felt, she was never again going to let the man see her exhibit one sign of weakness. She was going to participate in the decisions affecting her future—beginning right now!

"I don't care *what* you think I am," she retorted.

"Fine! That makes two of us." He swung around and headed for the door.

His unforeseen actions took her by surprise. "Where are you going?"

"Don't tell me you're suddenly concerned about me. How thoughtful of you, wife." The word "wife" was accented harshly.

"Of course not. I just don't want people to talk. After all, it *is* our wedding night."

"And you don't want people to talk? Don't make me laugh! You didn't give a whore's damn about appearances back in St. Louis. Or didn't you think some poor slob out in the territories would hear about your reputation? Did you think I was some backwoods hick who could be supplicated by a pretty face?"

"You *do* think I'm very pretty, though," she put in smartly, trying to throw him off guard.

"Believe me, you don't want to hear what I think." His eyes flaming, Cordell stomped from the room, slamming the door behind him.

Libby stared after him, the crash still resounding in her ears. A vast wave of emotions left her transfixed, her gaze riveted to the door long after he'd left.

* * *

Clenching his fists at his sides, Cordell headed for a shack at the edge of town. What he needed was a stiff slug of Chinook Griswald's rotgut in order to obliterate the evening from his mind. Then he thought of the ingredients the cagey old bastard put in the potent brew he sold to the Indians: alcohol, chewing tobacco, a handful of red peppers, a bottle of Jamaica ginger, and a quart of black molasses. He promptly changed course and headed for the Eagle Bird.

The saloon was empty except for the bartender snoozing at the end of the bar, and a fancy dude sitting at one of the five roughly hewn tables, laying out a hand of solitaire.

Cordell helped himself to a quarter-full bottle at the bar so's not to disturb the snoring bartender and took a seat at a table in a far corner. He propped his feet up on a chair and without ceremony upended the bottle.

For the first time in his life, Cordell had felt an overwhelming urge to wring a woman's neck and enjoy doing it. He took another snort of the fiery liquid. How could he let himself be so gullible as to think she'd keep her end of the bargain and not go through with the wedding? Why did he ever let Matilde talk him into this mess in the first place? Originally he'd agreed to Matilde's idea just to humor her.

He'd planned to investigate the girl before she arrived. If she checked out, he was going to make a final decision if they hit it off. He cursed the Pinkerton report's late arrival, but he had no one to blame but himself for letting things get out of hand. Again he took a big gulp. The sounds of unrestrained celebrating which continued to usurp the quiet of the mild evening air grated on him. The whole damned town was over at the hotel still hooting it up, and Cordell sat here alone. He emptied the bottle.

"What's the matter? Doesn't married life with *Katherine* agree with you?" The cardsharp, dressed in a black coat and red brocade vest, wore a particularly lewd, knowing smirk.

"What's it to you, mister?" Cordell snarled in a low,

dangerous voice.

"Sheldon Sharpe. I came upriver with Katherine on the *Benton*. Got a *real* good chance to get to know the little lady," the smirk slithered to his beady eyes, "if you know what I mean."

Chapter Thirteen

"Sharpe, you slimy bastard!"

Cordell's reaction was lightning quick. He sprang from his chair and smashed Sharpe in the mouth. The cocky little man flew back against a table and clattered to the floor into a limp mass. Sharpe came to as Cordell stomped to the door.

"We're not through yet, Chandler . . . not by a long shot," Sharpe groaned through the pulp of pain which was his face. Out of pure spite, he called out on a note of triumph, "Chandler, your precious lady has a delightful little mole just above her left breast."

Visions of Katherine lying willingly in Sheldon Sharpe's arms even as she traveled to become his wife haunted Cordell all the way back to the hotel. He wished he'd killed the gambler. But the fact was, Cordell had wed a wealthy whore. The truth slashed at him until he knew without question what he was going to do.

When he burst into the bridal suite, Libby was sitting quietly in the dark. Cordell lit the light. She'd changed into a blue silk kimono from Paris and her long, flowing black curls hung over one shoulder and down her back.

In two paces was standing over his dry-eyed young bride. She looked so innocent, almost childlike, that Cordell's gut ached. "I'm surprised you're still here," he said coldly.

Libby looked at the hard lines of his face. There was no sign of forgiveness. Yet all evening she'd listened to people tell her how truly fortunate she was to have snared Cordell Chandler. And while she'd waited for him to return, she'd done little else but think of him. At first she'd intended to tell him the truth and throw herself on his mercy, but the more she considered everything she knew of the man, the more she was swayed to try to make the marriage work— at least until she was safe from the reverend's wrath.

"Why wouldn't I be here? I'm your wife," she said calmly.

"Not for long."

"Now, how can you say that? *You* were the one who sent for me in the first place, remember?" She tried to sound flip in order to lighten their conversation, which was taking on an ominous tone.

"So I was reminded earlier at the Eagle Bird." He looked straight into her eyes, his gaze piercing enough to daunt the most strong-willed.

"The Eagle Bird?"

"A local saloon. I met one of your admirers there and we exchanged pleasantries." His scraped knuckles curled into a fist.

"Is that how you exchange pleasantries?" She nodded toward his hand, silently fearing what he was about to say.

"With the likes of one Sheldon Sharpe, yes."

Libby's face fell at the mention of the name. The man knew the truth about her. My goodness, she trembled, he didn't tell Cordell the whole sordid story, did he?

"I see by your response that you *are* acquainted with the little weasel." There was disgust in Cordell's voice. "Well acquainted, according to Sharpe, I might add."

"I hardly knew the man," Libby blurted out in an attempt to defend her unjustly tarnished honor.

Cordell's mouth tightened until his lips were white. In one fell swoop, he lifted Libby to her feet and tore open the top of her kimono to reveal the mole above her left breast, just as Sharpe had said. In open-revulsion Cordell snapped the length of silk shut. With a cold smile forming the most meager expression of civility, he said, "I'd say the man knew you well enough."

Short of revealing the truth about herself, Libby had no way of defending Sharpe's possession of such knowledge. Her mind raced, searching her memory to learn how Sharpe could know about the mole. Then it hit her: he'd been with Katherine when the two had walked into the cabin that first day Libby had stowed away and was slipping into Katherine's clothes. That was the only time he could have seen it.

Lacking a plausible explanation, she forced herself to lift unwavering eyes to Cordell. "He never touched me."

He cocked one dark brow. "And I suppose you are going to try to tell me that no man has?"

Libby's thoughts blinked back to St. Louis and the Reverend Ardsworth. She couldn't honestly give Cordell the answer he deserved. She dropped her gaze.

Sounding bored now, Cordell strode over to the feather-bed across the room before he said, "No need for you to try to think up some clever response. I already know the answer. Be ready to pull out at dawn."

"Then you're taking me with you?" Libby's eyes were wide. She'd thought she'd have to fight for the privilege.

He sat down and began unbuttoning his shirt. "Only as far as Helena. Once there, you're on your own, and I'll quietly get an annulment."

"You have my future all mapped out, don't you?"

"Every intricacy, right down to the fact that until we get to Helena, you'd best forget about indulging in your favorite pastime, or I'll leave you where you lie, if you understand what I'm saying."

Libby understood all too well. The man before her had a lot of pride. Learning the "truth" about his intended had deeply sliced into that dignity. She'd have her work cut out for her if she ever held out the slightest hope of convincing him that she didn't warrant his contempt.

Sharpe was wiping the trickle of blood from his chin when the bartender righted the chairs and table. "Hmph." The bartender looked around at the shattered glasses and broken bottles, then pointedly at Sharpe. "Someone's gotta pay for the damage. To my way of thinkin', it's you, mister."

Holding his swelling lip, Sharpe crawled to his feet. "I didn't throw any punches. Collect from Chandler," Sharpe sneered and stumbled toward the door.

The click of a hammer froze Sharpe in his tracks. The sound was all too familiar, and he swiveled around slowly to look into the double barrels of a shotgun.

"I know your kind," the bartender said, raising the shotgun, "so I keep my little persuader here," he glanced at his weapon, "for just such occasions. Now pay up before I gotta scratch my itchy finger and take a chunk outa your stinkin' hide."

Sharpe slitted his eyes, wishing he was on the other end of the gun. He'd show that saloon keeper! But he knew when he had a losing hand. Grudgingly he peeled off three bills and threw them on the bar. "That should cover the damage," he jeered.

The bartender waved the shotgun toward the door. "Get out. And don't come back."

Sharpe gulped down a bitter retort and swung on his heel.

"I'd be careful what you say about Dell's missus from now on if I was you. It ain't healthy to be talkin' about the lady the way you done. Folks in this town won't take kindly to it," the bartender hollered to Sharpe's back.

As Sharpe headed back to the boarding house he damned his luck, but found himself more determined than ever to put his plan to work. Second only to his love of riches was his love of self. Chandler not only had delivered a blow to his face; with one punch the man had destroyed Sharpe's chances to separate a few suckers from their money at the Eagle Bird. "You'll pay for this, Chandler. More than you know."

Still seething, Sharpe burst in on a sleeping Katherine. She rubbed her eyes at the light. "Who—"

"Who do you *think* it'd be?" Sharpe grabbed her. "That son-of-a-bitch Chandler?"

"Oh, for heaven sakes," Katherine pushed his hands away, "what's gotten into you?" she sputtered, then noticed his bruised face. "My God, what happened?"

In a voice heavy with revenge, Sharpe explained how Chandler had hit him and the events in the bar afterward.

"For someone who thinks he has it all figured out, that was a pretty stupid thing to do," Katherine hissed. "I thought the plan was to wait until they couldn't live without one another and then blackmail them. You made Cordell suspicious of his precious bride, telling him you know her mole—" Suddenly her face darkened. "How *did* you know about it, anyway?"

"You jealous?" He laughed and pulled her to him.

She slapped him away. "No.".

"Come on, sweetness. I saw it when we caught her putting on your dress in your cabin." He circled his arms around a now-mollified Katherine. "You know I only have eyes for you."

"And Cordell Chandler's money," she said astutely.

Keeping his voice light, he added, "Not to mention yours."

"We understand each other, Shelley. That's another thing I like about you."

"Isn't there anything else you like about me?" He squeezed her thinly clad breasts.

"You know what else I like about you," she said in a sultry voice.

"Then show me, baby."

Katherine rolled him onto his back and nipped at his neck. Quickly she cast off her nightgown and removed his coat and shirt. Then her greedy little fingers unfastened his trousers and clamped around his aroused manhood. Sharpe moaned and pushed at her head.

"Don't worry, honey . . . I intend to show you." Her eyes glittered with knowledge of the power she held over men. Inwardly a measure of satisfaction warmed in her cold heart that she was paying her father back for ignoring her. She lowered her lips to join her fingers.

Careful not to disturb his own pleasure, Sharpe maneuvered her so he could savor her body to the fullest and drive her wild. The woman was capable of total abandon and often as eager to experience all he knew about the wicked delights of passion. He'd never been able to enjoy such experimentation before, even with the paid whores he'd known, so Sharpe took full advantage of Katherine's willingness.

With senses burning for release, they reached the height of inflammed hungers before Sharpe roughly parted Katherine's thighs and plunged into her. Again and again he impaled her in a thrusting frenzy without regard for her sudden cries of pain, until his body shuddered in spasms and he slumped on top of her.

"Whew!" she panted, thoroughly satisfied. "You're an animal."

Sharpe moved to her side and traced his fingers downward across her drenched belly to toy with her mound of dark, curling hair. He plucked at a single strand. "So are you, sweetness . . . so are you."

Never one to idly revel in the aftermath of her conquests, Katherine was quick to get down to business. Disregarding preliminaries, she asked, "Now, what are we going to do about Cordell Chandler and his wife?"

"Don't worry. First thing tomorrow I'll see to it that we don't miss our chance with Chandler or his sweet little bride."

Chapter Fourteen

The night sky was rapidly fading into early morning gray when Libby left her room. Dressed in Katherine's best buff traveling ensemble, with three flounces on the back of the underskirt, and wearing a diminutive straw hat, Libby checked at the desk for Cordell and learned from a sheepish clerk that he was down at G.W. Bullet and Co. and had left word for her to join him there for breakfast.

As she left the desk the clerk chuckled. "We all thought you woulda ordered your vittles *in* this mornin'." Libby stiffened but decided to ignore the man's crude attempts at levity and headed down the street.

When she found the place and approached Cordell, he took one look at her and scoffed, "Is that what you plan to wear on the trail?"

"It is." She raised her chin. "And what's wrong with it?"

He looked from his plate to her hat. "Nothing, I guess — if you want to go around with a plate of fried eggs on your head instead of in your belly."

Libby bristled. Why, she'd never possessed such a lovely assortment of hats before. "Well, for your information, this is a very expensive hat," she said, recalling the price tag she had clipped from the brim. "And I like it."

"Suit yourself . . . dear wife." He gave an indifferent shrug and motioned to the chair next to him. "Sit down." He shoved the salt and pepper shakers in her direction as she took her seat. "Why don't you spice it up a little bit in case you get hungry later?"

"If you think you're going to upset me with your remarks, you're not going to succeed. I intend to prove to
you I'm not what you think. *Then* you'll have more to eat
than just your breakfast."

Cordell looked unmoved. "Oh? And what would that
be?"

"Your words."

"Madam, there's nothing you can do or say to change
my mind. Now get something to eat. We need to hit the
trail soon." Cordell stood up and put on his hat. "I'll be
out at the wagons." Without looking back, he strode from
the restaurant.

Libby watched him leave. All she'd intended to do when
she escaped from the reverend was to start a new life, not
make her life more complicated. First she'd been forced to
masquerade as Katherine for two months, then she'd
gotten in deeper to protect herself from the sheriff and
jail. But that wasn't enough; she'd let her own rashness
get her into a marriage with Katherine's fiancée. Even that
predicament seemed insignificant now . . . the real
Katherine and Sheldon Sharpe were lurking somewhere
nearby with knowledge that could send her back to the
reverend and disgrace a man who'd done nothing to deserve it. Goosebumps rose on her arms at the thought.

"Can I get ya' something t' eat, Miz Chandler?" asked
young girl, shyly fiddling with her starched apron.

"Oh . . . umm . . . yes. I'll have whatever is readily
available," Libby answered.

"Right away, ma'am. Ma'am?"

"Yes?"

"I just wanna say how pleased me and Pa is that Mr
Chandler got hisself a real nice lady like you."

"Thank you," Libby returned with a demure blush.

Not one person who knew Cordell Chandler seemed to
have an unkind word to say about the man. Libby felt a
twinge of growing regret that she wasn't the bride Cordell
Chandler had actually sent for.

Libby was hurriedly nibbling on biscuits, beans, and

bacon when Sheldon Sharpe paused in front of the restaurant and noticed her seated by herself. Now was the time to set his plan into motion. A sinister grin shadowing his lips, he entered and sat down across from her.

"Good morning . . . *Katherine*."

"What are *you* doing here?" She noticed the swollen bruise at the corner of his lip. Cordell.

"I saw you through the window and wanted to offer my congratulations. I only had time to compliment the lucky bridegroom last night. I know *Elizabeth Hollis* would want me to convey her best wishes as well, since she was unable to attend the ceremony," he said with a despicable arch to his lips.

When Libby heard her name, she cringed. "I can see you had quite a conversation with Cordell." Steeling herself, she asked, "What do you want?"

Sharpe rubbed his jaw and twisted his red moustache, his eyes glowing with malicious pleasure. "Now what makes you think I want something? His smile was evil. "Of course, if you ever felt the need to help out an old friend sometime—"

"Get to the point." Last night she'd felt sorry for the cardsharp after seeing Cordell's fist. Now she found herself wishing Cordell had done a better job on this low specimen of humanity.

"No point . . . just wanted to let you know I made arrangements with your husband's trail boss a few minutes ago to make the journey to Helena with your train. Won't that be cozy?"

Libby shot to her feet, sending a glass of water flooding across the table, but he cut her off before she could speak. "Better be *real* careful from now on, sweetness. I'd hate to have to spill the beans." He gave a malefic smile at her plate and unfolded a linen napkin to mop up the water.

"I'm not going to let you hurt Cordell."

As Libby twirled around to rush off, Sharpe ground out, "Don't tell me you have feelings for that fool *Chandler*." The girl was playing right into his hands, just as he'd planned. He rubbed his fingers together; he could already feel the new crispness of the money he was going to squeeze out of her.

"I have no intention of telling you anything." To the echoing sounds of his rude laughter, Libby bolted from the room.

"You don't have to rush off on my account, little lady," Sharpe mumbled to himself. He'd have to hurry before it was time to leave if he was going to make sure Katherine knew what she was supposed to do next. He was too close to big money to take a chance of anything going wrong.

Out in the first rays of sun, Libby pinched her eyes shut and let her head drop back. She breathed in big gulps of cool air. What Sharpe had said about her having feelings for Cordell was true . . . he'd been anything but nice to her, yet she did feel a need to protect him. And what he'd said about wanting a partnership in marriage kept takin on a definite shape in her mind.

She saw the bull train on the other side of the street an stepped off the plank curb to make her way over t Cordell.

"White woman coming," hollered a man nearby. All th men in the vicinity removed their hats and lowered the eyes.

Cordell was at her side, offering his arm before sh could assimilate such a phenomenon. The gesture su prised her after the words they had exchanged. "Appea ances, my dear," he said through curving lips. Sh gratefully accepted his escort and nodded to the thr men.

The bewildered expression on her face when she steppe on a pile of playing cards scattered in the street cause Cordell to comment. "No. The cards weren't thrown o here by some disgruntled gambler . . . the saloons use new deck for each deal to ensure against cardsharps mar ing them." Libby blanched at the mention of cardsharp but if Cordell perceived her discomfort, he did not men tion it. "With lots of extra cards, the gambling halls p the cards out to cover the dust and provide a cushion f ladies to walk on. You see, we on the frontier value o women. I'm sure you noticed the respect and deference the men paid you a moment ago . . . as I'm sure you observed that there aren't a lot of white women around. Hmph," came an expressive grunt of displeasure. "They say there are no old maids in Fort Benton. Most feel the best way to keep them from leaving is by providing the most genteel way of life possible out here."

"Do you feel the same way . . . about keeping white women out here, I mean?" she ventured, a small part of her hoping he'd had a change of heart and was beginning to soften.

"I made the mistake of letting you come, didn't I?" he said openly, his voice still full of bitter resentment.

While Libby could understand the extent of his animosity—after all, it must have been a shock to discover his fiancée had a strong penchant for any available man—she hoped the fact that he continued to treat her better than Katherine deserved meant he'd not entirely closed his heart to women and marriage. With Sheldon Sharpe tagging along on this trip, her task would be made all the more difficult.

Libby stopped, took a deep breath, and turned her head to look straight into the depths of Cordell's dark eyes. "Cordell, there is something I have to tell you."

Chapter Fifteen

"What could you possibly have to say that could make any difference?" From her look of dire seriousness, Cordell amended his position. "Let's go over there by the wagons, then you can tell me whatever it is that you find so terribly distressing."

With halting steps, Libby followed Cordell's lead. Next to the piles of merchandise, supplies, and hay lining the levee were three wagons hitched together, ready to be pulled by the eighteen oxen peacefully standing in their yokes.

Cordell noted her interest despite the trepidation paling her cheeks. "This is called a bull train, even though it's pulled by oxen. Oxen aren't as fractious as bulls. We move along pretty slow, but by using oxen, we don't have to haul feed for the animals; they graze along the way."

"I've never seen three wagons tied together like that before."

"That's why it's called a train. The first wagon is the lead wagon, the next the swing, and the last the trail. The one in the front carries the most freight," he explained.

"I see," Libby answered, trying to concentrate on Cordell's business, since the gold sparkle had returned to his eyes when he spoke about this part of his life. The man had an obvious love for his business, and Libby was determined to demonstrate a willingness to share in his life—every facet of it.

"No doubt you see dollar signs on each wagon," he spat caustically.

"You forget, I'm an heiress, remember?" she put out to immediately squelch that idea.

His countenance did not lighten. "What is it you wanted to tell me?"

Libby's shoulders slumped. He was being more obstinate than a badger. She sucked in her cheeks. Would she ever be able to convince him of her sincerity?

"I hope you will try to believe this is none of my doing, but Sheldon Sharpe told me this morning that he plans to be traveling with us."

Libby watched as Cordell's face took on the red flush of thunderous rage. When he spoke, his voice was deadly calm and he grabbed her arms. "Exactly where and when did you see Sharpe?"

Could he be jealous? Jealousy was not an emotion spurred by the indifference he professed . . . it was an emotion wrought with powerful feelings. It could be hatred, for she knew he was angry enough. Yet at times his actions toward her were gentle and considerate, and almost in spite of himself, tender.

"He came into the restaurant after you left." She lifted her chin. "I'm telling the truth, so you can let go of me now."

Cordell narrowed his eyes, the gold sparkle now drowned out by the opaque blackness. He stood there glaring at her as if she were no more than road dung. Libby began to wonder if she'd been right or not a moment ago . . . he was a difficult man to understand. Finally he let his hands drop to his sides and swung away from her.

"He said he already paid your wagon master, and there was nothing I could do to stop him," she said in desperation. *"Please do something."*

"I intend to!" He yelled at a tall man who Libby judged to be in his forties, from the gray twined through his light brown hair. "Gulch McKenzie! Get over here."

The man handed a rawhide whip to one of the scraggly bull whackers and came forward. "Yeah, boss?"

"You take money from some gambler to travel with

us?"

Gulch glanced at Chandler's missus. She looked awful ill at ease for a bride. The boss looked pissed himself. Jesus God, he'd had a bad feeling in his gut about that fancy dude, but the man had assured him there wouldn't be a problem. He scratched at the heavy whiskers on his chin. No use trying to get out of this one. "Yeah. There a problem, boss?"

"You might say that. Damn it!" In a fit of temper Cordell ripped the hat off his head and mashed it against his thigh. "Why in the hell did you go and take on a passenger?" he snorted.

"Ah hell, it seemed like easy money, and the man said there'd be no problem."

"No problem!" Cordell shook his head, running tense fingers through his wavy black hair.

"You want I should hunt the man down and give him back his money?"

"That won't be necessary, gentlemen," Sharpe said, coming up behind the men, carrying his bag, the sheriff keeping pace alongside him.

Sharpe smiled to himself. He'd made sure there was no way Chandler could use all his wealth and power to buy his way out of this. After Sharpe had left the restaurant earlier, he'd gone back to the boarding house.

Katherine was pacing the room. "It sure took you long enough to get back here with breakfast." She grabbed the covered plate from Sharpe's hands, plunked down on the single bed, and greedily began to devour the offering.

"You certainly don't eat like a lady, sweetness."

Katherine shot him a look of contempt. "I'm not exactly living like one, either."

"True," he snickered. "But you might want to ask what did take me so long."

"All right." She expelled a perturbed sigh. "Why were you gone so long?"

"I was spending some time with our little pigeon. And she played right into our hands. Elizabeth Hollis already has feelings for Chandler . . . but that's not the best of it."

"Are you going to keep me in suspense, or are you going to tell me?" she snipped, losing patience.

"Chandler and his bride are leaving town—"

"What? They can't do that before we're finished with them!" Katherine exclaimed.

"You needn't worry that beautiful little head of yours . . . I've already made arrangements to tag along."

"Fine!" she spat the word, jumping to her feet. "But what am I to do, stay hidden away in this flea-ridden rooming house?"

"Calm down." He placed his hands on her shoulders, pushed her back down on the bed, and settled himself next to her. "No one is going to leave you behind. I bribed some stupid stablehand to have clothes and a horse ready and waiting for you behind the boarding house after dark."

Her brows drawn in a shrewish line, she demanded, "And what am I to do with it, ride off in the darkness to who knows where?"

"You know I wouldn't allow that. The stablehand agreed, for a little extra cash, of course, to guide you to the bull train I'll be traveling with. Once we're far enough out of town, you can join us without fear that you'll be sent back. Then we'll both be on hand to make sure everything goes as planned.

"Sit down and finish your breakfast. I've got a little business to tend to with the sheriff before I join our happy newlyweds." Sharpe dug his fingers into Katherine's arms and ground his lips against hers before he scurried off to tie up all loose ends.

Cordell glowered at the gambler, resisting an overwhelming urge to finish the fight he'd started with Sharpe last night.

"Get the money, McKenzie. This man won't be traveling with us after all," Cordell sneered.

"Right up, boss."

"Wait!" A wicked, self-pleased smile twisted Sharpe's lips.

Gulch turned back, his face a puzzle.

"What are you up to, Sharpe?" Cordell stepped forward and grabbed Sharpe's arm. Libby moved closer to Cordell, fearing another confrontation.

Sharpe ripped his arm from Cordell's grasp. "Keep your hands off me, Chandler! Sheriff, are you prepared to do your duty?" he asked slyly.

The burly man stepped awkwardly forward, picking at his fingers. "Sorry, Dell . . . but if what Sharpe says is right, Gulch struck a deal in your name." With unconcealed contempt, he added, "He came to the office and showed me a law book which says I gotta stand behind him."

"The law? I'll show you the law, Sharpe!" Murder in his eyes, Cordell took a menacing step toward the cocky little bastard.

"Now, now, Chandler. I believe our bargain is legally binding; you should know that, you interested in holding public office and all." Sharpe's eyes gleamed in victory. "I'm certain you know of the consequences if you renege. I'll file suit against you. How will it affect your career aspirations when it comes out?" He noticed Chandler's face darken further.

"Seems you did your homework, Sharpe. But if you did, you also know I'm not about to let some two-bit cardsharp blackmail me."

"Then serve the papers I had you draw up, Sheriff. We'll all," he let his eyes slide to Libby, "just remain in Fort Benton together until the circuit judge makes his appearance. I've heard it can take months."

Libby felt the hairs at the back of her neck rise. She didn't dare stay in Fort Benton until the judge arrived; the reverend could very well get here before him. She had to do something to settle this impasse before Cordell lost his temper, attacked Sharpe, and landed in jail—with the real Katherine.

Chapter Sixteen

Libby urgently placed a hand on Cordell's arm. "May I have a word with you, please?"

"Later," Cordell returned sharply with a wave of dismissal.

Her dire circumstances would not allow Libby to remain a passive listener. She had to speak with Cordell now, before he settled this disagreement with fists or worse. She straightened her shoulders and moved into the middle of the group of men. "Gentlemen, I hate to interrupt, but I think if you will allow me a few moments' conversation with my husband, this business dispute can be resolved without further delay."

"What are you up to?" Cordell snarled without preamble.

Sharpe studied Libby's crestfallen face. Something in her nervous demeanor told him it would be to his distinct advantage for her to speak with Chandler. "Why don't you give the little lady a chance?"

"Yeah, Dell, it seems like it cain't hurt to at least hear her out," the sheriff chimed in.

"All right, you win," Cordell said, exasperated. "I'm not going to try to fight the lot of you. I'll listen to her. Come along dear." Cordell took Libby's arm and escorted her away from the others. His brows furrowed over black slits, he said, "You have five minutes. Now, what is it that couldn't wait?"

"Listening to the way Mr. Sharpe spoke, I was just

thinking that perhaps if we did take him along, it woul[d] ensure that he doesn't spread any gossip which coul[d] tarnish your reputation."

"*Your* reputation, you mean," he shot back.

"As your wife, the estimate of my worth affects your[s] as well now."

"Hmph, how fortunate for you," he grunted, not in th[e] least impressed.

Libby fixed an angry stare at him for a moment, the[n] continued. "If we take him, it also would be easier for yo[u] to keep an eye on me . . . so I don't embarrass you befor[e] you can get an annulment, if that's what you really wan[t] when we get to Helena," she threw out, hoping Cordel[l] would relent and agree.

Cordell's eyes flashed. "Don't you mean so it will mak[e] it easier for you two to be alone together?"

"I don't mean that at all. You're the one who keep[s] insisting that I want to be with the man, not me," Libb[y] persisted. "Maybe taking him along will even help prove t[o] you that I'm not what you think."

"Or give you two *more* opportunities to sneak of[f] together."

"What if I promise never to leave your side during th[e] trip?"

Cordell glared at her intensely. Just what he neede[d] would be to have to watch that pair every minute. No . . he would not take that bastard along to complicate mat ters further! "Even if you promise to disappear from m[y] life forever, right now, I'm not taking Sharpe along wit[h] us, and that's final!"

Libby pursed her lips. She was going to have to figh[t] for every concession with him, and this was one sh[e] couldn't afford to lose. He'd started back toward the me[n] when the idea came to her. "Cordell," she called out wit[h] hard determination in her voice, "if you take Mr. Sharp[e] along and give me a chance to prove to you that I'm no[t] what you think, I promise I won't contest the annulmen[t] if you still want one when we reach Helena."

"You *what?*" he choked, and swung around to stom[p]

back toward her.

She swallowed the urge to flee. "I said—"

"I heard what you said." He was back standing in front of her, his face burning with an incredulous glaze. "What makes you think you can contest the annulment?"

He was calling her bluff. This was no ordinary man. Of course, Libby had known that from the first moment she'd seen him board the steamer. She was going to have scramble to make him believe what she was about to say. But she was desperate now, and the words slipped out before she had a chance to polish her presentation. "I'll say that . . . that you and I have . . . have been together, which would preclude any possibility of an annulment." She bit her lip to keep it from trembling.

His brows shot up. "Together?"

"Yes."

"Together how?" he asked in a warning voice, wondering if she had the nerve to put it into words.

"As man and wife," she forced herself to say, immediately conjuring up a vision of the two of them lying entwined in a passionate embrace. Her past experiences with the reverend had at first tried to intrude into her mental image of Cordell. But she found that when she thought of Cordell touching her, the feelings of utter panic and anguish did not join with guilt to assault her senses. Instead she experienced a gentle warmth flooding through her breasts.

"Oh you will, will you?"

She took a cleansing breath and threw her head back. "Yes, if I have to."

"I'll deny it."

"If you do, then I'll be forced to prove that you know I—"

"Am not a virgin," he completed the sentence for her.

"That's not what I was going to say."

"Then by all means, finish whatever it is you are planning to use to hold over my head."

"I was going to say that I'll be forced to prove that you know I have a birthmark on an intimate portion of my

93

body. That should be proof enough."

He rolled his eyes. "My God, you never give up, do you?"

"No," she said with simple grace.

Cordell stared at the beautiful face, the finely etched features, the aristocratic nose with a slight upward curve, the full, delicately bowed lips, and the blue eyes the color of a Montana lake in summer. Pity she'd become such a loose woman! Her determination was almost admirable, though sorely misdirected and wasted on the likes of Sheldon Sharpe.

"Hell," he said, his patience taxed, "if you want that bastard along so badly as to try to keep me from ridding myself of you when we get to Helena, then you can have his company. But remember, if I catch you with him, or if there is even any *talk* about you two while we're on the trail, you'll come to regret it. That I promise you."

Her serious expression did not change. "You won't be sorry. And I'm not interested in Mr. Sharpe, regardless of what you may think."

"Chrissake. You're even starting to get inside my head." He rubbed his temples and strode off to grudgingly inform Sharpe and the sheriff that the matter was settled.

Sharpe had been leaning idly against the side of a wagon watching the exchange between Chandler and the girl. Sharpe was aggrieved that he hadn't been handed a better lot in life. He deserved everything that that fellow Chandler had. Why shouldn't he squeeze what he could get out of the pair? They probably had been coddled all their lives; they hadn't known the hardships he had, of being born a bastard and reared by a mother who'd raised herself to martyrdom, and never missed a chance to let him know that all concerned would have been better off had he not been born.

He had spent a poverty-stricken youth learning from the gamblers on the river until he was as good as the best of them. He'd left the shack that was his home with a vow not to return until he could show his mother how rich and powerful he'd become. Then he'd laugh in her face. His

94

expression turned sour. He'd heard the woman had up and died last year—before he had a chance to demonstrate how wrong she'd been. Her death had not pacified him. Sharpe was a driven man ... he would do anything necessary to prove to the world he wasn't the no-account his mother had called him.

Sharpe relaxed his features as Chandler approached. By the tension in the rancher's gait, Sharpe knew he'd won. The little fool had convinced Chandler to relent. Although Chandler's outward behavior when he was around the girl indicated he considered himself burdened with unwanted baggage, Sharpe sensed something else there. Maybe it was because of Chandler's fierce reaction last night in the saloon, or the way the man had allowed the girl to sway him just now. He wondered if Chandler himself was aware of it. But whatever was going on between them, Sharpe was going to find out and use it to his advantage.

"Well, do I toss my bag in one of the wagons, or do I have the sheriff serve the papers?" Sharpe asked with a twisted grin.

"Stow your bag in the lead wagon. Then get out of my sight before I change my mind," Cordell answered, barely civil.

Sharpe nodded and shuffled off, wisely holding his tongue.

The sheriff cleared his throat loudly to halt Cordell. "Oh . . . ah, Dell—could I have a word with you before you leave?"

"Sure, Clem."

The sheriff picked at his fingers. "In private?"

Cordell furrowed his brow in question as he and the sheriff moved out of earshot of the others.

Once the sheriff made certain they could not be overheard, he said in a hushed voice, "I don't want to alarm you and your missus none, but I thought you ought to know that that crazy Hollis gal escaped last night, her threatening Mrs. Chandler like she done. I ain't got proof, but I'd guess she had an accomplice. It looked like the cell was unlocked with the key and she just strolled out as big as you please while my deputies were busy elsewhere tending their duties." He noticed Cordell glance in Sharpe's direction. "I been thinking along those lines myself, though I cain't prove it. That gambler's just too slick."

"Thanks, Clem," Cordell said, his face giving away nothing.

"Just wanted to warn you to be on the lookout for trouble."

Cordell rubbed his chin before shaking hands with the sheriff. A distant gleam twinkling in his eyes, he said, "Looks like this trip just might provide a little more excitement than any of us anticipated."

Libby breathed a sigh of relief as Cordell approached. He did not seem nearly so agitated as he had a few moments ago. Could it have been his discussion with the sheriff? She felt a momentary queasiness—that they might have been talking about something other than Sharpe traveling with them—but dismissed it. Cordell certainly would not tell her. She was safe . . . for now. Sharpe was the only one who could give her away, and obviously he had not. Then she smiled to herself. The idea of trying to make her marriage to Cordell work was always on her mind now. The more she thought about it, the more appealing it became, until she could not ignore it. And she'd discovered her feelings had nothing to do with her predicament.

Her flight of fancy was interrupted by the sound of Cordell's harsh command: "Get 'em loaded and get 'em out."

Chapter Seventeen

Libby watched in dismay as Sharpe boarded the lead wagon and settled down beside one of the bull whackers. She'd done what she had been forced to do, but her victory with Cordell was hollow. Sharpe was sure to make this journey exceedingly complicated.

The sun was a white ball in the blue sky when the bull whacker laid his twenty-foot whip to the oxen. The train moved slowly down Front Street. It would turn west to climb the steep grade to the top of the bluffs rising over Fort Benton and connect with the Mullan Road, which provided a highway to the capital of Helena and the Deer Lodge Valley. Libby, who'd kept her place in the street, was unsure of where she would be traveling. Cordell rode up on his big palomino.

"Have you decided to stay here after all?"

"No." She looked around. Her options seemed few. "I'll ride in the lead wagon." She picked up her skirts and started to walk toward the train.

Cordell's booming voice halted her in the mid-stride. "Oh no you won't. I won't have you riding with Sharpe. Or have you forgotten our little deal already?"

"I haven't forgotten."

"Too bad your memory didn't serve you a little better last night. It would have saved us all a lot of trouble."

"Yes. I suppose you are going to have a difficult time explaining to all your friends what happened to your marriage after you have it annulled."

He shrugged. "Not at all."

"Oh? And what great tale are you going to invent this time?"

His eyes narrowed at her implication. "Folks have already seen you faint from the ordeal of river travel. They'll believe that after a couple of weeks with a bull train you decided you weren't cut out for life out here. Which, I might add, might very well become a simple fact."

"That way you'll no doubt get the sympathy vote when you run for office."

"I hadn't thought of it that way, but you could very well be right," he returned easily.

"Remember what happened to the last plan you came up with," Libby reminded him, wishing she could convince him to give their marriage a chance—instead of letting their conversations constantly erupt in argument.

"There was nothing wrong with my plan, only with one of the participants."

Stung by the truth of his remark and forgetting his command not to go near the lead wagon, she again started toward the only available mode of transportation.

"Don't even try it," he warned.

The unmistakable growl in his voice caused Libby to swing around and say, "If you don't want me riding in the wagon, then what do you suggest?" She stood with her hands shading her eyes, defying him to come up with a suitable placement.

He squinted at her for a long moment, then hollered, "Gulch!"

The man rode over to them. "What's up, boss?"

"I want you to round up a good saddle horse for Mrs. Chandler, and then catch up with us as soon as you can."

"Right up." Gulch wheeled his roan around and at a fast clip headed toward Harris and Strong Livery Stables.

Feeling uncharacteristically frustrated, Libby crossed her arms in front of her and cocked her head. "And what am I suppose to do in the meantime? Trot along be ind?"

"I hadn't credited you with much good sense—until now," he said wryly. "Think you could keep up, do you?"

He was issuing a challenge. Augusta's advice came to mind. Libby would have to show him she was cut out for the rigors of frontier life. "I'll keep up," she said proudly.

Cordell sat there studying her resolute stance, appreciating the curves of that luscious body. "You probably will."

He rode off, not looking back but painfully aware of her presence. An unsettled feeling surrounded him. He was a man of direction and conviction. And that woman, his wife, had somehow managed to get him to question his beliefs. He shook his head to clear it. How could he think he cared for a woman with Katherine's background? But even as he was forcing himself to put such ideas out of his head, his thoughts kept returning to the woman and the incredible strength of character she had just displayed.

It didn't take long for Libby to realize he wasn't going to rescue her from her own tongue. The wagons were moving at a slug's pace, so keeping up wouldn't be a problem. If only the ground weren't so rocky and uneven. She'd already stumbled twice when her foot flew out from under her and she landed splat in the dust. "Oh!"

By the time she looked up, Cordell was kneeling beside her. "I thought you said you could keep up."

"I can," Libby retorted distinctly. She tried to stand to prove her words, but when she put her slight weight on her ankle she let out a yelp, lost her balance, and promptly fell into Cordell, sending them both sprawling back into the dust with a thud. Cordell's arms instinctively wrapped round her before he purposely released her.

"Which is it? You say you can keep up, and then almost immediately sit down in the middle of the road."

"Isn't it time for tea?" Right after the words left her she clamped a palm over her lips, she was so startled by

99

her own nerve.

To her surprise she saw a whisper of a smile at th
corners of his mouth. Instead of saying something nasty
as she was expecting, his voice was filled with concern
He asked, "Which ankle is it?"

"The right."

Despite her protests, Cordell pushed her skirts up pas
her calves and unlaced her shoe. She flinched when h
pulled off the snug leather boot and his fingers poked a
the puffy flesh.

"How is it?" she asked nervously, fearing her injur
would give him the perfect opportunity to leave he
behind.

"Not bad." He gave a devilish grin. "Not bad at all, i
spite of the swelling." He sobered. "Shame it belong
to—"

"To your wife," she supplied, not wanting to hear hin
voice his low opinion of her again.

"Yes. To my wife," he mimicked. His eyes were blacl
ice when he grabbed her around the waist and supporte
her weight.

"What are you doing?"

"I'm putting you up on my horse with me until Gulch
gets here with your animal."

Reeling from such sudden intimacy, she gasped, "Yo
said you wouldn't touch me."

"Maybe I lied."

"But you're a man of your word. Everyone says so.'

"And you were supposed to be a virtuous young
woman. Now up you go."

Cordell settled her on the front of his saddle and
climbed up behind her. "Quit trembling. I've told you
have no intention of taking any liberties with you
Katherine."

Libby looked straight ahead, too afraid to turn he
head. She continued to tremble, but it wasn't from fea
of Cordell's touch. It was from the discovery that she had
found her special man, regardless of how disagreeable h

was being at the moment, combined with a remembrance of the reverend's unwanted touch. Somehow she had to put that horrible man from her mind every time she and Cordell came into contact if she was going to win Cordell as a real husband. A real husband? A lifetime mate? Yes . . she wanted Cordell Chandler as a lifelong partner. The thought was no longer merely a constant idea taking shape in her mind. It now had substance, flesh and blood and bones. Now all she had to do was figure out a way to make Cordell change his mind about her and the annulment before they got to Helena.

From her dreary little room Katherine took in the entire scene. When Shelley climbed aboard the wagon and the train started to pull out, she'd felt a momentary urge of desire to rush after them . . . but her better instincts took over. Shelley was much too greedy, and she was too wealthy for him to simply abandon her.

She snapped the curtain shut and moved to the tiny mirror propped up on the washstand. She smoothed at the stress lines around her eyes and studied her reflection: the simple calico Shelley had procured for her, her gnarled dark hair, her chipped fingernails. "Damn all men," she screeched. If it weren't for them, she wouldn't be forced to live like a common beggar.

A hammering at the door put a sudden halt to her rantings. "What's goin' on in there?" called out a gruff voice. Katherine froze. "You ain't supposed to have a woman in that room, Sharpe. Open up!" He rattled the doorknob.

"I'll see that you pay for this, Elizabeth Hollis," Katherine hissed as she hurriedly stripped a blanket off the bed, grabbed the few things she had left, and hoisted herself out the window. She threw a scarf over her head so no one would recognize her and scrambled around the back corner of the building toward a nearby clump of shrubs.

Her dress snagged on the branches and she w
scratched when she finally settled down to wait until t
stablehand came tonight to meet her. Once she joined t
train, she'd make sure everything worked according to *h*
plan.

Chapter Eighteen

Libby's thoughts raced as the horse trudged along under a pastel blue sky. Never had she imagined she'd find herself impersonating an heiress and marrying one of the wealthiest ranchers in the Territory of Montana. It would all sound like a fairy tale if it were not for one thing: Cordell Chandler thought her a soiled dove and intended to dissolve their relationship, such as it was, at the first opportunity.

Her first inclination had been to confess to prove she wasn't what he thought. The more she considered it, though, the more she knew she could not reveal her own soiled past. Oh, why was it that your past always lurked nearby, casting a dark shadow over all your hopes and dreams?

She brooded for a while . . . then an idea came to her. Why couldn't a sporting gal repent, if she were so inclined, and win the heart of someone like Cordell Chandler?

Cordell's mind was also busy reviewing events. He had come to this territory on foot as a fifteen-year-old orphaned war veteran from Pennsylvania, with no more than a bedroll, his knife, and a talent for carving steaks out of a steer's carcass for the miners in the gold towns. Those had been lean years. And now that he had built an empire and could think about settling down, marrying, raising a family, and giving something back to this glorious territory through public service, he had gotten himself hogtied to the likes of Katherine Rutcliff. Why in hell did she have to feel so damned good in his arms?

The lazy clopping of hooves distracted them and Libby swiveled in the saddle to see who was coming, causing Cordell to curse under his breath at what the feel of her body did to him.

"Come on, you son of an ass," Gulch grumbled, practically dragging an obstinate mule, which was throwing its head back in protest.

"Could that be one of your animals, Cordell?" Libby asked.

His face mirroring displeasure, he responded, "Why do you ask that?"

She stifled a smile behind her hand. "It seems to take after you."

"Very funny, my dear," he said dryly. "But as fact has it, that jackass Gulch has in tow happens to be your mount."

Undaunted by his attempt to deflate her newly discovered ego, Libby smiled brightly. "Well, then, I shall just have to look at that animal as another challenge, won't I?"

"Look at it anyway you want. You do ride, don't you?"

"Haven't I been riding with you all morning?" she answered evasively, not wanting to admit to any lack of skill. After all, it couldn't take much effort to sit on a slow-moving creature like that, she figured.

It was nearly noon, so Cordell called for the wagons to stop for the midday rest. Cordell dismounted and helped Libby down. Without a word he carried her over to a cluster of boulders, setting her down on one.

"The swelling's gone down. Looks like you shouldn't have any more trouble with that ankle," he announced after a quick perusal.

The sensation of his rough, warm fingers sliding over her skin sent a shiver up her spine.

"Are you cold?"

"Of course not!" She yanked her leg out of his grasp. "How could I be cold on such a beautiful day as this?" Libby looked away from him and slipped her foot back

104

into her boot.

Few trees stood on the lush green prairie. A gentle breeze swayed the long grass into blends of green, yellow, blue, and brown. For as far as she could see, there was open space. It gave her the feeling that there was room out here for everyone, no matter where you came from or what circumstances had brought you here.

"Since there doesn't seem to be anything wrong with your ankle, I expect you'll be ready when it's time to pull out," he said crisply.

Libby watched him walk away and her heart lurched. He was an incredibly handsome man. Her eyes settled on his backside and she marveled at its firmness.

"Mrs. Chandler?" Gulch approached, with a plate of beans he had hastily prepared over an open pit and a tin of coffee. "How 'bout something to put some meat on your bones? No offense meant, ma'am," he ended sheepishly.

"None taken, Mr. McKenzie."

"Gulch . . . everyone calls me Gulch 'cause I was at Alder Gulch during the big gold-strike in '63. I met the boss there in '65. He saved my bacon after a couple of claim jumpers speared me up good and left me for dead. Been with him ever since."

"You have?" Libby leaned forward, eager to learn more about Cordell Chandler.

"Yup. He was barely dry behind the ears then. But he took care of me 'til I was right healed. Him with only his pocketknife and a talent for cutting up beef got a job and supported us both until I could join him. By then he was already on his way to making a name for himself. Never met another like him."

"He was a butcher?"

"I guess you could say he was at first. We even made candles out of beef fat one winter. Did it late at night, and sold them to the miners. Then he got into buying and selling cattle. He's a real go-getter, that one. It wasn't long before he found a spread he wanted and bought it from some squaw man, and we settled on the ranch. It was just him and me until he brought his aunt from Pennsylvania to live out here on the ranch with us. She's his only living kin, you know."

"No, I didn't."

"Don't worry, you'll like Matilde. She can be a tad pushy, but her heart's in the right place." He laughed to himself. " 'Course, I wouldn't want to be on the wrong side of her. No siree!"

"Is there a Mrs. Gulch?" Libby asked, wondering how many people she was going to have to win over.

"Hell, no. The right gal ain't never come my way. I was beginning to worry that Dell wouldn't never get himself hitched up neither." His expression softened. "I'm right glad he got himself a real lady like you, ma'am."

"Yes, so am I," Sharpe said, sauntering over, a telling grin pushing his red moustache upward.

Gulch gave a harrumph, tipped his hat toward Libby, murmured "Ma'am," and went to grab himself a bite to eat.

Libby stiffened and stepped away, but Sharpe grabbed her arm. "What's your hurry, sweetness? I thought we might share our meal together."

"Here." Libby shoved the plate into his stomach. "It seems I've lost my appetite."

Sharpe spooned the beans into his mouth. "You don't know what you're missing, sweetness," he called to her retreating back.

Memories of what Cordell had said about her keeping her distance from the gambler made Libby quicken her pace.

From where Gulch stood near the cook fire with Cordell, they'd had a clear view of Libby and Sharpe.

"Sorry I took that gambler's money, boss. It looks like your missus don't like the dude any more than you do. And 'cause of me you're both plumb stuck with him, at least 'til we get to Helena," Gulch said, noticing the lady and that Sharpe fellow. "If you want, me and the boys'll teach him to keep his distance from Mrs. Chandler from now on."

Cordell had been intently observing the exchange. He responded absently, "Don't concern yourself. I'll deal with Sharpe. Let's get this train moving." He set his plate down and headed toward Libby. He'd told her to stay away from Sharpe. He could send her back to Fort Benton. Yet she'd seemed to be uncomfortable with the man. He wanted to believe what he'd witnessed was true. Of course, she probably knew he'd been watching her and was just putting on a good act for his benefit so he wouldn't send her and Sharpe back.

"This is your last chance for some lunch," Cordell said, joining Libby.

"Thank you, but I'm not hungry."

"Suit yourself. I guess if you get hungry later, you can always eat that meal on your head."

Libby's hand automatically went to her hat. "Very amusing, but I think I can manage without it."

"Then you might as well mount up."

Libby looked from the mule to Cordell, sank her teeth into her lower lip, and grabbed the saddle horn. Her heart was pounding. Somehow she managed to put her foot up into the stirrup. She could not tell Cordell she had never ridden before.

Cordell patted the mule's rump and it swished its tail. "What are you waiting for?" Cordell asked her.

She looked back at his resolute expression. He was waiting for her to climb up on the back of that beast. "You could help me up, instead of just standing there with your hands on your hips."

"You *are* a spunky little thing," he mumbled, locking his fingers together.

Libby smiled to herself and put her other foot in the cradle of Cordell's hands. That was as close to a compliment as Cordell had ever come. It wasn't much, but it was a start.

Chapter Nineteen

The mule hee-hawed and bucked, sending Libby into the dust. That didn't seem to satisfy the perturbed animal. It snorted and snatched Libby's hat off her head.

"You give that back!" she yelped and lunged for it.

"What's the matter? Are you afraid the poor beast will get indigestion?" Cordell smirked.

"Hardly," she shot back and popped the ruined bonnet on her head. The brim was ripped and strands of shredded straw hung drooping down the back of her neck.

Dusting herself off, she hesitantly asked, "Cordell?"

"Yes?"

"You said the driver of the wagon train was called a bull whacker, didn't you?"

Question filled his eyes. "Yes," he answered suspiciously.

Libby's narrowed gaze drifted to the offending mule and back again to Cordell. "Do they ever work as mule skinners?"

Cordell couldn't help himself; he let out a rolling laugh. "Actually, I think that mule had a better idea of what to do with that thing on your head." He plucked the ruined hat from her head and replaced it with his own wide-brimmed one. "This will give you better protection from the sun. Now up you go." He grabbed her around the waist and swung her onto the restless beast.

Libby clamped her thighs to the animal's sides; her hands clasped white to the saddle horn. The mule danced backward but quickly settled down and accepted its burden.

"Are you sure you know how to ride? Ladies don't usually sit astride like that," Cordell said, assessing the awkward way she had wedged herself across the seat. Strange . . . Katherine's father surely must have taught her how to ride properly.

"Of course. I'm still seated, aren't I?"

"That you are." In spite of an earlier resolution to rid himself of the woman as soon as possible, a lopsided grin crossed his face before it faded. "But might I suggest you pull your skirt down? Unless, of course, you have another reason for showing off those well-turned legs of yours."

"If I do, I can only guarantee you'll be the first to know," she retorted.

"Don't bother. What you have to offer doesn't interest me," he stated flatly and strode to his own mount.

"That maybe what you say now, Cordell Chandler," she whispered to his back. "And you may not know it yet, but somehow I'm going to make you care for me — if only you'd cooperate."

For nearly a week Libby had managed to stay away from Sharpe. She smiled to think of her success at thwarting Sharpe's efforts. Then her smile faded . . . except to keep up the appearances of a happy marriage by sleeping in the same wagon at night, Cordell had managed to stay away from her without arousing any curiosity. Despite her frustrations over Cordell, she was proud of herself for mastering the art of riding, although Gulch had confided that he had specially seen to it that the saddle had been altered so she could ride the mule sidesaddle.

"I don't understand why you sit the animal like you do," Gulch said.

"To demonstrate I can ride as well as Cordell," she lied for want of a better reply, finally realizing why the saddle was so difficult to endure, and so different from Cordell's.

"I'd wondered why a fine lady like yourself insisted on riding like a man. But that'll take some doing, to ride like Dell, ma'am. Dell's a natural to the saddle. Taught him myself, him being brought up in one of them cities back east and all. But if you're trying to prove that you ain't as weak as folks thought you was at the wedding, I'd say your keeping up as well as you've done is having the proper effect on Dell. 'Cause he's sure been watching you. 'Course, if you was mine, I wouldn't take my eyes off you neither."

Gulch opened his mouth to ask why she and Dell hadn't spent much time together, except at night, but thought better of it. It was none of his nevermind. Knowing Dell the way he did, Gulch found it difficult to understand why Dell didn't keep such a fine filly by his side during the day as well. Dell had always been most attentive when a new woman caught his interest. Gulch considered it all a moment longer, then concluded that a woman such as Dell's wife would be much too distracting for the success of the bull train, and he was never one to shirk his responsibilities. Dell sure had a lot more fortitude than he'd have if she were his bride!

But beneath his calm, indifferent exterior, Cordell's fortitude was crumbling. It wasn't easy keeping up appearances by sleeping in the same wagon with a beautiful woman each night, even if they were at opposite ends of it. He had lain awake at night expecting Katherine and Sharpe to try to sneak off together, but they hadn't. The report had stated that the young woman was a total shrew—spoiled, arrogant, demanding. She hadn't displayed any of those traits. If anything, she had gone out of her way to help out with the chores. She had taken her mount in stride. If she were trying to trick him or get him to soften, it wasn't going to work, though.

In the midst of a downpour, which had turned the brilliant blues and greens of the landscape into a muddy gray, they stopped for the night to make camp along the

Sun River. Cordell had forced Sharpe to take Libby's place on the mule and let her ride inside the wagon when it had started to rain. Cordell was full of surprises. He was kind and gentle at the same time he was firm and exacting with those around him.

Sharpe's red vest darkened to near maroon from the soaking it had taken by the rain, and his jacket and trousers clung to his body as he rode up alongside the lead wagon. He swiped at his sodden auburn locks. "You can wipe that smile off your face if you think my situation is comical because *you* are going to see to it that tomorrow I ride in the wagon with you."

Libby's face sobered and she glanced at the scraggily bull whacker to see if he was listening. The man ignored them and seemed to have turned a deaf ear, but carefully choosing her words she said, "I can't do that. You know neither my husband not I approve of your presence. So if you intend to continue traveling with us, you will simply have to abide by husband's directions."

Sharpe wanted to scream and strike out at the girl. But if Chandler carried through his threat, Sharpe would stand to lose his chance at a lot of money. "Then you better see that that husband of yours dishes out better directions," he sneered. He gave the mule a kick and jerked it toward the horses already stabled for the night.

Once the rain had let up, Libby climbed out of the back of the wagon and joined Cordell, who was driving the stakes in the ground for the cook fire. A light drizzle misted the air and caused her ebony hair to spring into a mass of curls, lending her a wild, untamed look. "What are you doing?" she asked, her curiosity piqued by a wealthy man doing such chores.

"What's it look like?" he fired back, equally as wet as Sharpe.

"What I meant was—why?"

"Simple. The men have other duties to tend to."

Libby stood mesmerized by all the little kindnesses and generosity Cordell showed his men. She'd tried to prove to him she was not the kind of woman he

111

thought, yet he continued to ignore her. Well, he was not going to disregard her for long, she'd see to that!

"In contrast to the pampered life you've led, there are some people who believe in carrying their share of the load."

"I have *not* led a pampered life!" Libby burst out.

"Then you won't mind taking over here for me," he returned. He cast a heavy iron pot into her hand and strode away.

This was her chance to show him that she wasn't just a fragile, coddled female. "Of course not," she called out. "You are about to find out I'm as good a cook as Gulch."

"That's not saying much," he threw back over his shoulder. "Anyway, I intend to make my meal from the leftovers from breakfast. Let the others suffer your cooking."

An hour later, after the rain had stopped and the men had slogged through the mud into camp, they were greeted with hot cups of coffee and a delicious stew Libby had concocted from beans, dried beef, and potatoes.

"This sure is mighty tasty, Miz Chandler," a mangy bull whacker said, shoveling the stew into his mouth, and dropping chunks on his dingy rawhide jacket.

"Thank you." Libby noticed Cordell out of the corner of her eye. He was second from last in line, still wearing his wet clothes, like the other men—all except Sharpe, who'd already changed into dry ones.

Libby dished up hearty servings for everyone until Cordell stepped forward and thrust out an expectant hand.

"Oh, no dear. Yours is over here." She reached for the specially prepared tin and offered it to him.

"What is this?" he growled, looking down at the cold, hard biscuits and a limp slab of bacon. "This isn't what the others are having."

"Of course not. I fixed this just for you . . . dear."

He scowled. "What do you *mean* you fixed this just

112

for me?"

As innocently as she could, Libby managed to say, "You were the one who said you intended to have leftovers. I merely put them on a plate for you, just like you wanted them."

Cordell's eyes narrowed. Libby flinched, expecting him to sling the plate into the mud and strike her. Instead a wicked smile took possession of his mouth.

"Just what I like."

"What?" she asked, puzzled by the sudden change in his attitude.

"A wife who follows directions."

Sharpe snickered, thinking about the lecture she'd meted out to him earlier. The men stifled chuckles and turned away under Cordell's glare as Libby filled the last man's plate and he joined the others.

This was the most responsive Cordell had been to her since their marriage. Perhaps just trying to be thoughtful and stand her ground wasn't enough with this man. Perhaps she should try an even sharper tack to prove to him that they were meant to be a match. The thought made her grin . . . to her delight there was the merest smile on Cordell's face as he stared at her.

He gathered another cold biscuit and bacon, slapped it together, and offered it to her. "Here. I'd like nothing better than to have you join me. We'll eat together this evening . . . sweetheart."

Libby looked longingly at the stew. She was hungry and that biscuit looked most unappetizing.

"I—"

"Now, I won't take no for an answer. Come along . . . dear heart. We'll enjoy our meal together."

"But I should remain here to serve the men, in case anyone wants seconds."

"They'll serve themselves," he said triumphantly.

This was becoming a war of wills, and Libby found herself pleasantly refreshed by it. It could even be a way to gain his respect. She would continue to try to prove to him she wasn't like the real Katherine Rutcliff and at the same time demonstrate that she wasn't going to endure being ill treated. Yes, she thought, she was going to woo the obstinate man, and at the same time give him a good run for his money—just as Augusta had advised.

Her mind made up, Libby said, "Cordell, you were right. I *have* been pampered too long. Starting right now, I'm going to begin working side by side with you and the men. And the first thing I'm going to do is dish the men up seconds so they can relax." She put her cold biscuit on Cordell's plate next to the other one. "You've worked hard too . . . dear. So I want you to be the first to have a second helping because you must be hungry."

Cordell's momentary triumph shriveled into silent rage as Libby toted the pot of stew toward the men and filled their plates.

"Oh, dear," she said sweetly to his retreating back. "I think it would be best if you went and changed. We certainly wouldn't want you to catch your death out here."

To whispered laughter, Cordell took his plate and disappeared into the wagon. A few moments later he stuck his head out the flap, a sardonic expression on his face.

"Katherine, sweetheart," he hollered. "Since you intend from now on to help your husband out, come into the wagon and give me a hand changing out of these wet clothes."

Chapter Twenty

Her hand on the stew spoon, Libby froze. He couldn't be serious, could he? She decided to ignore him and ladled up a serving of the hearty mixture.

"Katherine, dear, you'd better hurry along. You don't want to be the cause of me catching my death, now do you?" Cordell sang out to choruses of snickers from the men.

With shaking fingers, Libby plopped the stew onto the hefty ranch hand's plate. She surveyed the men's faces. Except for Sharpe, there was an unwritten consensus: they seemed to think it was a lover's game and expected her to go to Cordell. He wouldn't force her if she refused; she'd discovered that from their earlier confrontations. She could not refuse and instead further anger Cordell, not if she intended to prove to him that their marriage could work. Then the thought came to her that Cordell would not allow her to merely decline his directive, and she certainly did not want to test what his reaction might be.

"Katherine," he urged, his eyes narrowing.

She forced a smile. "I'm coming, dear," she returned through tight lips. She set the pot down and dished herself up a plate of stew. The succulent aroma wafted about her nostrils as she climbed inside the wagon. Cordell had reorganized the freight to create a cozy little space. He sat crosslegged in the middle of a pile of wool blankets.

"What's the matter?" she asked lightheartedly. "Can't a big man like you manage by yourself?"

He stretched out on his side, resting on his elbow. "I see you changed your mind." A lazy smile reached his eyes.

"I did?"

"Yes, you brought my dinner. How thoughtful of you," he answered, his voice holding a tight edge as he reached up and plucked the plate from her hands.

There before her stunned eyes he calmly began to eat—and ignored her completely.

"I thought you needed my help changing," she choked out, not certain whether she should be grateful or angry.

"Oh, I do. But I want to put some food in my belly first. One never knows how long it could take for you to help me remove all these wet clothes." His eyes danced. "Why, who knows, you might even find it necessary to change out of your own clothes," he baited her.

"And why would I want to do that?" she asked innocently.

Cordell had begun to watch her reactions. There was something about the woman that bothered him.

Libby licked her lips. Their wedding ceremony gave him reason to expect a husband's rights. She wanted to make their marriage work even more with each passing day. She swallowed the sudden lump of fear at a man's touch. Cordell Chandler was *not* Reverend Elijah Ardsworth, she stoutly reminded herself. Cordell's touch would come from the man she loved . . . yes, loved.

The realization struck her full force. It wasn't as if it was a sudden thing; her feelings for the man had been growing with each passing day. Bringing such a powerful emotion to the forefront of consciousness was something new, though. She actually did love Cordell.

Her childhood and all its ugliness reared up and threatened to reduce her to tears. She fought desperately within herself. Now was the time she must come to

116

terms with those ugly experiences if she was going to successfully put them behind her. A life with Cordell was too important and precious to her to allow the dark clouds of her background to overshadow her chances for a happy future. At that moment she made the decision not to let the memories of what the reverend had done to her plague her ever again.

Libby knelt next to Cordell. With trembling fingers she unfastened the top button of his shirt. She closed her eyes as his warm breath glided over her neck, sending a stream of sensual messages through her body.

A wet glob dropped on her sleeve, instantly ending her rapture. Her eyes flew open. "What is that?" She looked down at the stew oozing a dark, lumpy stain on the delicate pale blue blouse she wore.

Nonchalantly Cordell said, "I said you might find it necessary to change your clothes. I never have been very successful at eating in a prone position."

"Why, you pompous . . . I thought . . . I thought—"

"You thought *what?* That I'd turn to mush in your experienced hands the first time you came near me?"

"No!"

"Then what was it you thought, dear?" He took another mouthful of stew, silently challenging her to speak up.

"I think it's time I demonstrated to you exactly what I'm thinking." She leaned back and rested on her heels. She continued to shake, but it was from anger now. A rash impulse overtook her and without giving the consequences of her actions careful thought, her hands shot out, grabbed the plate, and dumped its contents over Cordell's head.

"What the hell!" he roared, his eyes snapping up to shoot warnings of imminent retaliation at her as he wiped the larger chunks from his hair and face.

Fearing his response, Libby scrambled toward the back of the wagon.

Cordell pounced.

"Oh!" she grunted as he landed on top of her. He

flipped her around until Libby came eye to eye with his glowering gaze. "Let go of me! What do you think you're doing?" she squealed, fighting the sensual feelings his hard body against her elicited as much as she fought to free herself.

"What do I think I'm doing?" he snarled.

"You deserved it, the way you've been acting," she panted, trying desperately to justify her actions.

She stopped struggling and stared into those incredible black eyes. The moment stretched out between them as Libby felt his heartbeat increase against her breast. Her tongue snaked out and moistened her lips, and she pressed them together. In the next instant Cordell snarled his fingers in the flowing mass of her ebony hair and pressed his lips hard on hers, demanding, forcing a response.

Libby felt not the slightest inclination to fight Cordell's kiss. Instead she slid her arms around his neck and delighted in the intimate contact. The absence of fear was another new experience for her and it served to reinforce her feelings for him. His lips were soft and warm. He tasted of salt and smelled of manly perspiration and stew, but to Libby it was the headiest of perfumes.

Cordell was not a man of impulse. He had lived a life of deliberation, carefully weighing all the possible consequences before acting. And here he was, not only straddling a woman he allowed himself to get stuck with, but enjoying it. The foolishness of his reaction to her nearness scorched his senses and he pushed her away as if he'd just been burned.

Libby looked hurt and confused. "If you think I'm going to succumb to your wiles and make it impossible to get an annulment from you, you're mistaken," Cordell said slowly, enunciating each word with cold precision. Then, in spite of himself, he broke out laughing.

Libby fought back tears. Delighting in Cordell's touch had been a new beginning, and now here he was accusing her of trying to seduce him like some common

118

whore. To make matters worse, he was laughing at her.

"Just exactly *what* is so amusing?" she demanded, determined to hold back the threatening flood of tears.

"You look like a little girl with the stew smeared all over your face."

Libby's tears dried. "Well, I have news for you, Mr. Cordell Chandler . . . you do not look any better yourself. If anything, you look worse with those pieces of bacon in your hair."

"In that case," he said dangerously, swiping at the food still on the plate, "I guess I'll just have to even the score." Before Libby could protest, he spread the contents of his palm down the length of her jet black tresses.

"You're insufferable! How am I ever going to get this bacon grease out of my hair?"

"I guess a pampered city girl like you is used to having some poor overworked maid tend to your hair for you."

"For your information, I am *quite* capable. Just show me how I can possibly get it clean out here."

"Think you can, huh?"

"Of course."

"All right. We'll just see." Cordell rummaged through a crate and came up with a bar of gardenia soap and two thick cotton towels. "Let's go."

"With you?"

"Maybe you've forgotten, but the state I'm in was *your* doing. Since we both are in dire need of a bath, we'll go down by the river together."

"Together?" she gulped.

"What's the matter, having a sudden attack of modesty? From what I read, plenty of men have seen that beautiful body of yours. One more isn't going to make much difference. And furthermore, we're married, if you happened to forget. But I have no desire to see you naked," he lied, "so you needn't unduly concern yourself that I'm going to bother to look."

Smirks greeted the pair when they emerged from the

wagon, towels slung over their shoulders, looking like two children who had engaged in a rousing food fight.

"Don't let us interrupt your supper. We're going to take a stroll down by the river. My wife and I have found it necessary to bathe."

Binkley, the boldest of the bull whackers, scratched his greasy red hair. "From the looks of ya two, it looks like ya already done washed up—in the stew."

As Libby frowned, the other men burst out laughing. Cordell seemed to accept it in stride and took hold of her hand.

His fingers were warm and his grasp possessive as he said, "Come along, Katherine."

The gleam of amusement in their eyes implied that the men thought Libby and Cordell had probably been engaging in marital activities when the stew had gotten in the way. Glad to be away from them, Libby marched through the shrubbery by the Sun River. At the muddy banks she stopped, unable to go any farther, having sunk knee deep in the sticky soft earth.

Cordell was ten feet ahead of her before he noticed she'd stopped. *"Now* what's your problem?" he barked.

"If you'd have taken a moment to look, you'd see I am stuck in the mud," she retorted, her temper flaring.

Cordell trudged back to where she stood, trapped in the gook. He surveyed the scene. "Well, for once it appears you're telling the truth." He laughed.

"Will you quit enjoying yourself at my expense and get me out of here?" She tried to lift her foot and the hem of her skirt only to sink further.

"You do seem to have a problem here, don't you?" He raised her skirt to see for himself and she batted at his hand.

"Don't tell me you've beginning to get another sudden surge of modesty."

"Just get me out of here so I can get washed up," she cried, exasperated.

"So, you're in a hurry to get cleaned up?"

"That's what I said." Libby's chest heaved in anger.

"All right. Never let it be said I didn't hurry to accommodate my wife."

Cordell bent down and with one swift motion plucked Libby out of the mud. The sensations at being held so close against his chest for the second time today were nearly overwhelming.

In three strides Cordell stood at the edge of the river. He waded in thigh deep. Without ceremony he dropped her.

Chapter Twenty-one

The swift current of the Sun River immediately claimed Libby. When she bobbed to the surface, Cordell discovered she was being swept away.

"Quit splashing around and swim back over here before I'm forced to come after you," he called out roughly. When she did not answer and sank below the surface again, the sharp edge in his voice turned to anxiety. Fear taking over, he yanked off his boots and yelled, "Hang on, I'm coming. I'm coming!"

He dived through clumps of debris brought by the storm and sliced through the choppy water. By the time he reached Libby she was treading water not more than five feet off the opposite steep bank.

Panting, he grabbed her above her waist. "You're safe now. I've got you."

A mischievous gleam entered her eyes. "I was fine before you came after me," she said innocently, squirming against his arm. Secretly, though, she was pleased he'd been worried about her.

He looked astonished. "You mean you weren't drowning?"

"Of course not. Whatever gave you that idea?"

"I can't imagine," he said deliberately.

With a calculating twist to her lips, Libby reached up and dunked Cordell's head under the water, then quickly swam out of his reach.

He came up sputtering.

"Whoever said you were a gentleman was wrong!" she called out, a safe distance away.

Swimming back to shore, Cordell rolled over onto his back and hollered, "And whoever said you were a lady must have been blind!" He stumbled to his feet and stopped to catch his breath, wondering why he was so concerned about her, cursing himself for being such a damn fool as to believe she needed help. She no doubt swam better than he did, and he'd risked his life to try and save that beautiful neck of hers.

With the ease of a fish, Libby swam back across the river and climbed out, dripping. Cordell tossed her a towel. Careful to maintain her modesty, she shimmied out of her clothing and wrapped the thick length of toweling around herself. "Now that we both are cleaned up and dry, where's our clean clothes?"

Clad only in a towel himself, Cordell looked Libby up and down. Moisture clung to her skin and he silently cursed himself for the urge he had to wipe every drop from that inviting body of hers. "Back at the wagons."

"Back at the wagons?" Her eyes grew round in disbelief. "What are you waiting for? Hurry and go get me something to put on."

"You got yourself into this situation. You have a choice. You can either walk back with me now—"

"The way I am?" she cried, horrified.

Cordell grinned, "Or you can head back by yourself later, because I have no intention of hanging around here like this," he announced, gathering his wet things and starting back without waiting for her answer.

"Wait for me!" Libby grabbed her soaking wet blouse and skirt and hurried after the big man, hopping over rocks and brambles, all the while hoping the men back at camp would be elsewhere tending to chores when they returned.

Libby was not to be so lucky.

Gulch, Sharpe, the bull whacker Binkley, and Mort sat in their same places, and each had a perfect view of the scantily clad pair.

"A-hem." Gulch was the first to clear his throat. "If we'd a knowed you two was in such an all-fired hurry to get back, we coulda been seeing to the oxen instead of sitting right in the way of a honeymoon couple rushing to their wagon."

Cordell's frigid glare put a stop to any additional comments from the men, who sagely gathered their plates and moved out of the line of fire. All, that is, except Sharpe, who let his eyes enjoy the length of shapely calf Libby displayed beneath her cotton wrap before he sauntered toward the coffee pot for a refill.

"Are you coming, Katherine, or do you intend to stand there and let Sharpe enjoy the view?" Cordell asked darkly.

Libby cast Sharpe an expression of disgust and climbed into the wagon after Cordell. He was standing right inside, staring at her.

"Well, are you going to turn your head so I can change?" she asked, feeling awkward and ill at ease with so little to cover herself.

Cordell continued to stare. "Do you usually ask your male companions to turn their heads while you undress?"

"Of course not . . . I mean . . . I don't have any male companions." Flustered, Libby tried to recover.

"No, I suppose not . . . your kind would more than likely call themselves customers."

"You're insufferable!" She was so busy angrily gesturing with her hands that she allowed the towel to drop around her ankles before she realized what she'd done.

Cordell sucked in an awe-inspired breath at the curveous beauty standing nude before him. Her neck was long and slender, her breasts high and full over a delicately small waist which curved outward to nicely rounded hips. At the top of her thighs a triangular mound of black hair pointed toward her intimate core. Her long, well-shaped thighs and calves led to an alluring pair of ankles.

In response Cordell released his towel. Libby swal-

124

lowed her first inclination to flee at the sight of complete male nudity before her. But instead of being paralyzed by fear, she was mesmerized by the beauty of his masculine form. Cordell Chandler had the broadest shoulders she had ever imagined; thick, curly black hairs covered his chest and narrowed downward in a suggestive line leading past a slender waist and hips to his manhood. Libby swallowed: Cordell was a very big man. She shifted her eyes to his powerful thighs. They were lightly dusted with wiry black hairs right down to the tops of his feet.

His body lust overtaking his judgment, Cordell reached out his hand palm up. With jerky movements, Libby placed her fingers in his and he closed his hand over hers. He pulled her up against him. Their bodies touching were igniting a fire somewhere in their souls.

Cordell gazed into the blue depths of Libby's eyes. Love radiated from an innocent center, causing him to dip his head and join his lips to hers.

Libby saw hunger and lonely pain in the blackness of Cordell's eyes. For an instant she thought of Caroline Arthur and the wistful way the young woman had been looking at him. She quickly put Caroline from her mind. Cordell was a man searching for someone to share his life with. And Libby desperately wanted to be that someone, to prove to him that he had found his special mate in her. As his lips closed over hers, she knew she would not give up until Cordell accepted her as his one and only.

Gently Cordell eased her down on top of the blankets and joined her there. "You are indescribably beautiful," he whispered hoarsely.

"So are you," Libby returned, gazing into the tenderness of his black eyes. All those terrible years enduring the reverend's touch were erased from her mind, and Libby found that being next to the man she loved really was a new beginning. With Cordell there was no need for enforced modesty . . . she found she wanted to share all of herself, everything, with him.

When Cordell made no effort to touch her, Libby urged, "Cordell, I want to feel your fingers on my skin."

If his wife had been anyone else other than Katherine Rutcliff, the wealthy slut, Cordell would have devoured her, he ached so bad. But the thought that she was just using him as another conquest gnawed at him and shrank his desire. He bounded to his feet.

"What's the matter?" Libby asked, confused by this sudden change.

"How many others have you invited to feel that velvety skin of yours?" It was an accusation, not a question.

"No one," she said simply.

"Get dressed," he ordered, furious with himself for his momentary weakness.

"But I thought —"

"I *know* what you thought." All the while he spoke, Cordell was angrily yanking at his clothes. "I already told you as soon as we get to Helena I'm going to get an annulment and then you can seduce as many men as you desire. Just don't think you are going to add me to your lengthy list."

"I don't have a list. And if you'd only give me a chance, you'd discover for yourself there hasn't been anyone else," Libby said quietly.

"Hah! What do you take me for, a fool?"

"No."

"Good. Then you better quit trying to get me into your bed so I won't be able to get an annulment," he said, and slammed out of the wagon.

Attempting to seduce her husband had been the furthest thing from Libby's mind — until now. Without realizing it, Cordell had given Libby the perfect solution to the problem of proving to the man that she wasn't the soiled dove he thought she was. Her face fell. Proving to Cordell she was a virgin was only half her problem. Then there was the little matter of telling him she wasn't actually Katherine Rutcliff, but the young woman

126

accused of attacking a man of God.

Libby drew her knees to her chest and rested her chin on the cotton towel. Hadn't she taken control of her life so far? Hadn't she proved that the reverend had been wrong about her? She had overcome all the adversity put in her way and succeeded. She was a lady; she was a strong lady. She wasn't quite sure yet exactly how she was going to go about it, but somehow, someway she was going to demonstrate to the obstinate Cordell Chandler that *she* was the *only* woman for him!

Chapter Twenty-two

The young messenger peddled his bicycle to the rickety picket fence and stopped at the gate. It was a warm day to have ridden all the way up the hill, and he wiped the sweat from his upper lip. He pulled the telegram out of his pocket and looked down at it. It was just his luck to have to deliver the message. His thin lips pinched, Herbert Wegian trudged across the weed-infested yard and bounded onto the porch.

Herbie looked over at the folded sheet one last time, forcing down the inclination to shred it and leave. But he was too proud of the job he did to let his personal sympathies interfere. He gave a resounding rap at the door.

"Herbie," the giant of a man greeted dourly. "And how is it that the Lord has guided your feet to my humble door?"

A shiver inched its way up Herbie's back. It wasn't something he could explain, but Reverend Ardsworth and his fiery preaching made Herbie sure he was bound to spend eternity in hell. He wasn't the only one who felt that way . . . there were others in the church youth group who feared the man. But they too were afraid to speak up, although all had whispered their support for the Hollis girl after they'd learned she'd run away.

The reverend's brows drew together. In a deep, booming voice filled with displeasure he demanded, "Well, speak up. I haven't got all day to wait for you to find your tongue. The Lord's work awaits me."

"I brought you this." Herbie's eyes slid to the wrinkled telegram as he held it out.

"Why did you not just say so in the first place?" Ardsworth snatched the piece of paper. When Herbie remained standing with his palm outstretched, Elijah's eyes narrowed. "What are you waiting for, boy?"

"My customers . . . I mean some of my customers *sometimes* give, uh, offer me a . . . a token of thanks for bringing their messages to them," Herbie stammered, fearing the reverend's wrath.

"You'll get your reward in heaven, boy. Now be gone."

"Yes, sir. Thank you, sir." Herbie scrambled for his bicycle, happy to get away from the daunting gaze of the reverend.

Herbie pulled the next two telegrams from his vest and glanced at the address. Now he had to peddle all the way in this heat to the wealthy section of town to deliver the next one. A pleased smile lit his face: at least he'd get a good tip for delivering the messages. Among the messengers at the telegraph office, Addison Rutcliff had the reputation as having an extremely generous pocketbook. "Hope these got good news, Mr. Rutcliff. Then I'll get even a better tip," Herbie muttered, giving the peddle his heel.

An evil smile tugged at the corners of Elijah's lips as he watched the boy's hasty departure. It always gave him such a powerful, righteous feeling of fervor to instruct one of the lesser of God's children, as was his divinely ordained right, about the sin of greed. These people were such weak souls, he thought as he went back inside the house.

Before he reached his study he'd opened the telegram and read its contents. "Marie! Get down here. Now!" he ordered.

A haggard woman, with little more than sunken hollows where once bright curious blue eyes had been, rushed down the stairs. As the mere ghost of a woman neared the huge reverend, she nervously straightened her worn gray dress and prematurely graying hair.

"Yes, Elijah? You called for me?" she asked in little more than a subservient whisper, wringing her blistered hands.

"Who else would I be calling for, woman? Especially since that devil's daughter fled her only chance to be redeemed."

His eyes flashed, causing Marie to shrink back. "I'm sure Libby will come to her senses in time, Elijah," Marie offered meekly.

"Yes, I'm certain she will." A cold smile pierced the straight line of his lips. "Sooner than she may hope." At the bewildered expression on the woman's face, Elijah added, "You see, that evil daughter of yours cannot hide from the hand of God. Her whereabouts has just been delivered unto me. and as soon as I am able to prepare for the journey, I shall be on my way to reclaim her soul."

Fear and confusion mingled on her trembling lips. "I do not understand."

"I shall attempt to explain it to you, then, although as a mere woman you are perhaps incapable of comprehending," he said condescendingly. "You see, this telegram from a concerned Christian gentleman named Sheldon Sharpe," he held it out, gloating, "states that your daughter was apprehended at Fort Benton, Montana Territory, before she could step off the steamer. The authorities are holding her in a jail cell awaiting my reply to Mr. Sharpe's message. So you see, no one can escape from God's humble servants when He is guiding the search for His lost lambs." A righteous, self-satisfied glow overtook him and he rested his knitted fingers on his ample belly.

Marie forced herself to say, "Elijah, you have me. Why not let Libby go and concentrate on reclaiming *my* pitiful soul?"

"No!" He backhanded her with such force that she slammed into the wall and slid to the floor. "You pathetic excuse for a human being!" he blazed. "I have no intention of letting the girl make a fool out me. Just as soon as I can make arrangements to have someone take over my duties while I am away, I'm going to reclaim Libby for God and bring her back where she belongs. I will *not* let it be said that Elijah Ardsworth allowed one of his poor lambs to stray without a determined effort to redeem her soul."

Marie dabbed the trickle of blood from the corner of her mouth. "May I accompany you, please, Elijah? Please?" she begged.

"Why should I pay passage for the likes of you?"

"Because I can help convince Libby to return to St. Louis without causing you any trouble," she said bravely. "I can help you make the girl see the error of her ways."

Elijah slitted his eyes at the scrawny bitch. He knew how to take care of anyone who resisted his guidance; he'd done it years before in Ohio. But she did have a point . . . he certainly didn't want the girl trying to get any of the townspeople involved, although he had no doubt he could handle the yokels.

He looked over Marie's bone-thin body. She'd been a real beauty once. He gave a disgusted snort at the haggard woman who cowered before him. No matter what they looked like, women did have their uses. Having her along would offer some benefits—until he had her beautiful daughter again, that is. This time little Miss Elizabeth Marie Hollis would not escape him—he would see to that!

"All right, my dear, I shall take you along. But I warn you: if you do anything, anything at all, to cause me even the slightest embarrassment, you will come to regret it. Do you understand?"

"Yes. Thank you, Elijah. I will not embarrass you, I promise. When do we leave?"

He glowered and took a threatening step toward her. "I already told you, woman, as soon as I can arrange for another minister to watch over my followers while we are gone on this mission of mercy. . . ."

Herbie's eyes rounded at the shiny silver dollar Addison Rutcliff flipped to him after scanning the message he'd received from Governor Potts. Still hoping for another coin, the boy said, "Thank you, sir. I hope the second one has good news too."

"Son, it could not have been better. As a matter of fact," he glanced at the name on the second message, "this one from a Mr. Sheldon Sharpe, bless his kind heart, has sent me news better than closing the deal I signed yesterday. Here." He dug into his vest pocket and flipped another coin in the boy's direction. "Get yourself an extra treat, and something for those you work with. Tonight I want everyone in town to help me celebrate my daughter's marriage to a fine upstanding young man in Montana Territory. The governor of the territory states there's a picture on the way. Too bad I don't have it now to show off this evening."

Herbie gaped at the distinguished older man. Everyone knew about Katherine Rutcliff's reputation. It just went to show you what money could buy. He quickly recovered . . . Addison Rutcliff was too wealthy and important to chance anything.

"Congratulations, sir. Will you be joining your daughter soon?" he asked, noticing the man's excitement. After all, there always was the possibility that the man could offer him another tip.

Rubbing his chin, Addison pondered what the boy had said. A gleam flickered into his shrewd eyes. "I had been planning to visit Katherine once I closed the deal I just signed. But of course, the final papers may take weeks or months to be drawn up and agreed upon by both sides," he said absently, to himself more than to the messenger. Addison looked blankly at the boy. "I couldn't, could I?"

"Couldn't what, sir?"

"No, of course not."

"What, sir?" urged the boy.

"Then again, why couldn't I?"

"Could or couldn't what, sir?" Herbie asked again, scratched his head, thoroughly confused by now.

"I am the owner of my businesses, aren't I?"

"Why, yes, sir . . . everyone in town knows that."

"And as owner, shouldn't I allow subordinates to take care of details?"

"If you think them capable, sir," Herbie answered, straightening his stance, now that such an important man had seen fit to consult him. Just wait until the other messengers heard about it!

"Capable or not, I'm going to do it. Thank you for the advice, son," Addison said, sending another dollar spinning in Herbie's direction. "When I return, stop by my offices. I think I could use a lad like you."

"Yes, sir!" Herbie saluted, he was so excited. Bewilderment overtook him and he asked, "When you get back from where, sir?"

"Why, Fort Benton, Montana Territory, of course. Thanks to your advice, I am not going to wait to visit my daughter and her new husband. And, of course, my precious Matilde," he wistfully mumbled to himself before again snapping his attention back. "Katherine was after me to make the trip to Montana with her. She will be delightfully surprised when I arrive so promptly, don't you think?"

"I'm sure your new son-in-law will find a visit from a man like yourself most enlightening," the boy said for want of anything better.

"Enlightening?" Addison laughed, then mused to himself, "How could I possibly *enlighten* any man who chose to marry my daughter?"

Chapter Twenty-three

His crafty eyes constantly shifting, Hobby Knubbleby scratched the bald patch on the back of his head. "What are ya smearin' yerself with dirt fer, lady? Egads, ya just took a confounded dunk in the river not more than a couple of hours ago. And now here ya go wallowin' like some sow 'bout ta go inta heat."

Katherine bit her lip to keep from giving the slimy little man a good tongue-lashing. "Need I remind you again, Mr. Knubbleby, that I am not paying for your company? I am paying you to take me to Cordell Chandler."

Hobby's gray eyes darted to a nearby hill. "In that case, yer highness, ya shoulda paid me off three days ago when we catched up with Chandler's bull train. Hell, if I'd a knowed at the time that dude hired me you was that crazy gal from the docks, I never woulda agreed ta take ya ta Chandler in the first place."

"Don't you mean if you did not have a cash box for a conscious?" Katherine snarled.

"A man's got ta do what he's got ta do ta make a livin' somehow. Besides, that frienda yers swore it was all a mistake, so I seen no harm in it. But I still don't get why we ain't just riding inta camp."

Katherine's temper burst and she threw a wad of bills at the man. "Here's your money! Now go on back to Fort Benton and get out of my sight!"

Not one to pass up a buck, Hobby dropped to his

knees and raked in the money. "Sure, lady. It'll be a real pleasure ta leave the likes of ya."

Grumbling to himself, Hobby's beady little eyes shifted to Katherine and back over the horses nearby. Then he snatched his horse's reins, mounted the nag, and scooped up the reins of the animal Katherine had been riding.

"What do you think you're doing?" Katherine demanded, experiencing a flicker of impotent rage.

"I'm takin' the horses back ta the stable. What ya paid me don't pay fer the horse." Making a mockery out of a gesture of respect, Hobby tipped his hat and galloped back in the direction of Fort Benton, leaving Katherine glaring after him.

Katherine expelled a sigh and took three deep breaths to calm herself. "Good riddance."

She set her eyes on a hill not more than a quarter mile to the south. She had observed Cordell Chandler and that Elizabeth Hollis person set up camp there not more than an hour ago, and head toward the river to bathe. She had watched with envious interest when Chandler had dived into the water after the girl. And her keen eyes had not missed the interaction between the two.

With a swift, sure motion, Katherine clamped her fingers at the shoulder seam of her red satin dress and ripped the sleeve. Not satisfied with her efforts to make it look like she had stumbled upon the train, Katherine picked up a handful of twigs and leaves and snarled them in her dark brown hair. As a final touch, she shredded the hem of her dress and rubbed patches of dirt across her bodice and down the skirt.

She took a steadying breath and headed toward the train, hoping to meet with Shelley first before she was discovered. She had nearly reached the camp when from behind fingers clamped around her arm.

"Ain't you an awful far ways from the nearest town, ma'am?" Gulch said.

"Thank goodness," Katherine whined, her eyes wide

and innocent, "I was so afraid I was lost forever."

"And just how did you manage to get free from jail and show up here?" Cordell barked, his black eyes sparking as he joined them. Clem had warned him to be on the look out for the woman.

"Jail?" Gulch choked, realization overtaking him.

"Yes. Don't you recognize her? She's the one who attacked that reverend back in St. Louis, the one who made quite a spectacle out of Katherine's arrival by insisting she was Katherine."

Katherine opened her mouth to retort, then thought better of it. She was here to help Shelley blackmail Elizabeth Hollis, not to raise Cordell's wrath.

"Please, you must forgive me for that . . . I was desperate. At least the sheriff finally let me go when he discovered it was a mistake."

"The sheriff told me you escaped," Cordell said point blank.

"It was a misunderstanding. I was finally released." She kept her gaze steady with Cordell's, intent that he not detect the yarn. "It upset me so much that I rented a horse and just left. I probably would have found my way to the next town if my horse hadn't thrown me. Luckily I happened on your camp, or I don't know what would have become to me." She hung her head but closely watched the big man's reactions from beneath her heavy lashes.

Cordell looked unconvinced by her story. He called out to one of the bull whackers standing near the animals. "Saddle up a couple of horses. I want you to escort this woman back to Fort Benton." He then looked pointedly at Katherine. "If what you say is true, you'd be better off to remain there until the next steamer arrives and can take you back to wherever you came from."

A towel slung over his shoulder, Sharpe was strolling back from the river when he noticed Katherine in the midst of another ruckus. For an instant the thought flashed through his mind to let the troublesome woman fend for herself . . . he pinched his lips and headed toward Katherine. No matter how much he'd like to turn and walk away, he knew if he were going to succeed with his blackmail scheme he needed Katherine's help.

"What is going on here, Chandler?" Sharpe asked, joining Katherine, Gulch, and Cordell. He fixed on Katherine an appreciative gaze. "And who is this lovely lady?" he added innocently.

Katherine immediately picked up on Sharpe's ploy, and pleaded, "Please, sir, don't let them send me back to Fort Benton. You must help me convince these men that I mean no one any harm."

"She looks harmless, Chandler," Sharpe said.

"A lot you know. No . . . *she goes.*"

"Can you spare the men or time it would take to return this lady to Fort Benton?" Sharpe shrewdly set out, knowing Chandler had to get his freight to Helena.

"You know damn well I can't."

"Well then, why not allow me to look after her until we reach Helena?" Sharpe offered, careful to keep his face neutral.

Libby climbed out of the wagon at that moment and spied Katherine. Her heart pounding, she took measured steps until she was standing beside Cordell. Absently she took his arm. "Wh-what is she doing here?"

"She says the sheriff discovered he'd made a mistake, let her go, and she left town and promptly got lost," Cordell answered, an open skepticism tinting his words.

"Do you believe her?" Libby asked in a shaky voice.

"Not for a minute." He studied Libby for a long moment, then added, "So I am going to have you keep an eye on her until we get to Helena."

"Me? Why me?"

"You're the perfect choice. With your experience she shouldn't be able to ply her wiles on you, my dear."

Libby bit her lip to stay a response.

Sharpe coughed to keep from chuckling. Chandler

had just outsmarted himself. Katherine remained passive, but Sharpe had known her long enough to know she was as delighted as he was.

Enjoying Libby's obvious discomfort, Katherine widened her eyes and clasped her hands in front of her in a display of deference. "Ah, Mrs. Chandler, since you're being gracious enough to watch over me, I wonder if you'd be kind enough to consent to accompany me to the river so that I might bathe."

Libby looked to Cordell for understanding, hoping he would support what she was about to say. Her throat dry, Libby quietly said, "I'm afraid that will not be possible. I have other duties to tend now."

To Libby's dismay, Cordell said, "Actually, I think it would be a very good idea. There is no doubt Miss ah . . . is in need of a bath." He suddenly turned to . . . Katherine. "If you aren't the person who attacked that reverend, then what is your name?"

"My name is Elizabeth Morris," Katherine said quickly, remembering Libby's full name from the poster the deputies had shown her. "That is one of the reasons for the mistaken identity. My name and description are similar to that of the wanted girl. But of course, that is where the similarity ends."

Cordell arched a brow. "Of course. As I was saying, Katherine, please accompany Elizabeth to bathe. And then you can take her into the wagon and give her one of those many dresses you brought. She can't go around like that."

Libby's shoulders slumped. "Very well. Follow me, *Elizabeth*."

"Thank you, Mr. Chandler," Katherine said in her most grateful tone. "You will not regret it."

"You needn't thank me. As soon as we reach Helena, I'm going to turn you over to the marshal and let him check out your story."

Katherine maintained her composure, but smoldered beneath her smiling face as she trotted after Libby.

Once alone with Libby inside the wagon Katherine's

demeanor reverted to that of earlier times. "Thought you could simply tell a few lies, move in on my fiancé, get me locked up, and then live happily ever after, did you? Well, little Miss Minister Beater, you better think again," she hissed.

"Why did you follow me?" Libby forced herself to ask.

"Why did *I* follow *you?*" Katherine mimicked. She threw her head back and laughed. "You stole my life and then want to know why I followed you? You must be joking." She pointed an accusing finger at Libby. "I have no intention of letting you take my place without paying for it. Just remember *that* when you're lying in your handsome husband's arms at night, Mrs. Chandler."

"Paying for it?"

"You didn't think I'd let you go without extracting some form of payment, did you?"

"But I don't have anything," Libby offered.

"You have a lot more than you realize," Katherine shot back viciously.

"But what?" Libby asked, confused.

"I'll let you know in due time. But for now, quit asking questions and do as you're told," Katherine advised darkly.

Libby kept a brave face as she opened the trunk and waited while Katherine rummaged through its contents. Katherine did not know that she and Cordell hadn't consummated their marriage, and somehow she had to keep Katherine from finding out. Libby knew Katherine did not feel anything toward Cordell, and he was too important to Libby to let Katherine ruin the best chance Libby had for real happiness.

"Why not wear the beige calico, it's—"

"Why don't *you* wear that frumpy dress," Katherine shot back. "That must be one of your selections. I'd never even consider anything so plain and homely." She pulled a dainty pink creation out and held it up in front of her. "This should do nicely."

139

"The calico is more practical," Libby added quietly.

"Practical for whom?" When Libby did not answer, Katherine added, "You can play your latest role of my keeper while we are in front of the others, but don't try to tell me what to do. Now let's go have that bath. You want Cordell to see me at my best, don't you?"

Chapter Twenty-four

As Libby led Katherine toward the water's edge, she chided herself for what she was about to do. She knew she would never be considered charitable for her actions. But she had no intention of meekly allowing Katherine to make her life miserable until they reached Helena.

During the last two months Libby had grown from a scared young girl into a mature, self-confident young woman. She'd taken control of her life; she now had a definite goal, a direction in life, and was determined to succeed. She'd learned to assert herself, and even while a shiver of foreboding inched up her spine, she swore she would never return to being that frightened young girl so easily manipulated again.

An impish gleam in her eyes, Libby purposely retraced the same course she'd taken to the river with Cordell. Katherine followed unsuspectingly. And like what had happened to Libby earlier, Katherine, too, sunk thigh deep into the sticky quagmire.

"Why, you little fool," Katherine bellowed, trying to free herself. "You did this on purpose!"

"Here, let me help you," Libby offered sweetly and leaned over to save the pink dress from the murky gook which would surely stain it.

"Put that dress down and help me before I expose you!" Katherine sputtered, floundering helplessly in the slime.

Katherine was making so much noise that Libby decided she'd best help Katherine out before the woman's screams brought the whole camp. Careful to remain on the edge of the sucking mud, Libby reached out her arm.

Katherine immediately took the proffered hand and with great effort climbed from the mire. "You did that deliberately, didn't you?" Her actions were so quick that Libby had no chance to get out of the way of the spinning mud that hit her square in the face.

"Next time you'll know better," Katherine spat triumphantly and lunged at Libby.

The two women rolled on the ground, Katherine screaming insults and Libby trying to protect herself while returning in kind each blow Katherine attempted to land.

Katherine's caterwauling brought Cordell and Sharpe running. Before Cordell could pull them apart, Sharpe stopped to laugh. "Why not let them finish their disagreement, Chandler? It might clear the air between them."

"Shut up and get over here," Cordell snarled and grabbed Libby.

Still kicking and swinging, Libby found herself being flung off her feet. Katherine darted at Libby only to find a hurting arm wind around her waist and hold her tight as well.

"She attacked me!" Katherine screeched. "First she led me into the mud, and when I asked for help to get out, she attacked me!"

Forcing himself to keep a straight face at the muddied sight the two women made, Cordell commented, "Isn't this the same place you came with me earlier, dear?"

Calmed and standing quietly at Cordell's side, Libby's expression hinted at guilt. "Yes, so I knew it would be a good place to bring Ka . . . ah . . . Elizabeth."

Cordell let a grin slip from his lips. From what he'd already seen of the woman's actions, he couldn't blame

142

his wife. And although he had no intention of saying so, inside he had to admire her spunk; she had held her own against that scheming Hollis person, who he still believed Elizabeth to be, though she insisted differently. "While I understand why you might wish to return to a familiar setting, I think you'd best go on downriver a-ways and leave Elizabeth here so you can both bathe without further incident."

Cordell cleared his throat to keep away the smile which threatened to break out on his lips. "Come on, Sharpe, let's get back to the wagons."

"I think I'd rather remain close by." He swung a sideways look at Katherine. "To make sure there are no further problems, of course."

Cordell lifted his brow. "No doubt your intentions are completely honorable. But I don't think there will be any further incidents. Isn't that right, *ladies?*"

"I certainly wouldn't think of starting anything," Katherine said innocently.

Cordell looked to Libby, his black eyes demanding compliance. "You needn't worry about me," she said, staring at Katherine.

"Good. Since we have your word that there will be no more trouble, I think it is safe for Sharpe and me to leave you two to your baths." He tipped his hat. "Ladies."

"Will you bring me back some clean clothing?" Libby called out to Cordell's back. At his silent nod of consent, she quickly strode further downriver before Katherine could say anything.

A short distance away Libby fond a delightful inlet where the icy water stood still and clear. The late afternoon sun had already begun to cool, so Libby wasted little time seeing to her bath.

"Here's a clean outfit," Cordell said, coming back.

Libby swung around. Cordell was standing only five feet offshore. He was staring at her, which gave her an idea. Without giving a proper assessment to what he might think of her actions, she took a buoying breath and stepped from the river.

Sparkling droplets of water glistened from her nude body and fell from the tips of her breasts. Her skin tingled from the chill and a healthy blush grew upward from her ankles under the heat of Cordell's admiring gaze.

Cordell openly watched his wife stroll from the water. Her blue-black hair hung in inky wet ringlets over one shoulder and down the edge of one full, tempting breast while the rest caught at her other shoulder and cascaded down her back. Her waist curved inward to such an extent that he was certain he could reach around it with his hands. Pelvic bones just below her flat stomach hinted at the rounded slimness of her gently flared hips. His eyes slipped further to hesitate at the softly, curling black hair at the top of long slender thighs.

Noticing the hungry look on Cordell's face, Libby stretched out her hand. "Cordell," she whispered, still astounded by her own boldness.

He snapped his head, immediately changing his expression to one of disapproval. "Whatever you're trying to do, it won't work."

Disappointment colored Libby's cheeks and embarrassment made her seek to cover her breasts with her arms. Quickly she said, "I merely wanted my clothing before I turn blue."

"Oh, sure . . . here you are." He awkwardly handed over a calico dress. Their fingers touched and Libby was astounded at the thrill she experienced by the rough feel of him.

Libby's breath caught at the sight of the dress. It was the same one Katherine had spurned only a short time before. Libby's first inclination was to insist Cordell bring her another dress. Katherine was sure to make an unkind comment. She started to return it, then quickly slipped it over her head.

"Thank you for bringing the dress so promptly," she said with a gentle smile on her lips. It was a simple act

144

of kindness, but it was a beginning.

"Just because I brought you a dress, don't think I've changed my mind about you."

"Oh, I won't," she agreed, standing before him, staring into the depths of those black, hypnotic eyes.

"Just don't." Cordell rocked back on his heels, unable to take his eyes off Libby.

"I wouldn't think of it," she repeated, a touch of sadness in her voice.

"Good," he muttered, while his eyes held a questioning gaze. "Now, I've got duties to attend to and you'd better get back to yours as well. I don't want that Elizabeth woman to try anything funny before we get to Helena."

"No, of course not," Libby said in little more than a trembling breath. Hearing the way Cordell said her name when referring to Katherine threatened to make her tell Cordell the whole truth. She sank her teeth into her lip; she couldn't take the chance of losing the man before she'd won even a small piece of his heart.

"So, despite what she told you, you still think she really is Elizabeth Hollis?" Libby questioned.

"Don't you?" he returned pointedly and swung around, not waiting for a reply.

She watched Cordell move away from her, then headed back to where she'd left Katherine. She could see Katherine in the distance, toweling her hair when a scruffy pup raced out from beneath a bush and charged her.

Libby reached down and picked up the squirming puppy. "What are you doing out here in the middle of nowhere?" It perked its ears and slurped Libby's nose. "You are a friendly little fur ball."

The puppy, the color of sagebrush, whined and gave her another lick. Tears came to Libby's eyes. She had always wanted an animal. Once, when she was ten, a small black dog had followed her home from school. The reverend had caught her feeding the scrawny animal a slice of bread, and he'd exploded with rage. He hurled a rock at the retreating dog, missing it and hitting Libby instead. Absently she fingered the raised scar on her forearm. She'd wanted something of her own to love. Instead, the reverend had whipped her and locked her in her room for three days with only bread and water.

Hugging the cuddly little critter, Libby fought off the flood of memories. Now she had her very own pet. She kissed its head gently and closed the distance between herself and Katherine.

Katherine rolled her eyes. "What is that cliché? Oh, yes . . . birds of a feather. Wherever did you find such a mangy beast?" She wrinkled her nose.

"He's not a mangy beast. He's a poor, homeless puppy and I plan to make a pet out of him."

"Much like yourself and Cordell Chandler, no doubt," Katherine sniffed with distaste.

Libby was not about to allow herself to fall prey to Katherine's cruel witticisms, so she directed, "We'd best be getting back."

"You needn't concern yourself, I haven't forgotten that you are supposed to be my keeper."

Back at the camp Katherine immediately headed toward Sharpe and the fire to get a warming cup of coffee.

Libby set the pup down and was scratching it behind its ear when Cordell found her. "What the devil are you doing with that coyote pup?"

"I found it down by the river. It must have lost its mother." She lifted it to her chest and smoothed its bushy coat. "I intend to make a pet out of it."

Cordell frowned. "Oh no you don't. You're going to return that animal to where you found it and be glad one of the men didn't see it first and shoot it."

"No!" she cried and ran to the edge of the wagon. She sank down along the wheel and hugged the pup to her.

Cordell hurried after her, intending to wrest the young animal away. His first inclination had been to

146

dispose of it before it could grow big enough to menace livestock. But seeing her response to the creature, he decided to be charitable and send it back to its mother.

When he found her, he stopped. She was sitting on the ground, rocking the animal and crooning to it. For an instant his mind visualized her cradling a child in her arms and his heart swelled. He blinked his eyes several times to clear the unwelcome picture.

"Katherine," he said softly, "do you hear that coyote howling in the distance? It's too close to be any animal except that pup's mother. The pup is a wild animal, Katherine. It must be returned to the wild."

Libby looked up, her eyes red and swollen. There was no mistaking the mournful cries. Regardless of the memories and how much she desperately wanted to keep the pup, Cordell was right, the pup had to be returned to its mother.

"There are times when loving means letting go," he added quietly. She sniffed back a sob. She wasn't about to let him see her break down over the animal. She gave the pup a big hug and handed it over to him.

Holding the struggling critter, his gaze dropped to her. If he hadn't received the Pinkerton report, he'd almost have sworn she was a poor, innocent girl who'd just given up her first beloved possession. He had to remind himself that she was Katherine Rutcliff Chandler, the pampered daughter of one of America's wealthiest businessmen.

Despite his resolve, the flicker of a question formed in the back of his mind. Was his wife really the wealthy slut she was reported to be?

Chapter Twenty-five

Horrified, Libby watched Cordell haul the squirming pup from camp. One of the bull whackers ran up to him with a rifle in his hands.

"Put the mangy beast down and I'll blow it t' kingdom come so it don't never up and kill no calves when it's growed," Binkley said, getting ready to set a bead on the helpless animal.

Cordell set the pup down.

Libby scrambled to her feet. She was about to race to its rescue when she saw Cordell knock the rifle from the mangy red-haired man's hands.

"No one is going to hurt that animal," Cordell warned, scratching the critter behind the ear. "Do you understand?"

"But —" the man started to protest.

"No . . . just let it be. I'm afraid my wife's taken a shine to the pup. And since she can't keep it, I'm returning it to its mother."

Bewildered, the man shrugged. "Sure, boss . . . whatever ya' say."

Cordell watched the pup scamper off toward the cries of its mother. Then he dismissed the bull whacker. Before he headed toward the fire, he caught sight of Libby. She was leaning against the wagon wheel, a grateful smile adorning her lips. It caused him to turn abruptly away.

"That little gal sure has you all wound up nice 'n snug 'round her pinkie, don't she?" Gulch chuckled, waving his little finger in the air. "Coyotes being the problem to the herds that they are, I'd a never believed you'd just let one up and saunter away the way you done, even for a new bride."

"Yeah, well, I did. So what of it?" Cordell grumbled. "And she doesn't have me wound around her finger, either."

"No. No, sure enough not," Gulch responded, taken aback by the forcefulness of Cordell's denial. His eyes darted to Katherine and back to Cordell. He rubbed his chin. He'd never seen a man so danged smitten as hell-bent on denying it as he was. He wanted to laugh to himself. Dell had always had the ladies falling at his feet. It must be a new experience for the rancher to find himself on the other end of the lasso; his heart was all tied up nice and neat by that little wife of his.

"I'm glad you disposed of that flea-ridden creature," Katherine sniffed, joining Cordell. "The last thing we need is to be infested by the filthy thing."

Cordell swung toward her. "What do *you* know about it?" he demanded.

Katherine clasped her hand to her throat. "Well, anyone can see it was just a wild animal," she said indignantly, then changed her stance to add innocently, "She should have consulted you before bringing it back to camp."

"As I suppose you'd have done," Cordell said skeptically.

"If I were Katherine, I wouldn't waste time giving my attentions to some dirty beast. I would save them all for my husband."

"No doubt you would," put in Sharpe, joining the pair. He ignored Chandler's dark look at Katherine's annoyance and sniffed at the concoction bubbling over the open flames. He rubbed his hands together in anticipation. "What smells so good? With all the com-

149

motion this afternoon, I've built up a healthy appetite."

"Yes, so have I," Katherine agreed. "I haven't enjoyed a good meal since I left the *Benton*."

"Well, I'm afraid you'll have to talk to my wife about your supper. You see, her culinary expertise is just one more thing she's begun cultivating since I married her."

The smug, superior expression died on Katherine's lips, and Sharpe rocked back and forth on his heels enjoying her discomfort. He did not want Katherine capturing Chandler's heart. The way she'd set about trying to work her wiles on the man since she'd arrived galled him. He was determined not to let anything interfere with the plan he'd worked out.

Sharpe cast Katherine a telling look. "I hope Katherine feels generous tonight, *Elizabeth*. Or you and I may find ourselves sharing the cook's cold leftover biscuits from breakfast."

"Nonsense."

"What is nonsense?" Libby asked, joining them by the fire.

"Oh, nothing," Katherine returned sweetly. Then her glittering brown eyes openly slid down Libby before she said, "That dress is perfect, my dear. It definitely is you."

Libby looked down at the beige calico and smoothed the wrinkled skirt. For a moment she quietly cursed the simple dress, which Katherine had earlier refused as beneath her, until Libby remembered that clothing wasn't the issue. What a person was on the inside was what was important, not what was on the outside.

"Why, thank you . . . Elizabeth. Cordell purchased it for me to wear on the trail," Libby said proudly and moved to Cordell's side.

Katherine narrowed her eyes, then recovered herself. "Indeed." She turned the charm on Cordell. "And did you select my outfit also, Cordell?" she purred.

"He did," Libby interceded, "for me. But what was it you were talking about before I joined you? Something being nonsense, I believe," she persisted, not about to allow Katherine's comment to drop.

"Our *guests* are concerned that you might decide not to offer them any of your wonderful cooking," Cordell said blandly.

At first Libby was tempted to deny them the meal. Certainly no one would blame her, the way Katherine and Sharpe acted. It would be no more than they deserved. Libby glanced at Cordell. His face was impassive, void of any emotion.

"I'm not sure there's enough," Libby said directly to Katherine. "You must understand, I didn't know we would be having guests for supper."

"Looks like you're out of luck, Elizabeth," Sharpe put in with a smirk.

Katherine's face burned with rage.

"But of course, I can always add more water to the stew and stretch it, I suppose."

The expression on Katherine's face mellowed. "I should expect so. Now when are we going to eat?"

"As soon as everyone is here." Libby ignored Katherine's sharpness and summoned the rest of the camp to supper.

Libby ladled generous helpings of the mouth-watering stew into everyone's bowl and then dished herself up a portion. Cordell was positioned on a rock near Gulch and Binkley, busy in conversation, the other bull whacker and ranch hand had moved off, and Libby certainly didn't want to join Katherine and Sharpe, so Libby took a seat on the wagon tongue.

Libby had been intrigued by Cordell since the first time she saw him boarding the steamer. He was such a handsome man with his black hair and eyes. And she'd found that when she was near him, despite his ill humor, she felt a special spark which touched her heart and made her feel alive. Touching him and kissing him brought her immeasurable joy. She had watched him with the others on this trip; he really was a good man in spite of the way he was treating her. Kind, considerate, caring, hard working . . . yes, she thought, those were the things that had spawned her love.

It was ironic that she'd been forced to endure the reverend's groping hands, and now, when she would welcome Cordell's touch, he resisted her. She reminded herself that anything worthwhile was worth striving for. But what if she managed to gain his affections and he found out she was an imposter. Would he still want her or cast her out? The thought troubled her, yet she was strong; she would take what came, one day at a time. She was patient; she would succeed. She had to.

After supper, Libby gave Cordell one last look and climbed into the wagon to wait for him. An idea came to her, and she set about combining their blankets into one bed instead of the two separate beds Cordell had insisted on. Outside, voices distracted her from her chore, causing her to stop and listen.

"What do you mean I can't go in there?" Katherine demanded angrily.

"It ain't no place for you," Gulch insisted. "That wagon's for Dell and his missus. You'd be just as cozy in the bed I made up for you in the last wagon."

Katherine fixed the man with her most malicious stare. "Well, at least let me go borrow a nightdress from the precious Mrs. Chandler."

Gulch hesitated, which Katherine took as consent. She put her foot up on the wagon, but Gulch immediately grabbed her and set her back down on the ground.

"Look, lady, I don't want no trouble. But I ain't gonna let you bother her no more tonight."

Katherine slammed her hands on her hips and spat, "I guess I shall just have to take the matter up with your boss, then, won't I?" She hoped the lowly trail hand would concede defeat and go away.

"You'll find Dell out checking on the oxen," Gulch directed, nonplussed.

Libby listened to the pounding footfalls leave the wagon and guessed Katherine had gone in search of Cordell. Quietly, Libby thanked Gulch for keeping Katherine away. She busied herself with finishing the task with Cordell's bedding. But keeping her hands occupied did nothing to take her mind off Cordell while she waited for the others to bed down for the night, and for Cordell to enter the wagon.

It was finally quiet outside. Katherine must have given up and gone to sleep in the other wagon. It seemed an eternity before she heard twigs snap and leaves crunch beneath the steps of someone coming nearer the wagon. In anticipation, Libby hurriedly arranged the stack of blankets around herself to offer Cordell a tempting glimpse of her. Her heart began to race when she saw it was Cordell entering the wagon.

Excitement flowed through her veins as she waited for him to say something. In the flicker of the lantern light, Cordell's black eyes flashed fire as they took in the creamy flesh exposed above the wool slanting her breasts.

"What are you trying to do to me?" he grumbled.

"Do to you?" she returned innocently.

"Don't try to tell me you don't know how you look right now."

"Of course I know how I look."

"Aha! Then you are trying to tempt me," he accused.

Libby was ready for him. She had been planning it all evening.

"Why would I be trying to tempt you? We've been sleeping like this in the same wagon since we left Fort Benton," she offered with a calm radiance she did not feel.

Her seemingly genuine answer momentarily stopped Cordell from further accusations. When he recovered himself, he said gruffly, "Don't try to tell me you

153

usually sleep in the buff. I know better."

"You do?"

"Yes, damn it!"

Although he'd fought the feeling since he'd entered the wagon, he'd felt a strange, glad warmth when he'd discovered his bedding had been moved and combined with hers. In his mind he could feel her hot flesh under his touch. Damn! What was wrong with him? She had planned the whole thing. Then, his senses taking control of his judgment, he descended on her.

Cordell's lips ground down on hers. There was nothing tender in their kiss. All the emotions which Cordell had kept locked away flooded forth. Anger, desire, passion coupled to explode inside him and he wove his fingers through her hair, deepening their kiss, unable to stop himself.

Chapter Twenty-six

Cordell's desire vaulted and he ached to take her. His tongue plundered her mouth, probing and gliding into her very depths. It seemed to be an endless kiss, a brutal, demanding embrace.

Libby was shocked by his forcefulness. But quickly she found herself a willing participant, delighting in their shared intimacy. It didn't matter that he had not come to her willingly; she was sure that with time it would happen. Her fingers wound through his thick black hair, reveling in his strength. Her tongue entered his mouth and made a thorough exploration before Cordell broke off the kiss and he pushed her away.

"What are you trying to do?" he snarled, raking his fingers through his mussed hair.

"Nothing a wife wouldn't do with her husband," she said without shame.

"Or a whore with any man," he returned cruelly.

"I am *not* a whore. And if you'd give me half a chance, I'd prove it to you," she returned with conviction.

"You may not have taken money for it, but that doesn't change what you are. And don't think I have any intention of becoming another one of your long list of conquests!"

Libby had all she could do not to giggle at such an outrageous notion. "I'd never think of you in such a way."

Cordell's eyes became mere slits. "And just how *do* you think of me?"

She shrugged. "I didn't know you had any interest in my thoughts. As a matter of fact, I thought all you wanted was to get to Helena as soon as possible so you could get an annulment."

"Don't try to skirt the issue," he said with anger.

"Never."

Cordell clenched his teeth. What was she trying to gain, the way she was acting? "Are you going to answer me?"

"Of course." She waited. Augusta was right . . . giving Cordell a run for his money had certainly ignited his interest — as well as his ire. If only the impression she was making on him could be redirected! She'd give him time.

"Damn it, woman . . . I asked how you think of me."

"You needn't get so upset," she stated calmly. "I think of you as my husband. And all I want is to please you . . . dear."

"Please me? *Please* me!" Cordell had managed his entire life without losing his temper over a woman, and now here he was near ready to burst. The concept was something new to him and only served to unsettle him further.

"It's not necessary to shout. You'll wake the whole camp if you don't keep your voice down," she advised softly.

"Why did you take it upon yourself to move my blankets?"

"It's cold tonight. I thought we might keep each other warm."

Making no attempts to wrap her nakedness in her own blankets, Libby reached for Cordell's.

"What do you think you're doing?" he asked tightly.

Libby turned back to him, the rosy crests of her breasts plainly visible. "Handing you your blankets, of

156

course. You did want them, didn't you?"

Cordell remained across from her, staring. He rubbed his fingers together. She was getting to him, with her exasperating innocent act! He was only human. He averted his eyes.

He hadn't gone near a woman since Caroline Arthur had sneaked into his room, paraded herself before him, thrown off her clothes, and climbed into his bed. Women were such a devious lot. He shook his head. And then, if he hadn't been so drunk from celebrating with his cowhands, he would never have taken her after the scandal she'd caused when he'd been engaged to her. He had to admit his memory was still rather fuzzy on that account, though. Strange, the lengths some women would go to, he thought before his attention was abruptly refocused as Katherine began to rise.

"What do you think you're doing now?"

"Since you persist in sleeping back in your own corner, I thought I would help arrange the blankets. After all, I was the one who moved them in the first place."

Totally frustrated, Cordell fought to hold onto his temper. "Just stay where you are!"

"But I want to help."

"No! You've done enough already!"

Libby smiled to herself. She was getting to him. All she needed to do was keep it up until she got him into her bed. She was sure when he discovered she was a virgin, he would realize how wrong he was about her.

How far she had come in a little over two short months. Before that she'd cringed at the very thought of any man ever touching her again . . . and now here she was boldly attempting to seduce a man. But Cordell Chandler was not just any man. He was the man she loved and intended to spend the rest of her life with — whether he knew it yet or not.

"And put some clothes on," he insisted.

"Why?"

"Because I told you to."

157

He waited for her to comply with his directive until he couldn't take her silent defiance any longer.

"Well?"

"Well, what?"

"Why aren't you putting on a nightdress?"

"I could lie to you and say I loaned Elizabeth my last clean one, but it wouldn't be the truth. Fact is, I was waiting for you," she said honestly. "But since you insist on sleeping on your own side of the wagon," she casually picked up one of his folded squares of wool and held it out to him, "here is your blanket."

"If you think you're going to trap me with that little act of yours, it isn't going to work!"

Before Libby could respond, Cordell rolled himself up in his blankets and turned his back to her.

Well, he was not going to cut her off that easily this time!

"Cordell?"

"What?" he said through gritted teeth, propping himself up on his elbow to look at her. He was not sure what he wanted to do most—have her beneath him or take her over his knee.

"It isn't an act."

Without another word he settled back down and pulled the blanket up over his head. The blanket effectively shut her out of his view, but it did not shut out his thoughts. For the longest time it troubled him that she'd slept with other men. He wondered why a woman with her background and breeding had dallied with so many. And he wondered why he should care.

Libby sat silently watching Cordell from across the wagon until it appeared he had dropped off to sleep. She grinned to herself . . . she was satisfied with his reactions. He had not been indifferent to her tonight. Spreading another blanket on top of her own pile, she slipped a heavy cotton nightgown over her head and turned out the lantern. She nestled back into the cozy cocoon she had made for herself.

"Not a bad start," she reflected over the evening's

events in the dark.

If only Katherine and Sheldon Sharpe weren't along to complicate matters, Libby was sure she could break down Cordell's resistance. She would just have to work around them and pray they didn't expose her.

From his bed, which he had laid out away from the other men, Sharpe waited patiently until the others were all asleep. Chandler and the Hollis girl were alone together every night in that wagon. Knowing Chandler's reputation with the ladies, there was no doubt in Sharpe's mind what was taking place. He just hoped the pair would fall in love during the process. Before he could put the next phase of his plan into action, he had to be sure the Hollis girl and Chandler had fallen for each other.

Sharpe continued his vigil until the fire had died down to a few glowing embers. Then stealthily he crawled to the wagon in which Katherine slept.

"Katherine," he whispered as he slipped into the small space made for her to sleep amid the cargo.

Katherine woke when a hand stroked her cheek. "Cordell, I knew you'd come," she said softly.

"Sorry to disappoint you, sweetness. I know how you hung on Chandler's every word tonight and batted those long eyelashes at him every chance you got."

"You! What are *you* doing here?"

"I didn't want you to get lonely for male companionship. Besides, it's cold out there."

"I might have known you were not just interested in me," she hissed.

"You know you're constantly in my thoughts, dear lady."

"Yes, the thought of the size of my purse."

"The size of something else as well," he said and joined her under the covers. He pushed her chemise up and clamped a hand on her breast. "I've missed you, baby," he panted, his lust and excitement growing.

159

Watching Cordell go into Elizabeth's wagon had kindled Katherine's need as well. It didn't matter whose body it was next to hers; any man would do to satiate her. With urgent fingers she plucked at the fastenings on Sharpe's trousers.

He stayed her hands. "Take it easy, sweetness. We have all night."

Katherine silently glared up at him as he sat up and shimmied out of his clothes. She could see the outline of his naked body in the moonlight which filtered in through the flap. "Pity you're not as big as Cordell Chandler. Now there's a real man."

In response to her comparison of him to Chandler, Sharpe brutally pounced on Katherine. Being unfavorably compared to another man, particularly Cordell Chandler, cut Sharpe deeply. He was jealous of everything Chandler had: wealth, position, respect, even the loyalty of his men, who Sharpe knew would put their lives on the line for the big rancher.

"So you don't find my body as inviting as Chandler's," he sneered, digging his fingers into her soft shoulders.

"No, I do not," she spat back, taking immense pleasure in the power she had to rile him.

He bit her neck and she squealed until he silenced her with his mouth. Breaking the punishing kiss, he said, "Maybe I'm built like that bastard and maybe I'm not, but in any event, I don't have any trouble satisfying you."

"I won't argue with that, Shelley honey." Katherine laughed, letting his hands rove over her hungrily.

Katherine threw her head back and strained against Sharpe's questing hands and tongue. An unintelligible rumble escaped her lips. He was doing delicious things to her body, fondling, probing, enticing, eliciting feelings so thick with anticipation that she thought she was going to scream if she didn't have him inside her.

She scratched at him until he mounted her and gave her a wild, frenzied ride, flipping and turning her until

160

ey had quenched their lusts in three different posi-
ons.

After he had poured himself into her, he gathered her
nto his arms and thoroughly kissed her. "Don't ever try
o tell me again anyone else has ever done the things to
ou that I have," he bragged.

"No, Shelley," she panted. "No one has ever satisfied
ne like you have." And it was true. She and the
ambler shared the same thirsts. Pity Sharpe wasn't
Cordell Chandler . . . but of course, she hadn't tasted
ne handsome rancher yet. The thought brought a
wisted smile to her lips.

Sharpe leaned on an elbow, feeling satisfied and
ninking that her smile was for him. "By the way,
weetness, if you expect me to vouch for your identity
vhen we get to Helena, you'd best behave yourself."

"I do not know what you mean."

"Your attempts to interfere between Chandler and the
Hollis girl is what I mean. I won't have you ruining
verything. You'll get your chance at the man when the
ime is right . . . and not before."

"But first we bleed them dry, is that correct?"

"You've got the picture. So don't try to change it
gain, sweetness."

"Are you threatening me, Shelley honey?"

"You know better. I simply want the best for both of
s." He softened the tone of his voice in order to keep
ontrol over the bitch. If she weren't useful to him,
e'd enjoy nothing better than watching her rot in a
Helena jail.

Chapter Twenty-seven

Under cool, bright blue skies interspersed with a few white puffy clouds, the bull train slowly moved along the Mullan Wagon Road toward Helena. Life settled into an uneasy routine for Libby. She helped out wherever she could, cooking meals and washing Cordell's clothes. Gulch had even spent time teaching her how to ride and shoot.

Cordell was a different matter. Libby hadn't made any headway with the obstinate man. And it seemed he made it a point to avoid her. In the morning he was gone on his horse before she awoke. After they'd stopped for the night, he'd return to sit across the fire from her and glare. But Libby wasn't daunted . . . she'd discovered he wasn't impervious to her. And she'd had time to figure out what she was going to do when they reached Helena . . . her plans contingent, of course, on Sharpe and Katherine.

Libby looked over at Katherine, seated near Cordell on a fallen log. Katherine continued her unkind jabs at her whenever she got the chance. At least Libby was grateful she'd managed to elude Katherine's efforts to speak privately with her. Katherine's sly attempts to seduce Cordell were wearing, too. The only reason Libby endured them was that Katherine's efforts had been no more successful than her own, and thankfully this was their last night before reaching the capital city.

Returning to the task at hand, Libby gathered up the evening's dishes.

"Cordell, honey, I'm speaking to you," Katherine said, perturbed that his eyes had followed the Hollis girl when she trudged off toward the creek bearing her load of pots, with Sheldon Sharpe trailing along some distance behind her.

"Maybe you were, but you'll have to excuse me, I have something to take care of which seems to require my immediate attention," he returned absently. He got up and left her staring, frustrated, after him.

"Ah, *Katherine*, there you are," Sharpe said to Libby, joining her as she finished scrubbing the dishes down by the creek.

Libby looked up. He was leaning against the felled trunk of an old, decaying pine, his hands clamping a tin coffee cup. "What are you doing out here, Sharpe?"

"My, my, you've changed. You used to address me as Mr. Sharpe. No longer the frightened little girl, are you, Mrs. Chandler?"

"What is it to you?"

"To me?" He shrugged. "I guess you could say it's no more than a financial matter."

Libby's eyes widened. Sharpe had hinted at this before. She set the pots down and drew herself up to her full height, jutting out her chin. "Well, I'm sorry to disappoint you, but I have no money."

"It's not your money I'm interested in, it's your husband's. And if you want to continue to keep Cordell Chandler as your husband, you'll make sure I share in, shall we say, a fair portion of his wealth."

Cordell stood hidden behind an outcropping of boulders not more than ten feet from his wife and Sharpe. When he saw Sharpe follow her from camp, he thought they were about to prove him right. The whole idea of them together gnawed at him, since he'd started to question his first impression of the young woman.

From the first day he'd gone to claim Katherine aboard the *Benton,* her actions had proved contradic-

tory to what he'd read in the Pinkerton report. Al
though she'd tricked him into marrying her, she'd a
first seemed the frightened virgin. Even her attempts to
seduce him had been awkward, done with an open
honesty, not with the flair of a wealthy slut. She'd
made no move to offer her charms to anyone while
they were at Fort Benton, or while on the trail. And
she'd gone out of her way to carry her weight.

When she'd risen to stand directly in front of Sharpe
Cordell had nearly given away his position, but a voice
inside had told him to wait. What he'd heard surprised
and pleased him: they weren't sneaking off to be to
gether. Sharpe was trying to blackmail her. His brows
drew together in question. He did not wait to hear her
answer; he wasn't sure he wanted to. He headed back
to camp. Not only had he learned what he'd set out to
but he'd gotten information which gave him something
else to think about as well.

Unaware that Cordell had been listening, Libby glared
at Sharpe, the slimy little weasel.

"No. I wouldn't give you a *cent* of Cordell's money.
even if I could, which I can't."

"Sure you can," Sharpe returned, "unless you want
me to tell Chandler that you're Elizabeth Hollis, the
sweet young thing who attacked that reverend." She
opened her mouth to retort, but he held up a hand to
stay her answer. "But I don't want you to answer now
I'll be generous with you, since you're new at this. We'll
be in Helena tomorrow. You have two days once you're
settled," he threatened, leaving Libby in shock to watch
him stroll along the creek, toss his cup in the bushes,
and bunch his hands into his pockets, whistling.

Katherine got up. Seductively toying with her thick,
dark brown hair, she walked over to Cordell at the edge
of camp near a stand of trees. In the firelight she
noticed that his expression bore an instant of uncer
tainty which she hadn't seen there before. Now was her

164

chance to capitalize on it. "Where did you disappear to? I was about to come looking for you," she said with coy concern.

"I was taking care of the call of nature, if you must know," he said tiredly.

Katherine was taken back for a moment, but quickly recovered. "I thought perhaps you were troubled about something." When he did not reply, she continued, determined and desperate to get him into her bed. "If there is anything I can do or if you need someone to talk to, I just want you to know I'm here and would be happy to listen."

"I'll remember that," Cordell answered blandly.

"I'm glad," she said with a sweet innocence she'd not known since she was twelve. She had lured one of her father's young stablehands to the carriage house and paid the frightened boy to touch her in those same hidden places she'd seen her father touch those painted women friends of his.

When Cordell started over to the fire, Katherine called him back. "Um, I don't suppose you'd consider helping me move a couple of the crates in the wagon so I could stretch out . . . I've been having cramps in my legs lately." She was giving her best performance and waited expectantly.

"Lead the way. It's the least I can do," Cordell grumbled and followed Katherine to the wagon.

Katherine did not believe in wasting a moment when she felt she had the upper hand. The instant Cordell climbed in and began reshuffling boxes, she cried, "Oh! My calf," and fell to the pile of blankets sobbing, "a cramp. I have a terrible cramp in my leg. Please, help me." She pulled up her skirt to show off her legs to best advantage and implored, "Please, would you rub it for me?"

Cordell arched his brow. Somehow he doubted the sincerity of her plight. He moved the last crate and was turning to leave when Katherine grabbed his arm.

"Please! Oh, it's *so* painful," she moaned.

165

"All right. Sit back, Elizabeth," he said sharply, relenting just to get it over with and get out of there before she was all over him.

Cordell bent over and tentatively began massaging Katherine's calf. The light from the lantern projected two enticing silhouettes on the canvas just as Libby returned from the creek, her arms ladened with pots.

"It ain't what it looks like, Miz Chandler. Honest." Gulch immediately stepped up to Libby and took her burden. "The boss is just being polite, that's all."

At first the urge to flee to the sanctity of her own bed washed over her. But she could not let Katherine try to steal her husband without a fight.

"Why don't you come on over to the fire and get yourself a nice hot cuppa coffee. It's getting mighty cold out and it'll warm your innards."

Libby took several deep, calming breaths. "I don't need a cup of coffee to warm me, Gulch. I feel plenty hot already, thank you."

Determination lining each step, Libby went to the wagon and threw back the flap. Cordell was leaning over Katherine and she had her hands on his shoulders. My God, he was just about to kiss her! How could he?

"Katherine!" Katherine exclaimed, telegraphing a look of guilt. "We thought you were down by the stream cleaning up after dinner."

Libby's eyes shot sparks of cold fury, another new emotion for the once malleable young girl. "So I see."

Cordell gave Katherine a push, sending her away from him. "No. You don't *see* at all."

"I think I see quite clearly," she said tightly, fighting to control the tears threatening her.

"And just what is you think you see?"

"You were about to kiss her."

"You believe that?" he asked darkly, his temper rising for some reason he did not want to recognize.

Libby folded her arms over her chest. "I do."

"Well, then, I don't want to disappoint you." Cordell reached over, yanked Katherine to him, and kissed her.

166

Libby gasped and swung out of the wagon, to Katherine's delight. She tried to deepen the kiss, but Cordell broke it off.

"Let her go," Katherine said in a sultry voice. "Jealousy will do a new bride good," she added in an effort to convince him to stay with her.

"She was jealous, wasn't she?" Cordell said to himself, ignoring Katherine's pleas. He climbed out of the wagon just in time to catch a glimpse of his wife tying the back of her wagon flap shut.

Cordell put his foot up on a rock, leaned his elbow on his knee, and chewed on his lip. His wife was jealous and the realization troubled him. He'd regretted kissing Elizabeth the moment he'd done it. Katherine had been horrified, and he'd hated seeing the hurt etched across her face.

Tommorow they'd arrive in Helena. He'd told her he was going to get an annulment when they got there. Now he found he didn't know what to do about her. She was becoming quite a dilemma for him, and he discovered to his chagrin that he was thinking about her more and more lately. Each time he saw her she set his senses whirling—more than any woman he'd ever known.

He was a man with a sense of direction; he lived a life of deliberation. Yet she constantly disturbed his sense of balance and caused him to act irrationally. Hell, he ached just looking at her. He'd made an effort to stay away from the train during the day because of her. But his equilibrium was thrown off the minute he returned to camp and she was there. No, damn it! He shook his head to clear it. He wasn't going to let a woman of her sort turn his neat, ordered life inside out.

"Boss, you gonna bed down or stand there staring at the ground all night?" Gulch called out from his bedroll.

Cordell frowned at Gulch. At that moment Cordell's mind willed his body to head for the wagon and put an end to his throbbing, hardening desire. Instead, he remained where he stood.

"I told her you were just being polite when you followed that Elizabeth person into the wagon," Gulch said on an awkward note. "Your wife's a downright nice lady. I'm sure if you went to her and explained it, she'd see reason."

"Yes. Reason. Trouble is, Gulch, I'm afraid, I already *explained* it to her." For the longest time before he headed for the wagon, Cordell stared into the fire, lost in thought, not even noticing the cold or dampness of the night settle around him.

Chapter Twenty-eight

Libby sat silent beside Binkley on the wagon box as the wagon bumped and rumbled closer to Helena. She had declined to ride, since she had eschewed the beige calico for fancier clothes—a pink-striped morning dress and a hat adorned with lace and silk flowers spewing rose-colored ribbons. Sharpe had ridden to the wagon once this morning to cast her a knowing smirk and tip his hat. Katherine was curled up in the third wagon, furious that she'd been forced by Cordell to wear the simple skirt and blouse Libby had offered.

Libby took a sip of the tepid coffee Cordell had handed her just before they'd pulled out of camp. He'd acted like nothing had happened the night before, chatting with the bull whackers, giving orders, then mounting his horse and riding out ahead of the train. She'd hoped he'd offer her an explanation, some slender thread of hope to hold onto. But he'd acted indifferent and preoccupied.

After Libby had run into the wagon and knotted the flap against him last night, she'd prayed he'd follow her and try to convince her it was a mistake. She'd even waited and for a while thought of going to him, but he hadn't entered the wagon until some time after she'd fallen asleep. It had taken a lot of newfound courage to confront them. Why hadn't she been able to stand her ground? She'd run and then spent a miserable night imagining the worse, fretting and condemning herself for being fool enough to continue such an ill-conceived charade.

"Up ahead there, ma'am, that's Helena. She's a ripsnortin' town, she is," Binkley pointed out, interrupting Libby's thoughts. "I hope we'll be there a couple days, at least. There's a lot t' keep a man entertained in Helena."

Libby thought of another one of Augusta Kohrs's lively descriptions of the area. It brought to mind the capital's history. Helena had risen in Last Chance Gulch, the site of a significant gold discovery. Situated along major transportation routes and near other mining towns, Helena became the center of population in the territory with over four thousand inhabitants. It was a bustling city which had officially been the territorial capital for only a little over a year and a half, winning a much-disputed vote on whether the seat of government should be moved from Virginia City to Helena.

Libby took in the sprawling, panoramic scene before her. "Oh, my, it *is* quite a city, isn't it?"

"Yes, it is," said Cordell, riding up. "Hold up a minute, Binkley, I'll take over until we get into town."

"Sure 'nuff, boss," the greasy redhead answered, halting the team.

Libby felt her nerves chafe as Binkley climbed down and Cordell took his place. Cordell looked positively handsome this morning in his denims, bleached muslin shirt, string tie, and jacket. He was clean-shaven and his black eyes seemed to twinkle with dancing gold flecks. When he took over the reins, his muscles flexed with authority, reminding Libby what a strong man he was. Without thinking, she moved to the far edge of the box.

"You needn't concern yourself," Cordell grunted. "I haven't put my hands on you yet, have I?"

She sighed, lowering her head. "No." But she wanted to shout, *Not because I haven't tried to get you to.*

"After I get you settled in the hotel and take care of Elizabeth and Sharpe, I'll see about that annulment." When Libby grimaced, he added, "You needn't worry, I'll get you a bank draft which should take care of your expenses until you're settled wherever you decide to go."

"Generous, aren't you," she mumbled, wishing he hadn't been a man of such strong conviction. It had helped him to resist her advances.

"I think so. If you will recall, this marriage was your doing, not mine."

"No. Not yours," she said miserably.

"If everything goes according to the plan, by tomorrow we'll both be free."

"Yes. Free." She bit her lip to keep from crying out that she didn't want to be free of him.

Libby sneaked a glance at Cordell. His jaw was set in a firm line. If she did not dispute the annulment, he soon would be out of her life forever. She'd come too far to allow that to happen without a fight. She would just have to step up her efforts to win over the obstinate man.

"Where will we be staying?" she asked, changing the subject to give herself time to think.

"At the Broadwater Hotel," Cordell answered shortly. He had been in a hurry to get to Helena to be free of the scheming slut. But now he found that tag distasteful, despite everything he knew about her.

"Cordell, why did you kiss Elizabeth last night?" she blurted out. It had bothered her all night and this might be her last chance to learn the truth.

"Because you accused me and pronounced me guilty before you had all the facts. I suppose one might say you drove me to it."

"Me? It wasn't my idea for you to kiss that woman."

"No? Then why didn't you give me a chance to explain that she had a cramp in her leg and asked me to massage it."

"You could have refused," she said lamely.

171

"Refused? Hell—that woman hung onto me like a leech. That's when you showed up."

"Then you weren't about to kiss her when I entered the wagon?"

"What do you think I've been saying?"

A feeling of relief washed over her. The openness of his confession gave her more to think about. What he'd said made sense. Katherine would do anything to ruin her chances with Cordell. She'd have to learn to stop and think before jumping to conclusions from now on. She couldn't just let him walk out of her life tomorrow. "Cordell?"

"What now?" He looked into those expressive blue eyes. It took everything he could muster not to get lost in those azure depths.

Cordell was still contemplating visiting his attorney when Katherine fired an unexpected volley, caught him completely off guard, and started another round of battles.

"I've decided I don't want the annulment."

"What?"

"I said that I don't want—"

He straightened his back, reeling from her untimely disclosure. "I heard what you said. But this is not your choice . . . it's mine. And I have *no* intention of spending the rest of my life with a common whore." After the words "common whore" slipped out, Cordell could have cut out his tongue. What had he been thinking of? Of course he couldn't stay married to someone like Katherine Rutcliff.

Cordell clenched his teeth and whipped the oxen onto Broadway. The sooner he unloaded the lot of these troublesome people, the sooner he could get his life back in order!

Libby paced back and forth across the plush flowered carpet. Cordell had left her with Gulch at the lobby

172

entrance with orders to secure two rooms—one for Gulch and one for Cordell and his bride. Then the infuriating man had departed with Sharpe and Katherine after a short conversation Libby was unable to decipher.

The spacious room was decorated in heavy carved rosewood. Tatted lace graced the enormous bed. The daintest doilies covered a nightstand and nearby table, and imported lace hung at the windows, wherein offered a southern view of the pine-dotted mountains in the distance. It was the most exquisite room Libby had ever seen, but for all it mattered, it might have been a smelly old stable until Cordell Chandler was there to share it with her.

A knock at the door ended her musings. She opened it to an eagerly smiling bellboy who bobbed his head. "I have you bags, ma'am."

"Yes, thank you. Bring them in." Libby stepped back to allow the boy to cart Katherine's trunk and Cordell's bags inside the room.

The young lad set his burden down, collected a tip, and left. The door was still wide open when Libby bent over to start unpacking.

"Is this Room 212?" a richly attired woman of at least sixty asked. She was dressed in a deep moss green velvet overskirt with a deeper green satin crinoline. Lace bunched up about her double chin and a generous bow knotted at her throat hung down over her ample bosom. A matching bonnet bordered with ostrich feathers graced her snow-white hair.

Libby noticed that for a woman of her size she seemed to flutter about the room, constantly animated as she peeked into suitcases and drawers and fingered everything within reach.

"I'm afraid you must be in the wrong room. This is my room," Libby said finally, after recovering from the woman's bold onslaught.

"Oh, but I was told at the desk this room belonged

173

to Cordell and Katherine Chandler. Of course, that silly man must have made a mistake—you obviously aren't Katherine. You see, I met the girl myself some time ago when I was in St. Louis. I was there making arrangements for my nephew, Cordell . . . that's Cordell Chandler. He's a simply wonderful rancher. Lots of cows, you know. But of course, you've never heard of the man unless you've been to Deer Lodge. That's where we live. Well, most of the time, at any rate. He's pretty well known in the territory," she said as an afterthought, stopping to catch her breath. Taking in hand long-handled glasses hanging on a gold chain around her neck, she looked Libby over from head to toe.

"My, but you're a pretty little thing. Oh dear, I must be going. I have an appointment with my doctor. The dreary old scavenger insists I lose weight when all I came to him for was my gout. He just *won't* let me enjoy my few remaining years in peace. He has me on the worst diet . . . toast and milk! Can you imagine anyone existing on toast and milk when the world is full of appetizing delicacies? But look at you . . . of course you can't." She slapped a gloved hand to her lips and breezed over to the table to inspect the edibles.

"Did the hotel deliver that luscious bowl of fruit? What a foolish question, of course they did. They sent one to me when I arrived." She reached out, snatched a big, juicy apple, and bit into it. "This is wonderful. Much better than toast and milk, don't you agree?" She took a handkerchief out of her pocket, wrapped up the apple, and stuffed it in her purse. Libby hid a smile. "Can't let the doctor have the upper hand, you know. Why—forgive me, my dear—as usual, I've been rattling on. People tell me I never settle down. Seems to be a curse. Not that I mind . . . I meet the most delightful people this way. Well, I must hurry off. Busy, busy, you know!"

The woman was like a whirlwind. After she'd gone,

Libby took a deep breath and plopped down on the bed. She felt like she'd just been through a tornado. Gulch had said Matilde Chandler could be a formidable woman, a force to be reckoned with. Libby could see it in the way the woman had swished into the room, dominated the conversation, and left before Libby'd had a chance to say half a dozen words. She surely could daunt a less stout-hearted soul. There wasn't a doubt in Libby's mind that living in the same house with Matilde Chandler would mean there'd never be a dull moment. But Libby had liked her immediately.

"*Aunt* Matilde," Libby whispered. "What an enchanting lady." Libby smiled to herself, but her smile faded as the realization hit her: Matilde knew Katherine. Now Libby began to worry what she would do when Matilde found out about the masquerade; worse yet, what would *Matilde* do?

Libby got up and closed the door, then continued hanging her gowns in the wardrobe as she fretted over this latest problem.

Five minutes hadn't passed when there was another knock at the door. With some apprehension Libby opened it.

"I just don't understand it," Matilde Chandler gushed, out of breath from bustling back up the stairs, seemingly confused. She reached into her purse, removed the apple she had acquired from the room moments earlier, and took another bite. "I checked and this is the right room. Room 212. My nephew and his wife are supposed to be in this room. So, my dear, who are you?"

Chapter Twenty-nine

"I do not understand where you are taking us?" Katherine complained. "Why are we not staying in the same hotel as you and your *wife?*" she demanded.

"I told you when you found your way to my train what was going to happen when we reached Helena, didn't I?" Cordell said dryly.

"Yes . . . but I thought you'd changed your mind, especially after last night," she beseeched, a distinct uneasiness overtaking her.

Sharpe's eyes narrowed ever so slightly. "Last night?"

"Yes!" Katherine shot Sharpe a quelling look, then turned innocent eyes on Cordell. ."I thought after you kissed me that—that things would be different."

"Well, you thought wrong."

Katherine's mouth quivered in surprise. She was certain she'd changed his mind, even though he hadn't stayed with her last night. A hint of desperation entered her voice, for she'd missed her monthly and now feared the worst. "But I am not who you think I am . . . my name is not Elizabeth Hollis. It is Ka—"

Paying scant attention to her ravings, Cordell interrupted. "Look, I don't care what you say your name is . . . you'll have a chance to tell it to the marshal."

An inner glow warmed Sharpe's heart, and he toyed with his thin red moustache. Katherine deserved exactly

176

what she was about to get for not listening to him. Expectantly, he looked forward to her begging him to help her out. He planned to let her sit behind bars for a while this time. Maybe she'd pay attention to him from now on, and even be grateful after he saw fit to vouch for her. He was still smiling to himself when they stopped in front of the marshal's office.

An I-told-you-so grin on his face, Sharpe helped a reluctant Katherine down. Cordell had already disappeared into the marshal's office. Katherine swiveled around in Sharpe's arms. "Shelley, honey, you're not going to let him have me arrested, are you? What about our plan?"

"Oh, yes, our plan . . . maybe if you'd stuck to it you wouldn't be in this predicament now, sweetness," he lectured, enjoying her panic.

"Help me, please, and I swear to you, I'll do exactly what you say. You just can't let them put me back in a jail cell, you just can't!"

Flanked by a man of medium build with slicked-back light brown hair, Cordell returned saying, "This is the woman I was telling you about, Matt. The one who's accused of attacking a minister."

The marshal looked the pair over, then waved them inside. "Come on in and let's get this over with."

"No! This is all a dreadful mistake!" Katherine pleaded.

"Until I check out the story you told Dell here, I'm afraid I'll have to lock you up."

"Looks like we don't have any other choice right now, sweetness," Sharpe whispered. Even if I did, he thought, you have to learn you can't try to cut me out by thinking you can move in on Chandler yourself, Katherine Rutcliff.

Katherine tried to stand her ground, but Sharpe took her by the arm and ushered her inside. The room was larger than the jail in Fort Benton. Wanted posters

177

hung tacked three deep to one wall. An assortment of rifles and six-shooters adorned another. There were three battered desks with a varying degree of clutter. In the next room at the back of the outer office were four cells, each with a bed and washbasin.

"You'll have to come on back with me," the marshal said to Katherine. He moved toward the rear of the room.

Katherine looked beseechingly from Sharpe to Cordell. Not receiving any support, she raised her head, pinched her lips, and let Sharpe escort her into a cell.

"Take care of yourself, sweetness. I'll be in touch." He turned to leave the cell.

"I'll say you'll be in pretty close touch, Sharpe." Cordell slammed the bars in his face.

"What in the hell is this all about?" Sharpe demanded, and grabbed the bars. "What kind of a joke is this? Get me out of here!"

"It's no joke, Sharpe," Cordell said.

"Mr. Chandler here has sworn out a complaint for your arrest," the marshal added.

Sharpe shot steely daggers of hate at Cordell. "What for?"

"I overheard you try to blackmail my wife down by the creek last night, Sharpe. I believe it's called extortion."

Katherine smirked. "At least I won't be lonely now."

"Shut up, bitch. Chandler," Sharpe called out to Cordell's back, "if you get me out of here, I'll give you some real interesting information about that little wife of yours. I guarantee it'll be worth your while."

"Save your breath, Sharpe. I'm not interested in anything you have to say," Cordell returned and shut the door, effectively putting an end to Sharpe's entreaty.

Smugly, Katherine smiled at Sharpe. "You weren't too smart trying to blackmail the Hollis girl down by the creek, were you? You were so stupid, you didn't even

178

bother to check to see if you were being followed!"

"I don't know what you have to smile about, no one is going to take my word you're the real Katherine Rutcliff now. It looks like we're both going to be *guests* in here for a while, *sweetness.*"

"Two down," Cordell said to himself with a twinge of mixed emotion at what he was about to do as he walked into the law offices of Elgin and Bayless. He was glad to be rid of the Hollis woman and Sharpe, but confusion surrounded him when he thought of his wife.

The plush law office walls were decorated in a fine blue and gray stripe, accentuating a thick patterned rug and heavy mahogany furniture. The attorneys' botanical interests were evident in the varied assortment of potted plants set in clusters about the room.

"Ah, Dell Chandler, haven't seen you for quite some spell," a portly attorney greeted him, clasping his hand. "Something I can do for you?"

"Yes, Hiriam, there is."

"Come along, we can talk in my private office." Hiriam Bayless glanced at the fob watch hanging from his protruding belly and led Cordell into a pleasantly appointed room. After they were seated, Hiriam leaned back in his chair. "What can I do for you, Dell?"

"I want you to draw up the necessary papers for an annulment."

The balding man's eyes went round. "An annulment? Is this for you?"

"Yes," Cordell said darkly.

Ignoring Cordell's apparent displeasure with the topic, Hiriam laughed. "I didn't even know you were married. When did this happen?"

"A couple of weeks ago at Fort Benton," came the curt answer.

"Who's the lucky bride? Anyone I know?" Hiriam asked, his curiosity piqued.

Cordell moved to the edge of his chair, his face dark. "I'm not here to discuss the details of the wedding. Your firm pulls in a hefty fee every year from my business. All I want is for you to take care of the necessary paperwork."

"Calm down, Dell. I won't pry, since you obviously prefer not to talk about it. But you know, in order to get an annulment you can't have, ah. . . ." He cleared his throat. ". . . You can't have . . . *consummated* your marriage. Due to your past, shall we say, reputation, the judge will probably have a few questions for the lady. Therefore, I would advise you to get an affadavit from your wife swearing that *nothing* has happened between you. It could save a lot of time and headaches."

"What if she refuses?" Cordell asked, thinking how Katherine had said she didn't want the annulment.

"Well, then, of course, an annulment could take some time, or it may be impossible, for that matter." He fidgeted with his pudgy fingers. "You *do* know that a divorce could be a nasty blot on your record, should you decide to run for office."

Damn, things were complicated! Cordell had never intended to marry Katherine Rutcliff after he'd found out the type of woman she was. He should have known she'd trick him. He'd always believed in living his life openly, honestly; he detested the idea of having to play her game and trick her into wanting an annulment. But knowing her as he did now, that's exactly what he'd have to do. Worst of all, a part of him didn't even want the annulment. He was attracted to the raven-haired young beauty. But he couldn't get her past trickery out of his mind. No; an annulment was the best thing.

"If I run for public office, people will have to accept

me as I am. Just draw up all the necessary papers, Hiriam. I'll get her to sign them."

Cordell left the attorney. The sun was setting when he entered the Holdup Saloon, ordered a bottle of whiskey, and took a seat at the only free table in the place. A well-kept man of small stature was tinkling the piano keys and four cowhands sat around the next table with a fancy dude, playing cards. Cordell poured himself a generous slug and polished it off without hesitation.

"Damn her," he muttered into his glass. Six months ago he had known exactly what he wanted. He'd let Matilde convince him Katherine Rutcliff would make an ideal wife, although he'd had a bad feeling about Matilde's idea. "I never should've listened to Matilde," he groaned and poured another drink. It was lonely on the ranch and he wanted children. "Hell, cows never gave a man this much trouble," he grumbled into still another glass of the fiery amber liquid.

Next to him one of the cowhands threw down his cards and stomped out. "Hey, mister, want to sit in? We could use another player," the gambler called out.

Cordell still hadn't decided exactly how he was going to get Katherine to sign the annulment papers . . . and he wasn't going back to the Broadwater until he did. He shrugged. A good game of cards might even serve to take his mind off the woman. "Why not?"

Cordell was a fair gambler and held his own for several hours. The liquor had dulled his senses, or he might have had a bigger pot in front of him. "This will have to be my last hand, fellas," Cordell announced near midnight.

The gambler dealt the cards and bets were placed. One by one the cowhands folded with "two rich for my blood" or "I'm out," until it was between Cordell and the gambler.

"Give me two," Cordell said.

As the gambler dealt the cards, he watched Cordell's reactions. Feeling sure that he was about to win the rest of the rancher's money, the gambler covered the last bet and called the hand. Cordell turned over a royal flush, winning the pot.

"You're a pretty good player," the gambler said. "I could have sworn you were bluffing."

Cordell was only half listening; his attention was on one of the saloon girls, whose amorous attention was on a cowhand across the room. It made him think about his willing wife who sat alone back at the hotel while he played cards in this smoke-filled room.

Without warning, Cordell sent his chair spinning backward and rushed toward the door.

"Where you going in such an all-fired hurry, friend? You forgot to collect your winnings," the gambler hollered, scooping up the coins.

Dismissing it all without a backward glance, Cordell headed straight back to the Broadwater Hotel. He was tired of having to deny himself. Since Katherine wouldn't give in to an annulment, it was about time she started learning exactly what a real marriage was all about!

By the time Cordell neared the hotel, he'd convinced himself that he could enjoy his husbandly rights and still eventually get a quiet divorce. At that moment, though, divorce was the last thing on his mind.

Chapter Thirty

Matilde stood at the door, holding her lorgnette in front of her quizzing eyes and waited for Libby to explain her presence in Katherine's hotel room.

"Well, young lady? You must have some kind of an explanation."

Libby's eyes were big, her lips slightly parted in startled surprise. She couldn't begin to try to tell Matilde Chandler that she had the wrong room again. She certainly couldn't attempt to convince the woman she was Katherine. Matilde had already met Katherine. What was going to happen when Cordell introduced her as his wife?

Two options occurred to her. She could tell Matilde Chandler that Cordell had married her instead of Katherine and then try to keep aunt and nephew apart, or she could be truthful and hope for the best. Somehow, neither one seemed to fit the situation. From the looks of Matilde Chandler, she was growing impatient. This is it, Libby, you can't just close the door and pray she'll disappear, she said to herself, and took a steadying breath.

Libby opened the door wider and stepped aside, extending her arm. "Please, won't you come in?"

Feeling a little befuddled, Matilde moved past her, removed her gloves, and asked, "Now, just who are

183

you, my dear girl?"

"I'm an acquaintance of Katherine's," Libby said, the idea just popping into her head. "Please, do sit down. I'm sure Katherine will be along shortly."

"Well, why didn't you just come right out and tell me who you were the first time I was here?" Matilde brightened noticeably. "Of course, I know I can't really blame you . . . friends tell me I never give people a chance to fit a word in sideways once I start talking." She furrowed her brows, as if the realization just hit her. "You don't think that's true, do you?" She waved off the implication. "Naturally you do." She answered her own question, as was her custom. "Oh, I am relieved, though. I was so worried after I got Augusta Kohrs's telegram. She said that after Cordell married Katherine, something seemed to have gone wrong between them."

Libby hid her surprise at Augusta Kohrs's powers of perception. "Augusta didn't mention anything to me."

"You know Augusta?"

"Oh, yes. We had many pleasant conversations during the journey."

"She's such a dear. We've been friends for years. But back to the wedding . . . did you notice anything out of the ordinary?" she asked, concern momentarily taming the lines of animation etched across her features.

"No . . . I didn't. Augusta didn't mention anything to me, either. Cordell seemed to appear—" Libby began before being cutting off.

"It was nothing Augusta could put her finger on, mind you. Just a feeling, she said. You see, I arranged the marriage. Of course, you must know that, since you're a friend of Katherine's," Matilde babbled on, making herself comfortable. "Augusta's such a dear to keep me informed. Otherwise I might not have even known that scoundrel of a nephew of mine had gotten married. Dell's not really a scoundrel, you know. He's

184

one of the finest men I've ever known, even if he has a tendency to be a bit stubborn at times. You know how men are, though. Or do you?"

"I —"

"Of course, you probably don't. Forgive me, I don't know what made me think that in the first place. But a young lady as beautiful as yourself must have plenty of beaux. Whatever possessed you to accompany Katherine? Not that we don't have a whole passel of handsome, eligible gentlemen who'd find a lady as cultured as you delightful company. You know, I could tell the first minute I met you that you were a young lady of quality . . ."

Libby continued to listen politely as Matilde jabbered on in a steady stream, asking questions and often animatedly answering them herself before Libby could even open her mouth. Matilde had a heart the size of Montana, Libby thought. Each passing minute, Libby's admiration for the vivacious older woman grew, and Libby found herself wishing that dear old soul was indeed her aunt.

"You never *did* answer my question," Matilde said unexpectedly, leaning forward in her chair. "Why did you accompany Katherine? Oh dear, I don't believe I've even let you introduce yourself. Do forgive me, my dear."

Libby smiled broadly, amused by the ball of energy that was Matilde Chandler. "My name is Elizabeth. But I've enjoyed our conversation so much that I do hope you'll call me Libby," she said, crossing her fingers in hopes that Cordell's aunt would forget to ask her her last name.

Matilde took Libby's hands in hers. "Libby, what a charming name, child. It fits you so well, too."

"Thank you." Libby beamed. "Traveling up the Missouri on the *Benton* with Katherine was a last-minute decision." Libby chose her words carefully, not wanting

185

to tell another lie. "Katherine asked that I be with her during the trip. She did not want to be lonely." *Lonely,* Libby thought, remembering Katherine's relationship with Sharpe. "After the wedding, it didn't make sense for me to remain in Fort Benton, so we traveled together to Helena. And here I am."

"Well, I'm so glad Katherine has such a dear friend. I didn't spend a lot of time getting to know Katherine when I was in St. Louis, but if she's anything like you, my dear, Dell has made a match he can be proud of," she gushed.

This was Libby's chance to find out why Cordell had allowed his aunt to select a bride, so she hesitantly put forth, "I know it's none of my concern, and Katherine never told me, so I hope you won't think I'm being too forward, but I've often wondered why a man such as Cordell Chandler would allow someone else to chose his bride for him. I mean, because he seems so forceful," Libby amended.

"You mean a man like Dell, who could have had his pick of eager girls? Including Caroline Arthur," Matilde added, speaking more to herself. "Despite appearances, he's a lonely man. Oh, I know—it seems hard to believe. But living out on the ranch away from people and working as hard as he does . . ." Her voice trailed off in momentary reflection.

Her face grew serious. "Dell nearly *did* marry once, but discovered just in the nick of time that Caroline had gone and gotten herself in a family way," she raised her eyebrows, "if you know what I mean."

"Cordell has a child?" Libby inquired, wondering why he hadn't married the mother, or ever mentioned the child even once.

"Oh, no," Matilde answered, scandalized. "The child wasn't Dell's . . . seems Caroline couldn't stand to wait for Dell while he was away selling cattle. She got lonely, so she said, and took up with some no-account,

186

although she claimed to love only Dell. Still does, always mooning over him.

"Anyway, after Caroline lost the baby, she tried every way she could think of to get Dell back. But it kind of made him gun-shy. So I took the buffalo by the horns last year and convinced him, to try and find himself a woman." She tittered. "You'll never know all the talking I had to do to get him to agree to bring Katherine to Montana. I'm so happy I did now, though. The boy deserves all the happiness in the world, and now it looks like he's finally found it . . . but don't ever breathe a word of this outside this room." She slapped a hand to her cheek. "Why, Dell would be simply *furious* with me. He's such a proud man, you know."

"Caroline Arthur," Libby barely whispered, finally understanding why the girl had stared at Cordell so wistfully at the wedding reception . . . and why people seemed to be uneasy when she'd mentioned the girl's name.

Matilde continued to talk nonstop for another twenty minutes, but all Libby could think of was how she'd said Cordell deserved all the happiness in the world. She wanted him to have that happiness. And she desperately wanted that happiness to be with her.

The gravity of the deception of the Arthur girl attempted to put over on Cordell troubled Libby when she thought of it and her own masquerade. How could she hope to be considered any different by the man, the way she'd deceived him? And she continued to mislead him.

She remembered her own circumstances and stiffened her spine. She'd made a decision: the reverend was not going to put his hands on her again, that's why she had run away. She'd done what she'd had to do, and she'd matured because of it. And she'd learned a valuable lesson: each person was responsible for his own happiness. You could let life's devastating experiences get the

187

better of you, or you could learn from the past and use it to make a brighter future. There was not a doubt in Libby's mind what she had to do.

"My goodness, look at the time. I've been going on for nearly an hour." Matilde abruptly stood up and straightened her skirt. "I must be going, or that doctor of mine will undoubtedly have a fit. Please, do tell Katherine I'm so sorry I missed her. But tell her I'll welcome her into the family tomorrow night at supper with Dell. I've already left the boy a note, telling him I'll not take no for an answer. He's so hard to get a hold of, you know. I already left three messages for him at the desk earlier. You'll also join us, of course," Matilde said enthusiastically, and was gone before Libby could decline.

Libby sank onto the bed, exhausted and distraught, mumbling, "Tomorrow night, dinner with Cordell and his aunt. What am I going to do?"

His mind made up, Cordell strode into the hotel lobby, picked up his messages, and collected his room key from the desk. Now that he'd made up his mind not to deny himself any longer, he wondered just how she'd act when he informed her of his change of heart—as far as their intimate relationship was concerned. She'd been trying to seduce him, but how would she feel when she learned he intended to be a husband in every way, and still seek the dissolution of their marriage?

"Boss, I was wondering where you got to," Gulch said, leaning in the doorway of the dining room.

Cordell had just started up the stairs, but when he heard Gulch's voice, he turned and went toward the man. "I took care of Sharpe and that Hollis girl. They won't be bothering anybody for a while." When Gulch looked confused, Cordell continued, "You knew I was

188

going to take the girl to the marshal."

"Yeah, but what about that Sharpe fella?"

"I took care of accommodations for him, too. Seems he thought he could blackmail Katherine last night," Cordell added, careful not to elaborate.

"What could he possibly have to use against a sweet little gal like your Katherine?"

"Tried to invent something," Cordell returned evasively, not about to tell anyone else about Katherine's unsavory past. Pity his wife wasn't the sweet little lady everyone thought she was.

Gulch shrugged. "Can't say as I ain't unhappy to see the last of that pair. They was nothing but trouble, those two." He licked his dry lips. "I sure could use a bottle and a warm, willing woman tonight. At least, how 'bout joining me and getting us something to wet our whistles with?"

Cordell looked in at the empty tables in the grandly designed room and thought about Gulch's comment about a warm, willing woman. He pictured his wife, a frilly blue nightdress outlining her luscious curves. He didn't have to remind himself what he'd intended when he left the card game.

"Sorry, Gulch—I've got a wife waiting for me, remember?"

Gulch watched Cordell take the elegant stairs two at a time. He wished he had a woman half as special. He headed back to the table, then suddenly remembered he'd forgotten to tell Cordell about Matilde. "Dell," he hollered up the stairs, "Matilde's staying at the hotel and she's been looking for you."

"Yes, I know . . . I got her messages," Cordell yelled back, causing two aging patrons to raise disapproving eyebrows. He gave the pair a cordial nod, disarming them with the magnetism of his smile, then added to Gulch, "How *is* the old dear?"

"Still as full of the devil as ever." Gulch chuckled,

thinking of how Matilde could convince the hardest-headed person.

"Guess I'll find out for myself soon enough. One of Matilde's messages was to let me know that Katherine and I are having supper with her tomorrow night at seven."

Chapter Thirty-one

Libby was lying in bed, continuing to trouble over the dilemma of what she was going to do when Cordell's aunt met them for dinner tomorrow, when the lock on the door clicked. For an instant her heart stopped. Fright filled her: it would not be Cordell. Perhaps an intruder was trying to break into her room! Frantically she looked around for something to protect herself with. In the filtering moonlight she spied a heafty vase of fresh cut flowers.

The pounding between her ears was deafening as she tiptoed across the room.

Just as the door swung open, Libby raised the etched glass vase. There, silhouetted in the doorway, was a big man. Libby gasped and held her breath. Her hands shook so, she feared she'd drop the exquisite vase if the man took another step toward her.

"I sincerely hope you don't plan to make a habit of greeting your husband that way," Cordell drawled, and lit the lamp on the table.

Libby let out a long sigh of relief and set down the vase. "What are you doing here?"

"This is my room, too, if I must remind you."

"No . . . it's just that it's so late. I thought perhaps . . ." her voice trailed off.

"Perhaps I wouldn't return to my wife? Well, I have

returned. As a matter of fact, I have been thinking."

"Oh?" she ventured, afraid to ask more.

"Yes. Since you don't seem to want an annulment, I've decided there's no longer any reason to deny myself the pleasure of your company while we're married," he said with a lopsided grin.

"The pleasure of *my* company?" she repeated, her mind blocking out the words *while we are married*. Her heart thumped as she swallowed the thoughts of Reverend Ardsworth which had reared up before her. Don't be silly, Libby, she reminded herself. This is what you've been wanting—to show the man you aren't what he thinks. Now's your chance . . . don't let it slip by.

"Is there a problem with that?" he asked innocently enough, watching her reaction.

Libby stepped slowly toward him, her mind swiftly plotting her next move. Standing directly in front of him, she looked up into his unreadable black eyes and said softly, "No."

"Good, then." He swooped her up into his arms and carried her to the bed. God, she felt like she was made to fit into his embrace. His body heated up under the touch of her skin against his forearms. He lowered her to the bed and sat on the edge stroking the side of her velvety cheek.

There was no doubt in Libby's mind: from the way the gold flecks danced in his smoldering black eyes, she knew there would be no more waiting. She was going to become a woman tonight—Cordell's woman. There was no way around it. And even if there was, this is what she had been wanting: to demonstrate to him that he'd been wrong.

Her chest began to rise and fall at an alarming rate with the anticipation of what she knew was about to come. Cordell wanted her and she wanted him. She held the thought that their coupling would be a new beginning for them. This time together would plant the seed that would grow strong and span a lifetime, nurtured by their love for one another.

"Do you intend to be one of those wives who just lies there stiff as a plank when your husband comes to you to exercise his rights?" Cordell asked in a drawl, interrupting Libby's daydreams.

"Only if it is a plank you desire," she answered, surprised by her own audacity.

"My God, a woman like you is every man's dream and every husband's nightmare," he grumbled. At that moment he ached, wishing he didn't know about her background—and her penchant for chasing after the nearest man.

"Am I your nightmare?" she purred, and reached out to run unsteady fingers across his lips.

"The worst kind." He grabbed her hand and held it tight for a moment before drawing it to his mouth and gently nipping at the silken skin of her fingers.

Cordell leaned over and pulled her into his embrace, pressing his lips to hers. Her breath caught at the unrestrained passion of his kiss. Fine threads of enchantment spun a web of tumultuous sensations throughout her, and she wound her arms around his neck.

"Am I still the worst kind?" she panted, reeling from the magnitude of their kiss.

Slipping her nightdress over her head to reveal taut, rosy breasts, Cordell rasped, "The absolute worst."

Softly, caressingly, his hands closed over the delicate mounds; his fingers toyed and explored every darkening wrinkle which rose at his touch. His own need burgeoning, Cordell let his mouth and tongue suckle at the throbbing spheres. Again and again he buried his head, taking in mouthfuls of her and squeezing the lush breasts against his flaming cheeks.

"Relax, my love, there's no need to be tense," Cordell murmured. "I'm not going to do anything we both don't want."

"I'm not tense," Libby insisted, forcing herself to

relax. "I'm excited, since this is my wedding night. Doesn't a bride have the right to be a little nervous, even though we are having a delayed honeymoon?" She let out a nervous giggle.

"By all means a bride has that right. But there's no need . . . tell me there's no need."

"There's no need," she whispered mechanically, mesmerized, through lips swollen from their passion.

Cordell was beyond arguing, beyond caring. His wife was making him experience feelings more intense and urgent than he thought possible.

"What do you need?" he urged. For some reason he had to hear her say the words.

When Libby remained silent, Cordell prompted, "Tell me, darling." He splayed his fingers up the satiny soft skin of her sides and kneaded her breasts. "Tell me you want me."

"I—I want you."

Cordell kissed and licked each nipple, forcing Libby to moan and throw her head back, arching and pressing herself to him. "Now tell me you need to have me," he prompted.

He dropped a trail of fiery kisses down toward her belly and beyond, his fingers roving over her thighs to nudge her legs apart.

"I c—can't," she stammered.

"You can and you will," he said in a deep voice, immersed in her entire being.

Cordell ran his hands over the sensitive flesh on the inside of her thighs to caress the dark, curly triangle of hair at the apex of her open legs. "Say it, darling. Tell me."

"I—"

Cordell's lips captured hers, effectively silencing her feeble protests, grinding and demanding, coaxing and forcing Libby to concede and stay her hesitancy.

When he left her at last, breathless, Libby looked up into his eyes. Gone was the constant message of disdain, the open resentment. In its stead was unhooded passion, the roaring of a sensual blaze which only she could satiate.

"Tell me," he demanded with an urgency which brooked no more delay.

"I need to have you," she breathed, beyond herself.

The words were like a dam bursting within him, and he gathered her into his arms, crushing her to him.

"I want you to undress me," he said, at last holding her from him.

"Me?" she croaked.

"Yes, Katherine, you," he whispered against her ear. He took her hands and guided them to help him off with his jacket. Then he set her to unbuttoning his shirt and releasing it from his waistband.

Libby willingly followed his lead, hesitating only when he called her Katherine. She reminded herself that he was making love to her, though, not Katherine; he was married to her; he was her husband.

"Now the pants. Unbutton my pants and slide them down my legs." Cordell patiently waited, quietly enduring her awkward movements and one instance when she caught the hairs on his legs in the folds of his denims.

He flinched, causing Libby to shrink back. "I'm sorry, I didn't mean to hurt you."

He cupped her chin and cast her a genuine smile. "You didn't hurt me, little one," he soothed, despite the fire in his voice. "Now the underwear. Remove my underwear. I want you to know me."

Libby swallowed hard. She had seen a man naked only twice: Cordell briefly, when they were on the trail, and then the reverend, when he exposed himself to her. She remembered thinking how ugly the reverend had been; his manhood had seemed to be purple with anger.

She took a breath and bit into her lip as she slid the last of Cordell's clothing from him. When she saw him spring free and proud, she gasped: there was nothing ugly about him. She found all of him handsome—

beautiful, even; she reached out hesitantly to touch him, causing him to groan.

She lowered her eyes and said with honesty, "You're beautiful."

"No, my love. It is you who are truly beautiful. Every single inch of you." He kissed her eyes. "Your eyes." He kissed her nose. "Your nose." He kissed her lips and chin. "Your lips, your chin. Every part of you," he said, leaving a trail of molten fire everywhere his lips touched.

"Oh, God, you make me forget what you are," he mumbled unintelligibly, and proceeded to evoke a heightening response from his wife. His mouth became unquenchable, nibbling and savoring, consuming and devouring until they were both panting.

"Touch me again," he demanded.

"I'm — I'm not sure how," Libby said, hoarse from passion.

"Give me your hand."

Libby placed her hand in his and he wrapped her fingers around him, squeezing them and showing her how to move around him in an up-and-down motion. "Oh, woman," he moaned thickly, beginning to lose control.

Giving him pleasure intensified Libby's emotions and the love she felt for him. She wanted to know he was receiving as much as he was giving, and she circled him with her other hand, applying pressure in a rotating motion.

"Lie back. I want to pleasure you for a while," Cordell instructed before he exploded from the ecstasy she was giving him.

Oh, yes, she thought, this is what giving love to each was all about. Sharing oneself freely and fully . . . offering and receiving without shame. Demonstrating that each belongs to the other. She lay back and tried to lie still, despite the searing heat feeding her hunger for him until he spread her thighs once more.

Cordell hooked his arms under her thighs and drew her, open, to him. At first Libby was shocked when his tongue swirled and touched her but spiraling tingles engulfed her, causing her to squirm and shudder from the uncontrollable sensations.

His tongue stroked and dipped into her, simulating long, slow strokes, then flicked and lapped until he fastened his mouth to her and suckled and skimmed over that most sensitive spot. Libby bucked wildly, unable to stop herself. Time and time again he brought her to peak after potent peak.

He stopped and looked up at her. "Now tell me you want to feel me inside you."

His pupils were dilated, his black eyes glistening with gold flecks which openly bespoke his passion, his desperate need to hear her say the words she wanted to say, to experience their joining.

"Oh, my love, I do want to feel you inside me," she whispered eagerly.

Cordell immediately positioned himself over her and without hesitation plunged into her moist heat. To his utter shock she cried out when he drove through her virgin's barrier, causing him to stop and support himself on his elbows over her.

His face registered the unexpected surprise that he had just taken a virgin; the jarring impact on his mind sent his head spinning. He studied her face for a moment. There was only an open, loving innocence there which further stupefied him and forced him to mumble, "My God, how can you be a virgin?"

Chapter Thirty-two

From beneath half-lidded eyes heavy with unspent passion, Libby breathed, "I told you I was a virgin. You're the only man I've known; the only man I'll ever care to know." She pulled him to her and began to move, drawing him deeper within her.

When he'd discovered she was a virgin, Cordell's first inclination had been to withdraw . . . but he was well beyond being able to resist. His blood throbbed through his veins until he was so fully engorged he knew he had to seek release. And when her muscles pulsed around him, he felt as if he'd been ignited. He began long, hot thrusts, lunging in and out almost involuntarily.

Libby kept pace with him, wildly taking delight in his incredible possession. He might not know it yet, but there was not a doubt in Libby's mind: Cordell was claiming her as his mate. As the sensations skyrocketed, Libby twisted and bucked, losing all thought except for the mind-shattering emotions riding her until wave after sensual wave caught her, and Cordell groaned into her mouth before convulsing and holding her to him so tight she was sure they had truly become one, joined for all time.

Cordell wiped Libby's wet black locks back from her forehead. Confusion mirrored his features. "I don't understand you," he muttered before disengaging himself to lie on his back next to her.

For an instant Libby nearly blurted out the truth about herself. She'd proved she wasn't the type of woman he'd thought. But she feared his response should she tell him she was not Katherine. Instead, she quietly laid her head on his shoulder and remained mute, listening to his heartbeat, praying she could somehow win his love.

Cordell lay awake for hours, conflicted at the knowledge that the woman sleeping beside him had been a virgin. All this time he'd been convinced, he'd never doubted the Pinkerton report. How could there have been a mistake? The report detailed how she'd been caught naked with the fiancé of another woman, and there were other descriptions of her amorous forays. The answer came to him. Katherine had merely toyed with all those men, letting them take their pleasure — short of ever consummating the act. Since she had a wealthy and powerful father — Addison Rutcliff — those men would never have dared to force her to go through with what she'd begun. Although a part of him wanted to believe her, there was evidence branding her a tease — a wanton, rich coquette, with the best coy act he'd ever witnessed.

She was too close for him to be able to think clearly. The warmth and scent of her nearby kept him from retaining his perspective. With a myriad of emotions assaulting him, Cordell gently ran the back of his hand along the side of her cheek, then slid from the bed.

The first rays of dawn were casting shadows about the room when Cordell collected his clothing and dressed. He hurriedly wrote Katherine a note instructing her to meet him in the dining room tonight, since he had pressing business to attend to and would be out all day. He left the note on the dresser, where she was sure to find it, and left the hotel.

Libby turned over and reached for Cordell just before

she heard the door close. She sat bolt upright to discover he'd gone. She grasped his pillow up and hugged it to her. She had slept little, reliving every treasured moment of their joining. It had been a beautiful experience, and she'd learned that with the right man, intimacy took on a very special meaning.

Her heart full, she got out of bed and went to the window. The mountains off in the distance were dark, high-rising shadows against a lightening sky dotted with black fringes of wispy pines. Below she noticed Cordell leave the hotel, hands in pockets, his stride determined.

Her heart overflowing now, Libby returned to bed. She ran her hand over the rumpled sheets. A smile tugged at the corners of her lips. There was evidence of their lovemaking, and the pungent fragrance of it assaulted her. Last night had proved Cordell was not impervious to her. It had moved their relationship past the initial phase. Now she had to figure out what she was going to do tonight at dinner with Cordell and his Aunt Matilde.

Libby stood in front of the small, gilt-edged mirror and fanned the plume of her white evening bonnet. She smoothed her point d'esprit lace vest with Louis XIII cuffs. She adjusted the deep blue chatelaine bow at the waist of her embossed velvet gown. The light blue of the gown matched her eyes and the neckline accentuated the cleavage of her bosom. Even the blue-black of her hair, coiffured in ringlets swept back and tied with a satin ribbon, lent a dramatic aura to her appearance. "At least I'll look my best tonight," she said to her reflection, then left the room.

"Miz Chandler, you sure do look mighty fine this evening," Gulch said, a big grin on his angular face.

Libby blushed at the open compliment paid her by the ranch hand, dressed now in new denims and a red aid shirt with string tie. "Thank you, Gulch. And you ook like you're dressed to go dancing tonight. Could it e with a special lady?"

"Ah, heck, no." He flushed and shuffled his feet. No fine lady like you would look at a sidewinder like e," he stammered, flustered.

"Nonsense. Any lady would be lucky to have some-ne like you."

"Shucks, you're too kind," he returned awkwardly, nd fussed with his hair, fluffing the graying strands at is temples.

Libby put a sympathetic hand on his forearm. "Don't orry, Gulch, someday your lady will come along. I irmly believe that there is someone for everybody. ook at Cordell and me . . . I never dreamed I'd be so ucky as to marry someone as special as Cordell. I just ope I can make him happy," she said absently, forget-ing for the moment that Gulch was Cordell's dearest riend.

"Don't you worry none—you'll make Dell happy. He ust needs a little time to adjust to being hitched, an' ll. He may be a mite stubborn and pigheaded, but e'll make you a good husband once he settles into the dea. Ever'body can see how much you two love each ther," he said, thinking that the newlyweds ought to uit trying so hard for perfection and just let nature ake its course.

She gave him a benign smile void of the turmoil hurning within her. "I'm glad I've got you on my ide."

"You can count on it. Say, where's Dell? I hear tell you two are having supper with Matilde tonight."

"I was just on my way to meet him in the dining room. He had business to take care of today."

"Well, you just go on into that dining room and hook up with Matilde while you're waiting. She'll fill you in on Dell—and how to handle him."

Libby looked a little apprehensive, and Gulch added, "Don't you fret none, you'll like Matilde. Like I said, she can be a handful. But if she takes a shine to you, you couldn't have none better on your side. And you being the fine lady you are, there's no doubt she'll take to you, ma'am."

"I certainly hope so, Gulch," Libby said, wondering what Matilde Chandler would say if she found out that she'd been impersonating Katherine. *Katherine*. Libby hadn't seen her since Cordell had driven off with Sharpe and Katherine after they'd first arrived in Helena.

"Ah . . . Gulch?"

"Yes, ma'am?"

Libby hesitated. Dare she ask about Katherine?

Gulch noticed her hesitation. He liked the gutsy little lady and wanted the best for the pair, so he urged, "If there's something I can do for you, or help you with, you just gotta ask. I'd be mighty pleased to do what I can. Is there something I can do for you?"

"I haven't seen Mr. Sharpe or *Elizabeth* since we arrived. Are they staying at a different hotel?" she asked hopefully, worried that Katherine could show up. If Matilde saw Katherine she would surely spoil everything, and ruin Libby's chances before she could secure Cordell's love and somehow explain the truth.

"Rightly so, ma'am. Them two is enjoying other accommodations right now." He fought down a smile.

"Other accommodations?"

"Yeah. They're cooling their heels behind bars." He slapped his thigh and let loose an inarticulate sound expressive of mirth.

"They're in jail?" Libby said, her eyes widening.

"Sure 'nuff. You know, Dell done gone and told that gal that's what he intended when she showed up at the bull train. Don't think that one thought he'd go through with it, though . . . she didn't know Dell. That

202

man's always been true to his word."

"But you said *they?*"

"That Sharpe fella, too."

"What did Mr. Sharpe do?"

"You'd know more 'bout that than I would."

"Why?" she ventured, fearing the answer.

"Dell told me that Sharpe fella tried to get money outa you for something." He scratched his head, bemused. " 'Course, he didn't tell me what." He looked at her questioningly. "You wouldn't want to tell me, would you now?"

"I—"

Libby was momentarily taken aback. Had Cordell been spying on her and Sharpe? He hadn't mentioned it, or for that matter, confronted her. Yet he'd seen Sharpe jailed. Was he attempting to protect her or his money?

"It makes no nevermind. You don't have to say a word. At least that cardsharp won't be bothering you none for a spell. But remember I'm your friend, if you be needing one."

"Thank you, Gulch," she said gratefully, letting out a sigh of relief. She glanced at her watch, wanting to end what was becoming a difficult conversation and prepare herself for an equally difficult evening ahead. "It's nearly seven o'clock. I'd best be going. I don't want to keep Cordell waiting."

"Yessum, ma'am. Relax and be yourself tonight. Matilde'll love you," he said earnestly, and strode off to enjoy a good bottle and card game.

Libby put one foot in front of the other, mumbling to herself, "Relax and be myself." I'm afraid this is not going to be a very relaxing evening, she thought, clarifying the plan she'd formulated in her mind. Now all she had to do was make sure everything went according to schedule.

* * *

Cordell entered the elegant dining room in the Broadwater Hotel. Tables covered in white linen were set with gleaming china and fine flatware. Fresh cut flowers stood tall in the center between glowing candles. Finely dressed patrons sat at the tables enjoying cordial conversation.

He seated himself at the table specially reserved for him when he was in town. It was the best table in the room, positioned near the large-paned window and offering a view of the whole room while affording privacy by means of three strategically placed potted plants.

"Mr. Chandler, especially for you, sir." The waiter beamed, presenting Cordell with his favorite libation. "It's is always good to see you, sir."

Cordell accepted the offering. "Thank you. It's good to know I am remembered."

"I would never forget a man such as yourself, sir. There are many of us who are hoping you will be Montana's next treasurer," the spindly ex-miner said. He'd grown up in the territory, and living so close to the political core of the area, shared the concern for Montana's future that many of his aspiring contemporaries did.

The man began to scurry away, then returned to Cordell's table. He thrust out his hand, a leaf of flowery scented stationery folded in his fingers. "Sorry, I nearly forgot . . . this message was delivered for you a few moments ago."

As Cordell read the note, a smile came to his lips. Matilde was going to be late, as usual. He had to laugh to himself: his aunt had been born nearly a month late and had made it her life's vocation never to be on time since. She'd probably be late to her own wedding, were she to marry.

Cordell looked up to see his wife standing in the doorway. She was stunning, easily the most beautiful woman in the room, the most beautiful woman in the entire territory. Visions of their lovemaking rose up to trouble him. The feel of her, warm and willing in his arms; the scent of her, lingering with him even when she wasn't there . . . it all preyed on his mind. She moved toward him with such grace that despite himself he felt a certain pride when the other men in the room turned to watch her.

Libby smiled brightly as Cordell rose and pulled out her chair. Matilde was not here yet. So far Libby was safe from discovery . . . but the evening was just beginning.

Chapter Thirty-three

Libby cast Cordell her brightest smile. "I missed you this morning," she said, hopeful he'd softened toward her after what they'd shared last night. He was elegantly dressed in somber black trousers and matching vest and coat. Every ounce of him radiated strength. Remembering Katherine's comment to her father when they first boarded the steamer, Libby smiled: Cordell hardly fit the image of a hick rancher.

Cordell's eyes narrowed. "You were very good. Did you really expect that one night with you would change my mind, though?"

Libby's heart lurched, but she was not defeated. And she was not about to let him see he'd struck a nerve with his stinging comment. "No." She lowered her eyes before raising them, a mischievous gleam challenging him. "But I suppose it's comforting to know that an annulment is out of the question now."

Cordell glared at her. For an instant he wondered if she'd planned her own seduction. Her emotions had seemed so honest—and she *had* been a virgin. She was right, though: an annulment was not possible now.

When Cordell had left the hotel that morning, he'd gone directly to his attorney's sprawling home, rousing the man from a warm bed. Wearing a nightshirt and cap, his feet bare, Hiriam Bayless had received Cordell in his study.

"Bring me a robe and slippers, Frances," he ordered the petite elderly housekeeper. "And after you bring us some coffee, light a fire to take the chill out of the room." The woman scurried off and Hiriam turned his attention to Cordell. "Well, Dell, what's the meaning of dragging me out of bed at this hour of the morning?" he blustered.

"I need your advice."

"It's your wife, isn't it? No, no, you don't have to bother answering . . . I can see it in your face. An annulment is no longer possible, is it?"

Cordell did not answer.

"I thought as much. You're going to have to introduce me to this little lady." He sent Cordell a secret, knowing message with the slightest twitch of his lips. "Perhaps you need to rethink your decision."

"No, I do not," Cordell said forcefully. "What I need is for you to come up with a legal solution."

"There may be no legal solution besides divorce, Dell." He tented his fingers, a sly spark flickering into his eyes. "Since you seem to find an annulment out of the question—"

"I've given it some thought," Cordell said defensively, remembering the night of the card game and his idea to get a quiet divorce since he'd decided to bed his wife.

Hiriam's slippers and robe arrived. He put them on, cocking a brow at the rancher. Dell was in deeper than he probably realized. "Since you so obviously find her, shall we say, pleasing, why not enjoy the lady and then do what many others do?"

"And just what *do* many others do?" Cordell asked in a voice filled with warning.

Hiriam fidgeted. Cordell Chandler was a man of principle. "You must be aware that many of our country's finest citizens have been united in marriages of, shall we say, convenience—which fulfill a public image and at the same time allow both parties a certain latitude to enjoy the company of others without the responsibility of commitment—except on paper of course."

"Of course. You're a heartless bastard, Bayless."

Hiriam was astounded by the sheer vehemence of Cordell's remarks. He cleared his throat. "Then the only other thing I can suggest to you is to make her want the dissolution of your union. Ah, Frances, the coffee, at last," Hiriam said as his housekeeper entered, relieved at the interruption of what had become a most uncomfortable conversation.

Cordell accepted the hot cup of steaming coffee and stared thoughtfully into it.

"I said, an annulment appears out of the question now," Libby repeated, bringing Cordell back from his musings.

"Yes, it is, unless, of course, you decide you may wish to end this farce of a marriage yourself," he said too obligingly to suit her.

"I don't look on our marriage as a farce at all . . . dear," she said sweetly. She glanced about. "Where is your aunt? I thought she was supposed to be here tonight. I am *so* looking forward to seeing the dear lady again," she said innocently, careful to mask her delight that thus far everything was proceeding according to her design.

"Matilde's always late." His gaze drifted around the room. "Speaking of Matilde, there she is, with the Van Lindens."

Libby's head snapped around. Matilde Chandler was across the room, speaking with a diminutive elderly couple. Her hands virtually flew as she talked, adding to the effervescence of her character. Dressed in an exquisite creation of fur-trimmed silk, an oval pouf draping the sides of the pleated silver gown, Matilde was the epitome of ostentation. Crimson ostrich plumes rose high above her head and bobbed as she talked.

"Why don't you escort your aunt to the table?" Libby suggested, busy contemplating her next move.

As Cordell weaved through the maze of tables, Libby dashed out the French doors. Her chest heaving, she hurried around the side of the hotel, taking a note she had prepared earlier from the small satin purse at her wrist.

Standing hidden behind the massive pillars at the dining room entrance, Libby peeked around the corner to see Cordell greet his aunt with a big hug. The warmth he displayed for the older woman gave Libby a good feeling. Cordell obviously cared about his family, and he wasn't afraid to show it.

"May I be of assistance, ma'am?" the desk clerk asked, noting her strange behavior.

"Oh!" she startled. "Oh, yes . . . yes, you can." She thrust out her hand, a neatly folded slip of paper held between her fingers. "Would you mind waiting five minutes and then delivering this to Mr. Chandler?"

The bewildered man followed Libby's gaze. "But ma'am, Mr. Chandler isn't more than twenty feet away."

She cast him a conspiring smile. "I want him to be surprised." She handed him the note and a generous tip from the money Cordell had given her to purchase what she needed. "Thank you . . . please don't tell Mr. Chandler who it's from." After a moment she asked, "Where is the nearest necessary?"

"You must go back through the lobby. It is the second door to the left of the registration desk."

"Thank you," she said, and sauntered off.

The man was left gaping after her, wondering if all the Chandler women were so eccentric. He shrugged, looked at his watch, and waited. Who was he to worry about what the rich did, so long as he got paid for his services.

"Dell, darling." Matilde planted a smacking wet kiss on his cheek, then looked him up and down with her jeweled spectacles. "Marriage must agree with you—you look wonderful . . . doesn't he, Howard?"

"Quite. Good to see you again, man," the aging gentleman said.

The two shook hands. "And you, sir." Cordell nodded to the matron at Van Linden's side. "Ma'am."

Matilde clasped her hands together. "Love to you two." She dismissed the couple. "Now, I simply cannot wait another second to see your lovely dark-haired Katherine. I'm so pleased. I just knew when Addison Rutcliff wrote to me that you and Katherine would be the perfect match. Did I tell you what the doctor is trying to do to me? I'm simply going to waste away to nothing if he has his way, the way he's trying to starve me, and the only reason I came to Helena was for my gout. . . ." Matilde continued chattering in a lengthy, unbroken chain of words, taking Cordell's arm and grabbing a roll from the table before fluttering across the room.

"My dear boy, I thought you said Katherine was here," Matilde said, confused, munching the biscuit with the relish of a child enjoying a piece of candy.

"She was just here," Cordell said as the desk clerk tapped him on the shoulder."

"Mr. Chandler, I'm supposed to give you this." He handed over the note. "Miz Chandler." He nodded to Matilde.

Cordell read the note and arched a brow. "Who gave you this?"

"Don't know. I was just told to deliver it, sir."

Cordell rummaged through his pocket and tossed the man a coin. "Thank you. You didn't happen to see Mrs. Chandler, did you?"

"She asked after the . . . ah . . . you know," he

210

looked sheepishly at Matilde, "the little room, sir."

"Thank you." Matilde waved him off. "Dell, sit down. I do believe we're beginning to make a spectacle of ourselves standing here. Katherine will be back shortly. You know how we ladies are. Besides, I'm utterly famished."

"Auntie, dear, I'm afraid you're in the habit of making a spectacle of yourself *wherever* you go."

"I know." She tittered. "But it is *such* fun. People should enjoy themselves, don't you think? Oh, of course you do . . . what's in the note?"

"It appears that Gulch wants to see me. Something to do with Marshal Hillard."

"Well, why didn't Gulch just come to the table? I haven't seen him in ever so long."

"He said it's a private matter. You know Gulch . . . he's more comfortable with a bedroll out under the stars. If you'll excuse me?"

She watched Dell's handsome back, reflecting to herself, "As a matter of fact, I haven't seen that nice Marshal Hillard for some time, either." Mentally she put a visit to the man on her list of things to do.

Libby waited until Cordell went up the stairs and swiftly made her way over to Matilde. "Miss Chandler," Libby greeted and sat down.

"I'm so glad you could come. Didn't I tell you to call me Matilde, though? I must have. But if I didn't, you simply must — all my friends do. Have you seen Katherine? I still haven't, and I can't understand why. You know, everyone seems to be so busy these days . . . there's not enough time. Oh, dear," she clasped her palms to her cheeks, "there I go again, babbling on, not giving you a chance to answer. *Have* you seen Katherine?"

"I just left her. She had an accident with her gown and is changing. She wanted to look especially nice this evening. I'm sure she'll be along presently."

"Yes, of course." She lifted her spectacles in Libby's direction. "That's what you said last night," she mused.

For the next hour and a half, Libby engaged in what she only could describe as a comedy of errors as she alternately entertained a perturbed Cordell, who had returned from his wild goose chase of Gulch, and a confused Matilde, making one explanation after another, ordering dinner and even managing to consume part of it. There were two trips to the necessary and three notes, calling each of them away for various reasons.

Libby had accidentally spilled wine down her gown. She'd let out a piercing squeal, jumped to her feet, and knocked her chair into a man about to take a bite of cream pastry, causing the confection to splatter all over his face. Once, when Libby was nearly caught, Matilde sighted her doctor and immediately scurried off, not wanting to be discovered gorging herself on potatoes and steak just as Cordell returned unexpectedly.

Cordell only half-listened to Matilde's jabberings about Katherine and the delightful girl who'd kept her company. He was annoyed at waiting for Gulch, who never did show up. Matilde's prattling about Libby never once raised his suspicion, since Matilde was in the constant habit of collecting new friends wherever she went.

Finally unable to endure such a disjointed meal any longer, Cordell stood up and announced that he was going out for a peaceful drink before retiring.

Libby breathed a long sigh of relief when she saw him walk out the front entrance. She immediately joined Matilde, who pleaded a splitting headache.

"Must you leave so soon?" Libby asked sweetly. "I realize supper was a bit harried—"

"Harried? Why, I've never experienced anything like it in my entire life. It was most . . . most . . . ah, exhilarating, to say the least. Of course, we must do

212

this again tomorrow night, when perhaps we can all have a chance to be together. I'll stop on my way up to my room and write Cordell a note." She furrowed her brow. "Although the poor boy has had his share of notes tonight, don't you think?"

Libby slumped in her chair, disbelief tightening her lips. "Tomorrow night?"

Chapter Thirty-four

The hotel lobby hummed with activity. Guests milled about the refined public rooms decorated with distinction, while others strolled from the elegant hotel bundled warmly against the cold morning. Matilde flitted down the stairs and about the clusters, cheerily greeting friends and strangers alike before boarding her coach and instructing the driver to hurry the horses along to the marshal's office.

Without delay, two fine grays moved the carriage along the dusty streets, bumping over ruts deep from last winter's storms and up the hill to the jail.

When the carriage stopped, Matilde alighted, tripped, and stumbled. Marshal Matt Hillard had been coming out of his office and opened his arms just in time to stay Matilde's fall.

She looked up into his dancing silver eyes. "Matt, I was coming to see you, but I never expected to be received with so much warmth."

"For you, dear lady, a hug is never enough," he said and gave her a kiss on the cheek before releasing her.

"Matt Hillard, you always have been a heartbreaker. If I were thirty years younger, I'd have my father get the shotgun and you'd find yourself with a bride."

"Ah, heck, Matilde, you don't have to be thirty years younger — I'll go round up a preacher right now." He started off down the walkway until Matilde called him back. "Young man, don't you dare leave an old lady standing out in the cold."

"I'd never leave my favorite visitor outside without an escort." He rushed to the door of the jail and signaled for her to enter.

Matilde swished past him and immediately began fingering the posters on the wall. "I haven't seen you in ever so long. So after I left Cordell last night I thought, now Matilde, tomorrow morning you just take yourself right on over to see that darling Matt Hillard. And here I am. I thought for sure that by now you'd have taken a wife."

"You know I've been waiting for you."

"Such poppycock! But I love to hear it. You heard, of course, that Dell finally married. You know, if I hadn't found someone for him, he'd also probably still be a bachelor. Perhaps I should look for a wife for you too. She is such a delightful girl. Addison Rutcliff's daughter, Katherine. Wait until you meet her, she is the kind of girl who would make any man proud. She—"

"She's an imposter. *I* am Katherine Rutcliff. That girl is impersonating me; she attacked a reverend," Katherine screeched from her cell inside the adjoining room.

Matilde slapped her hand to her chest, scandalized by the outburst. "Matt, whoever *is* that raving person?" she demanded, all gaiety gone from her voice.

"Don't pay her any mind. She's been raging all night. Never stopped once even to take a breath, that one. Yesterday Dell brought her in with some gambler who tried to blackmail his missus. Her name's Elizabeth Hollis. She was on the steamer with Katherine, and according to Dell, she got demented when she landed at Fort Benton. Tried to say she was Katherine. 'Course, folks knew better. Seems she escaped and tried to tell Dell they let her go. But he knew better 'cause the

215

sheriff warned him before they left town. I'm keeping her until they decide what they want to do with her."

"Oh?" Matilde said, remembering Katherine's friend, Libby, and the strange dinner she'd had the night before.

"Lies! All lies!" Katherine shouted, ignoring Sharpe's effort to silence her. "I am Katherine Rutcliff. Matilde Chandler, you visited my father and me in St. Louis to arrange the marriage. Just come in here and you'll see for yourself that I'm telling the truth!"

"Why don't we go next door and have a cup of coffee in peace and quiet." He started toward the door.

"No, no . . . I think I'd like to speak with that young woman."

"I don't think that's such a good idea. That one's a real shecat, she is. Now, come on, I could use something to warm my insides."

Matt opened the door, but Matilde was not to be put off. She ignored him and barged through the heavy door into the cell room.

Matilde lifted the spectacles to her eyes. "Oh, my goodness gracious! Katherine!"

"Yes, old woman. Katherine," Katherine sneered. "Now get me out of here and I'll consider telling Papa to go easy on you fools for locking me up."

"Didn't you marry my nephew?" Matilde asked, astounded to find the young lady she'd personally selected for her Cordell, though she knew he never would've married the girl if he hadn't found her enchanting. Now Matilde was horrified by the type of person Katherine Rutcliff had just shown herself to be.

"I always thought you had little sense," Katherine snipped impatiently. "How could I have married that bastard when these imbeciles threw me in jail?"

Matilde crinkled her brows. "Then if you didn't marry Cordell, who did?"

"What does it matter?" She shot a superior glare of

anger at Matilde and the stunned marshal. "A simple laundress, Elizabeth Hollis, married your precious nephew. Now get me out of here!"

Matilde listened quietly while Katherine's face turned blotchy red as she ranted and raved, demanded and threatened. After a full ten minutes, she turned her fury on the marshal. "Since you know the truth at last, you idiot, open the cell!"

Matt ran his hand down his face. "Matilde, you said Dell has got himself a good marriage. You think we ought to let that one," he thumbed in Katherine's direction, "out right yet?"

Matilde looked the pair over thoroughly with her spectacles, then suggested, "Why don't we go back out to your office and discuss it . . ."

The smell of cheap perfume and cigar smoke assaulted Libby, causing her to rouse from sleep. She snuggled closer to Cordell's warm body and ran her fingers lightly over his hirsute chest. She lay next to his naked form; his chest and muscular thighs pressed against her own cotton gown.

Last night he'd come to her again. She'd been awake, worrying what she was going to do about another dinner with Matilde Chandler when Cordell had swaggered into the room.

"Have you been drinking?" she asked after noticing the sour odor of whiskey. His black eyes were unusually bright, and the scent of perfume hung from him.

"Only enough to erase you from my mind," he said darkly.

"Doesn't look like you were too successful, since here you are." The thought that he could have been with another woman, the way he smelled, rose up and threatened to turn her into a shrew of a wife, but she fought the urge down.

"No, damn it. It seems I still hunger for that ripe body of yours." He pulled her into his arms.

It was another major triumph for Libby. He'd sworn he'd never touch her again, and she'd feared he'd gone to some other woman; the scent he bore gave it away. She'd told herself not to mention it, but the words seemed to tumble out of their own volition. "And am I your second choice for the evening?" she asked as indifferently as she could manage.

"You're not a choice at all." His body betrayed him, tautening, growing hard through his trousers.

Libby's chest began to heave. "No, I am not, am I?"

"Never," he murmured against her soft curls, and nibbled lightly at her ear, whispering his need. She wasn't his choice, she'd been right. He'd never wanted her kind of woman as his wife. But she *was* his, and he craved her like an addiction.

Libby's arms slipped up to his collar and she twisted at the buttons before sneaking her heated fingers inside the bit of bleached cotton. Cordell shuddered against the magic her fingers worked across his chest. He picked her up and kissed her, then crossed the room and lowered her to the bed.

"You're the worst kind of woman: one who could destroy a man if he let you. But you, my hot little wife, as long as you belong to me, are going to be touched only by me . . . as often as I desire . . . when and where." He held her from him, his black eyes riveted to her blue ones. "Until you ask to dissolve this marriage."

Libby stared back. From the intensity of his hunger, she did not have to question him further about another woman; she had her answer. His words should have acted like a bowl of ice water . . . but Libby had become sure of herself and what she wanted from life. And she wanted Cordell.

"I'm going to undress you, slowly, layer by layer, peel

away your clothing until you lie before me and open to my touch," he said, his hands beginning to strip away her clothes.

When Libby lay there naked, Cordell sat back and let his gaze drink in every inch of honey alabaster flesh. "Now I want you to undress me. The shirt and jacket first. Ah, good. Now the boots and socks. Now the pants, my seductress." Cordell groaned when Libby's hand brushed his turgid maleness.

It was Libby's turn to absorb his male body in the soft flickering lamp light. He was all muscles and golden brawn — muscular power. Without words his body told her what he wanted.

"You like what you see, don't you, my wanton witch?"

"Cordell, I—"

His fingers went to her peaked breasts, sending sensual messages arcing through her. "I want you to say it."

Libby moaned and rubbed her chin against his hand. Her eyes heavy-lidded with passion, she answered thickly, "I love what I see."

He began a fine, heavenly torture with his fingers and tongue, spreading fire everywhere he went, causing Libby to writhe from the sweet agony. She was enthralled that she could respond to him in such a wild, uninhibited way. Over and over he moved up and down the length of her, forcing her to cry out her need for him.

"Cordell, I beg you, I have to have you," she begged, surprising herself with the strength of her plea.

His heart thundering in his chest, Cordell captured her lips with vigor and plunged his tongue into her throat. He wanted to devour her, every inch. A storm raged within him as he tasted and feasted on her mouth, grinding and savoring, while his hands worshiped the fiery buds of her erect nipples.

When his lips left hers, Libby implored, "Cordell, *please*."

Cordell rose over her. "Open for me, wife, all the way," he commanded in a voice thick with passion.

Libby's response was involuntary; her thighs spread and she lay beneath his burning gaze, moist with a naked readiness, longing to receive his throbbing staff. He plunged into her with a mighty thrust. Slowly at first, he began to pump her full with simmering desire. Then his languid motions took on more urgent, potent movements. Coiling gyrations engulfed her and she reared up, throwing her hips against him in a frenzy of consuming bursts.

Cordell collapsed in the drenched intensity of their lovemaking, remaining mute against the spinning emotions which screamed inside him to speak words of love. And he knew if he didn't stay away from her from now on, he never would let her go, regardless of the consequences.

Libby lay still, waiting for him to say the words of love she desperately longed to hear after she'd offered herself to him so freely, so eagerly. Then the scent of the strong perfume from some other woman again assailed her nostrils. He could have had any woman, but he'd chosen to be with her despite what he thought her to be. If only he would choose her in every way!

The man beside her was no ordinary man . . . if only she could come up with an exceptionally brilliant plan to win him over before the reverend could reach Fort Benton and force her to return with him.

Chapter Thirty-five

It had not taken Reverend Ardsworth long to make preparations and leave St. Louis for Fort Benton. He had a single purpose: to reenter the life of that dark-haired girl from Satan and reclaim her. He swore she would reap the Lord's wrath for her evil deeds. He knew his feeble wife hoped to temper the retribution he'd planned, but nothing, nothing would stop him from punishing the girl for her sins!

Addison Rutcliff had been in such a rush to reach his daughter and see Matilde again that he'd chosen to take the Northern Pacific Railroad to Bismarck, Dakota Territory, before boarding a steamer to travel the rest of the way to Fort Benton. He journeyed with a song on his lips, happy to have heard that his flesh and blood had finally managed to turn her life around.

One of the reasons for Addison's stellar success in business was that he took the time to learn the background of people and places he was involved with. From fellow travelers Addison had learned that prior to the coming of the railroad, Bismarck had been named Edwinton. But the town's fathers adopted the name of the German Iron Chancellor, hoping to attract German settlers.

221

Walking up the gangplank, Addison asked one of the gruff crewmen, "How long is the trip to Fort Benton?"

"You in a hurry, mister?"

"I suppose you could say that. You see, my daughter was recently wed there. I missed the wedding. And now hope to meet my new son-in-law, Cordell Chandler, and congratulate them both."

"Dell Chandler?"

"You know the man?" Addison asked, his interest piqued.

"That I do. One of the finest men in the territory, he is. Heard the little gal he married is a real fine lady. Folks really took to her, they did. The womenfolk of the town went all out to make the wedding something special, so it's told."

Addison's chest swelled with pride. Katherine had done him proud after all. He'd see that his wedding gift demonstrated just how pleased he was. "Thank you for reassuring an old man. Now, how long did you say the river trip would take? I'm even more eager to get to Fort Benton now."

"No more than eleven days, sir . . . sometimes quicker. Won't take no time at all."

Black puffs of smoke billowed from the stack on the *Red Cloud* and mingled with the clear azure sky. Addison Rutcliff paced the deck, taking in the picturesque landscape that was the treeless prairie beyond the cottonwood-lined banks of the muddy, churning river.

Addison had a grand time aboard the steamer; it was the first vacation he'd taken since his dear wife had died so many years ago. With every turn of the paddlewheel he moved closer to his daughter and her new husband. They stopped at the Big Knife River, above Tobacco Gardens, above the mouth of the Yellowstone and Porcupine Creek. The eighth day out the steamer ran all night.

"A couple more nights and you'll be with your

222

daughter," the captain announced to Addison. "Bet she'll be thrilled, from what you been telling me."

"Yes. I plan to see that they get a very special wedding gift. Even when she was a little girl I was never able to hide things from Katherine." He grinned to himself. "But my coming to visit her so soon after her wedding is one surprise I'm sure Katherine will never have anticipated. You know, captain, I can hardly wait to see the look on her face."

Reverend Elijah Ardsworth's moods were particularly black: he'd been able to raise only enough money for his wife and himself to travel in what he considered lowly steerage, a stuffy corner room on the main deck near lowing cattle and squealing pigs, not to mention all the filthy disciples of Satan who spread their vermin-riddled belongings nearby.

To make matters worse, the sky had turned black, ripped open, and let loose sheets of rain as they stood at the rail in one of the spaces not cluttered with what Elijah considered the dregs of humanity. "Here, Elijah, please—take my blanket, I don't need it," Marie offered, fearing the cold would make him particularly ugly after they bedded down.

"I should have left you back in St. Louis," he sneered. "Then I could have continued to serve the Lord in meager comfort instead of being stuck here with a bag of bones who couldn't warm a man's soul, let alone the rest of him." He looked about to make certain no one was close by. Satisfied he wouldn't be seen, he pushed her into one of the many isolated crevices created by stacks of crates. He stripped her of the crude woolen square, tore off the bodice of her dress, and fell heavily on top of her.

Marie bit her lip and endured his lewd groping and grunting until he had satiated his lust and rolled off her. Without preamble he fastened his trousers and dragged her back to their tiny room, where soon he was snoring and snorting satisfaction, deep in sleep.

Marie gathered herself into a tight ball, pulling her ruined, threadbare gown closed at her throat. Silent tears of hopelessness slid down her hollow cheeks. Please, God, don't let him harm my baby girl. Let her find happiness far away from us. Even if I'm never allowed to see or touch or hold her in my arms again, Marie prayed quietly, the tears flowing more swiftly now.

Sunday morning dawned bright as a jewel. Marie had changed into the best dress she owned, a worn gray cotton with long sleeves, a neat white collar, and stiff white cuffs. The reverend, dressed in his usual dour black, stood at the rail, tapping his thick fingers impatiently against an upright he leaned into.

"Ah, Reverend and Mrs. Ardsworth, I hope you will join us. Reverend Barksford is holding services in the main salon," said the wife of a well-dressed couple. Marie guessed them to be in their early forties.

"Why, we'd be pleased, wouldn't we, Elijah?" Marie asked before realizing her error.

Elijah Ardsworth glowered at the pair and sent his wife a particularly venomous look. "I'm sure you'll excuse my wife and me if we choose to worship according to the tenets of my own church."

The couple gave Marie a sympathetic nod and moved off, confused by the man's strange behavior.

Once they stood alone again, the reverend lashed out at Marie with all the force of his anger. "Don't you *ever* presume to speak for me again, bitch. Although that stupid captain made the mistake of having some idiot heathen hold services aboard this tub, it does not mean I condone such actions. And we certainly could never, do you hear me, *never* attend such a travesty!"

"Elijah, I am so sorry. It is my pitiful soul. But I

224

will learn. I promise you, I *will* learn." Marie hung her head, fearing he would strike her once more. "I should never have been so presumptuous. It won't happen again."

"It better not! Or else I just might decide to baptize you in the river. The Lord might even smile on your immersion at my hand. My efforts to cleanse your sorry soul in the glory of His will could finally earn you your place in heaven," he said crazily. Then his face darkened. "Just don't get any stupid ideas and forget why we're here—our mission is to reclaim the lost soul of your daughter from the devil's grasp. And no matter what, I don't intend to let Satan win this time! The girl will soon realize the error of her ways and come to repent!"

"Elijah, I will help you," Marie reassured him, swallowing the lump of fear threatening to close her throat.

He grabbed her shoulders, bruising her with his grip. His eyes glinted fire, he curled his lip. "Of course you will. And in a few short weeks we will be in Fort Benton and collect that wayward daughter of yours. Then she'll learn at last that no matter how far she tries to run, it'll never be far enough."

Chapter Thirty-six

"Knock, knock," Matilde chirped and entered the room without the slightest embarrassment over the rumple of clothes directing her focus to the couple lying in bed under a satin quilt.

Awakened from sleep by Matilde's singsong voice, Cordell turned over and yelled, "How the devil did you manage to get in? Bribe the hotel clerk, did you?"

"Hadn't thought of that. But I'll remember the suggestion next time, if I find the door locked." She waved off his apparent anger. "You simply did not bother to lock the door last night." Her bright, astonished eyes settled on Libby, who gasped and ducked beneath the covers. "Good morning, my dear. My, but you've got a glow about you this morning."

Libby shimmied further beneath the covers in an attempt to hide her obvious nakedness. She was almost afraid to breathe for fear that Matilde was about to expose her at any instant.

"Might I suggest that you try knocking and then wait to be invited before you enter next time, Auntie dear? You'd be much less apt to end up in a situation you find shocking."

"Oh, nonsense. Nothing you could do could shock me, Dell. I practically helped raise you, if you recall."

"In that case, it shouldn't bother you if I personally

escort you out." Cordell rose and wrapped a blanket around himself as Matilde squealed and grabbed the big knotted bow at her throat, scandalized.

"You shouldn't be running around like a half-naked savage. Get something else on this minute," she instructed. "There are ladies present."

Cordell looked serious. "I'm just about to take care of that, Aunt Matilde."

Cordell took her arm and gently shoved her through the door, throwing it shut behind him. "You two will meet me downstairs for breakfast, won't you? They have the most delicious berry muffins dripping with butter this morning," she called through the door.

"I've got business," Cordell returned. Having let the blanket drop, he stood before his wife in all his muscular glory. "You can have breakfast with Katherine in about an hour."

"Not unless I take a tray to the jail," Matilde said to herself.

"What?"

"I said I'll come back; I have letters to mail," Matilde improvised and flitted down the hall, a pleased grin on her lips.

"Don't rush." Cordell took the last two steps to the edge of the bed and threw back the covers.

"I—I thought you didn't want anything to do with me," Libby said, uneasy that she lay before him naked in the bright light of morning.

"I don't," he breathed, drinking in her beauty. "I don't want to do this." He kneeled down and placed a lingering kiss on her lips, still swollen from their passion of the night before. "And I didn't plan to do this." His hands slid down her cheeks and caressed her breasts, causing the nipples to peak at his touch. "And I certainly didn't plan to do this." Knowledgeable fingers lit fires of desire everywhere he came into intimate contact with her yielding body.

227

"And I know you didn't plan for this," Libby murmured, caught up by the incredibly powerful messages of her own reckless heart. She pushed him back against the pillows. Straddling him, she began to run her fingertips up his chest.

His distended manhood pressed against her demanding entry, and Libby joyfully guided him into her hungry body. Together the tension rose in tendrils of hot, blazing heat, sensations propelling them beyond endurance until in unison their bodies found release in wave after liquid wave.

Not waiting to cradle his wife in his arms, Cordell shoved himself away and threw on his clothes. "I don't know what the devil you think you're trying to accomplish by seducing me. It isn't going to work," he shouted, angry with himself for forgetting the kind of woman he had married, despite his intentions to enjoy her body while he remained married to her.

"Oh, I'd say it worked quite well," she said pertly, ignoring his comment about her enticing him. She determined not to let him see how his continued unwillingness to admit his feelings hurt her. "You might as well stop fighting it—"

"Fighting *it?*" he demanded.

"*Us.* I *am* your wife. I *love* you. And eventually you'll come to realize that you love me too," she said boldly.

"Not as long as I can help it." He stormed through the door, crashing it behind him. Stomping down the hallway, Cordell wasn't sure whether he was furious with the girl because she insisted she loved him, or furious with himself because he was forced to admit he had feelings for her too, despite his earlier resolve.

Matilde sat primly on the patterned settee in the public room, waiting until she saw Cordell stalk down

228

he stairs and out the massive double doors. She took one last look at the dining room and all the aromatic pastries that beckoned before she fought down the inclination to indulge herself and headed up to the young woman's room instead.

This time she rapped according to custom and waited until the disheveled girl, dressed in a blue silk robe, hesitantly creaked open the door.

Libby's eyes saucered when she saw Matilde Chandler. Dressed in a commanding peach morning gown of striped muslin and matching peach Gainsborough hat, Matilde stood to her full five-feet-eight-inch height. "Aren't you going to invite me in . . . *Libby?*"

"Oh . . . yes. Yes, of course." Flustered, Libby toyed with her tangled black curls. Although Cordell was perhaps not aware of it yet himself, he was just beginning to respond to her, and Libby feared that Matilde Chandler would unmask her and then Libby'd never be able to win the obstinate man over.

Wanting to take the girl's measure, Matilde strode into the spacious room and turned to face her squarely. "I think an explanation is in order, don't you, my dear?"

"An explanation?"

"Please, I know that I enjoy my gift for speech. And I do have the tendency to rattle on. But in this case, I think it is past time that we got right to the point. I helped raise Cordell after his mother ran away with some sweet-talking peddler. That's why the right wife for the boy is so important. He'd never admit it, but it left a lasting impression on him. He's a strong man because of the hardships he's endured, and he deserves a good woman by his side." True to her nature Matilde gabbed on, giving Libby even more insight into the man.

Libby raised her chin to demonstrate her equal will. "I quite agree with you."

229

"Then you'd better start by telling me exactly who you are." Libby opened her mouth to answer, but Matilde cut her off. "And I want to know why Dell referred to you as Katherine, not to mention what you were doing in his bed this morning."

Libby could feel her blood pressure rise. Despite all the flippant pageantry associated with Matilde Chandler, the woman was no one's fool. She was keenly observant and not about to be put off by some hastily invented tale.

"Why don't you sit down?" Libby said, passing her the bowl of fruit. "An apple, perhaps?"

Matilde cast a yearning glance over the luscious offering, red, purple, and orange. "No. No, don't try to cloud the issue with food, young lady. I want the truth, and I want it now!" she exclaimed, then snatched up an apple and stowed it in her purse. "For later."

Libby hid a smile. She took a deep breath and said a silent prayer that she could win Matilde Chandler over to her side.

"I've told you who I am—"

"Elizabeth, is that correct?"

"Yes. My name is Elizabeth Marie Hollis . . . Libby."

"I see. Then at least you were telling me the truth about your identity when we met."

"I never intended to lie to you, ma'am," Libby said honestly and stiffened against the high-backed chair.

"I told you to call me Matilde. That stands—for now, at any rate."

"Thank you for that, at least."

"You needn't thank me. I want to know what you were doing in Dell's bed this morning," Matilde asked, confused by the sudden thought that Cordell had attempted to pass Elizabeth off as Katherine, maybe thinking he could pull the wool over her eyes."

Libby studied her fingernails for a moment. She started to bring them to her lips, as she had when the

230

reverend lectured her before he pronounced punishment. Then her eyes caught sight of the lengthening tips. She hadn't chewed her fingernails since she'd met Augusta aboard the *Benton*. She returned her hands to her lap. She was not going to revert to old habits brought about by fear. She was no longer that frightened young girl.

"I suppose you wouldn't believe that he got the wrong room last night?"

"I am not naive." There was an edge to Matilde's voice.

"Then there is no need to deny what we'd been doing."

"None whatsoever."

"I love your nephew. And although he may not admit it, I think he is coming to have feelings for me also," Libby blurted out.

"It is quite apparent you two share a certain, shall we say, physical attraction. But have you forgotten that Cordell is recently married, to a young woman who is supposed to be a friend of yours, no less?"

"Then you noticed it too?" Libby asked hopefully, ignoring all else.

"My dear, if you think you are going to break up his marriage, you had better think again."

"Oh, no, no, I'd never do that," Libby said earnestly. "All I want is for Cordell to be happy."

"Then perhaps you should take the first stage back to Fort Benton and return to St. Louis without further ado."

"I'm sorry, but I can't do that."

Matilde narrowed her eyes. Somehow, she was sure she was missing part of this addling puzzle. "Can't or won't?"

"Both, I suppose."

"Well, in that case, would you mind telling me why Dell called you Katherine this morning?" Matilde probed, not about to settle for less than the whole story. And at the same time she was becoming more and more intrigued by the girl. Matilde could see the love in Elizabeth's eyes when she spoke of Cordell; the caring radiated from every pore. Matilde knew Katherine was in jail. But, of course, rather than simply informing the girl of her knowledge, Matilde wanted to hear Elizabeth's side—particularly after becoming privy to Katherine's true nature yesterday morning.

Libby stared long and hard at Matilde before she finally admitted, "Because he—he thinks that—that I'm Katherine."

Matilde's mouth fell open. "What?" She quickly composed herself. "Oh, dear," her hand went to her cheek, "then who is it Dell married?"

"He thinks he married Katherine Rutcliff," Libby said evasively, still unable to lay out the entire series of events.

"He thinks . . . I see. Or at least I *think* I see." A troubled line sketched her forehead. "Let me see if I have this straight. Dell thinks you are Katherine. And he married Katherine—"

Libby moved to the edge of her chair. "That's right."

"Only he actually married you."

"Yes." Libby's tongue shot out and she wet her dry lips.

"Well, that's something to think about." Matilde sighed, took the apple out of her purse, and crunched into it. When only the core remained, she set it aside and suggested, "Now I think I'd better hear the rest of this story. And don't leave anything out."

Wringing her hands, but determined not to shrink from the truth, Libby poured out her story. She told about stowing away on the steamer, intent on becoming a laundress once in Fort Benton, and how she came to impersonate Katherine Rutcliff. Libby attempted to gloss over the flaws in Katherine's personality, not

232

wanting to speak ill of someone who was not present and able to defend herself.

But Matilde would have none of it and persisted until Libby told about Katherine and Sheldon Sharpe, and the Pinkerton report describing Katherine's numerous indiscretions. Even Libby's decision to continue the impersonation after landing at Fort Benton, when Cordell had mistaken her for Katherine, tumbled out. Libby had not intended to describe what she'd done to trick Cordell into marrying her, but Matilde managed to gain that knowledge as well. By the time Libby had finished explaining, she had told Matilde the truth about everything except the reverend.

"My goodness, child . . . that is quite an incredible tale. So strange, in fact, that I find it believable. But I have one question," Matilde said, taking another apple from the basket. She withdrew a dainty monogrammed handkerchief from her sleeve and proceeded to polish the red-skinned fruit until it shone.

"What's that?" Libby ventured, holding her breath, half-afraid of what to expect.

"Just what do you intend to do when Cordell finds out about the real Katherine?"

Chapter Thirty-seven

For a long moment Libby stared at Matilde Chandler. Her question about what Libby would do when Cordell found out she wasn't Katherine had been troubling her for weeks now — ever since she'd come to want a lasting union, for that matter.

"I see that my question seems to be causing you distress."

Tears hovered near Libby's lower lids when she said, "I love Cordell, and I don't want to lose him."

Matilde leaned forward and took Libby's hands in hers. When Libby did not immediately meet her gaze, Matilde crooked a finger, hooked it under Libby's chin, and drew her face up until their eyes fastened on each other.

"You really do love my nephew, don't you, my dear?" Matilde said, her eyes ferreting out the truth.

"It's that obvious?"

"Aside from the fact that you've said so twice, yes. The eyes are the windows of the soul. And in looking into your eyes, my dear child, I can see that there is that special kind of love which flows from the heart; it is the kind of love that is experienced once in a lifetime. And when it does happen, it fills one's cup with a fountain overflowing with joy and happiness," Matilde reflected wistfully.

"You speak as if you've known that kind of love."

A sad glow came to Matilde's face. "Yes, I have . . . many years ago. But I lost him due to my own foolishness and fears. Yet, though we had a short time together, I've always had the memories to treasure in my heart." She shook her head to clear away her own reminiscences. "But seeing how you feel about Dell, and watching him, I realize I don't want your chance together to slip away just because of the unfortunate circumstances of your beginning. While I was visiting Marshal Hillard I saw Katherine—"

"You did?" Libby gasped.

"You needn't worry yourself, child. I saw Katherine Rutcliff's true nature. I also saw the kind of company she keeps, that seedy gambler friend of hers. Her behavior while I was there left little doubt that they deserve each other." True to her nature, Matilde went on at great length about her less-than-cordial conversation with the spoiled young heiress.

A sense of foreboding mirrored in Libby's eyes, prompting Matilde to add, "Oh, don't be concerned about Katherine or that Sharpe person. I was visiting with Matt Hillard, the dear man; he owes me a favor or two. Anyway, after I discovered the kind of person Katherine was, I made arrangements for her to enjoy her present accommodations a while longer . . . at least until Cordell has left Helena." Matilde smiled, pleased. She became serious. "I think you should tell Dell the truth."

Libby's face took on a blue pallor as the blood drained from it. She knitted her fingers together, spanning the distance from the bed back to the chair where Matilde sat. Libby faced her squarely. "I can't do that."

"You can't keep up this charade indefinitely, either."

"Only until I'm sure of Cordell's love . . . then I'll tell him the truth. But I can't take the chance of losing him."

"He means that much to you?"

"Yes . . . I just wish he weren't so obstinate."

"That's always been one of his more enduring qualities, I'm afraid."

"And most irritating."

"True," Matilde agreed.

"Somehow, I have to make him realize that we belong together."

Matilde threw up her hands and shrugged. "Well, then, if you intend to persist with this, I'll simply have to help you. . . ."

Libby and Matilde were still chatting, enjoying coffee and hot-cross buns when Cordell returned. Deep frown lines etched his face. Every time he looked at Katherine he wanted to devour her, she was so beautiful. Every time he thought of her with all those men, he wanted to choke that graceful neck of hers. He tried to force himself to remember that he'd been the first to possess her totally, but her past haunted him nonetheless.

He recalled thinking that the others had undoubtedly been thwarted in consummation of their relationships with her because they feared the wrath of her wealthy and powerful father. No doubt she'd have cried rape and had the poor slobs arrested in order to protect her tarnished honor. But knowing that so many others had stroked her willing flesh, had caressed and tasted of her freely, drove him to keep to his original plan of seeing their union dissolved—and the sooner the better.

"Dell, I'm so happy you've returned in time to share a little breakfast with us," Matilde said cheerily.

Cordell looked at the near-empty basket of fruit and the empty platter which had no doubt once contained a mountain of warm rolls. "Looks like I'm a little late."

"Nonsense . . . why, I'll just rush on downstairs and see to another plate." Matilde was on her feet and gone before Libby could protest.

The instant the door closed, Cordell turned on Libby.

"I see you haven't wasted any time trying to enlist Matilde's aid. But if you think you can fool her and pretend to be the devoted wife, hoping I'll soften toward you, you're sadly mistaken!"

Libby calmly poured a cup of coffee and offered it to him. "I was doing no such thing. She was merely having breakfast with me—at your suggestion, I might add."

"You might as well not make it a point to grow too fond of her."

"And why not? She's a delightful lady."

"Because you won't be part of the family much longer," he said with a conviction that he himself questioned.

The sting of his retort caused Libby to walk to the window and look out. Montana was a glorious kaleidoscope of magnificent ponderosa, larch and lodgepole pines, jagged boulders, lofty mountains, flowering prairies, and fertile valleys, all beneath a pearlized blue sky. She breathed in the beauty of it all. She felt a kinship with the land and never would return to the big, dirty city again. And she was not going to let Cordell dismiss her from his life!

Cordell came to stand behind her. Her hair smelled of mint and mingled with the lily fragrance of her perfume. No wonder men found her irresistible. Cordell himself could hardly keep his hands off her.

Feeling his breath hot and moist on the back of her neck, Libby swung around and found herself wrapped in his arms. She gazed into the black depths of his eyes. A jumble of emotions assaulted her. He wanted her, she could feel it in his touch and see the hunger in his face. Another emotion silently spoke of his stubborn pride and determination to rid himself of her.

"What was that little game you were playing at dinner last night?" he questioned, startling Libby. She was certain she'd successfully carried off the complicated charade.

She tried to disengage herself, but he held her tight. "I don't know what you mean."

"I think you do."

"What gives you that idea?" she asked innocently. All the while her heart was thudding against her chest at his nearness.

"The message I received from Gulch, for one thing. I saw him this morning and he didn't know anything about any note. Denied sending it."

His eyes were boring into her now, warning her that she was in trouble. "I—"

"She's trying to cover for me, Dell," Matilde said, standing in the doorway, her arms laden with pastries.

Cordell dropped his arms from Libby and went to Matilde. "You seem to be making a habit out of barging your way into our room, auntie dear."

"Not me. I told you I was coming back."

Once they were seated and Matilde had eaten a berry pastry, Cordell said, "What did you mean, Katherine was trying to cover for you?"

"I sent the note in Gulch's name," she admitted, covertly winking at Libby.

"Oh you did, did you? *Why?*" he asked, not at all convinced.

"Because I wanted to spend some time alone with your beautiful wife. Now that she's part of the family, I wanted to welcome her and get to know her better."

There was something which didn't ring true about what she said or the ease with which she said it, but Matilde had always had her own unique way of doing things.

"Thank you for seeing that I got some breakfast. We don't want to detain you. I'm sure you've got business elsewhere," Cordell suggested.

Unmoved, Matilde waved him off. "You don't have to be polite. If you want me to leave, just say so."

"Good-bye, Auntie."

"Very well." She heaved a sigh. "I know when I'm not wanted. I'll see you two tonight at the Elgin dinner party. It will be such fun introducing my new niece to everyone." She brought her hand up to stay Cordell's response, knowing he was about to refuse. "No, now don't you say another word. You can stop by my room and pick me up at six-thirty. That way you'll have two gorgeous women to escort. Kiss, kiss, you two. I can hardly wait until this evening," she squealed with anticipation, and like a whirlwind whipped from the room.

Chapter Thirty-eight

Libby went to the wardrobe and began rummaging through Katherine's gowns. She wanted to look especially good for Cordell tonight. The green velvet would never do; this was June, and something which suggested summer and brought out the color of her eyes would serve her better. She had to sparkle for Cordell tonight. She'd already worn the blue . . . she thumbed through another dozen gowns, discarding each in turn.

"What are you doing?" he asked.

"I don't have anything to wear tonight."

Cordell rolled his eyes. "I wonder how many poor husbands have heard that before. Well, since Matilde has seen to it I have no choice about attending Elgins' flashy dinner party tonight, get one of those concoctions you call a hat and I'll take you shopping."

Libby look confused. "Cordell, you don't have to buy me anything. I'll find something."

"Don't try that sweet, innocent act on me. I know better, remember."

The inclination to argue surged over her and she fought it down. She had Matilde on her side, and they'd come up with a plan to win him over. Now all she had to do was follow it and ignore his attempts to provoke her into doing something stupid. Biting her tongue, Libby grabbed her hat and followed Cordell from the hotel.

They wandered along the busy streets, peering in shop windows filled with finery. It was a new experience for Libby and she felt like a child about to receive her first doll. It was a pity, she thought, looking at her own reflection dressed in Katherine's expensive clothes, that she had to rely on Cordell's generosity.

They passed several laundries as they strolled through town. Inside, girls glistening with perspiration wiped soddened locks from their eyes while they toiled over the boiling tubs. Libby's breath caught: she could have been one of those girls.

"What's the matter, haven't you ever seen anyone doing an honest day's work before?"

"Not only have I seen girls doing an honest day's work, I've spent many days working over hot tubs myself," came the reply.

"Somehow I find that difficult to believe." Cordell grabbed Libby's hands, pulled off her gloves, and examined her palms. He rubbed the softened skin, causing a moist heat between her legs to make her uneasy. With her hands still in his, Cordell observed, "Those hands," he ran his thumbs along the inside of her palms again, "are as soft as a child's."

"Some children have to work hard too," Libby retorted, remembering her own childhood.

"And some are coddled, like the daughter of Addison Rutcliff."

"Perhaps even the daughter of Addison Rutcliff had to pay a price," Libby returned, Katherine's anger over her lonely childhood rising up before Libby.

There was something about the inflection in her voice that caused Cordell to release her and walk ahead along the boardwalk. "Here we are."

He strode into the milinery shop. The interior was properly decorated with a feminine flair. Generous roses papered the walls and lace adorned the windows. Gold

241

and white chairs, set at angles, faced a rack of ready-made gowns in a rainbow of colors.

"Ah, Dell darling, what brings you to my humble shop?" cooed the petite modiste.

Libby stepped from behind Cordell and the delicate features of the ravishing redhead fell. She was dressed in the finest of eastern fashion. A rose-beige princess gown, the back draping tucked around the front of the skirt, was arranged into a semihobble, with a ruffled trim detailed into a sweeper at the bottom. The woman's red curls were swept up and tied with matching ribbons.

Libby stepped forward and took Cordell's arm. "We came to select a gown for this evening."

"I see," she said stiffly. She turned from Libby as if she were transparent and smiled at Cordell. "And for what occasion am I to dress your friend, Dell?"

"Miss . . ." Libby checked the name lettered on the door. "Devaux, I'm not Cordell's friend," Libby corrected sharply.

Lynette Devaux cocked her brow in a hostile expression. "Oh? Then Dell, why ever would you accompany this person?"

"Lynette, *this person* is my wife."

Lynette's tiny hand clasped at her throat and her unease became overly apparent by her shifting stance. "I am at your service, of course, Mrs. Chandler. What may I show you?" Her demeanor was immediately transformed into that of a humble shopkeeper, and she ushered them toward the chairs.

"Don't be too hard on her, Katherine," Cordell whispered and stretched out, pleased at the way his wife was handling herself. He'd seen Lynette's cutting tongue in action before.

Libby recalled the snobbery of the women in St. Louis for whom she'd done washing, and she decided to try to imitate them. "Do you have any sky blue silk? I

242

equire a ballgown styled with a deep décolletage, a eart-shaped neckline exposing my shoulders. No leeves, but a midnight blue trim with frills," Libby nstructed.

"But Mrs. Chandler, midnight blue trim?" Lynette vhined.

"If your establishment cannot meet my needs, per-aps we should shop elsewhere."

The modiste's chin squared. "Mine is the finest shop f its kind in Helena. Of course, I can meet the needs f Cordell Chandler's wife."

"Very well, if you'll show me your wares," Libby met er hard gaze, "I'll make my selections."

Lynette nodded and scurried off. "Katherine, Lynette s an old and dear friend. Remember that," he warned, olding back a smile. Few females could daunt the ormidable Lynette Devaux. But naturally, Katherine Rutcliff would not let any woman better her, although ʌynette had caused her to pause. The thought gave Cordell an idea he fought to beat down.

Returning triumphant, Lynette's arms were filled with dress form sporting a light blue silk. "My dear Mrs. Chandler, you are in luck. I just happen to have de-igned the very thing you described." A sneer curled her ips. No one was going to treat her like a simple hopkeeper and get away with it, not even Dell's wife. Thoughts of Dell turned her eyes a deeper green. For ears she'd longed to catch the elusive rancher, and now ʌe sauntered in with a total stranger and announced he vas married.

The surprised look on Dell's wife's face softened the dges of Lynette's mouth. "If you'll follow me, Mrs. Chandler, I'll have you fitted in no time. And then Dell an return late in the afternoon and pick the gown up or you," she offered smugly.

"That'll be fine," Cordell answered for Libby before he could say a word.

Deflated by Cordell's eager acceptance, Libby allowed herself to be led behind a curtain in the back. There she was poked and turned, twisted and measured.

"Ouch!"

"I *am* sorry, Mrs. Chandler," Lynette begged, drawing back the pin in her fingers. "I'll be more careful next time."

"No doubt. Now please help me off with this gown."

Lynette Devaux did not see the gleam enter Libby's eyes as she helped slip the gown over Libby's head. The toe of Libby's shoe settled heavily onto the delicate ruffle, causing a loud ripping noise to slice through the tense silence. "Oh dear, I am sorry, Miss Devaux. I'll be more careful next time. I do hope that tear won't cause you too much extra work. The gown will be ready for tonight, won't it?"

Lynette glowered, having been bested. "It shall be ready." Lynette set the torn gown aside and hurriedly ushered the pair toward the door.

Another gown caught Libby's eyes and she stopped to admire it. At Cordell's urgings Libby tried on the creation and found that it fit perfectly.

When Cordell saw how beautiful his wife looked in the gown, he announced, "Wrap it up. We'll take both dresses."

Thrilled to have two beautiful gowns of her own, Libby hurriedly changed back into her original dress and rejoined Cordell.

"Why don't you go on ahead and browse in the next shop, Katherine? Lynette and I have some business to attend to."

Reluctantly Libby left the dress shop and strolled along the sidewalk. She glanced back over her shoulder, waiting for the longest time for her husband to leave that woman's side . . .

* * *

By the time Libby had climbed from the tub, Cordell was gone. While she was soaking, he abruptly announced he was going to dress and head downstairs for a drink. While sharing accommodations and acting like a happily married couple for appearance's sake had been part of the bargain at first, after they had made love, Libby was sure things would change more rapidly than they had. At least she'd made some headway, and she was not about to give up! Wrapped in thick toweling, Libby stared at the frothy blue creation hanging on the wardrobe door. If the gown hadn't been so extraordinary, Libby would have been tempted to leave it where it hung. But she had to impress Cordell's associates this evening.

She barely managed to slip into the bodice of the gown and only luck and force of will allowed her to fasten the tiny cloth buttons. "Lynette Devaux," Libby groaned. The shrew had deliberately taken in the seams!

Frantic, Libby checked the time. The shiny brass hands on the porcelain clock were approaching the hour when they must leave. There was little time left before they were to meet Matilde and depart for the Elgins' party, and Libby had no other gown to change into.

When Cordell had gone to pick up the two gowns he'd purchased earlier, he'd returned with only the blue one. Lynette Devaux had said she'd send the second gown to the hotel later that evening, explaining that the hem needed attention. Libby had thought it strange when Cordell relayed the message, since the gown had been in flawless condition when she tried it on. Now she understood perfectly: the woman had meant to put her in this predicament.

"Knock, knock," Matilde sang and breezed into the room. "You really should start locking that door, my dear. One never knows who might be on the other side." She turned the lock. "Oh! My goodness! You look as if the breath is being squeezed out of you. But

245

the gown is absolutely stunning." She stepped forward "Will you be all right this evening?"

"Only if I don't try to move or breathe," Libby said wishing she could get her fingers on that modiste "What am I going to do? Cordell should be back i twenty minutes."

"Do you have a needle and thread?" Matilde asked examining the gown as she helped Libby out of it.

"Yes, but there's no time."

"Nonsense. Did Dell have a chance to tell you that when we were growing up I used to sew for the family? I'm not just another pretty face, you know," she said, causing Libby to smile at the old dear. "Scissors, too.'

"We'll never have it altered in time," Libby fretted, explaining what had happened. She rummaged through Katherine's trunk and pulled out a small bag containing needles, scissors and thread. "The thread doesn't exactly match."

"It'll do. Hurry now, thread several needles, then si back and relax."

Libby did as she was told and moved across the room to sit on the edge of the bed. She watched as Matilde snipped the delicate buttons and with ease moved them over just enough to allow Libby breathe.

Matilde looked up. "Put on another petticoat, it'll make the gown appear even more dramatic."

Libby slipped into the satin undergarment and let Matilde help her on with the gown. They had just finished the last button when the key turned in the lock. "Quick, go put a little more color on your cheeks," Matilde instructed, "while I keep Dell entertained."

"Why, Dell, you look simply ravishing," Matilde crooned when he stepped into the room. "We've been sitting here waiting for you to return. Isn't Li— Katherine the very picture of elegance? I can see by the way you're gawking at her that you quite agree. Go give

246

your wife a kiss, boy." She shoved Cordell toward Libby, who stood expectantly near her wrap.

Cordell wore a black sack coat with quilted lapels, striped trousers, and a gray double-breasted waistcoat. The collar folded down on a shirt of soft white. A string tie held with a gold clasp completed his attire and matched the golden sparkle in his black eyes.

Cordell's eyes studied Libby from head to toe. The critical way he surveyed her gave Libby cause to wonder if he knew what that Devaux woman had deliberately done.

"Aren't you going to give your wife a kiss?" Matilde pressed.

"I do not need you to instruct me in proper decorum," he glibly stated. But fact was his wife took his breath away.

"Well, then, if you two are done enjoying the view, I suggest we leave," said Matilde. "I, for one, do not want to miss a bite of those delicacies." She whizzed from the room, leaving Cordell and Libby with little choice but to hurry after her.

"Our coach is over there." Cordell made a sweeping motion with his arm, directing the ladies to the ornate lacquered carriage. He swung open the door and took Libby's arm to offer his assistance.

Libby stepped inside the carriage and froze. There, proud as a fanned peacock and looking as well-dressed, sat Lynette Devaux, a self-satisfied smile curving her full red lips.

Chapter Thirty-nine

Libby froze at the sight of the Devaux woman. What was she doing there? She had a lot of nerve to be sitting there so calmly after what she'd done!

"Do sit down, Mrs. Chandler," Lynette said sweetly, although she could see the cold dislike in the modiste's eyes. "I do hope you found the gown a perfect fit."

"Why, yes, I did. No doubt you've been in business for many years, you have such expertise, Miss Devaux," Libby returned gaily, masking the urge to bare her nails toward the schemer. "I've never had quite such a . . . a form-fitting gown before. Why, the way you sew, I'm surprised your shop wasn't simply bursting with customers when we were there." Libby quietly added to herself, *seeking alterations.*

Lynette bristled and waited silently while Matilde bundled in, leaving Cordell no choice except to sit next to his little snip of a wife. The chit had on her most beautiful creation, which brought bitter bile to Lynette's throat. Even the magnificent gown she wore tonight held a sorry second place to the one that Chandler's wife had ordered. Lynette ran her fingers over her own lime satin gown. She'd dazzle them tonight after Cordell's wife was forced to leave due to the mishap she had planned with the gown. A secret smile twisted Lynette's lips. The seams couldn't possibly hold together all evening. Then Cordell Chandler would come to realize what a mistake he had made by marrying the troublesome girl.

Lynette laid a gloved hand over Cordell's. "It was so thoughtful of you to invite me to join you and your aunt tonight . . . oh, and of course, your wife."

Matilde choked, causing Lynette to turn her syrupy attention to the elder women, who for once held her tongue.

Libby was furious, but was not about to give the woman the satisfaction of watching her create a scene. How could Cordell invite that horrible woman? He had spent some time alone with her earlier that afternoon. Libby's heart threatened to sink, thinking they might be lovers and had planned to spend the evening together. But she was not going to let her fears ruin her evening.

In stony silence they rode to the Elgins' home. The carriage rocked and rumbled through town and out along a dusty road for what seemed to Libby an eternity. At last it came to a halt in front of a sprawling frame house. Split-rail fencing lined the long drive, dotted silver in the moonlight.

"Thank you, Dell," Lynette purred and hung onto his arm as he helped her alight, expecting his wife to pliantly walk behind them, beside his batty aunt.

"Lynette," Cordell pried her fingers from his sleeve, "I think I should escort Katherine inside. Don't you agree?"

Lynette pinched her lips, swung around, and strutted toward the house, not waiting for Cordell.

A pleased warmth spread across Libby's stomach when Cordell offered his arm after helping her and Matilde from the coach. She'd anticipated that he planned to ignore her all evening. She thought she was going to have to work for his attention. He'd invited the dressmaker along, obviously to show her that he was serious when he'd said he wanted the dissolution of his marriage. And Libby had been sure he instructed the woman to stitch the seams so the gown would be too tight.

Walking by his side now, Libby was no longer quite so certain. But one thing she did know, she wasn't going to let him go without a fight!

"Enjoy yourselves, ladies," Cordell announced once he'd ushered Libby and Matilde around the spacious parlor. It was filled to overflowing with guests of every description and dress and eager to meet the rancher's new bride.

Overstuffed furniture surrounded doily-covered tables which held Tiffany lamps all draped in red, white, and blue streamers celebrating the nation's centennial. Over the mantle hung the Stars and Stripes. It was a comfortable room which bespoke wealth.

For what seemed like hours Libby forced herself to smile and laugh and listen to farsighted men talk about statehood for Montana. She circulated among the guests, delighting men and women alike with witty stories of traveling up the Missouri River.

The revelers made speeches, read poems dedicated to the great nation, and sang rousing choruses of patriotic songs.

"I see you have managed to charm old Elgin and his wife, not to mention the rest of the guests," Cordell said blandly. He offered her a glass of spirits and lifted his own in toast. "To Mrs. Chandler, the little lady who tamed one of the most opinionated group of Westerners I've ever met. Not to mention weaving her magic around them."

"I'll drink to that," chimed in Hiriam Bayless. "Chandler, when you came to me the other day, I never dreamed Katherine here was such delight." Hiriam colored when Cordell's face turned murderous.

"It's all right, Mr. Bayless," Libby interceded, not about to let the new information that Cordell had sought the attorney's advice daunt her. "Like most newlyweds, Cordell and I have some adjustments to make."

Bayless sent a lopsided frown toward Cordell, then hiccupped. "We're all rootin' for you, *Mrs.* Chandler."

Libby's gaze shifted to Lynette Devaux. "Yes. Everyone."

"Lynette, I almost forgot," Cordell motioned for the redhead. A smug twist on her full lips, Lynette waltzed over to Cordell and looked up at him with unhooded, adoring eyes. Libby stiffened her stance, fearing the worst. "I want to thank you for taking time to come tonight. But it appears that it hasn't been necessary. My wife did not have any difficulties with her gown after all."

Lynette's smile dissipated and she huffed, "Well, since you don't seem to be in further need of my *services* any longer," cold eyes shifted down the seams of Libby's blue silk, "I will allow Mr. Bayless to escort me home." With a curt swish she swept her skirts aside and wound her arm around him.

After the others had moved off, Libby stayed Cordell's leave. "You invited that woman along with us tonight in case I had a problem with my gown? I thought . . ." Her voice trailed off.

A spark Libby could not define glittered into his eyes. "You thought I was interested in her?"

Libby dropped her eyes and thought of denying his observation, but he would know. "Yes."

"It's not what you thought at all. I've known Lynette a long time. She's not what a woman could consider a friend. I was afraid she might have sabotaged your dress. You two did not exactly hit it off this afternoon. She has a tendency to be a bit jealous and vindictive."

"So I discovered. It was lucky for me your Aunt Matilde happened by early, or I might not have been ready on time."

Overhearing the conversation, Matilde joined them, waving her lorgnette in the air with a flourish. "My dear, most things in life don't come about simply because of luck. Isn't that right, Dell?" At Cordell's warning frown, Matilde changed subjects. "Come along, you two, it's time for dinner. I sneaked a peek, they are having a simply sumptuous spread; it looks so American, the way it's all laid out amidst those little flags. We simply must hurry. I don't want to miss a bite."

"What about your diet, Aunt Matilde?" Cordell reminded her with a laugh, masking concern for the aging lady.

She cast him a smile of annoyance. "Don't worry, Dell, I already ate the milk and toast today that the doctor ordered. And don't think I won't tell Katherine here that it was your idea I check on her before the party, since we all know how Lynette can be," Matilde added flippantly.

Libby's head snapped around. Cordell was glaring at his aunt now. "Is—is that true? You were concerned about me?"

"Appearances," he answered blankly, but his eyes gave away more than he'd intended. In spite of himself he had looked out for her. The knowledge caused Libby's throat to choke up.

Brightening with a spark of hope, Libby winked at Matilde. "Yes, appearances."

"Oh, poppycock! It's no more than anyone in love would do—even if he won't admit it."

The rest of the evening was a success. With Matilde's help and support, Libby dazzled them. Cordell didn't have a chance. The two ladies took the party by storm, Libby with her sweet warmth and Matilde with her bubbling flamboyance. The very people Cordell had thought would reinforce his decision to seek a quiet dissolution of the marriage had deserted him.

Cordell was still reflecting on this when an excited messenger pushed his way into the party. "Custer's been massacred! He's been massacred!" the man yelled, and thrust a scrawled note into the host's hand.

Hiriam read the crumpled piece of paper and then looked up, a serious expression on his face. "Ladies and gentlemen," he shouted, silencing the partygoers. "It is my sad duty to inform you all that on June 25, General George Custer, the commander of the Seventh Cavalry, and nearly two hundred and sixty men were

252

slaughtered at the Little Big Horn by an overwhelming band of Sioux and Cheyenne."

Three women fainted and others stood silently clasping their hands over their mouths in utter shock. A quiet fell over the celebrants.

"I guess that was the great Indian fighter's last stand," drily commented one of the gentlemen.

"What a horrible thing to say," argued another. "Custer was a great Indian fighter."

"He was vain and egotistical," inserted Cordell.

"Capable, though," Hiriam insisted, joining the group of men who had gathered around Cordell. Libby stood mute, numbed by such news, although men down through history seemed to find it necessary to kill their brothers. Greed, hatred, and the desire to possess land which did not belong to the white man, Libby surmised, had brought about the slaughter. Secretly she sympathized with the plight of the Indian and understood what it meant to be driven to desperate acts which could only bring far-reaching and devastating repercussions.

Libby was left in the parlor as the disrupted celebration came to an end with the men adjourning into the host's study to pore over maps of the territory in order to pinpoint the site of such a bloody massacre.

"Are you ready to return to the hotel, Matilde?" Cordell set out, returning from an hour's debate over Custer's annihilation and the man's character.

"You know how I am at the party. I intend to stay until the last crumb has been eaten, regardless of all the uproar. But you two run along . . . the Archers have already consented to give me a lift. Kiss, kiss." She blew them a sign of affection and flitted away among the lingering guests.

Cordell turned to Libby. "Don't tell me you aren't ready to leave."

"There is no way I can keep up with your aunt. I'm ready."

In the carriage alone with her, Cordell instructed the

driver to spare the horses, then leaned back against the seat and slipped his arm around her shoulders. She nestled against him in such a natural gesture that Cordell felt himself softening further. Despite his resolve, he was coming to view Katherine in a different light.

The Pinkerton report had classed her as little different than a wealthy slut giving away favors. Cordell hadn't found her to be like that at all. She had been a virgin. Perhaps she'd had a reason, or maybe there were extenuating circumstances which had caused her to become such a loose woman. Perhaps she had changed. For miles Cordell pondered the troubling question of whether one's past should be allowed to destroy the future . . . and whether a person should be judged solely on past deeds.

Cordell was still lost in thought when the carriage lurched sharply, tossing Libby onto his lap.

"Sorry, Mr. Chandler, we've thrown a wheel," the driver announced, sticking his head into the coach to catch sight of the couple.

Embarrassed by Cordell's arms around her, Libby scrambled to right herself, but he held tight. "Guess you'll have to take one of the horses into town and bring back another rig."

"That'll take hours, sir," the man announced, stifling a yawn.

Cordell looked deeply into Libby's eyes illuminated by the full moon. In a voice heavy with hunger brought about by her nearness, he said, "Yes, it will, won't it."

Chapter Forty

Libby watched the dark form of the driver mount a carriage horse and gallop off into the black shadows cast by the brilliant moonlight, his coattails flying behind him. She knew she should have asked Cordell why he didn't get out to assess the damage before sending the driver for help, but something held her back. All around the coach the sounds of night assaulted her ears. Crickets chirped in rhythm with the lonely howl of distant coyotes and the songs of night birds. Even the gentle howl of the wind through the trees murmured a knowing rustle.

Cordell's warmth and hardness pressed through Libby's skirts and caused her to fidget at the sensations that his nearness was causing. She swiveled around to find herself encircled in his strong arms. His moist, warm breath caressed her forehead, raising goosebumps along her spine—and an overpowering need.

"I—I shouldn't be s—sitting on your lap like this," she stammered, uneasy to be pressed so close against him. Touching him was almost more than she could stand, she wanted him so fiercely.

Cordell brushed his soft lips back and forth across her forehead. "No, you shouldn't," he whispered. "It could prove our undoing."

"Our *undoing?*" Libby thought she was going to

dissolve into him, she was becoming so stirred up inside.

"Yes," he breathed. "Undoing this," he unfastened the top two hooks at the back of her gown, "and this," another hook fell away, "and this."

The velvety tone of his voice mesmerized Libby. A long silence followed as Cordell waited for a response. He expected her to respond. His body shifted and Libby found herself left with only her thin chemise to cover her heated nakedness. There was an unbridled intensity emanating from him, issuing a silent order for Libby to yield, to unfurl her own passion and become a willing, active partner in the lovemaking she was certain was about to occur.

She felt dizzying sensations when Cordell ran fiery fingers up her neck to cup her cheeks between his hands. *"Katherine."* The name was like a poem on his lips. If only he were sighing her name. "I want to you to undress me too, now."

"Oh, Cordell, I want you to love me. I do want you to—"

Cordell's lips urgently took possession of Libby's breaking off her pleas. He savored her warm, willing mouth, exploring that dark satiny cavern with his tongue. She smelled of ginger and magnolias, which mingled with the fragrance of pipe tobacco and wine from the celebration.

"Here?" Her eyes widened at the outrageous notion. "Make love inside the carriage? On the seat?"

"Here." He patted the leather seat, breathing, "Right here. Such a forbidden place will only serve to heighten the passion between us."

Nervously, Libby silently agreed; making love in the coach would add excitement.

"Take off my jacket first," he said, silently challenging her.

With wavering fingers Libby slipped the dress coat

from his shoulders. "Now the shirt." Button by button Libby freed the linen fabric until Cordell sat before her, his magnificent chest bare and rippling with tensed muscles. Libby ran sensitive fingers up and through the clumps of ebony hairs, the sensations echoing her need to be filled by him.

Suppressing the inclination to rip away his remaining clothes and take her without further hesitation, Cordell found his voice quiver with the tension vibrating within him. "Now the boots . . . then the pants."

Kneeling before his seated form, Libby stripped off the last of Cordell's clothing. In front of her eyes his stiff maleness sprang free, and she reached out and tentatively stroked the hard shaft. The flesh was soft and heated, and it throbbed against her hand.

Cordell groaned and in one torrid motion scooped Libby up into his arms, ripping away her lacy chemise and dropping it to the floor of the carriage beside the rest of their clothes.

Libby glanced down at the shreds of lace laying at her feet. Her gaze drifted back up the length of Cordell to his eyes. For the longest moment they stared at one another. The two of them fit together well. The scent of newly rubbed leather assailed her. And his words about making love in the coach enlivened her senses. Libby had no doubt in her mind that she wanted him. Her warm body felt like it was ready to explode.

"Here, lie back . . . I'm going to show you what a spell-weaving witch you are." Cordell covered Libby's body with his own and began to suckle at her swelled breasts. His teeth nipped at the coral tips extended into blossoming buds, while his palms rubbed over her, his caresses causing agonizing delight.

"But what if someone happens along?" Libby worried, in between panting breaths.

Cordell looked up briefly and grinned. She seemed to have such an innocent modesty. He brushed an errant

257

curl from her forehead. "You needn't worry that silken head of yours. This road is rarely traveled. More than likely, we'll be alone here for hours."

"Hours?" she repeated weakly.

"Hmm. Hours and hours." Cordell's lips rained kisses across Libby's breasts and moved lower. Sweetly, suggestively his tongue ignited her senses.

She was so aroused that her legs opened of their own volition when his tongue twined through the dark curl of hairs at the top of her thighs.

Her woman's scent caused his yearning to explode and he plunged his tongue into her while he wrapped his arms around her thighs and positioned her closer to his searching mouth.

Libby let out muffled cries as he brought her closer and closer to the brink of ecstasy. When she could no longer tolerate the sweet agony, Libby arched and strained toward him, squirming, tensing, and biting her lip to keep from crying out her need.

"It's all right, my love. Show me how much you want me, how much you need me," Cordell urged.

Libby nodded wordlessly, too lost to what Cordell was doing to speak. She didn't want him to stop. She wanted to experience everything with this man — the physical side of love which joined two souls in the deepest way possible.

Her hands embarked on their own intimate exploration. Then how he had called her his love reverberated in her consciousness. "Did — did you mean what you said?" she forced herself to ask in a breathy voice.

"You know I always mean what I say," he answered and moved over her, pressing her against the smooth leather, to kiss her lips.

"I mean about my being your love," Libby entreated between possessive kisses.

Cordell raised himself up on his elbows. His face reflected a troubled mind. Confusion and indecision replaced the determination which had always been mirrored there.

He gazed into her eyes. "I'm making love to you, aren't I?"

His answer was evasive, but Libby viewed it as another step. She smiled to herself: until recently he would have launched into a tirade had she broached such a subject.

"Yes, you *are* making love to me," Libby acknowledged, accepting what he offered instead of questioning him further.

He didn't reply. His arms surrounded her and ran delectable fingers up and down her back and over her buttocks, cupping them and swiveling her around until he lifted her on top of his masculinity.

"Cordell—" she rasped, but he had no intention of not completing what he'd begun. She was wet and ready for him when he slid himself into her. The tight fit reminded him how she seemed to have been made just for him.

He held fast to her buttocks and began to move within her . . . slowly at first; long, deep strokes; pausing between each powerful movement so Libby could draw him deeper into her. The tips of her fingers trailed erupting streaks of fire where she touched him, causing him to murmur unintelligible words.

His invasion was so mind shattering that Libby felt a thousand surging tingles overcome her and she strove harder and harder, faster and faster to lose herself in him. Again and again he drove into her honeyed heat, relentlessly the friction building and building until a prism of colors blasted out before them and she collapsed on top of him, satiated and deliciously drained.

They were drenched with the hot beads of their exertions and surrounded with the musky odor of their lovemaking. For the longest time they remained joined until Libby shivered as a wave of cold air whistled in through the curtained window of the coach. Cordell reached down and grabbed his dress coat and wrapped it around Libby.

"We'd best get dressed," he advised in a husky voice when he felt her shudder again. "I don't want you taking cold. We will be pulling out for Deer Lodge Valley and the ranch the day after tomorrow, and I want you feeling well enough to ride by my side."

Libby looked into his black eyes, now reflecting gold in the moonlight. Although he hadn't openly spoken words of love, he'd admitted he was making love to her. That admission had given Libby cause to hope that she would gain his love. He wanted her by his side when they left Helena. Could it be because he was coming to care about her? Or was he still intent on keeping an eye on her so he could seek the dissolution of their marriage once he reached his home? Whatever his reasons, she decided she would speed up her efforts to win the man she loved.

Back in the hotel room, next to his slumbering wife, Cordell lay on the bed, his arms crossed behind his head. He was unable to sleep. He'd decided to take Katherine to the ranch with him. Somehow it made sense to get her on his own turf. Maybe there, where he was in total control, he would be able to convince her to sign the divorce papers; heaven knew, nothing else he'd done so far had worked. Even with this latest decision, which was sure to prove successful, Cordell did not find comfort.

He'd lied to Katherine when she'd asked why he'd taken Lynette along with them to the centennial celebration. He'd planned to flaunt Lynette Devaux to demonstrate to his wife that he intended to obtain a divorce one way or another. But when he'd seen Lynette for what she was, a vicious she-cat who would delight in

260

humiliating his wife, he could not stand to see anyone cause Katherine any discomfort.

He reviewed the evening. Katherine had charmed all the guests—both men and women. She had even won stodgy old Hiriam Bayless to her side. And she had demonstrated compassion and much insight when news of Custer had been delivered.

He lit the lamp by the desk and turned the shade so as not awaken Katherine. He settled himself at the desk near the window. There on the corner, hidden beneath a stack of his business papers, was the Pinkerton envelope. Cordell ran his fingers through his mussed hair and shuffled through the wrinkled sheets over and over again, rereading it as he had been the last few days, wanting, hoping to discover something he'd missed before; hoping beyond prayer that some kind of explanation for Katherine's behavior was contained within those pages.

He pounded his fist on the table, sending the report flying. "Nothing, damn it!"

Realizing his outburst might have awakened Katherine, he got up and checked on her. She had to be exhausted; she did not stir. He gazed at her for a moment. She was even more beautiful in the muted lamplight.

Still feeling restless, he paced the room. He didn't want to admit it to himself, but he was becoming much too fond of his little wife. If he didn't do something fast to rid himself of the black-haired beauty, he would be lost; he would find himself irretrievably in love with her. . . .

Chapter Forty-one

The morning sunshine streamed into the dining room through glass-paned French doors and spacious windows. Cordell was sitting at a corner table, intently staring into his cup of coffee, when Libby joined him.

"Good morning," she offered with a smile.

"Yes, I suppose it is," he said absently. Then, as if he had just actually realized who it was, he shot to his feet and pulled out a chair. "Join me."

"Thank you for letting me sleep late. I must have been more tired than I realized. I'm famished after last night, aren't you?" Libby asked before she realized the implication of her question. A blush colored her cheeks and she dropped her eyes.

"Last night's activities certainly could build a healthy appetite," he said, settling back across from her.

"I meant—"

Cordell held up a palm. "I know what you meant."

Libby gazed into those incredible black eyes. He was mocking her, the insufferable man! Last night they'd shared something special; they'd made love. Not simply in the physical sense . . . she was certain of it. No . . . they'd come together with more than their bodies. They'd come together with more than raw lust; their hearts had come together as well.

"No . . . I'm not sure you do." A hint of emotion

seeped into her voice. "But you will," she added with conviction. Immediately she brightened. "Well, now, have you ordered yet?"

Once breakfast was over, Cordell had the answer to the dilemma which had been troubling him all night. He was going through with his plan to gain a divorce, despite the nagging feeling to the contrary. Seeing Katherine's expression tighten when flaxen-haired Caroline Arthur stopped by to renew their acquaintance, Cordell almost decided not to proceed to separate himself from the one woman who was beginning to haunt his conscious thoughts.

Cordell rose. "If you'll excuse me?"

"But I thought we'd spend the day together. You've been saying I should see all of Helena, and since this is our last day here, I thought—"

"Perhaps Matilde will take you on a tour. I have urgent business to finish up before we leave tomorrow morning. Be sure to dress for dinner; we're entertaining important guests."

Libby watched Cordell saunter directly toward that topaz-eyed Caroline Arthur's table. So *she* was his urgent business! The muscles in his powerful thighs rose and fell beneath the tight trousers as he moved, and Libby had to swallow back the feeling of warmth churning in her stomach.

The woman must have left Fort Benton immediately after they did. Was she following Cordell? He *had* nearly married her once, Libby thought, troubled. Caroline had tried to trick him into marrying her, only she hadn't been successful because he had found out in time she wasn't carrying his child. Libby chewed her thumb, a nervous habit she'd overcome since fleeing the reverend's house. Would Cordell be sorry he hadn't wed Caroline Arthur when he discovered her own deception?

"My, my, but you're so busy watching that dear nephew of mine that you completely missed my grand

263

entrance," Matilde announced with her usual effervescence, standing over Libby in a fine gray morning dress which complimented her white hair. She threw out her arms. "Shall I go out and do it again? I relish making a stir, don't you know."

Libby's attention snapped back to the dear old lady who stood at the table nibbling on a muffin she had snatched from the basket in front of Libby. "Oh, Aunt Matilde, I'm sorry . . . what did you say?"

"Nothing of any great importance, dear." Matilde noticed Caroline spring from her seat and hug Cordell before he pulled a chair close to the beauty and joined her.

"That's the soon-to-be *Mrs.* Robert Kirkland. He's a prominent member of the legislature. I wouldn't concern yourself about her if I were you, dear. She and Cordell—"

"I'm not concerned, and I know about her and Cordell," Libby shot back much too quickly.

Matilde watched the young woman's reactions. She wished Libby would tell Cordell the truth before things got out of hand. But she'd promised not to interfere. Whatever prompted her to make such an absurd declaration? She shrugged off the contradictory thoughts. If events precipitated a change of heart, she'd simply overrule her previous decision. Matilde's mind made up, she reached for the butter. "Well, good. Then let's have a big breakfast, and we'll spend the day overindulging ourselves at Cordell's expense."

The exquisite golden satin ball gown Libby had chosen for the evening fit her as if it had been made for her, not purchased off the rack at Lynette Devaux's shop. Considering the Devaux woman's feelings, Libby felt fortunate that Lynette hadn't done something to this gown, too, besides having it delivered too late to wear to the centennial celebration after she'd sabotaged the other gown.

Ruffles studded with glitter draped seductively low across her breasts and shoulders. The bodice was nipped in, showing off her tiny waist. The skirt billowed out in row upon row of scalloped ruffles banded with ribbons. Low-heeled pumps with rosettes on the toes peeked out from her hem. A halo of tiny yellow flowers worn as a garland secured ebony curls cascading over her milky shoulders.

Cordell returned to their room as she was putting the finishing touches to her ears with shimmering diamonds. He had dressed in the latest evening wear and gone out earlier to check on the seating arrangements. "Are you ready to go . . . to dinner? My God, you look stunning!" he exclaimed, his eyes admiring the golden goddess before him.

"Thank you." Libby smiled to herself. She'd made the desired impression on him. "I wanted to look my best." *Although I'm surprised you noticed, the way you were carrying on this morning with that Arthur woman,* she longed to say.

"And you do." He offered his arm. "Are you ready to go down to the dining room?"

Arm in arm they strolled down the hall and into the graciously decorated room. Finely dressed couples turned to admire the striking couple, and whispered about the wealthy rancher and his beautiful wife.

They approached a long table set with elegant silver and stemware. Sparkling china and enormous bouquets of fresh-cut flowers adorned the table. Matilde was busily engaged in conversation with two distinguished elderly gentlemen. Middle-aged matrons sipped champagne, and young ladies hung on every word of their escorts' conversations. Libby was pleased to be a part of such a wide assortment of patrons until her gaze settled on Caroline Arthur, an angelic vision in frothy white.

"Why don't you join Matilde, dear? I won't be long,"
Cordell announced abruptly and left Libby to go to
that Arthur woman and slip an arm around her.

When the pair strolled out onto the dance floor and
began to waltz among the other guests, Libby fumed.
How could he devote so much time to that woman
after the way they'd made love last night?

Libby spent an hour trying to ignore Cordell's behavior. But he was paying such close court to the Arthur
woman: holding her too tight while dancing, escorting
her among the guests, sharing a glass of champagne,
never once leaving her side.

"Does it bother you, my dear?" asked a powerfully
built, impeccably dressed gray-haired man holding a
pipe inches from his lips. He joined Libby, who was
standing alone.

Libby's attention whirled toward the stranger. "Bother
me?"

"Caroline and Chandler."

"No . . . no, of course not," she fabricated, a blush
rising to her face. "Sir?"

"Robert Kirkland. Caroline became my intended right
after you wed Chandler."

"Weren't you both at our wedding in Fort Benton?"
At his nod, Libby continued. "You and Caroline must
have been in a terrible rush to reach Helena this soon
after being in Fort Benton at the same time as Cordell
and me. Do you have business here?" she probed,
having to know why Caroline had shown up so soon,
the way she did.

"I am a member of the legislature. So it is important
that I be in town at this time. As for Caroline . . .
well, she has her own reasons for doing things."

"I see."

"I'm afraid you're rather transparent, Mrs. Chandler,"
he keenly observed.

266

"Mr. Kirkland, if I show concern about my husband and your fiancée, it is merely because I am still a bride and have yet to accept fully the ways of politics out here in the west."

"Well said, fine lady. But if your husband is being a little too attentive to my Caroline, it is to gain some type of response from you and no one else. You see, Caroline and Dell have been friends for many years . . . were engaged once. But even if Caroline still holds out any hope of landing Chandler," he said candidly, "I doubt if he's interested.

"Caroline is no fool. She's not going to let a man of my wealth slide through her greedy little fingers. No doubt that's why she badgered me immediately after our wedding to take the first stage for Helena. Besides," he shrugged, "I love her despite her faults, and I will take care of her. So you see, that makes us the perfect match."

The knowledge slammed into Libby and she had to support herself against a nearby chair to keep from losing her legs. The man knew of Caroline's intentions and chose to stand idly by. Then a sadness for Robert Kirkland engulfed her. Love was meant to be shared, returned. And to go through life loving and not being treasured and valued would leave an emptiness unfillable by other pursuits designed to serve as a substitute. Her heart went out to him.

"Can I get you something?" Concern filled his voice.

Libby recovered herself and laid an understanding hand on his arm before she politely said, "No. If you'll excuse me, I do think I need to powder my nose."

"Would you like me to find someone to accompany you? You look a bit pale."

"You're very kind, Mr. Kirkland. But actually, I'm fine."

"Of course."

Libby cast a long glance at Cordell and Caroline

Arthur, then swept from the room with such grace that men stopped their conversations and stared.

But it wasn't only the men who watched Cordell's wife. Caroline's eyes, too, followed her with sharpened interest.

The instant Cordell's attention was drawn from his wife back to Montana's politics, Caroline excused herself and strolled in the same direction she had seen that snip of a girl go.

Libby was sitting quietly, gazing into the mirror and trying to assimilate everything that had happened to her the last few months, when Caroline boldly joined her.

Caroline smirked. "You look like someone who's just come to realize she's made a big mistake. Perhaps I can help. I know what it's like to be in love with a man who doesn't return that love."

"Cordell," Libby said in no more than a troubled whisper.

Caroline smiled to herself. It had been so simple to plant the seed of doubt in the girl's mind. All she had to do now would be to carefully play on the little snip's weaknesses. Caroline glanced in the mirror and fussed with her pale curls. "I know this may be difficult for you, but maybe I can help. Cordell and I were engaged once. And I'm undoubtedly closer to Dell than any woman ever has been—or ever will be." She smiled benignly, studying the girl from beneath lengthy blonde lashes.

Libby felt herself tense, but was determined not to expose the inner agony she was experiencing, although she was fully aware of the circumstances surrounding Cordell's proposal to Caroline Arthur. "If you're closer to my husband than any woman has been or will be, why is it that he did not marry you?"

Caroline was momentarily caught off guard, but just as quickly recovered. "My dear, it's not because he didn't ask."

"Oh? How enlightening. It does seem a bit odd, though."

"*What* does?" Caroline shot back before she realized she was about to be outdone.

"Seeing the way you look at him, it would seem you would have readily accepted such a proposal," Libby returned, not about to allow victory to such an obvious predator.

Caroline's lips tightened. Her ploy to prey on the girl's assumed insecurities wasn't working. She'd have to implement another tack.

Matilde, who had witnessed Libby's retreat followed by Caroline a few minutes later, had stuck her head in the door in time to overhear Libby's slapping retort. Matilde had intended to intercede if necessary, but Libby was proving to be a spunky little thing, perfectly capable of holding her own. A satisfied smile on her face, Matilde returned to her seat at the dining table. There was more substance and grit to Dell's little wife than she'd originally thought . . . just what Dell needed. Feeling totally self-satisfied, Matilde scooped up a spoonful of gooey chocolate dessert and slid the confection into her mouth, savoring the sweet, rich taste and creamy texture.

While Matilde stalled Cordell's efforts to put a stop to what he had started, the battle of wits between Libby and Caroline continued.

Caroline gave a wicked smile. "My poor dear, everybody in the territory knows that Dell has worshiped at my feet for years. I shouldn't tell you, but," she shrugged indifferently, "since no one would believe you anyway, you see, Dell and I came up with this little plan for me to marry Robert Kirkland so Dell can acquire the man's land. Unfortunately, Robert has been most uncooperative about selling. So after I'm Robert's wife, Dell and I can still be together, and between the two of us Robert's land will simply fall into Dell's hands."

"Then why did he marry me?" Libby demanded, visibly shaken.

"Silly goose. To provide a cover so no one would suspect."

The way Cordell had been paying court to the pale beauty gave her story credence, and Libby's new self-assurance began to pale. With as much dignity as was left over, Libby stood and said proudly, "It was a nice try, *Miss* Arthur. Oh, I believe that you still desire my husband, but I'm afraid I find your tale ill-conceived and farfetched. More along the lines of a story that would come from a jilted lover."

With Caroline's mouth agape, Libby made a grand exit, leaving the Arthur girl speechless. But once Libby was back in the dining room and caught sight of Cordell staring after her, her chest began to heave and her heart raced. When Cordell excused himself and took a step toward her, Libby fled through the French doors. She did not want to face him now . . . not yet. Her mind was whirring with the events of the last few months, and after her less-than-pleasant conversation with Caroline Arthur, Libby had a decision to make. . . .

Chapter Forty-two

Outside in the brightly shimmering moonlight, Libby walked quickly to the edge of the gardens and paced back and forth for what seemed the longest time before crumpling onto a stone bench set beneath a group of majestic pines. What kind of response could Cordell be hoping to gain from her by sending Caroline Arthur to say those awful things? Did he expect her to concede defeat? Was she supposed to perish after her confrontation with that winsome blonde predator? What Robert Kirkland had said also caused a rude awakening. Although she and Cordell had made love with tenderness and what had seemed genuine affection, he was parading the beautiful Caroline Arthur in front of her so she would seek a quiet annulment.

Caroline Arthur . . . she hadn't seemed to be such a cloying schemer when Libby had seen her at the wedding. And then she remembered how the Arthur girl had tried to trap Cordell into marriage and had nearly succeeded with those paternity claims of hers. But how could he seek Caroline's aid now? Or had he? Troubled thoughts surrounded her, threatening with their awesome consequences.

She took a handkerchief from her reticule and blew her nose. If she continued to refuse to leave quietly, would their lives be a combination of incredible sensual pleasure and heartbreaking pain? Would she forever live in fear, forced to accept his indiscretions at will? No . . . she could not exist that way, despite her love for the man. She had come to have too much respect for herself to allow herself to lose that hard-won esteem.

Libby sat out underneath the tall pines, mulling over her life, until a chill overtook her. Her teeth had begun to chatter, and she rubbed her arms to chase away the goosebumps. She couldn't remain out here any longer; the night was growing too cold. She stood and smoothed her skirt, her mind made up. She had undergone an intense inner struggle, but finally settled on what she would do. The time for games was over. . . .

Cordell's brows drew together when he noticed the haughty way Caroline calmly strolled into the room right after his wife had made a rather hasty exit. He had a gut feeling Caroline had thoroughly delighted in contributing to the look of anguish he had noticed on Katherine's face. Anger gnawing at him and a new protectiveness springing forth, Cordell was in the process of following after Katherine when Caroline interceded.

"Well, darling, did you miss me?" Caroline cooed, taking Cordell's wrist and drawing the drink he held to her lips. As she took a sip, her eyes never once left his face. Although he seemed distracted and she didn't like the way his attention was riveted to the French doors, she was confident she could win him back. Then she wouldn't be forced to marry that dreary, stuffy old Robert Kirkland for his money. After all, she was sturdy pioneer stock — like Cordell Chandler. They belonged together and he would come to realize that, she was sure of it.

"Why would Dell miss you when he has that simply devastatingly beautiful young bride?" put forth one of the finely clad men in the group with whom Cordell had been speaking.

"Not to mention our important discussion about the upcoming session of the legislature and the heated debates likely to ensue."

"Or Custer's massacre."

Caroline frowned at each of the men in turn. She was furious that anyone could conceivably compare that little snip of a wife favorably to herself. More favorably, no less! Although a coy expression came over her features, underneath she wanted to personally slap each one of their smug, craggy faces.

"Maybe you gentleman haven't noticed who Dell has chosen to spend his time with this evening," she rejoined, her pale eyes glittering.

"And maybe you have forgotten who your fiancé is," Robert Kirkland said to Caroline, puffing on his pipe as he joined the cluster. He turned to Cordell. "That's a mighty fine wife you have, Chandler. Had the pleasure of speaking with her earlier. A real jewel, that one."

Cordell had been silently listening to the various conversations since Caroline had joined them. He was not a man to make rash comments. He had learned the hard way to think through what he was going to say; it had paid off.

Cordell removed Caroline's clinging hand. A bland look on his face, he said, ignoring Kirkland's obvious captivation with his wife, "Kirkland, it's good to see you. Been hearing a lot of good things about your record in the legislature."

Disregarding the pouting Caroline, Robert Kirkland extended his arm to Cordell. "And I've been hearing that you have a growing number of supporters who want to draft you for a seat in government. You'd be a mighty fine ally to have when the Indian vote comes up again. Particularly since this messy business with Custer at Little Big Horn."

Caroline stiffened, crossed her arms over her chest, and tapped her satin-encased toes as the men became

273

engrossed in a heated debate over what should be done with those wild, rampaging Indians. It irritated Caroline no end that Cordell should be taking such an interest in protecting a bunch of worthless savages when, as far as she was concerned, everyone knew the territory, as well as the country, would be better off if the red menace were entirely annihilated.

"Robert, honey," Caroline rubbed her hand seductively against his arm, ignoring the pungent smell of pipe tobacco, which irritated her even further, "do you have to talk business now? It's such a lovely party. Shouldn't we be enjoying it? After all, I did my part to help Dell earlier. Now I want to have some fun."

Awkwardness veiled the group, and one by one the men excused themselves and drifted toward other guests engaged in less upsetting conversations.

Once only three of them remained, Kirkland looked pointedly at Caroline, although his comment was meant for Cordell. "I never thought Chandler needed help with the female population." Then he turned to Cordell, his sage eyes probing Cordell's. "Just what was it that Caroline was helping you with?" he inquired bluntly.

"She offered to enlighten my wife as to the unpredictable nature and responsibilities of being part of a busy ranch," he said, casting aside Kirkland's question with his usual ease.

Kirkland looked unconvinced, but during his tenure in the legislature he had learned when to pursue and when to accept issues at face value. "Well, I'm sure Caroline could offer expert advice about life on a ranch. I do hope you also gave her some pointers on what to expect when Chandler here joins me in government." He slipped a possessive arm around Caroline. "This little lady knows how to charm the most ardent dissenter and sway a man to any cause that suits her."

"Yes, she's always known how to twist things to her advantage." Cordell was getting bored with the conversation and wished he had never involved Caroline. Having another woman explain the rigors of frontier life had seemed like a good idea at the time, a way to convince Katherine to return to St. Louis. But it had been a tactical error . . . he was sure of it now.

He'd known Caroline still had her bonnet set for him. Then it hit him; Caroline had undoubtedly said more to Katherine than she'd asked. And for the second time tonight he found the thought did not at all please him. He shot Caroline an assessing look. She'd make Kirkland a fine wife, since the man knew of her past and how to handle her moods.

Red blotches heightened Caroline's color. After what she had done for Dell, that was the thanks she got. She was tired of playing the innocent little pioneer daughter. It had always served her purpose, though. "But Dell, darling, you're going to give Robert here the wrong impression. You know I was only trying to help an old friend out of a bad marriage."

Cordell remained impassive, yet inside he would have liked to strangle Caroline for her catty comment, the overzealous schemer. It wasn't uncommon for friends to help each other out when it was called for out here in the west. But Caroline had made sure with her implication that she had been involved in something less than honorable with his wife. Yet with only the most honorable of intentions, so she said. And the worse part about it was that what she'd said was partly true, he had suggested Caroline talk to Katherine.

Cordell cocked a brow and shrugged. There was no longer the slightest doubt, he had made a bad strategic error asking for her assistance. He would have to face the problem of Caroline and put an end to her conniving machinations once and for all.

He had wanted Katherine to agree to the annulment. But when he saw the lengths that Caroline had gone to bring such a devastated look to Katherine's face, he knew he'd made a mistake. And that he should care bothered him no end.

"I'm afraid in your overexuberance to help out a onetime friend, you mistook my intent—"

"I did not!" she blasted back, losing control and not caring who overheard her. "And what do you mean, *onetime friend?*"

Faces turned, their attention drawn to the sweet scent of scandal. Cordell's opponents on the Indian question in particular moved closer, eager to enjoy what they deemed would deflate the momentum the man was garnering among voters.

"I think you know," Cordell answered in a calming voice, not desiring to cause Robert Kirkland undue embarrassment.

"Maybe Caroline does, but I do not. If you'd be good enough to enlighten me," Kirkland demanded, his pride on the block, his fists clenched.

Not wishing a confrontation with a man years his senior, as well as one who'd become a recent ally, Cordell took a step backward, a sympathetic expression to his lips. "Kirkland, the subject isn't worth arguing over. Caroline and I grew up together and some thought we would wed someday. They were mistaken. Caroline is about to become your wife. I'm sure she'll do everything in her power to make you happy. And as everyone knows, I already have a wife."

Caroline drew in a breath, displaying shock. "No! I thought—"

"Caroline," Cordell murmured, "everyone knows we were once close. But that has been over for a long time, and you have Robert now."

Suddenly a hard, cold realization struck her: Cordell Chandler would never be hers. Her previously assured expression collapsed. For better or worse, her future lay with Robert Kirkland. She raised her chin. "Yes, and I'm most fortunate I do." She swung adoring eyes to Kirkland.

Listening nearby, Matilde ordered additional cream

276

for her coffee and sat stirring it. She had been tempted to follow after Libby and then somehow restrained herself. Cordell Chandler could take care of himself, of that there was no doubt.

Of course, she'd been prepared to leave her seat had Cordell not handled Caroline with his usual panache. Her heart gladdened that the boy was in the process of extricating himself from the pair without bloodshed and with everyone's pride intact. A few years ago she'd have been tending bruises. She smiled to herself at how Cordell had matured into a true statesman, as well as one of the best damned ranchers in the territory.

She lifted her cup in silent toast to Cordell, gave the glaring Caroline a knowing grin, and sipped at the hot liquid confident that things were coming along nicely.

Kirkland looked aggrieved. "You best make up your mind, Caroline. I've been very patient with you. But there is a limit, you know."

"Robert, you're the only one I love," she crooned, cementing her future with the elder man. "But you've never understood my relationship with Dell. Has he. Dell?" She added, seething that everything was turning out all wrong; she could be in danger of losing both men.

"Caroline, we don't have a relationship any longer. Now if you'll excuse me, I have a wife to look after." Cordell bowed curtly and left the pair staring after him.

Strangely, his words about his wife conjured up a quiet pleasure deep within him. The vision of his wife on the trail, fighting to prove to him that they did indeed belong together, clarified before him, sinking hooks into his being, propelling him forward with steps weighted from a decision suddenly made. Yes. He had reached a decision. . . .

Chapter Forty-three

"What are you doing alone out here?" came the familiar voice. Cordell parted the branches and stepped into the clearing, silvered in the shadowy moonlight.

"I had a decision to make," Libby said stiffly.

His brow shifted into a questioning angle. "A decision?"

"Yes," she swallowed the spoonful of hurt threatening her determination, "about our marriage."

He studied the shifting shadows that played across her face. It was a beautiful face . . . a small upturned nose, big blue eyes, thick lashes, and full, sensuous mouth drawn into a serious line . . . intuitively he knew his ploy tonight had backfired. It had been too successful. He'd convinced her that he had no intention of ever being faithful, and if she insisted on staying with him, he would never let her feel secure or loved, the way a wife should.

He should have been happy that he'd finally prevailed over the conniving one. But he wasn't so certain she was conniving any longer. Even if she was, he'd made a decision. Now, seeing how much he'd hurt her with Caroline, as well as with Lynette the night before, he felt the guilt washed over him like acid. And he came to realize that he had not made a sudden decision, but that for some time his feelings had been changing.

"Don't you think I should be included in all decisions affecting our marriage?" he demanded, suddenly perturbed that she could make a determination without consulting him.

Libby's mouth quivered and she pressed a finger against her lips to still them. "You have made it perfectly clear where you stand on the question of our marriage," Libby shot back.

The rustle of bushes and crunch of dried leaves caught their attention.

"I thought I would find you two out here," effused Matilde, swatting at a tree limb which had caught her fancy chapeau. "You are missing such a delightful party inside. But then again, no one could blame you, Dell, for wanting to get your lovely bride alone. Don't dally too long or people will being to talk. You—"

"I don't give a hooter's damn what people say. What are you doing out here?" he asked. Matilde was so used to interfering, he'd seldom felt the inclination to stop her. But he was no longer in the mood to be so indulgent.

"Cordell, Matilde is your aunt." Libby defended the dear soul. "She cares about you."

Matilde waved Libby off. "Don't let Dell upset you. He certainly doesn't rattle me. I've taken care of his ornery hide long enough to let his stubborn streak get the better of me. . . ." She continued to chatter, hoping she'd disarmed the volatile situation. They were the two people she loved most in this world. Yes . . . she loved Cordell's bride too. Although she hadn't known the girl long, she instinctively knew Libby was the right one for her favorite relative. "And you'd best be forewarned, child, that he can be too obstinate for his own good sometimes. But what I recommend is—"

"Aunt Matilde, that's enough!" Cordell shouted. "No doubt you had the best intentions coming out here, but if you'd be so kind," he took her by the shoulders, turned her around, and headed her back in the direction from which she'd come, "I need some time *alone* with my wife. *Now.*"

The tone of his voice brooked no dissent, and the way Dell had said "his wife" was encouraging. In a meekness that was rare, Matilde chirped, "As long as everything is under control here, I suppose I'm not needed."

"No. You're not. Go back inside and play hostess until we return."

Matilde looked back over her shoulder at Libby standing quietly behind Cordell. Oh, how she prayed they'd work out their problems—they just had to! "Well, if you're sure I can't provide moral support or something."

"We're sure," Cordell answered for them both before Libby could respond.

"All right. But don't be long," she advised and reluctantly left the feuding pair alone.

Cordell watched his aunt's departure. He waited until he was sure the whimsical woman made another of her grand entrances inside the French doors.

Libby also watched Matilde's retreat. The old dear meant well. There are some things in life, though, that one has to handle for oneself. Matilde could not salvage Libby's marriage to Cordell. A marriage could work only if both husband and wife were willing. When Cordell turned toward her, the indulgent expression on his face became one of extreme perturbation.

"We need to talk," he said quietly and motioned for her to sit back down on the bench.

"I think we've spent more than enough time talking. You've made it plain from the beginning that you want me out of your life. But what I don't understand is, if you didn't feel anything at all for me, why did you go to so much trouble to protect me from that gambler and his accomplice? And why did you make love to me

280

the way you did if you're . . . you're still interested in . . . in Caroline Arthur?"

Cordell could feel the pain radiating from her despite the proud tilt to her chin, and at that moment he wanted nothing more than to gather her into his arms and hold her. Honesty had always been his most loyal confederate; he'd forgotten that of late. Now was the time to realign his life, bring back his original plan of taking a wife to be a partner and raise a family with. And despite Katherine's past, he now knew she was the one with whom he wanted to do exactly that.

"I protected you because you are my wife," he answered without pretense. "And about Caroline Arthur, I made a mistake. I'm not interested in her. Haven't been for a long time now. We were close once. Engaged, as a matter of fact. I'd have married her if I hadn't found out she'd lied to me about carrying my child." Cordell watched for a shocked reaction and was pleased when she remained unshaken by his confession.

Libby recalled the discussion she'd had earlier with Matilde about Caroline, and without comment allowed Cordell to continue.

"Turned out the baby was some drifter's, but she lost it. Speculation was that it was a self-induced abortion. Caroline always lands on her feet, though. Most folks out here are quick to forgive, seeing how so many of them have rather checkered pasts of their own."

What Cordell had just said about people forgiving gave Libby the smallest flicker of hope. Would it be possible that he could forgive her someday? "What about tonight?" she blurted out, having to hear the sordid truth whether it dealt a final blow to their marriage or not.

"Tonight was a mistake."

"A mistake? What kind of mistake?"

"Can't we just leave it at that?" he said, not wanting to hurt her further. preferring omission to admission.

281

Libby studied the handsome man standing over her. He was probably the most rugged man she had ever seen. There was nothing effeminate about Cordell Chandler. He was the epitome of masculinity. Tall, broad-shouldered, with muscles which bulged through the fabric of his finely tailored trousers . . . hair the color of a moonless midnight . . . eyes which could seduce a nun . . . a personality that every mother prayed to God would shine on her daughter and bestow the glory and magic of the Chandler name. He was a man who had experienced enough life to know what he wanted and to appreciate it when he found it. And Libby couldn't let it rest; she had to hear a full explanation, whether it left her devastated or not.

"No, we can't. Caroline Arthur said some things inside that I can't ignore."

"What did she say to you?"

"She told me that you didn't love me and that the two of you intended to wait until she had married Robert Kirkland and then she'd see to it that you got some land of his that you've been wanting." Libby poured out the story, leaving nothing out, in spite of the wad of dread threatening to close her throat.

As Cordell listened his fists flexed and he had to beat down the urge to go back inside and squeeze that delicate white throat of Caroline's. He'd never meant for her to spin such a tale. Caroline had taken it upon herself to embellish her finely woven tapestry of lies.

When he didn't respond right away, Libby urged, "Is it true? Did you seek out her help so I'd agree to the annulment?"

Cordell combed his long, slender fingers through his hair. "Oh, God, Katherine."

Libby's brows drew together in sober realization. "You were responsible. It was your idea for Caroline Arthur to say those awful things to me."

Without waiting for his reply, for fear a heart-rending

282

sob would escape her constricting throat, Libby whirled around and started back down the winding path, intending to retain even a small measure of her shrinking pride. Wounded as she was, she still was unable to say the words which would terminate her dream of a life with Cordell.

In two strides Cordell caught her arm and swung her back around to face him. "Damn it, Katherine, I've tried hard enough to rid myself of you. I admit to asking Caroline Arthur to talk to you about the tough life on a ranch, in an attempt to get you to agree to a quiet divorce. But I swear, I never told her to say those awful things. That was strictly her idea. And after I saw you leave, I made sure Caroline understood that she has no place in my life any longer.

"Damn it to hell," he grabbed her arms, "I've tried to tell myself that you mean nothing to me; that you are no more than a wealthy, loose woman looking for some unsuspecting backwoodsman to marry and give you respectability. But these past weeks I've watched you around the men on the trail and with my friends and associates here in Helena. You've carried your weight and never complained. You've captivated everyone you've come in contact with . . . and, so help me God, that includes me," he confessed. "I may come to regret it. But I love you, Katherine," he rasped, openly.

The tears stung her eyes. He loved her. *He loved her!* Cordell Chandler, the most sought-after rancher in the Territory of Montana, loved her—Elizabeth Marie Hollis. Then the name Katherine hit her full force. Cordell was pledging his love to her, but he thought her another woman—a woman of loose morals. He still loved her. He was willing to set the past aside. Only a strong man, a man truly secure within himself and his position, would make such an admission. If they were going to have a new beginning, a real marriage with a strong foundation, she had to be honest with him too. Libby

283

took a deep breath and searched his face. Despite the outcome, she could no longer continue with the masquerade. She had to tell him the truth.

"Cordell?"

His hands went around her back and he pressed her into him, watching the play of moonglow across her face. "What, my darling?" he whispered.

"If . . . if we are going to start fresh and build a real life together, I have to be honest with you—"

"There's no need, I know about your past. Let's just put it behind us and start from now and go forward. I love you and that's all that matters."

"No," she said simply, scrambling out of his embrace to face him squarely. "You don't know. I'm not who you think I am."

He had read the Pinkerton report. There was nothing she could say that he didn't already know. Complaisantly he crossed his arms over his chest and said in an obliging voice, "Then who are you?"

Libby gulped down the overwhelming urge to take flight. She had gone this far. There could be no turning back now. "I'm an impostor. I am not Katherine Rutcliff."

Chapter Forty-four

For a heart-stopping moment Cordell just stood there staring, an unreadable expression on his face. It was too dark for Libby to read his eyes. "You are telling me you lied to me about who you are?"

Libby took a recovering breath. "No. Not exactly. If you'll remember, it was Captain Massie and you who assumed that I was Katherine Rutcliff when we met."

"And where did the man get such an idea?" he asked darkly.

Libby lowered her head, feeling overwhelmed. It was like a snowball rolling downhill, gaining momentum until it couldn't be stopped. Her moment of truth was here. She fought to retain her resilience. "Why don't we discuss this later when you've had time to absorb the idea?"

She tried to pull away from him, but in the blink of an eye Cordell swept her up and strode down the path back toward the hotel.

"What are you doing? Where are you taking me? I demand to know!" She struggled to free herself.

"It's a little late for you to be demanding anything!" he snarled and kept walking.

Cordell stomped past the amused and horrified guests in the lobby, with Libby flailing her arms and legs to no avail.

"Sir, may I be of assistance?" a scandalized bellman rushed forward to ask.

"I'd say for the first time since I've seen them together they're doing fine," Matilde interceded, holding up her bejeweled lorgnette, and peering through it at the pair. "Just stay out of their way. That will be all the help they need." Then she threw back her ostrich-plumed head and gave a hearty laugh.

"Put me down!" Libby demanded. "How will this look for a man of your standing in the community?"

"I don't give a damn how it looks!" Up the stairs he stormed, his face darkening, his eyes a thundering black.

Gulch, all duded out in jacket and string tie, was escorting a saucy-looking buxom woman in scarlet satin from his room when his eyes settled on the sight coming toward them. "Lord, what's up, boss?" he shouted. Then his eyes shifted unsteadily to Libby. He nodded toward her in awed respect. "Ma'am."

"Here," Cordell managed to get the key from his pocket and flung it to Gulch, "Open the door to my room."

"But —" Gulch hesitated, his eyes moving between the two faces. One was angry, the other merely bewildered.

"Just do it!"

"Right up." Gulch scratched his head, but immediately left his confused lady friend to carry out Cordell's instructions. "Will there be anything else, boss?"

"Hang the *Do Not Disturb* sign on the door, then get out!"

"No! No! Don't go," Libby implored. But Gulch only cast her a glance of silent sympathy, bobbed his head in deference to Cordell, and backed awkwardly out of the room. He hadn't seen the boss so angry in a coon's life, and he was just glad it wasn't he who incurred the man's wrath. He liked Dell's missus and quietly hoped that the pair would resolve whatever had stood between

286

them.

Once they were alone, Cordell dumped Libby on the bed without ceremony. When she tried to scramble to a far corner, he pounced on her and pinned her arms over her head.

"Let me go!" she snarled, squirming wildly to extricate herself from his grasp. He held tight, the heat from his hands sending tingling sensations through her.

"Are you sure that's what you want? Or perhaps you want something else?" he asked cruelly, not certain what he wanted to do with her after hearing such a shattering confession. On one hand, he was almost relieved that she wasn't Katherine Rutcliff and on the other, he felt driven mad by such an explosive piece of information.

"No!" she shrieked, scared by the sudden change in the usually even-tempered man.

His face was no more than a breath away, his eyes boring onto hers. "Then you had better start talking, and this had best be good!"

"I'm not Katherine Rutcliff—"

"So you've said. Just who the hell are you?" he petitioned, barely able to contain his spiking anger.

"My name is Elizabeth Marie Hollis," Libby managed, surprised she was able to find her voice.

He was glaring at her. "You mean Elizabeth Marie Hollis *Chandler*, don't you?"

"That wasn't my idea, if you'll remember. You were the one who came up with the plan to get married."

"To Katherine Rutcliff. And we were not actually to go through with it," he added with a snarl.

"Yes, to your precious Katherine Rutcliff, who forced me into this charade in the first place." She glared back at him for a moment, then amended, "No. That's not entirely true. I was desperate, so I let Katherine and that friend of hers force me into masquerading as her."

She had piqued his interest now. The situation was

obviously more complicated than he had thought at first, and one way or another, he was going to get to the bottom of it! It had taken some deep soul-searching to decide finally to accept Katherine as his wife, knowing about her past and all. And now he'd just learned he had not married Katherine after all. It was beginning to make sense: his trouble believing the Pinkerton report; the girl's innocent act that had indeed been real; her awkwardness when they'd made love. Even that scene at the paddlewheeler. It hit him with a cold, sobering force, causing him to sit up and give the girl a chance to collect herself.

Libby rubbed her wrists, which ached from his grip. She was frantic to escape. He must hate her now. Now she'd never be able to make him love *her* before she told him the truth. Now he'd never forgive her for tricking him.

"I think you better leave," she said quietly, her voice shaking.

"Leave? Leave!" He threw up his hands. "You expect me to *leave* after dropping that little bit of dynamite on me?" He flung himself off the bed and paced back and forth across the thick, patterned rug, his hands clasped behind him. After the third pass he stopped directly in front of her, his hands on his hips, nose to nose, and said with deadly calm, "First of all, this is my room, if you've forgotten. I'm certainly not going to be kicked out of my own quarters. And second of all, no one, I repeat, *no one* is going anywhere until you explain everything to my satisfaction, at which time I will decide what is going to be done. Do I make myself clear, *Elizabeth?*"

"Libby. Call me Libby."

He leaned on the bed with his fists on each side of her. "All right, Libby. Start explaining. And don't leave anything out," he warned.

Libby gulped back the lump of fear in her throat.

288

Cordell wasn't going to settle for any more lies. But she could never tell him about what the reverend had done to her. He would think she had encouraged the evil man.

"As I said, I let Katherine and Sheldon Sharpe force me into masquerading as her—"

"So the real Katherine Rutcliff is in jail with that gambler Sharpe?"

"Yes," she admitted. She waited, hoping (yet despairing) he might want to rush out and rescue his precious Katherine so she, Libby, could disappear.

"Well, continue," he said. "I want it all. Including how they could *force* some innocent girl into doing such a thing."

There would be no delaying the truth. "I assumed Katherine's identity because I was a stowaway. I was afraid she would have me thrown off the boat. I had nowhere else to go."

"You were that eager to get to the Montana Territory?" he said skeptically.

"Yes. I had seen a handbill and hoped to find honest work. With Katherine's help I was able to fool everyone onboard the ship. For nearly two months I was the daughter of an important man. I was treated with respect and kindness. And I made many friends," she added proudly.

Although he was already certain of the answer, he asked, "Why did Katherine force you to assume her identity in the first place?"

"She wanted to spend time with Sharpe," Libby said candidly, "before she was forced to marry you."

"How do you know that?" he quizzed bitingly, his pride pricked. A strange relief mingled with his anger, he finally had the answer of how Sharpe had come to describe the mole Kath . . . er . . . Libby had above her left breast; the real Katherine must have told him to add credence to the story.

289

"Because I heard Katherine and her father arguing outside her stateroom before the ship left the docks in St. Louis."

He rubbed his chin. "I see." After a moment's contemplation, he added, "What made you continue the ruse after the ship docked at Fort Benton?"

"Because . . ." her voice trailed off, choked by mushrooming anxiety.

"The truth, Libby. Because why?"

"Because Captain Massie . . . he . . . ah . . . he had a *Wanted* poster with my description on it," she stammered, cold dread freezing her to her position on the bed.

Cordell stiffened and seemed to study the ceiling for a moment before he said, "You were the one who attacked that reverend?" Disbelief fringed his voice. She hardly seemed the type to use violence.

"It didn't happen the way it sounds," she pleaded. "He—"

"He deserved it, right?"

Tears began to roll down her cheeks and her lower lip trembled. "Please, I—"

"It's all right," he said in a soothing voice, his anger diffused by her tears, "you don't have to tell me about the reverend until you are ready. I won't press you. But once you were alone in the hotel room back in Fort Benton, why didn't you just disappear?"

"I had met you by then. All the way up the Missouri River you were a vision, a dream of a way of life with someone I could never hope to have. And then when I saw you and had heard the kind of man you were, I just couldn't let—" She ceased, too embarrassed to continue.

"You just couldn't what, Libby?"

"Let Katherine . . . ah—"

"Let Katherine marry me?"

"Yes, if you must know," she blurted out.

290

"Why, Libby? Why couldn't you let the real Katherine marry me?" he probed. He had to have the answer.

"Because all the way up to Fort Benton, Augusta Kohrs told me what a good man you were. And in that hotel room when you were so angry and could have stricken me, you didn't. Instead, despite your anger, you treated me with the respect due a lady, the respect Katherine didn't deserve."

"So you decided to save me from Katherine. Is that correct?"

Libby hung her head, then immediately snapped it up again to say, "In a manner of speaking, yes."

"Then why didn't you just tell me the truth and let me deal with Katherine, instead of going through with the wedding?"

"I hadn't intended to go through with it at first. If you'll recall, I was following your script. I even fainted on cue. But when you overplayed your part, I guess my temper got the better of me."

"Whatever do you mean?" he demanded, intrigue beginning to gather about him.

"I had been thinking that if I married you, I could buy myself some time. You're important . . . if the reverend came here looking for me, he wouldn't dare try anything with you around."

"So the only reason you married me was so I could protect you from this man of God," Cordell demanded, his fists clenched, the veins standing out in his neck from the tension. "And all this time you have merely been play-acting, playing another part, starring in yet another role, another masquerade?"

"Yes . . . no! I mean—"

"What is it, Libby? Yes or no?" he pressed. "What *do* you mean?"

All color drained from Libby's face. What was she going to do now? Could she dare to tell him how she felt? Would he laugh in her face and throw her out of the hotel? Would he prosecute her and then have her thrown in jail and sent to prison?

He grabbed her arms, his fingers digging into her with a raw forcefulness she had never seen him display before. Before he had exhibited a quiet strength of will, he had been a charismatic leader with sheer determination. Before her now was a man she'd never seen before . . . a dangerous man who could crush her like an ant, if he chose.

"Tell me, Libby. Tell me! Yes or no?"

Her heart was pounding against her chest so loudly she was sure he could hear it. Her head was throbbing, interfering with her ability to think. There was no escape. The only thing she could do would be to tell him the truth and hope for the best.

"All right, I'll tell you. The answer is no!"

His grip did not loosen. "What answer, Libby? The answer is no to what?" he commanded. He had to hear her say it. He had to know.

"I haven't been merely acting the part of your wife!" she practically screamed.

"Then what have you been acting?" he shook her. "What?"

"I haven't been acting. I haven't! I fell in love with you, if you must hear it. I love you! I do!" she sobbed, covering her face to keep from seeing the disgust she was sure would be there.

He released her and settled down next to her. Quietly, attempting to lift her chin with his forefinger, he said, "Look at me, Libby."

"I can't," she whimpered louder, releasing a flood of pent-up sentiment. "I just can't."

"Look at me." He pried her fingers from her face.

His expression held no malice, no hatred. His lips were drawn in a serious line, his black eyes sparkling golden rainbows, as if he were holding back great feeling. But he said nothing. He was waiting for her to say more. Was he waiting for her to justify herself? She'd never apologize for loving him.

"If you're waiting for me to express my regret for what've I've done, you're going to have a very long wait. I'm not going to say I'm sorry," she blurted out suddenly, "because I'm not. I'll never be sorry for loving you. Never!"

"Neither will I," he murmured with great emotion, nearly causing Libby to make real use of the fainting couch. "Neither will I."

Chapter Forty-five

Libby thought for sure her heart was going to burst from Cordell's simple, honest admission. He had just stated that he was glad she was his wife, hadn't he? She had to be sure she wasn't deluding herself.

"Cordell?"

"Yes?"

"Am I so in love that I just imagined you say that you're happy I'm your wife instead of Katherine?" She held her breath, praying she was right.

Cordell pulled her into his embrace and stroked the wisps of hair at her temples. "Yes, my little vixen, that's what you heard me say. In my heart I've loved you for some time, but I was too stubborn to admit it even to myself. But I do . . . I love you, Elizabeth Marie Hollis Chandler. I love you."

"You mean you fell in love with me even though you thought I was a loose woman who would destroy your life? Even though you thought I had bedded many other men?"

Cordell gave a bittersweet laugh at the thought. "Yes."

"You must really be in love with me, then." Libby threw her arms around his neck and thoroughly kissed him.

"What do you think I just said?" he offered, breathless, when they finally came up for air.

"Oh, Cordell, you'll never be sorry. I love you so much."

"With you, my darling, there's no doubt in my mind I'll ever be sorry." A smile curved his lips before she shifted her head and poked him in the nose with her headdress. "And now you won't have to wear those awful flowered things on your head anymore, since I assume they belong to Katherine."

Nearly beside herself with joy, Libby grasped the decoration with the colorful birds and flowers and tossed it to the floor. She then ran her trembling fingers along his face.

"My wonderful, brazen little wife, I love you." With those words, he began to bestow tender kisses up her neck to cover her face.

Cordell had been understanding and supportive. The realization that she had been granted the true love of such a man caused joyous tears to flood her eyes. A girl was lucky to find a kind husband, a man who would provide shelter and put food on the table. But to have a man like Cordell Chandler was every girl's fantasy. She felt truly blessed. She had found herself a very special man.

"I'm so glad you told me the truth. It shows you have come to trust me . . . that we share more than our bodies; we have come to share a unity of spirit. Now we share all of ourselves with each other — no holding back any longer, my love." When Libby remained quiet, Cordell held her from him. He looked deep into her eyes.

He was patiently waiting for an answer. He expected her to tell him she had no more secrets. She bit her lip.

"Libby, dearest," he breathed, "just promise me you won't ever lie to me again."

She had a choice now. But how could she explain about what the reverend had done to her? Those awful groping hands. No . . . she could never do that . . . *never.* She crossed her fingers. "I've told you the truth, I promise." *I just haven't told you the entire truth,* she thought miserably.

Libby settled back while he began to make love to Elizabeth Marie Hollis for the first time. Then, while his mouth kissed her eyes and nose and nibbled at each earlobe in turn, Libby began to fret. She had not told him the whole truth . . . what would she say when he asked her about the reverend? And he would ask — of that she was certain. Cordell was not a man to let anything slide. He was thorough and exacting. Would he be able to accept her after the reverend had put his vile hands on her? He'd forgiven her when he thought her to be Katherine Rutcliff, a loose woman. But relief had poured over his face when he discovered she wasn't Katherine. Dear Lord, what was she going to do?

Libby's mind continued to conjure up all sorts of horrible images until Cordell slid the top of her ball gown below her breasts and his lips fastened on a crested nipple. Then everything but Cordell and what he was doing to her slipped from her mind.

"You know, it's funny," he crooned, kissing her distended nipples, "the first moment I laid eyes on you, I didn't want to believe you were the kind of girl described in that Pinkerton report."

"But eventually it really didn't matter?" Libby giggled when his tongue swirled around the outside of her breast.

"No, my precious one, it didn't really matter," he echoed. "What matters is that you are mine. Now, I want you to show me that you are." He cast her a devilish grin. "I want you to accede to my every whim."

"Your every wish is my command, sir."

"Sir? I like that. But I like even better that you know how to be a dutiful wife." He chuckled knowing that the beautiful woman lying before him would never be *the dutiful wife,* and loving her all the more because she would be a woman to stand beside him, not in his shadow. She was exactly the kind of woman he wanted. "Now I want you to stand up and slowly unbutton your dress."

Gracefully Libby rose. Never once taking her eyes off her husband lazily reclining across the rumpled bed, leaning on his elbow, Libby worked the cloth-covered buttons loose. When the last fastening had been disengaged, she smiled at Cordell and let the gown fall to her feet.

Cordell's eyes assayed her lace-clad hips and thighs. "How deliciously decadent you look, wife."

Libby was delighting in their sensuous little game. "Thank you, sir."

"Just what I like—a grateful little vixen." He lifted his foot. "Take off my boots," he ordered.

Libby knelt at the edge of the bed. Her cheeks were high with color. She slid the polished footwear and socks from him and massaged his feet, reveling in every inch of her man.

"You know how to please a man."

"No one but you, my love. No one but you," she said in a voice thick with desire. "Let me make you even more comfortable."

Cordell grabbed her hands and brought them to his lips. "Not yet, my impatient little imp. The best things in life are to be savored, to be sipped and enjoyed, every taste partaken of as if it were a fine and delectable fruit." Cordell licked the length of each finger in turn, his tongue stroking along the tips of her ignited fingertips. "Now kiss me and then we'll continue your lesson."

He pulled Libby to him and dipped his lips into hers. He sucked and licked until she opened her mouth, beckoning him to taste her. He curled his tongue and she slid hers along the center, in and out in sensuous

297

rhythm.

"Where did you learn to kiss like that?" Cordell asked after a lingering kiss.

"Mmm . . . from my husband," Libby purred.

"Bright girl. You have already learned the right thing to say."

"I have the best teacher."

"Then let's go on with your lesson. You do want to continue, don't you?"

"Oh, yes, sir."

"Then lie back and open your legs for me. I want to see if I am pleasing you."

The top of her inner thighs were glistening with the evidence of her pleasure. Cordell ran his hand tantalizing over her dark mound and followed the path of sheen on her thigh. Libby whimpered and watched him lift his fingers, fragrant with her juices, to his lips, to sip at the taste of her.

"And am *I* pleasing to you?" Libby rasped, mesmerized by what he was doing to her.

"Release me from my trousers and you will see for yourself," he whispered and arched toward her, his pants straining against his arousal.

His manhood swung free and stood straight before her.

"Take hold of me," he directed, watching her reaction to him in the golden lamplight. "That's right," he moaned when her soft hand closed around the silken shaft. "Now slide your hand up and down. Ahh," he groaned at the friction created as she brought him close to exploding, "that's right, my love. Faster. Rub it faster."

Libby's tongue darted out and Libby bent her head and lapped at his shaft. All the while her mouth savored him, Cordell strained against her, peaking their surging excitement.

For over an hour Cordell introduced and demon-

298

strated the world of sensual pleasure and delight to Libby. He sucked and licked, probed and explored every inch of her heated body, taking her to new heights. He taught her the meaning of agonizing desire, and lust, then the honeyed agony of patience when she would have taken him into her and ended her sweet pain. He took her beyond teasing stimulation until every nerve screamed that he take her and end her urgent need.

She squirmed, nearly out of control. "Cordell, I can't stand it any longer."

He looked up from his ministrations. "Then tell me what you want."

"You," she panted in between gasping breaths. "I want you."

"What do you want me to do to you?"

Burning with pulsing need for him, Libby had long ago lost any false modesty she might have had. "I want you inside me," she begged.

"What do you want inside you? What part of me?"

Her fingers snaked out and caressed him. "This part of you."

Libby was drenched; beads of sweat trickled down her face, plastering her hair against her head. A smooth sheen spread over her shiny, wanting body. Her legs were spread wide.

"Open yourself to me, Libby," he repeated. Lying next to this beautiful, wanton woman, Cordell took himself in hand and jerked at the head of his maleness. "See my pleasure. It is waiting for you to open yourself and test your desire for me."

"Don't make me wait any longer. I cannot bear it," she pleaded.

"I would never let you suffer," he groaned and eased into her.

Libby hooked her fingers around his shoulders and dug his nails into him. "It feels so good, so incredibly good," she cried.

"That's right, my love. It feels so good for both of us." He began to pump, then stopped and withdrew his length before returning even deeper. Over and over he prolonged their release, wanting this time never to end, wanting to suspend the glorious moments.

Libby arched and strained against him, pushing herself to grind, then rub mindlessly with his beat. Her legs wrapped around him, pulling him into her very depths.

Long, langorous strokes built their ardor beyond convention until they escaped the perimeters of consciousness, exchanging the known limits of wild, raging rapture for the transcendental mysticism of their union.

This night their bond was forged, and each left an eternal mark upon the other. And as they lay together returning to this earth, Libby wondered whether what they had shared would survive the coming weeks and a reverend determined to destroy her happiness.

Chapter Forty-six

Katherine shivered against the chill of the dingy cell. There would be hell to pay before she was done with Cordell Chandler and that little bitch who had tricked her. She paced the floor like a caged animal, sending dust motes into a whirl in her wake. She stopped and looked over at Sharpe. The little weasel lay on his side, curved into a ball, sleeping as peacefully as a newborn.

"Wake up!" she shouted. "How can you sleep when we need to get out of here?"

Sharpe scratched his wiry red hair and squinted over at the screeching woman. "What do you want now? You know there is nothing we can do, so relax. You heard the marshal and that old broad talking . . . as soon as Chandler leaves town you'll be released."

"That'll be too late!" she screamed, near hysteria, unconsciously placing her hand on her belly without giving deliberate thought to the seed which she no longer doubted had taken root within her shortly after they'd left St. Louis. "Don't you understand? I have to stop them before my father gets here or he'll cut me off! Now think of something, if you expect to share in my wealth!"

"You mean if you have any wealth left when your father discovers the truth, don't you, Katherine dear?"

"You bastard!"

"There's no need for you to be carrying on so, Miz Rutcliff," the marshal said, coming into the room. "Looks like you two'll be leaving these fine accommodations this morning."

"So," she slapped angry hands on her hips, "at last you acknowledge who I am. I'll have your star for this, you . . . you incompetent moron!"

"No use slinging names, ma'am," the marshal shrugged, "it was an honest mistake. What with you keepin' company with this known gambler here." He turned to Sharpe. "Consider yourself lucky, mister, that Cordell Chandler dropped the charge of extortion against you and said to let you out once he'd left town. Otherwise, you'd be keeping me company a lot longer."

Katherine glared with hatred at the marshal. "Oh, I almost forgot . . . a message arrived at the telegraph office and was delivered to the hotel this morning. Mr. Chandler thought you should have it without delay. Seems your pa is on his way and is eager to link up with you and your new husband." A knowledgeable grin on his face, he took the sheet from his pocket and handed it to Katherine.

For what seemed like hours, Katherine waited on the edge of her bunk, holding the message so tight that her knuckles were white. Fear rose in her throat, but she wasn't defeated yet!

The sun signaled noon when a rumpled Katherine and a stubbled Sharpe finally stepped into the brilliant sunshine. Her steps were determined, as she stomped toward the nearest hotel. Sharpe trailed behind her, still hoping to reap a healthy monetary reward from Katherine. At the same time, he wondered why he let the woman lead him around like she did.

It was certainly not the type of establishment she was accustomed to, and Katherine expelled a huffy breath

302

and negatively assessed the plain, bare floor of the lobby of the tidy hotel she'd chosen. She stepped up to the abandoned desk and slammed her hand down on the bell.

"Service! I am waiting!" she screeched.

"What are y'all hollerin' for?" returned a dumpy clerk, adjusting his suspenders as he resumed his duties.

"We need accommodations *immediately.*"

The clerk cocked a bushy brow. "And a bit of a bath too, if my nose serves me right."

"Your nose is none of my concern. Just see to our rooms!"

He took two keys out of the rows of boxes behind him and held them over the register. "That'll be three bucks . . . in advance."

Katherine reached for the keys, but he snatched them back. "You'll get your money. But now just give me those room keys," she commanded, not used to being denied, especially in such a base establishment as this.

"My ma didn't raise no fool. No money, no room."

Katherine turned and huffed out of the hotel.

"What do you propose now?" Sharpe asked, suddenly questioning why he hadn't kept his distance from her back in St. Louis and continued to make his living as he'd always done. Disgust rippled through him. It was the first time he'd had the slightest feelings for a woman—and she'd turned out to be as rotten as he was. If it hadn't been for Chandler, he could've remained in Fort Benton and taken more than a few rich suckers.

She swung on him, her eyes wild. "It's simple. It's *your* turn to pay a few bills. You can get off your ass for once, find yourself a card game, and cheat a few nobodies—I don't really give a bloody damn."

Sharpe puffed out his chest, tweaked his thin red moustache, and went in search of a game, Katherine following along behind him, harping. The mouthy bitch still had to depend on his trade.

There was a slim chance he could end up with a goodly slice of Chandler's money—enough so he'd never have to concern himself with earning another penny again. Surely Chandler would pay to protect his wife's sordid past from getting into the newspapers and hurting Chandler's political chances.

Inside of an hour, Sharpe had found a saloon filled with what looked like easy pickings. He was seated at a table across from three well-dressed men, dealing cards from the bottom of the deck. In front of him a pile of coins had grown from the one he had lifted from an unsuspecting saloon patron's pocket to four neat stacks. He had given Katherine enough to pacify the spoiled bitch, who incessantly nagged and prodded. It had disturbed his usual concentration. He breathed a silent sigh of relief . . . at least she'd finally left him to ply his trade. He dealt the cards. One more hand and he'd have enough to see them through until they could reach Chandler's ranch.

When the pot suited him, Sharpe showed his hand. "Gentlemen, read those little ladies and weep." A slow grin spoke of his self-assurance.

Greedily he stretched out his hands to rake in the gold.

"We don't take kindly to cardsharps around here, mister." The butts of two six-shooters smashed down on Sharpe's fingers. In unison came a thud and the crack of bone breaking.

"Eee yowww!" Sharpe screamed in excruciating pain. One man grabbed him from behind while another pummeled his face with a fist. Sharpe crumpled to the floor. "No!" he pleaded through a pain-ridden mouth, blood spurting from his split lip. A heavy foot stamped on his hands, further bloodying the masses of broken bone and twisted flesh. The haze of agony thickened and Sharpe lost consciousness before the last heel had finished with him.

"Well, you stupid fool, you're finally coming around," Katherine snipped when Sharpe opened his eyes.

Through the net of pain that was his hands, Sharpe made out the fuzzy images of bars and Katherine's frowning face. Panic began to overwhelm him as his memory assimilated the events of the last few hours. For the first time in his life he'd been plying his trade for someone else's benefit, and he'd been caught. He shook his head . . . he couldn't believe it—he, Sheldon Sharpe, first-class gambler, had been caught cheating!

Desperate, he threw himself at the bars, ignoring the pain. "You've got to use your influence and get me out of here! I'm in here because of you!"

Katherine stepped back, disgust in her eyes. "I might have been able to, if you hadn't been so careless in selecting your marks. You managed to pick a judge and three legislators, you dunce." She gave a snicker and moved toward the door.

"But you can't leave me here. You can't! What will happen to me?"

"More 'n likely, you'll be tried and sent to the territorial prison at Deer Lodge," the marshal interjected. "And since you picked the wrong suckers this time, no doubt you'll get a right speedy trial at that."

"Deer Lodge?" Katherine laughed. "Why, Shelley honey, just think how close by you'll be. Cordell Chandler's ranch is in Deer Lodge." She placed a gloved hand on the marshal's chest, her big dark eyes casting innocence. "Sir, may I please have a moment with the accused? I won't be long."

The lawman gave Sharpe a cursory glance, then moved out of the cell area.

"Quit worrying, Shelley honey. After I've taken care of that little twit and am married to Cordell, I'll see to

305

it that you are freed."

"Then do it now," he urged, past caring about appearances. He'd been in prison once before and had sworn he'd never be incarcerated in such a stinking hellhole again.

"I'm afraid until I am the influential Mrs. Cordell Chandler and have Papa's blessing and the backing of the Rutcliff name, there's little I can do. Don't worry, though; I always get what I want. *Always*. And this time won't be any different. . . ."

His arms burdened with an assortment of packages, Addison Rutcliff disembarked from the steamer he'd taken on the last leg of his journey to Fort Benton. Now he strode purposefully toward the Overland Hotel. Anticipation roiled his blood. His little girl had married at last! No longer would he have to worry about Katherine's sexual escapades. Whistling merrily, Addison stepped up onto the plank sidewalk only to collide with a tall, dark-haired woman.

"Oops," Addison grunted, the boxed gifts tumbling to the ground. "Forgive me. I was so engrossed in thoughts of seeing my daughter and meeting my new son-in-law that I fear I was not watching where I was going." A smile crept up his face. "You see, Katherine is my only child, and I was unable to attend her wedding, so I purchased all these." He fanned his hand wide, indicating the jumble of presents.

"Katherine? That wouldn't be Cordell Chandler's Katherine, would it?" Augusta Kohrs asked, remembering the governor giving the bride away, because her father could not be in attendance.

"Why yes. Do you know them?"

"My husband and I had the great pleasure of becoming acquainted with Katherine on the trip upriver. I'm Augusta Kohrs." She offered her hand, a genuine smile

306

adorning her spirited face.

He clasped her fingers. "Addison Rutcliff."

"Your daughter's a wonderful girl . . ."

Addison listened rapt with interest as Mrs. Kohrs sang Katherine's praises. If he didn't know better, he'd almost have wondered if she was talking about someone else, Katherine's behavior had undergone such a drastic transformation. He had worried that his daughter would sabotage the arranged match. But miraculously, from the dear lady's description of the wedding and the reception, the pair seemed to be well suited. Inwardly he breathed a sigh of relief; he'd had finally found the answer to years of misery over Katherine.

"You have no idea how good it feels for a father to know that his daughter has married well. Thank you so much for watching over my little girl."

"It was my pleasure."

Addison began scooping up the gifts. "Now, if you'll forgive me, I'm anxious to see Katherine. At which hotel are they staying?"

Augusta's face fell. "I'm sorry. Dell and Katherine left for Deer Lodge by way of Helena weeks ago . . . he seemed quite eager to get his bride home."

Disappointment cast a momentary shadow over his features before he composed himself. "Quite all right. I suppose that will give me a good excuse to go to Deer Lodge for a visit." The idea of extending his time away from his businesses suddenly agreed with him. He tipped his hat. "If you'll excuse me, I want to see to travel accommodations as soon as possible."

"Con and I are leaving for home with a brief stop-over in Helena first thing in the morning. We're their neighbors, you know. You're welcome to accompany us. I know Con will enjoy the company."

"Thank you. I accept your generous offer . . . once I get settled at the hotel, I'd consider it an honor if you and your husband would consent to join me for a libation. I want to hear all about your trip upriver with Katherine." A self-satisfied grin crossed his lips. "Won't they be surprised when I appear on their doorstep . . . ?"

Chapter Forty-seven

With each ripple of the Missouri River that splashed against the bow of the ship, the steamer carrying Reverend Elijah Ardsworth and his wife moved closer to Fort Benton.

Rested and filled out from the absence of bone-grinding work on the ship, Marie Ardsworth was beginning to feel more like herself than she had in many years. Gone were the dark violet shadows from under her sunken eyes. Gone were the purple bruises from her body, which had colored her bony frame. And gone were the constant fears which had made her shoulders stoop, lowering her once-proud head. Elijah Ardsworth had been forced to temper his verbal and physical abuse due to the close quarters and questioning remarks from fellow travelers. He spent more time on deck than with Marie, leaving her to enjoy female companionship and express ideas, opinions held inside for far too long.

Sitting on the edge of the bed in their tidy compartment, Marie was all aflutter with excitement at the prospect of dining at the captain's table. "Elijah, you *must* hurry. We don't want to be late for supper this evening!"

He pivoted around to shoot daggers of hatred at the scrawny bitch. He clenched his fists, itching to instill the fear of God into the heathen woman. Lately she'd been forgetting a woman's proper place, not to mention the shame of her past.

In a low voice, a rumble of dire foreboding, he said, "Never attempt to give me directives again, you pathetic excuse for a human being."

"But Elijah—"

"I said *never!*" He struck her with the back of his hand.

Marie flew off the bed and hit her head on a nearby table leg, slumping into an unconscious heap.

"Stupid bitch. It'd serve you right if you died," he drawled. He grabbed a thin, limp arm and dragged Marie into a sitting position. Crouching over her, he squeezed her chin into an upright position and slapped her face. "Wake up before you force me to make you regret it."

Dazed, Marie stroked her swelling face and massaged the cut at her temple. Focusing her blurry eyes on him, she lifted her chin. Perhaps it was the relative security of her surroundings, the close proximity of help, or one too many days living in terror of what he threatened to do to her, but over the last weeks, Marie had come to a decision.

She'd let down her precious, beautiful daughter for years; she'd failed Libby miserably. Elijah had terrorized both mother and daughter, treating them like vermin and worse. Although she'd prayed her child had escaped to a better life, Marie had been given a second chance by God to protect her only child. For that, at least, she was grateful. This time she was not going to meekly allow him to ruin her child.

"Get to your knees and pray that the Lord will forgive you your guilty, pitiful life," he preached in that disgusting, boastful voice of his.

With great effort she managed to climb to her feet. Tears of all those lost years overflowed her eyes and streaked down her cheeks. Trembling, she wiped them

310

away. "Ever since I married you, I admit I've been guilty and pitiful. And I do pray the Lord will forgive me. But not for giving life to my daughter, as you've so often reminded me. I pray he'll forgive me for standing by and doing nothing while I let you mistreat and abuse an innocent child." She swallowed the lump of fear his presence had always elicited in her. "I have turned my head and pretended not to see what you, a man who is supposed to be a servant of God, was doing."

He took a step toward her and she backed up against the door. "Through me, God is punishing you for your sins. And will continue until you repent and cleanse your evil soul." He raised his hand. "You will never talk that way—"

"Don't threaten me anymore, Elijah." Marie sniffled and wiped her nose. "I've lived with this shame for too long. And I've lived with the guilt of my silence for the last time, do you hear me? For the last time." She blinked back more tears. "If you lay a hand on me or my daughter in violence ever again, I'll—"

"You'll *what?* Cry for help? Hah! Who'd believe you, a woman with no self-respect? You're alone in this world. With no where to go. Do you hear me? *All alone.*" With that, his lips curled into an evil, self-confident smirk, silently bespeaking any number of calculating designs for the two women's futures.

Losing her burst of fortification, Marie let out a beleaguered cry and fled from their quarters.

Elijah changed hurriedly. He'd have to join that skinny hag before she said something out of turn. He smoothed his shaggy brows with his index finger. There was no doubt in his mind that he could control the bitch. And when the time came, he'd wreak the Lord's ultimate vengeance upon both mother and daughter for their unforgiveable sins. . . .

* * *

Libby snuggled deeper into the mound of blankets in which she was nestled inside the covered wagon. She could hardly believe her fortune . . . despite her sin of assuming another's identity and then tricking Cordell Chandler into marrying her, she'd been blessed with an understanding and supportive husband, not to mention one who was the most beautiful, rugged man she'd ever seen.

She chewed on the end of her thumb. How was Cordell going to react when he discovered her dark secret of having attacked the reverend? The wheel hit a rock, pulling her musings back to the present. Through the split in the canvas she could see the sun peeking over the top of pine boughs lining the well-traveled road to Deer Lodge, sending pillars of golden light through the early morning shadows. Libby crawled to the back of the wagon and peered out.

"Good morning, dear heart," Cordell said, riding up to the wagon and leaping off his horse to join his wife.

Libby pressed herself into his welcoming arms. "It is now."

While the driver kept the team moving at a steady pace, Cordell held Libby. Pin by pin he released the silk of her hair and stroked the curling strands.

"Yes, my darling, it certainly is." He bent his head and united their lips in a gentle kiss meant to reassure, to hearten, to convince her of his love.

Cordell spent hours in the wagon with Libby describing the scenery, pointing out birds and animals, and telling her of her new home. They talked of his childhood and how he'd come to the Montana Territory penniless and built the empire in which she would soon share. They talked of Aunt Matilde and of Gulch, who had remained in Helena to escort Matilde back to the ranch when she was ready, and Cordell told openly of his friendship with Caroline, reassuring Libby that she need never worry about her again. And they discussed Katherine and Sharpe, and all the events leading up to the present.

All the while they laughed and whispered, his hands petted her back or toyed with the fine hairs on her arms—not in an intimate way which silently spoke of foreplay, but in a way meant to reaffirm the bond that had already been forged. And as he sat next to her, his arm lightly drawn over her shoulders, Libby temporarily let go of all her worries.

For the remainder of the trip Cordell and Libby experienced the idyllic interlude of lovers cosseted away from an intruding world. At night they made delicious, wild, abandoned love, savoring all the fruits that passion had to offer. During the day Cordell kept Libby at his side; he either rode with her in the wagon or had a horse saddled and took her with him while he surveyed their progress.

On the last day out, Cordell took over the cooking chores to relieve the cook, so he could ride ahead and ready the ranch house for their arrival.

"Morning, sleepyhead." Cordell strode over to the wagon and helped Libby out, giving her a smacking kiss in front of the men.

She rubbed her eyes. "How long have you been up? I shouldn't have overslept." She stretched. "I plan to help with the cooking."

"I've been up for hours. Got to keep strong coffee ready for the hands at all times, you know. Sit down by ther fire and I'll get you a cup."

"You're going to make a cowboy out of me yet." Libby laughed, thinking about how the men had to have their coffee to get themselves going.

Appreciative eyes rolled down her gently rounded curves. "Not much chance of that," Cordell said.

"That's for sure," seconded a mangy bull whacker, who immediately moved away at Cordell's glance.

313

"What's for breakfast?" Libby asked.

"How does a *hoss thief special* sound?" Cordell grabbed a plate and headed for the fire.

"Oh, dear. No. I—I couldn't eat horsemeat," Libby choked out, taking a quick count of the mules and horses nearby.

Three of the men hid chuckles behind their coffee mugs while Cordell grinned at her innocence. "Would a plate of *spotted pup* sound better?"

Good heavens, *not dog* was her first thought. Then she grew suspicious as the men sauntered off or turned their heads in amusement. "All right, Mr. Chandler," she chided, "exactly what are you offering me to eat?"

"Is *Moonshine, Swamp Seed,* or *John Chinaman* more familiar?"

"You know perfectly well it is not." She made a playful grab for the pot.

"Those are just pet names the cowpokes gave to the dish, nothing to worry your beautiful head about. Sit back down," he directed, leading her to a place of honor he had prepared by rolling a good-sized rock over near the fire and padding it with blankets. "I'll serve." He returned to the pot and dished up a healthy portion and handed it to her.

"*Pet* names, huh?" Libby took a bite. "Hmm, rice and raisins with cinnamon. This is wonderful."

"I spruced the rice up specially for you, my love." He hesitated for a moment as if mulling something over. " 'Course, the men like it this way better too, and so we'll make better time." A lopsided grin graced his full lips. "And the sooner I'll get you home into my bed—"

Libby looked around, scandalized. "Cordell! The men will hear."

"Don't think that every one of them isn't envious."

Oh, precious Lord, she loved this man. As they ate, she considered all that he was. He could be hard and take charge when necessary; he could be pliant and

314

giving; he was charismatic; he was thoughtful; he could be teasing or serious. In the final analysis, he was everything a man should be and more, so much more. But most important of all, he was hers.

"All right, woman, let's get beans and sourdough biscuits going, then I'll show you my favorite secluded pond."

Visions of partaking of that special lagoon with Cordell caused Libby to eagerly fetch the beans, molasses, bacon, and pepper while Cordell assembled the sourdough starter, flour, baking soda, and salt. He took the heavy iron kettle, poured water over the beans, and hung them over the fire to simmer. Their culinary preparations complete, Cordell saddled up and gave Libby a boost into the saddle.

To the trill of birds, Cordell and Libby rode from camp to a spot where the creek widened and the flow of water ebbed, forming a lush basin surrounded by secreting pines and tall grasses.

"I hope you know this isn't going to be a quick dip," he huskily put forth.

Libby slid from the horse and began unfastening her blouse. "Umm, you're wicked," she murmured.

"And you're about to find out just *how* wicked." A pat on the rump sent his horse off to graze nearby, and Cordell tore at his clothing. He had meant to take her leisurely. But that nice, rounded bottom of hers rubbing against him all the way out here had driven him to a feverish brink.

Libby finished stripping off her clothing and splashed into the pond, one step ahead of Cordell. He surged toward her and, spasms pouring through him at the heated touch of her flesh against his, drenched her with kisses.

"More," she groaned.

"I'll give you more, my little delight."

"I'll never get enough of you." She laughed, her voice

315

rich with desire.

Fleet seconds lapsed before they were joined in liquid splendor. Fiercely they moved against one another in wild rhythm, building immense, nearly unbearable friction until the rivulets of their passion mingled with their wet resplendence and they found a glittering release in the spasms which racked their bodies.

For two hours they explored, tantalized, and were lost in each other until Cordell carried Libby from the water and gingerly set her on heavy tufts of grass. Lying beside her, toying with her fingers, he said, "Tomorrow, my love, we'll be home. Then you'll never have to fear anyone again."

Libby turned her head away. Her lips quivered, thinking of the reverend and her black secret. "No," she forced out, "I'll never have to fear anyone again."

Chapter Forty-eight

Cordell had described his ranch before they arrived, but Libby's breath caught as she stood inside the fence surrounding the front yard, surveying the two-story white plank house with deep green shutters. This was her home. *Her home!* She walked around the house and counted twenty-seven windows. It was the finest house she had ever seen.

"You like it." It was a statement from a self-assured man who had succeeded in life and had no reason to apologize for what he had.

"It's marvelous," she squealed, clasping her hands in front of her like a child at her first birthday party.

"Well, then," he scooped her into his arms, "let's have a look inside."

She giggled mirthfully, hugging his neck.

He strode toward the front door. "I bought the farmhouse complete with furniture, stables, corrals, ricks of hay, and implements, as well as cattle, sheep, goats, and grain."

"I love this place already. Does being a rancher keep you very busy?" she ventured, a gleam of impishness in her eyes.

"I have Gulch to take care of running the ranch."

"Good. Then I can have all your time." She toyed with his hair, delighting in the coarse texture of the

317

shiny black strands as she wound them around her fingers.

Forcing himself to ignore what she was doing to him with those inviting hands of hers, he said, "I'm afraid my mining, real estate, water rights interests, and politics take up a fair amount of time." Her face dropped. "Don't worry, my love, nothing is going to keep me separated from you for long." He nudged the door open with his boot and stepped into the spacious parlor.

Libby giggled.

"What's so amusing?"

"I think I like being carried over the threshold."

"Then I'll make a point always to carry you inside."

"What if I should grow plump?"

"My love, whether you are thin or plump, I'll never tire of holding you in my arms, and as long as I've the strength, I'll carry you wherever you desire."

She thought her heart was going to burst with love. And she knew that he would be her rock, the balance in her life. He would be her stability; someone who would always be there.

He set her down and she gazed in awe at the opulence of the rose patterned rugs, lace curtains, velvet tufted chairs, and carved rosewood tables laden with exquisite porcelain and bronze statuary.

To Libby's horror the cook came into the parlor, wiping his hands on his stained apron, and let go a wad of tobacco on the edge of the carpet. "How do, ma'am." Not waiting for a reply, he turned his attention to Cordell. "Me and the boys has got ever'thin' ready, jus' like you sent word, boss."

"Thank you, Murphy."

Libby stood quite still, reeling from shock at the darkening stain on the floor while Cordell introduced the craggy cook.

"You can join the others in the bunkhouse, Murphy," Cordell suggested when an awkward silence ensued.

"Thank ya." He bobbed his bald head and grinned at Libby. "Ma'am. No disrespect meant, but me and the other cowpokes don't cotton with bein' inside no big house." Noticing the bemused look on her face, he added, "There's two things a cowboy's 'fraid of more'n anythin': bein' cooped up inside some big house where he cain't look up and see them stars winkin' at him in the sky at night, and gettin' hooked up with a good, God-fearin' woman!"

Once the little man had left, Libby's horrified gaze shifted from the brown blotch on the rug to Cordell. "Don't worry about cleaning it up, we don't out here. It's a kind of custom, you might say," he reassured her. "Not too many of the men make such use of the floor."

Libby was not appeased. Such a disgusting habit was the first thing that was going to change around here, she decided.

When her bewildered look continued, Cordell added, "I don't itch to sleep outside. And I love being hooked up with a good, God-fearing woman. So don't let it bother you."

She knew he'd meant to appease her fears. But the mention of God caused her to recall her secret troubles: what if Cordell was a deeply religious man? He would surely cast her aside when he discovered what she'd done to a' minister.

"What is it, Libby?" he asked, lifting her chin in the crook of his index finger.

She swallowed her hesitation. "I suppose I was wondering if you're a religious man."

"Don't worry, I'm not a heathen, if that's what you're wondering about." When she didn't look relieved, he elaborated. "I believe that there is a greater being, but I think a man can worship his God in different ways

319

than just going to church once a week and dropping a couple of coins in the plate. Does that set your mind at ease?"

At Libby's nod of assent, Cordell took her arm and escorted her through the house, proudly introducing her to her new home. At the end of the tour, Libby mumbled, "I didn't notice any closets."

"Not many of the houses in these parts have them. You see, closets are taxed as if they are another room. "So," he shrugged, "we have wardrobes."

"Oh."

After they were refreshed, Cordell spent the rest of the day presenting Libby to the ranch hands, explaining the operation of the spread and describing the special breeding stock of Shorthorns and Herefords he'd brought in, which vastly improved the quality of his cattle.

Libby was enthralled by the workings of the ranch and eager to add her own special touch, as well as take over the running of Cordell's house. The first several days she watched closely and learned how to make soap and candles, and how to roast coffee. She took over the cooking and cleaning, often scrubbing up the tobacco juice stains from the rug and floor. By the end of the week she was feeling so confident that she invited the men to join them for supper.

"That's right, put it in the middle of the parlor. Right there," she directed the bearded wrangler toting a bulky armload of nailed slats.

"You sure you want this crate of sawdust in the middle of this here fine room, ma'am?"

"That's right. Thank you."

"Yessum." The bewildered man set the strange piece down, scratched his head, raised a confused brow, and scurried from the house, muttering. It wasn't his nevermind to question the rancher's wife.

Satisfied with her handiwork and confident that her idea would work, she retired to the bedroom to ready herself for her first dinner party as hostess in her own home. Inviting the ranch hands was the perfect way to practice before entertaining Cordell's friends, associates, and all the people he'd invited out to the ranch from Fort Benton and Helena. He wanted them to witness their reciting their wedding vows, using her real name as Cordell had suggested, just to make sure there could be no question of the legality of their marriage.

By the time she returned to the parlor, six spruced-up cattle hands bolted awkwardly to their feet, their hats in their freshly scrubbed hands. Libby wrung her palms together, anxious that everyone find her efforts adequate. For a long moment the conversation was forced until Murphy reached for an appetizer and stubbed his toe on the crate brought in earlier.

"No offense meant, ma'am, but if you don't move that there box, me and the boys are likely to jest up and let fly a chaw into it."

Cordell threw his head back and roared when Libby's hand flew to her breast in shock at his candor. "Murphy, if I'm not mistaken, I'd venture to say that that is the very reason why my wife had that box of sawdust brought into the house in the first place."

Murphy looked down at the shaven chips and rubbed his jaw. "Right enough? Well, I'll be jiggered if the little lady didn't come up with a galdarned useful idea."

After that everyone laughed and relaxed, making the evening a success. Linen tucked into their collars, the cowboys sat around the formal dining table, slurping soup and shoveling slabs of beef into their mouths. Lively conversation whipped around the table. Libby was surprised at the colorful language and Cordell was amused that the men had come to feel so at ease that they were forgetting themselves.

One of the hands had just told how he'd come by the name of Panhandle, and everyone was laughing when a crash at the door interrupted the joviality.

Matilde whirled into the room, a tornado in sparkling burgundy satin. Gulch trailed behind her, heavily burdened with hat boxes and carpetbags. "My goodness, don't stop on our account! Everyone *knows* laughter works wonders for the soul," she gushed.

"Aunt Matilde," Libby cried happily and rushed from her seat to embrace the old darling.

Matilde gave Libby a quick hug, then stepped back and fluffed out her gown. "Nothing personal, child, but I didn't stop a mile from the ranch to dress for dinner just to let my gown be crushed." Her attention immediately shifted to Cordell. "Wipe that smirk off that handsome face of yours and come escort your aunt to the table."

"Gulch," Cordell said, forcing back a chuckle, "stow Matilde's bags upstairs in her room, then join us. Murphy, get a couple more chairs." He strode to Matilde and offered his arm.

Dinner went better than Libby could have hoped for. The conversation was relaxed and lively. And the men remained until their bellies were full, and they got the hankering for some good rotgut and a smoke.

One by one Libby bade them good evening as they excused themselves. This was the first time she'd been hostess in her own home. *Her own home:* the thought warmed her breast. Never in her wildest dreams had she imagined she'd end up with a husband like Cordell and a family like Aunt Matilde and the ranch hands, who treated her with the respect due the wife of Cordell Chandler. If only she were deserving of such regard!

"Libby, dear, you look like you're a thousand miles away," Matilde observed, breaking into Libby's musings.

"Oh, I'm sorry . . . I suppose I was." Libby looked

322

around. Cordell had joined the men to discuss plans for riding out tomorrow to inspect the herd.

"Well, what if you and I clear the table, then engage in some woman-talk?" Matilde asked gaily, hovering around the table and scooping up the china.

Once they had the dining room back in order, the two women retired to the parlor and settled onto the settee.

"Well, my dear, how do you like my . . . ah, nephew's home?" she chattered brightly, then caught herself. "I mean *your* home, of course."

"It's more than I could ever have dreamed of. And Cordell is more of a man than I ever thought I'd—" Libby choked up.

A serious look covered Matilde's face. "My dear, have you told Cordell the truth yet?"

Libby's face remained impassive. She still hadn't told him all about the reverend, but she wasn't about to share that with Aunt Matilde, either. She forced a look of contentment and said, "Yes, and Cordell was wonderful about it."

Matilde laid a comforting hand over Libby's. "I am so glad it's all out in the open now. I just *knew* everything would be all right. Cordell is special, even though he can get rather touchy on occasion."

"Very." Libby cleared away the emotion threatening to close her throat and quickly changed the subject. "What about you?"

"Me?"

"Yes. You're such a dear lady," Libby said candidly. "Why didn't you ever marry, if I may ask?"

Matilde fidgeted with the fringe on her shawl. "I suppose some people are meant to find that someone special, and some people aren't. Me? I found food instead. Oh, my—don't look so sad for me, child. Actually, I've had my share of gentlemen friends and a pretty full life—even if I do say so myself," she added a bit too brightly.

"But—"

Matilde silenced her with a hand. "I'm not unhappy, dear. And there's few things I'd change." For the merest instant her thoughts shifted to the one man she'd loved and lost, but she quickly put that out of her mind. "Now, why don't we go see how much of that tart is leftover before I toddle off to bed and leave you with that dashing nephew of mine?"

Libby followed Matilde to the kitchen at the back of the house. In spite of the woman's protestations to the contrary, there was a sadness, an emptiness under the surface which no amount of food could fill. Libby made a mental note to herself: if it was up to her, Aunt Matilde would never feel lonely again!

Chapter Forty-nine

Libby awoke feeling as if she'd been reborn. She and Cordell had spent the rest of last night making love and talking until nearly dawn, when he'd had to tear himself away to tend to the workings of the ranch. Honestly and openly he'd told her about his relationship with Caroline, leaving no chance of further question in her mind.

He'd answered her every question, filling in the details of a lonely childhood and the loss of his family when he was just a youngster. He explained about Katherine Rutcliff and his original intention to let her come to Montana at Matilde's insistence. His plan had been to get to know Katherine before the question of marriage was decided upon, and how things had gotten out of hand due to Matilde and her overzealous enthusiasm, and the trouble on the docks at Fort Benton.

Through his vivid descriptions Libby experienced his pain and joy, his inner longings, his fears, hopes, desires and frustrations. She came to know him as the consummate male he was and even shared bits of her own childhood, careful to delete the unseemly portions.

If only she could bring herself to confide in him the whole truth! He'd told her he would wait until she was ready to tell him about her problems with the reverend. Despite what he'd said, she still wondered why he'd

325

never pressed for answers. Last night she was almost tempted to tell him about herself and accept the consequences, but something had held her back, and she'd decided to hold onto her newfound happiness just as long as she could.

Humming quietly to herself, Libby went to the kitchen and fixed herself a cup of coffee. She was sitting at the work table gazing out the window when a loud crash followed by a ruckus and angry voices assaulted her ears. Recognizing the all-too-familiar voice, Libby's heart raced with fear as she hurried to investigate. *Please let me be wrong,* she quietly prayed.

"Let go of my arm, you mangy son of a dog!" Katherine screeched, wrenching her sleeve free of Murphy's grasp.

Murphy fought off the raining blows. "Ya stop that right now, 'fore ya force me to load ya up and toss ya outside on your duff."

"You'd better not touch me," she yowled and took a swing at Murphy's head. Her aim missed. In her determination, she'd put all her strength into the blow and ended up landing on the Oriental carpet with a thud. "Ooh!"

Libby reached the entryway in time to see Katherine swipe at her hat. "Oh, my, what . . . what are *you* doing here?"

With as much dignity as Katherine could garner, she gathered herself to her feet and straightened her dusty beige skirt. With a haughty tilt of her shoulders, she glided into the parlor and sat herself down as big as you please. "What the devil do you think I'm doing here? Cordell Chandler is my fiancé, if you've forgotten that little fact. And I intend to take my rightful place here with him."

Horrified, Libby's gaze shot to Murphy, who was scratching his head, as they followed Katherine's lead into the room. "It's all right, Murphy."

"Ya sure, ma'am? If'n ya want, I'll be mighty happy to oblige ya and show that one," he thumbed toward Katherine, "the other side of the door."

"I'll call if I need your help. Thank you, Murphy."

"Yessum." He bobbed his head and was gone.

"Well, now," Katherine huffed, "before you sit down, get me something to drink. I'm parched after such an uncivilized trip." Then as if she'd forgotten her command, she sneered, "We need to have a little talk." Her lips twisted into a smile, denoting her intention to destroy what fragile happiness Libby had found.

"Where is your friend?" Libby asked hesitantly, fearing that Sheldon Sharpe was lurking nearby to make the situation even worse.

"My friend?"

"Mr. Sharpe," Libby elaborated.

Katherine gave an apathetic flip of her wrist, forgetting her request. "Oh, the gambler." She rolled her eyes. "He'll be in Deer Lodge shortly, I believe. Sit down. You're irritating me, standing over me like a worried little sparrow."

Libby gasped before she could catch herself as she took a seat next to the vindictive young woman.

"You needn't concern yourself about him. The stupid fool managed to get himself arrested. Seems he tried to cheat the wrong men. On top of that, they discovered an old *Wanted* poster on him. I'm sure he got a speedy trial and will be spending the next five years in the territorial prison. Of course, if you feel the need, I'm sure he'd welcome visitors," she said sarcastically.

Libby stiffened and raised her chin. "I think you'd better leave."

Not in the least abashed, Katherine slid over on the settee until they were nose to nose. "You, Elizabeth Marie Hollis *Chandler,* might as well think again."

Feeling confident, Katherine got up and began to saunter about the parlor, noting the rich furnishings and doing a mental accounting of the display of wealth within the house. "I believe when your precious Cordell finds out about you, he'll see things much differently. And naturally I intend to be here for him—to console the man, of course."

"Of course." Libby's lips were tight when she said, "Since you have already taken the liberty to show yourself into the parlor, why don't you take the liberty to show yourself out?"

"I have *no* intention of leaving. You see, I'm here to stay." Katherine glared at the young woman. There was no doubting it, the girl was no longer an awkward child. There was a self-assurance about Libby which Katherine had not expected. But she was not about to allow the pretender to get in her way.

At that, Libby's breath caught.

"Don't tell me I've struck a nerve, my dear *Mrs. Chandler?*"

Katherine's smile was so venomously sweet that Libby had to steel herself in order to hide her anxiety. "I'm afraid you made the long trip out to the ranch for nothing—"

"I think not. You see, I doubt a man like Cordell Chandler will want you when he finds out who you really are."

Inwardly, Libby breathed a sign of relief. Thank God Cordell already knew her true identity! She could be done with Katherine before Cordell returned. "If that is why you came, I'm afraid there is absolutely no need for you to remain any longer."

Unimpressed, Katherine cocked a brow. "Oh? And why should I leave?"

"Staying won't help your cause. You see, I already told Cordell about myself."

Katherine's face sagged, momentarily deflated. Then the flicker of an idea took root and her expression became hard, desperately obstinate. "Even if you did, which I doubt, it won't do you any good."

Libby moved to the edge of her seat and leaned forward. "There's nothing you can say to him to destroy our marriage."

"Maybe not. But there is plenty I can say to the rest of the citizens of this fine, Christian territory about his sweet, innocent little wife which will forever ruin your precious husband's chances of holding political office. And when I'm done, you'll never be able to hold your heads up around these parts again."

"I've done nothing to be ashamed of," Libby cried, panic beginning to close in on her.

"No? Well, even if you *are* as innocent as a daisy, who will believe that when I'm through telling my story?"

"You wouldn't hurt Cordell just to get back at me, would you?"

"I'll do whatever I have to. I'm sure you understand that . . . *Mrs*. Chandler. Particularly considering what you have done to me. I have no qualms of destroying his career."

"That won't destroy our marriage."

"No. I suppose not, if he still wants you, knowing who you really are. There's just no accounting for taste these days," she added with a cruel smile. "But knowing how much you seem to love the man, I don't think you'd allow him to make such a sacrifice." By the look of devastation on Libby's face, Katherine knew she'd won. She gave an indifferent shrug to her shoulders. "You'll just have to give him up."

Before Libby could even think of formulating an answer, the sharp click of footfalls drew their attention to the doorway. Libby's hand flew to her mouth. "Oh, no," she whispered behind a trembling hand.

"What is the meaning of this?" Matilde demanded entering the parlor, her hands on her hips, her lined face as hard as a man's fist.

"Aunt Matilde, I—ah—we—"

"We were just having a *friendly* little discussion," Katherine said sweetly, rising to greet the older woman

Not giving a single thought to their less-than-pleasan meeting back in Helena, Katherine stretched out he hand, expecting a warm return, since she'd met Matilde Chandler some months back and the woman had been eager for the match at that time.

Matilde bristled. "My, but you have put on weigh around the middle since I met you, Katherine."

"I suppose I could say the same about you, but didn't come here to exchange insults," Katherine re turned, hoping that no one would guess her secret yet

"I heard what you seem to consider *friendly*. And you can be advised, young woman, that I have no *intention* of allowing you to come into our home and threaten *any* of the Chandlers." Matilde stepped next to Libby and put her arm the girl's shoulders.

"But she," Katherine pointed an accusing finger in Libby's direction, "married your nephew under false pretenses." Her voice rising to a high pitch, she contin ued, "You *know* I was supposed to marry him. She had me arrested so she could take my place . . . so she could marry Cordell *for his money*. So she—"

"Enough! I know all about the wedding. Libby told me the truth."

"You believe her?"

"My *niece* does not lie. That I know for a fact, so there is no use attempting to malign her character any further."

"If you know about the wedding, then how can you stand there and defend her?" Katherine implored, nearly

330

exhausting the innocent guise she had quickly adopted to gain Matilde's support for her cause.

"Quite simple, actually. Libby is married to Cordell. And *happily*, which is more than could have been said if the boy had married you, from what I've heard. Now, I suggest you take *Mrs*. Chandler's advice and find more suitable accommodations for the remainder of your stay in our territory."

"I'll show you to the door," Libby said, a sober determination coloring each word.

White-hot anger seared Katherine's features; her eyes sparked; her lips quivered with rage. And when Libby reached to take her elbow to escort her out, Katherine wrenched her arm back and flung herself into a corner.

"What do you think you're doing?" Matilde commanded in a take-charge voice, so unlike her usual bubbling self.

Feeling her position strengthened, Libby advanced to where Katherine stood.

"You'd both better sit back down and decide if you really want to alter the bright future Cordell Chandler expects to have," Katherine threatened, fully prepared to carry out the menace she posed.

"Don't you try to blackmail me," Matilde warned.

Fearing Katherine would make good her threat, Libby stepped in front of Matilde. "Wait! We can't let her destroy Cordell's future because of me."

"Nonsense," Matilde insisted. "She wouldn't dare—"

"Oh, but I would." There was a calculating calm in her voice. If it weren't for the simple fact that her father would be arriving shortly and Katherine wanted him to be presented with the perfect picture of her wedded bliss, she'd have delighted in destroying Cordell Chandler's future that moment, and that of his little bitch of a wife's, too. But after receiving that untimely telegram from her father, Katherine had hired a coach

331

with Sharpe's winnings and ordered the driver to lay the whip to the horses. She knew she was only a few days ahead of the man. It called for whatever measures were required to make sure her father received the best impression she could present.

"I have nothing to lose by making sure your story is in every newspaper tomorrow." Katherine bluffed, waiting for a reaction. When the two did not resist, she directed, "Sit down, ladies. I think at last we understand each other." She bided her time until they were seated. "Now, all we have to do is come to a satisfactory agreement. I don't think that should be too difficult, do you?"

Cordell had returned and stood unnoticed in the doorway. A skeptical lilt to his deep voice, he inquired "*What* shouldn't be too difficult?"

Chapter Fifty

The room was filled with such tension that Libby's head began to pound; she wanted more than anything to take flight. She looked over at Matilde, who had straightened her back and sat stiffly quiet, her hands folded in the lap of her burgundy silk robe. Katherine, too, sat erect. But there was an aura of arrogance to her pose which only reinforced Libby's dread that the woman fully intended to ruin Cordell's future.

"I asked, *What* shouldn't be too difficult?" Cordell repeated, the crease in his brow deepening. His cold, hard eyes settled icily on Katherine. "What are *you* doing here?"

Katherine's lips pinched. *Damn* her father for threatening to cut her off if she didn't marry the man! She'd always instinctively fought her father's threats. If she'd only known what kind of man Cordell Chandler was, there'd never have been a problem in the first place. He certainly was no hick rancher, as she'd originally surmised. Cordell was strikingly handsome, with coal-black hair, those intelligent black eyes, and strong features. Her eyes surveyed him from head to toe. She heaved an inward sigh; he possessed such a muscular, deliciously masculine body that being married to him would have held many untold rewards.

"I'm here to become Mrs. Chandler."

"What!" Disbelief flooded his voice.

"I said, I'm here—"

"I *heard* what you said." He crossed his arms over his chest. "You do realize that I already have a wife, with whom incidentally, I happen to be quite satisfied. I'm afraid you're out of luck."

Katherine was beginning to seethe. He was not taking her seriously, the pompous idiot. Well, she'd just make sure he did develop an appreciation for the gravity of the situation—and fast! "No, I'm afraid it is you and that precious little wife of yours who are out of luck. And if you don't agree to my terms—"

"Your terms!" Cordell laughed, incredulous. "I suggest you leave before I bodily pick you up and *throw* you off my land myself." He took two steps toward her, a murderous gleam in his eyes.

Libby leaped to her feet. "No, wait!" She grabbed his arm. "Please, she'll ruin your life!"

Cordell took hold of Libby's arms and held her from him, searching her troubled blue eyes. Matilde cleared her throat, drawing Cordell's attention from his wife.

"Dell, dear, I think if you allowed me to explain, I could clear up this little inconvenience in no time at all."

"Little inconvenience!" Katherine howled.

Cordell sent Katherine a silencing frown before turning his attention to Matilde.

"What do you have to do with this?" He thought a moment. "Besides, of course, sticking your nose in my business in the first place."

Scandalized, Matilde's hand flew to her throat. "I've always had only your happiness in mind, Dell."

"In that case, why don't you head back to your room and leave me to settle this mess?"

Matilde would never be considered anyone's fool. She could tell from the warning look in Cordell's eyes that now was not the time for debate. Retaining her dignity, Matilde stood up, snapped the throat of her robe shut, and chirped, "If that's what you want, dear."

"It is," he stated flatly and sent her a daunting look which brooked no further comment.

Matilde laid a comforting hand on Libby's shoulder. "Don't worry, Libby dear, Dell will take care of everything." With that she strolled from the room.

Katherine applauded. "Bravo, Cordell honey. Now, if you'll just dismiss that person," she waved in Libby's direction, "you and I can get down to business."

Cordell glared at the nervy woman. "Do you have anything else to say before I throw you out?"

Katherine remained rooted to the spot. "I'm not going anywhere."

"Cordell, please, sit down," Libby pleaded. *"Please."*

Cordell heaved a sigh; he wanted to be done with Katherine Rutcliff, and for some reason Libby was trying to shield her. Only because of Libby's insistence did he grudgingly seat himself.

Libby announced sadly, "I am the one who is going to leave."

Cordell was at the end of his patience and announced darkly, "You, my dear wife, are not going anywhere."

"I—I have to, or she'll ruin your career," Libby blurted out.

Katherine rose. "If you'll point me to the kitchen, I think I'll have something to drink while you two work out the details. Incidentally, Papa will be here in a few days, and I want him to see how happy his only daughter is."

His composure shattered, Cordell lunged for Katherine, but Libby pulled him back. "Please, just listen to me while she's in the kitchen." The furious glint in his black eyes softed before her supplication. *"Please."*

335

Cordell ran his long, tapered fingers through his wavy hair. "All right. I'll hear you out." He gave Katherine a look of disgust. "Down the hall to the back of the house, third door on the left."

The instant Katherine sauntered off, Cordell pulled Libby down on the settee with him. His fingers dug into her arms. "What the hell is this all about?" he demanded, not about to let anyone come into his house with threats such as the Rutcliff woman had issued.

"Oh, Cordell," Libby burst out, and buried her head in his chest. For a few long minutes she sobbed against his fine jacket, leaving a dark, wet stain over his heart.

When she'd calmed, he lifted her chin and gazed into her swollen red face and eyes. Even in her present state she was beautiful to him. He nuzzled her neck. The fragrance of gardenias clung to her hair. He cursed Katherine under his breath. If that troublesome woman weren't in his kitchen, he'd have whisked Libby to their room and made wild passionate love to her.

He took out a handkerchief. "Here, blow your nose."

"Thank you." Libby put the hanky to her nose and blew. "Oh, Cordell, she's going to ruin your career. She's going to tell everyone about our wedding and my past, and how I had her arrested so I could take her place. She said she'd make you into a laughingstock all because her father will disinherit her if she isn't Mrs. Chandler when he arrives. He'll be here in a few days. She means it. What are we going to do?"

"Throw her out," he said calmly.

"No . . . no . . . we can't."

"Why not?"

"Because I'm not going to let her jeopardize your future on account of me. I can't!"

Cordell took her into his embrace and stroked her silken hair. "Calm down. I'm not going to send you away. Even if you left, I'd find you and bring you

336

back. I certainly have no intention of marrying Katherine Rutcliff, regardless of the circumstances."

Libby sniffled. He'd never actually marry Katherine, but he wouldn't have to really be married to her to fool her father. The glimmer of a plan lit her face. "Cordell, what if you only pretended to be married to Katherine while her father is here? After he leaves, she can go on her way still a wealthy woman. That should satisfy her, and then she'll have no reason to want to lash out at me through you. I could pretend to be her maid."

"If you'll remember pretending to get married is what got this whole mess started in the first place," he playfully kissed her, "although I wouldn't change a thing if I had it to do over again. But as far as this charade with Katherine is concerned, the answer is no."

She pushed him away. "Cordell, just consider it for a moment. It can work, *really* it can. I *know* it."

"No, love . . . I think the best thing would be to send her packing and tell Addison Rutcliff the truth when he arrives."

"Please, Cordell. I'd never forgive myself if your life was ruined because of me."

"My life could never be ruined as long as I have you."

"Then you'll do it? For me. Oh, please, Cordell, it will only be for a few days. *Please,*" she begged, certain of the soundness of the plan.

She was sincere, and so excited about the prospects of helping him. But he was perfectly capable of handling any threat Katherine Rutcliff could possibly pose. Still reluctant, he relented to humor his crazy, wonderful wife. "I should probably have my head examined. And will undoubtedly come to regret this, but all right. I'll play the woman's husband—but only for a few days—"

"Only as long as Katherine's father is here," Libby

337

reiterated, her face lighting up.

"No longer than a week. Do you hear me? No longer than a week. After that, I either want the man sent back to St. Louis or told the truth, regardless of the consequences. And I want you to know I'm going along with your harebrained scheme *only* because I love you."

"Oh, thank you. You won't regret it. It'll work . . . I know it. And with Aunt Matilde's help, Mr. Rutcliff will never suspect. Now all I have to do is convince Katherine to accept a compromise."

An indulgently skeptical expression crossing his face, Cordell added, "Yeah, that's all." He paused and then suggested, "Shall we go and talk to her?"

"I'll handle everything." With the exuberance of a child, Libby swung her arms around his neck and gave him a wet kiss. "Don't worry about a thing." She leaped up, grabbed her skirts, and dashed toward the kitchen. Halfway down the hall she stopped and swung around. "Oh. I love you too!" she called out, and blew him a kiss.

Cordell watched her disappear through the door. Shaking his head, he grumbled to himself, "There's nothing to worry about. After all, what could possibly go wrong?"

For over an hour Libby argued with Katherine. At first Katherine was adamantly opposed to such an outrageous notion as tricking her father into believing she and Cordell were married.

"It won't work! My father will find out; he's much too perceptive; he'll know something's wrong. Besides, even if it *did* work, how long could this charade go on before someone who knows you're Cordell's wife visits the ranch and destroys our precious game?"

"Stop worrying . . . it'll work. You want to remain in

338

your father's good graces, and I don't want you trying to ruin my husband. If we work together, inform the men working here at the ranch of the plan, and practice our parts, everything will be fine."

"Fine? Ha! What about the length of my father's visit?" Katherine reminded her skeptically.

"We'll give him a few days and then have one of Matilde's friends in Helena send him a telegram saying he's urgently needed back in St. Louis on business."

Katherine scratched her head. "Business always did come first with my father . . . but I just don't know. He'd eventually learn the truth. What then?"

"He doesn't have to know the truth ever. You can wait a few months and then return to St. Louis, and tell your father that you divorced Cordell."

"Why would I do that?"

"You've always been good at excuses. You'll think up something reasonable by then," Libby urged. "Your father has always accepted your explanations before, you told me as much."

"True . . . but—"

"Aunt Matilde can give credence to whatever story you come up with. You said yourself that they've been friends for years. It'll work. I know it!"

Katherine gazed out the gingham-curtained window at the miles and miles of nothing but outbuildings, a tidy vegetable garden, and an assortment of filthy animals. Suddenly she almost changed her mind.

She longed for the excitement of the city, the hustle and bustle . . . she craved a return to the pampered life. She'd been a wealthy young lady, admired and sought after by the most eligible of swains; she'd reveled in having her every desire satisfied by a bevy of servants. Knowing she could never adjust to life as a rancher's wife, even after Cordell was elected to a seat in government, Katherine condescendingly agreed to the scheme.

"Don't worry. With Cordell's cooperation and Aunt Matilde's help, your father will never suspect a thing," Libby said.

"He'd better not, or I'll make sure that the whole sordid story appears in every newspaper from Deer Lodge to St. Louis," Katherine threatened. "And you can start our little charade now by readying my room and personally seeing that I have a hot tub and fresh clothing waiting for me when I've finished the meal you are going to prepare. Um, let me see . . . I'll have two eggs, ham, and muffins. Oh, and grind some of those coffee beans over there," she pointed toward an open sack on the counter. "I've been waiting to be offered proper hospitality ever since I arrived."

Libby pursed her lips, but went about the task. She'd have liked nothing more at that moment than to shove Katherine out the back door and lock it. There was no doubt in Libby's mind that Katherine would be insufferable, demanding, and generally impossible. Libby scooped up a handful of coffee and cranked the grinder with a vengeance.

Katherine drummed her fingers on the arm of her chair while Libby heated the water and brewed the coffee. Katherine waited until the steaming cup was placed at her fingertips, then casually looked up, her eyes glittering, and snipped, "Where's the fresh cream?"

"There isn't any."

"Well, I can't drink this."

Libby sucked in her cheeks, which flamed with fire. Her calm exterior did not give way to the inner fury she felt in that moment. Instead of giving in to the urge to leave fingerprints on Katherine's milky white neck, Libby settled into the chair next to Katherine and smiled. "Then don't." Libby quietly reached for the cup and, to Katherine's utter surprise, sipped its contents.

Katherine's eyes narrowed ominously. "*I* suggest —"

"No!" Libby cut her off. "*I* suggest you remember that you have a lot to lose if you're not careful."

Katherine threw back her head and laughed. The little twit had just challenged her to a game of wits. "My, my . . . I do believe that the next couple of weeks are going to prove very interesting. Very interesting indeed."

Chapter Fifty-one

The sun had just risen over the horizon and promised a day to rival the hottest of summer when Libby stepped from the house and bid Cordell a lingering good-bye.

Libby delighted in the warm rays on her back as she strolled among the thick patches of buffalo grass and sprigs of wildflowers after watching him ride out toward the range. A basket dangling on her arm, she snatched sprigs from the bright colored assortment and dropped them into the wicker container; they'd make the perfect bouquet for the dining table.

"Libby. Libby, child," Matilde sang out from the rear porch, and waved Libby back toward the house. Impatient for the girl's return, Matilde barreled across the yard, wiping her hands on the once snowy-white apron now streaked from her efforts at cooking. "I've been trying to fry that infernal bacon, but all it does is spit at me. Much like that *houseguest* of ours," she said plaintively. "I'll be so relieved when Gulch, Murphy, and the rest of the men return. I don't know *why* Cordell had to go and insist on surveying the herd just now." The impish sparkle in her eyes left no doubt that she knew exactly why Cordell had removed himself from the ranch this morning—the constant bickering was more than anyone could endure. "Look at these nails." She splayed her fingers out in front of her. "Less than a week ago, I sported a manicure of perfection. Oh, well." She sighed.

Libby hid a grin. "Come on. I'll finish getting breakfast while you sit and talk to me."

As they returned to the house and Matilde took a place at the table, she continued her objections.

"What about that lazy good-for-nothing staying with us? Oh, I *wish* Addison would hurry and arrive so we could get this over with. I *never* should have agreed to such a scheme. I thought he'd have been here by now."

A little more than two days before, Matilde had stood horrified by Libby's plan to trick Addison Rutcliff into believing his daughter and Cordell were married. It had taken a lot of convincing, but the older woman had finally accepted her role in the plot.

"I simply can't go along with such a subterfuge. Addison is a longtime friend. Why, I'd *never* be able to hold my head up again if this got out. No . . . I won't be a party to this," Matilde insisted.

"Aunt Matilde—" Katherine began, joining them.

"I am not your aunt. By the way, how could a young woman of your breeding behave as you do?" Matilde cut in.

In the midst of yet another squabble, the door opened and Cordell came into the kitchen.

Libby's exasperation was obvious to him as he returned unexpectedly for the tally sheet he'd forgotten. Unable to ignore his wife's tense expression and leave her to settle the problem, he scrapped his plans for the day. He took over and defused the tension with his usual panache.

"Aunt Matilde, dear, Libby's plan will allow everyone concerned to save face. Addison will go home a happy man. And six or eight months from now, Katherine can go home and tell her father she obtained a quiet divorce." Cordell continued to reassure all parties until everyone but himself was satisfied. He itched to take

343

Katherine by the scruff of the neck and boot her off his property. But he'd agreed for Libby's peace of mind and would see this outlandish plan through.

All parties apparently mollified, the waiting for Addison Rutcliff's arrival began in earnest. After two more days at home, Cordell threw up his hands. Refereeing three women was more than any normal man could handle, so he packed his gear and rode out to the range to join Murphy and Gulch as he'd intended earlier, wisely leaving Libby in charge of preparations.

"Where's my breakfast?" Katherine shouted at the two women standing near the barn.

Libby cast a harried Matilde a sympathetic nod of understanding and with purposeful steps strode to the house. She pushed past Katherine, standing with her hands on her hips, still in her blue satin robe.

"Well?" Katherine demanded.

Libby whirled on her. "If you want to eat, the first thing you'll have to do is get dressed. Then take yourself out to the chicken coop and collect the eggs." Katherine bristled and opened her mouth to retort, but Libby silenced her. "This is a working ranch, not a luxury hotel. As long as you choose to remain under this roof, you will be required to make yourself useful."

Unimpressed, Katherine indifferently wound an errant curl around her finger. "People of your class were born to make yourselves useful for the benefit of people of mine."

Libby's fists clenched. Katherine had been trying to provoke her every chance she got. "Yes, history has numerous examples of what has happened to the upper classes who've shared opinions similar to yours and had no appreciation for the feelings of others. Take, for example, Marie Antoinette."

Katherine subconsciously rubbed the back of her neck. She hadn't been able to better the twit since she'd arrived. Taking in an indignant breath, she jutted out her chin and huffed, "Well, I no longer want to eat, anyway. I've lost my appetite. I'm going back to bed."

A mischievous smile pulled at Libby's lips. "Pity. Aunt Matilde and I were just about to have cake. Since you have been putting on weight, it's just as well you've lost your appetite."

"Why, you—" Katherine snarled at the implication of the beheaded queen's infamous words, and at the reference to her growing stomach. In a huff, she stormed from the kitchen. Of course she was putting on weight; she was pregnant. That was another story. According to her best calculations, the baby was due in approximately four and a half months. An evil smile came to her lips. She'd take care of that little problem at the right time.

"What was all that about cake?" a bewildered Matilde asked, coming into the house.

"Oh . . . nothing. I just thought perhaps you and I might enjoy some for breakfast."

By late afternoon the three women sat in the parlor, surrounded by an uneasy, unspoken truce. Matilde was knitting blue booties for the baby she planned to spoil as soon as her nephew got down to serious business and got his wife with child. Katherine sat regally in a corner chair, reading a dime novel she'd obtained from the luggage the twit had been using as her own. Libby moved about the room, dusting and polishing furniture she'd already rubbed to a glowing shine.

Fully expecting to pass another day waiting for Addison Rutcliff, the three women were biding their time with an effort at civility. The thud of hooves clopping into the yard broke the stillness. Libby rushed to the door and swung it open thinking Cordell had changed his mind and returned early as he had before.

"Cord—" Libby started to call out, then broke off as two strangers approached in a wagon drawn by two fine matched bays.

Katherine was right behind Libby and pushed her aside when she recognized one of the men. *"Papa!"* she cried and ran to greet the older man.

"You sure about this, girl?" Matilde asked Libby as she watched Katherine. "You can still rethink this foolishness."

"It's not foolishness, Aunt Matilde. It's the only way I can make sure she doesn't destroy Cordell's future."

"That one can't hurt Cordell. Don't you ever believe it," Matilde insisted. But the plea in Libby's eyes stayed any further comment. "All right, let's go welcome Cordell's 'father-in-law.' "

Katherine glowed when Addison climbed down and enveloped her in his arms. "Daughter, I am so terribly proud of you." Tears welled in his eyes. "You have managed to turn your life around. All the way upriver I worried that I'd made an awful mistake. But after I talked to the Kohrses in Fort Benton and accompanied them to their ranch—they were kind enough to provide my transportation here—I knew I'd done the right thing, sending you to marry Chandler."

It was the first time Libby had ever noticed Matilde act shy and retiring. The older woman inched forward to greet Katherine's father. An unaccustomed blush heightened Matilde's color and caused her voice to squeak when she greeted, "It's so good to see you again, Addison."

He took Matilde's hands in his and said with a catch of emotion, "Matilde, I can't *tell* you how happy this old man is right now."

"Oh, Addison, your Katherine is." She sent Katherine a look meant to scorch, but Katherine only smirked, knowing she had the upper hand. "So much more than I . . . ah . . . we ever could have imagined. I can't put

346

into words how I feel having her here."

Libby hung in the background while Matilde directed the unloading of Addison's bags and an assortment of gift boxes, then dismissed the wagon driver with a message to thank the Kohrses for so graciously providing Mr. Rutcliff an escort. The threesome chatted and Katherine gave her father a tour of the yard and outbuildings, bragging about her plans to improve the house, proudly describing all the work she'd already done.

"Only in your dreams," Libby said behind her hand.

"What did you say, miss?" Addison asked, turning to the beautiful dark-haired girl who, in a soft way, resembled his own daughter.

"Her? Surely you can't be referring to my maid," Katherine snipped.

"If I were you, daughter, I'd think twice about having such a lovely creature in the same house." Addison chuckled at the joke he'd made, but Katherine was not amused.

"Libby, sir. My name's Libby."

"You needn't concern yourself about her, Papa. She's leaving in the morning anyway. Cordell hired her so I wouldn't have to keep house. But I plan to take care of my husband all by myself." Triumph glowed in Katherine's face.

"Cordell will never allow that," Matilde said, astounded by Katherine's nerve.

"If Katherine wants to begin taking responsibility for her own home, why not?" Addison asked, proud of his daughter's display of initiative.

"Yes. Why not, *Auntie* Matilde?" Katherine parroted.

"Well . . . well, because Cordell hired Libby here to help me as well. And I, for one, certainly don't intend to do without help," Matilde quickly added.

Addison took Katherine's and Matilde's arms and walked them toward the house. "No one could ever ask that you do without, Mattie. Oh, and Libby, would you

347

see that one of the hands takes my luggage to my room?"

Libby's gaze shot to the pile of leather and boxes the driver had unloaded outside the fence. "You certainly don't believe in traveling light, sir," she observed.

"No. Not when I intend to be spending several months with my daughter and her new husband."

"Several months?" Libby mimicked, dismayed. Cordell was going to be furious when he found out.

"Yes. I've worked long and hard enough, neglecting my daughter for far too long. From now on I plan to spend my time making up for it." He turned to Katherine. "Guess I should have mentioned it in my telegram. But enough of that; I want you to unwrap your wedding gifts as soon as I get settled."

Libby's shoulders slumped. What had she gotten them all into?

When Cordell hadn't returned by seven-thirty, Katherine ordered Libby to serve dinner by eight. Matilde gasped, but kept still under Libby's warning gaze.

"Libby, set out the good silver tonight. We'll be celebrating," Katherine ordered. A sudden idea flickered into her mind and her eyes sparked. "And we'll have *cake* for dessert tonight. Do you think you can manage that?"

Libby bit back a retort and meekly nodded before scurrying from the room to throw a quick cake together. As she got to the door, she heard Addison Rutcliff say, "Aren't you expecting a lot from the girl?"

"Hardly. She's just a servant." A vengeful smile spread over her lips. "Besides, she likes cake. She said as much herself this morning."

Libby smoldered all the while she fried the potatoes and put the thick steaks into the pan. Katherine had been demanding and totally unreasonable from the moment her father had arrived. *Remember, this was your idea,* a small voice lectured. *You've come too far to let her upset you. Eventually she'll be gone and you'll have the rest of your life with Cordell.* Another thought intruded into her mind. *Sure you will, silly girl. You'll have Cordell, until he finds out what you did to the reverend. Then just how long do you think he'll let you stay? You lied to him. He'll never trust you again.*

Her steps heavy with the burden she carried, Libby managed to set a mighty fine table, the crowning touch a bouquet bursting with color. She'd picked it that morning. The lamps lit, the candles flickering, Libby stood back and surveyed her work. The dining room was spacious. In the middle, an enormous mahogany table and a heavy sideboard graced a fine braided carpet. On the wall a huge elk reflected its majestic beauty in a gilded mirror.

As Libby was straightening the forks, Katherine, escorted by her father and followed by a chattering Matilde, entered the room. "I ordered dinner for eight. Why isn't it ready?" she demanded.

Libby bit back an answer. "I thought you'd want to wait for Cor . . . ah . . . Mr. Chandler."

No sooner had Libby gotten the words out than the back door crashed open. All eyes shot expectantly toward the sound. A moment later Cordell bounded through the door and down the hall, with eyes only for his wife. "Libby, darling." His voice trailed off and his outstretched arms dropped to his sides when he caught sight of the elder man stiffly glaring at h'm in question.

Chapter Fifty-two

For what seemed like an eternity, Libby held her breath as the two men scrutinized one another. Addison Rutcliff's steady gaze shifted from his daughter to his daughter's husband and then to Libby. His face remained impassive, but Libby thought she saw a interrogatory flicker in his eyes before he thrust out his arm to Cordell.

"Cordell, son." The tears of a long-held worry at last spilled into his eyes.

"Mr. Rutcliff—"

With a welcoming jab to Cordell's shoulder, Addison insisted, "Please, call me Addison."

Katherine saw her chance to begin her plan to win Cordell away from that twit and rushed forward as if on cue. With practiced innocence she clutched Cordell's arm and gazed adoringly up into his eyes. "I'm so happy finally to have my two most special men together." She reached out and pulled Addison to her. Then she reached up on tiptoe and gave Addison a peck on the cheek before she turned to Cordell and said, "I know Papa's arrival interrupted our usual routine, but haven't you forgotten something?"

Ever so slightly, Cordell narrowed his eyes at the brazen young woman. There was no doubt of her intent. She was going to use her father to try to gain an advantage every opportunity she got, and to start with, she expected him to docilely buckle under to her machinations. He freed his arm from her clinging fingers and stepped back. "Not a thing."

For an instant Katherine was tempted to shower Cordell and his whore of a wife with a string of invectives. *Have prudence, Katherine,* she told herself. As if she were scolding a young boy caught trying to snatch a cookie, Katherine teasingly reprimanded, "You naughty bridegroom, you neglected to kiss your *new wife.*"

Cordell's eyes darted to Libby, who stiffened at Katherine's bold ploy. Looking at Cordell, Libby carefully kept her pose placid and said, "If you excuse me, I'd best get supper on the table before it's stone cold."

Before Libby could make an exit, Katherine rubbed her hand up Cordell's arm. Snaking her other hand around his neck, she began to draw him to her, her tongue slowly licking her puckered lips.

Libby grabbed a water pitcher from the table and swung around so rapidly that she bumped into Katherine, drenching the front of Katherine's fine striped dress.

"Why, you imbi—" Katherine caught her sudden rush of temper and immediately calmed. "It was an accident," she amended. "Sop up the spill while Cordell and I go and change our clothing. Then you may serve dinner." She dismissed Libby with a turn of her back and suggested to the others, "Why don't you make yourselves comfortable around the table? We'll only be a moment." She paused for effect, then giggled slyly, "Unless, of course, we become otherwise engaged."

All through dinner Katherine gushed sweetness. She hung onto every word her father and Cordell uttered; she was animated, she conversed with Matilde, whose own incessant chatter displayed her anxiety. Only once did Katherine come close to losing her temper when Libby failed to offer her a second helping of dessert with the comment that Katherine should be watching her waistline.

"I've never had to watch my weight in my entire life," Katherine spat.

"It's never too late to start," Libby returned before she could stop herself. She shot a furtive glance at Cordell and was heartened when he had to choke back a grin: Katherine was, for once, on the receiving end of a sharp comment. Although Libby had never intended to behave so poorly toward another, a smile inched its way to her lips.

Never one to allow anyone the last word, Katherine gathered herself up in her chair and said haughtily, "Libby, I know this is not the most opportune time," she reached out and laid her hand over Cordell's, a nasty light in her dark eyes, "but Cordell and I have decided we won't be needing your services after tonight."

"I thought we'd settled that issue earlier," Matilde said startled, dropping her fork.

Katherine turned on her venomous charm. "Auntie Matilde, I know you require help, but you're my family now and I intend to take care of my relatives from now on."

Libby felt her throat closing from the tension. She just couldn't allow Katherine to dismiss her as if she were discarding a worn pair of slippers.

"Well, what are you standing there for? You need to get the kitchen cleaned up and pack so one of the hands can take you into town in the morning," Katherine snipped, pleased that she'd managed to settle the problem of getting that common laundress out of the house.

Libby hesitated. She could put an end to Katherine's

game, but the reflection in Katherine's eyes warned Libby that Katherine wouldn't feel the slightest reluctance at destroying Cordell's career. Libby bit her lip and turned to head back toward the kitchen when Cordell's low, menacing voice halted her retreat.

"Wait just a moment. You aren't sending Libby anywhere." Cordell proceeded to put an end to any further attempts to dislodge Libby.

For the remainder of the evening Cordell listened to the tangle of lies Katherine cheerily interlaced. Silently he cursed himself for allowing this deception and made the decision that in the morning he was going to have a conference with Addison Rutcliff and put an end to the situation once and for all.

Cordell almost had to shake his head at Matilde. Her behavior was unusual even for her, and he could only describe it as girlish. She tittered and fluttered her lashes at Addison's every word. The changes in Matilde's behavior brought vague memories of long ago, when Matilde had left for an extended tour of Europe after a broken engagement. Cordell rubbed his chin. Not Katherine's father, Addison . . .

Cordell excused himself and strolled from the house after refusing Addison's offer to accompany him for a smoke. Out in the cool night air, Cordell stuffed his hands into his coat pockets. He gazed up at the silver-studded black cloak of the night sky.

As he left the house and walked past the stables and out into the fields, a shroud of peace enveloped him with the songs of crickets, owls and coyotes. This was his home, as it was Libby's. He picked up a clod of rich brown earth, still warm from the heat of the day. His heart filled with pride and an undefinable sense of fulfillment surrounded him. Here they would raise their children, a houseful. Here they would live and love. Here he would cherish and care for Libby, and protect her from the harm he knew had been her childhood.

And here they would grow old together.

Thoughts of Libby heightened his need to hold her in his arms, to run his fingers over her silken flesh, and to make love to her. He could stand it no more; he turned to walk back toward the warm yellow light that glowed in the curtained windows.

Libby pulled the gingham curtains shut, finished wiping off the work counter, and went upstairs to her room. It was a pleasant room, done in earthy chintz and patchwork. She ran her hand gently over the bedspread, each colorful square sewn by a loving hand. A sadness enveloped her: tonight she would sleep alone beneath the blanket's padded warmth, without the man she loved lying next to her. She wouldn't be able to snuggle against him and find security in the knowledge that he really was hers.

A heaviness upon her shoulders, Libby undressed and slipped into a plain bleached muslin nightdress. A flicker of candlelight bathing her in its yellow glow, Libby was settled onto the bed when the doorknob creaked, snapping her out of her reverie.

Cordell slipped into the room. "My darling," he whispered, "I couldn't stay away from you, even for one night." His boot heels pounded across the floor and an instant later he was seated next to her, holding her in his arms.

"I'm so glad you came." Her body fit along his and she felt his uninhibited response throb against her.

Slowly, languorously, he kissed her, his tongue igniting her senses and enflaming her entire being, until she wanted nothing more than to become a united extension of the man she loved. Continuing to devour her mouth, Cordell ran fiery fingers up her thighs, gathering the yards of gown until he slipped the garment over her head.

Her hands reached out and bared his skin. The sight of his muscled nakedness never ceased to fire her insatiable hunger. Moments stood still as they explored one another until a noise outside the door called a halt to their lovemaking.

"What was that?" Libby gasped.

"What was what?" I didn't hear anything but the pounding of your heart," he said, wrenched from the heavy-lidded moments shutting out the rest of the world.

She wiggled free, wrapped herself in a blanket, and walked toward the door. "No . . . no, I'm sure I heard something."

"Come back here. Now," he ordered and stretched out his arm. Lying across the bed, Cordell presented a vision Libby had to fight against. Her eyes caressing every inch, she leaned against the door and listened, but not a sound came from the hall outside.

Without the slightest attempt to disguise his eagerness, Cordell rose and strode to Libby. "I told you to come, woman."

"But—"

"No," he murmured and with great ceremony lifted her into his arms and carried her back to bed, thrusting the quilt aside with his foot. As if she were a most delicate flower, he lowered her to the smooth, cool sheets and immediately slid his body along the length of hers.

In minutes under his ministrations her willing body was hot and moist for his. Fears of discovery slid from her mind and any thoughts about outside sounds were forgotten as the torrent of their passion exploded into a frenzied rhythm. Pulsing cascades enfolded and enthralled them as he plunged deeper and deeper into her encasing warmth until the only sounds they heard were the thunderings of their hearts.

Addison Rutcliff remained frozen against the wall in the hall outside Libby's bedroom door. There was no question in his mind about the base animal sounds echoing from that young maid's room. His daughter was still a bride and already her husband was being unfaithful to her. He'd wondered about that relationship when Chandler had first walked in. It'd seemed odd that the young man's gaze had settled on the girl instead of on his wife.

Addison stayed until he was certain his presence would not be detected, then crept downstairs. He was thankful that the house was dark. At least Matilde would not have to learn what her nephew was about. He purposefully made his way to Katherine's bedroom; light shone from under the door. She was still up . . . pacing the floor and wondering where her errant husband was, no doubt.

He scratched at the door.

Combing her long, dark hair, Katherine held a sensuous pose, expecting it to be Cordell, furious as a badger, since she'd taken it upon herself to settle into his bedroom.

When she opened the door, her sensuous pout dropped to surprise. "What? Papa!"

He pushed past her and stood inside the room, his fists clenched at his hips. "We need to talk. Hurry up and close the door."

Fear that she had been found out wrinkled her brow as Katherine followed his directive. Once they were alone in the solitude of Cordell's private sleeping quarters, Katherine mustered her courage, ready to invent yet another tale, if necessary. "What is this all about, Papa?"

His face softened and he reached for her hand. "I'm sure you must be wondering where your husband is."

"Well, I, ah—"

"It's all right." He patted her icy hand. "I'm just thankful I'm here to help you."

"To help me?"

"Yes. I understand now why you were so eager to let

Libby go. I saw Chandler go into her room earlier."

Katherine couldn't believe the nerve of the little twit. Katherine had thoroughly expected her to be brought to heel. But instead, she had shown more spunk than Katherine thought she possessed. Maybe she could turn the situation to her advantage. Katherine directed her eyes toward the floor as if in shame and sorrow, letting her father enfold her in his arms.

"I'm sorry you had to find out, Papa." She sniffled. "I've been trying so hard to handle this on my own."

"If that's the kind man Chandler is, I think tomorrow morning we'll get you packed up and leave the bastard to his little maid. You're too good for the man."

His comforting words had provided the perfect excuse to allow Katherine to return gracefully to her previous life. She would not have to come up with any more lies. She could simply leave after breakfast tomorrow. This was the intended climax to the ruse they'd planned. It would be so easy! But something held Katherine back from agreeing. Her pride had suffered. No one bested Katherine Rutcliff, let alone some twit of a launderess. No . . . Cordell Chandler was supposed to be hers, and he would be until she was ready to throw him over. But the fact was, she wanted the man and she was going to have him!

"Katherine?" Addison held her from him and looked into her troubled eyes. "Don't worry, I'll see that the marriage is annulled. I'll take care of everything. You'll see."

She sighed and forced the tears to stream down her cheeks. "I'm afraid there's one thing you can't take care of, Papa."

"There's nothing that Rutcliff money can't take care of, daughter."

"Yes there is," she cried in her most pitiful voice.

"What is it, child? You can confide in your father.

357

Tell me." He smoothed her hair and stroked her back, offering comfort and reassurance.

"Oh, Papa," a gush of sobs exploded from her, "I'm afraid I'm pregnant. I'm going to have Cordell's child."

Chapter Fifty-three

It had been a week since Addison Rutcliff had arrived, and Cordell was about ready to explode; Libby had finally broken down and told him that the man planned to stay for months. Sneaking in and out of his own wife's bedroom was wearing his nerves paper thin. He'd had to climb out the window after midnight, dressed only in a blanket when Rutcliff had come to request that Libby attend to a chore for him, and he'd been the brunt of Gulch's jokes because of it. Cordell's restraint was hanging by a thread.

If Libby hadn't pleaded with him to be patient and explained her plan to have Rutcliff receive a telegram, Katherine and her father would have been gone from the ranch the morning after the man had arrived, and their lives would have returned to normal. Then there was Matilde. She was acting like a silly schoolgirl over the elder entrepreneur. For a woman who had held herself so ably apart from interested men for years, Matilde was openly losing her heart.

"Dell," Matilde approached Cordell after dinner as he was brushing down his horse, "there's something I need to discuss with you."

"You mean about Addison Rutcliff," he glibly answered, brushing the magnificent stallion.

"How did you know?"

"The whole ranch is buzzing with it. You haven't exactly been trying to hide your feelings."

"I never told you this, but I knew Addison a long time ago—"

"You mean he's the one you were engaged to before you went away to Europe."

"My God, you were just a child then," she said, astounded, then remembered what an exceptional man Cordell was. "You've always had the most amazing memory. No one can put anything over on you, can they?" She let out a nervous, high-pitched laugh. "You don't mind, do you? I mean, Addison being Katherine's father, and you having to continue the charade a little longer—until I can figure a way out of this mire."

"Auntie, if Addison Rutcliff will make you happy, Libby and I can endure his daughter a few more days. But now you are going to have to tell him, or I shall."

Matilde clasped her hands together, delighted that Cordell would accept Addison. An instant later she hugged Cordell to her. "Don't worry, everything will work out fine. Addie has asked me to take a walk in the moonlight with him in half an hour. I'll think of something by then."

Matilde skipped off, humming. Cordell watched after her, shaking his head.

Addison laid a blanket on the porch swing for Matilde and held her elbow while she hefted herself up. As they sat together, Addison shifted his foot back and forth so they continued to rock while they talked of old times.

"I should have married you, Matilde. I was wrong to let you slip away so many years ago . . . can you ever forgive me for behaving so rashly?"

"I've never forgiven myself. You didn't know I was going to come back after I ran away. I've always been flighty," she admitted, thinking how she'd suddenly left town after he'd proposed, she'd been so afraid of commitment.

He took her hand and kissed her fingers. "Oh, Mattie, do you think two old folks like us—"

"We're only old on the outside," she insisted.

"You're not old, even on the outside. To me you will always be a beautiful, unpredictable flower. If you'll agree, after I settle this unfortunate mess Katherine has gotten herself into, we'll be wed."

Matilde was so excited that she nearly leaped off the swing. "Oh, Addison. Yes, yes, yes!" she cried. "Of course I'll marry you." In her exuberance she assumed her dilemma had miraculously been eliminated. "And you needn't concern yourself with Katherine and Cordell anymore. I'm so glad you know the truth. Now Libby and Cordell can get on with their lives, and so can we. . . ."

Addison stiffened at Matilde's babblings, but his response went unheeded as she proceeded to make her usual outrageous plans for the future. It wasn't long before Addison was wondering all over again how he could've let such a vibrant woman get away and marry Katherine's plain, passive mother, bless her soul. Life with Matilde would add spice to his existence; it would never again be dull. But first he'd have to settle up with Cordell Chandler. . . .

Cordell was bent over his account books, busily applying pen to paper, when Addison entered the spacious mahogany-paneled study. Shelves laden with books and walls hung with masterpieces painted by the most talented Western artists of the day made the room elegant, yet comfortable.

"Chandler, we need to talk," Addison said rigidly, coming to stand in front of Cordell's desk.

"Yes. I think it's about time," Cordell returned in a voice which bore no trace of his usual easy charm. "Please," he waved toward a nearby leather sofa, "make yourself at home."

Addison eschewed a seat. "I think what I have to say can better be addressed from a standing position."

"Suit yourself." Cordell put down his pen. If there was going to be a confrontation, he was ready for it. Katherine had smugly overplayed her part, attempting at every turn to undermine the bargain they had struck. The woman clung to him like a leech whenever her father was in sight. She never missed the opportunity to make Libby's life miserable with her demands and snide remarks. And he'd constantly found himself in the position of having to thwart Rutcliff's every move to have Libby sent away.

Addison hooked his thumbs in his vest. "It's about time Libby —"

Rudely, Cordell cut him off. "I'm not sending her away, if that's what this is all about. And I think it is about time —"

It was Addison's turn to interrupt. "It is about time you, my son —"

"I'm not your son."

"I'm well aware of that fact. But as I'd begun to say, I think it's about time you quit sneaking into your wife's room. I may be getting on in years, but I'm not as thick-headed as everyone here seems to think," he announced, despite the fact he'd just learned the truth — a bit of information he sagely suppressed.

Cordell cocked a brow. "So it would appear."

"Speaking of appearances, I think an explanation is in order. I want to know exactly what's been going on here. I have a right."

"Yes, you do, sir."

For over three hours the two men talked. Cordell explained the whole sordid story, leaving out nothing. It

362

was time Katherine be taken in hand, particularly if Matilde and Addison were going to be married.

Addison had been angry at first, his anger shifting from Cordell and Libby to Matilde and finally coming to settle on the culprits: Katherine and Sheldon Sharpe. While he listened to Chandler, Addison's mind drifted to thoughts of Katherine's pregnancy. Now he knew the child could not be the rancher's. That left the gambler.

Once both men had been satisfied, Addison made his apologies and went in search of Katherine.

"Here you are, daughter," Addison said silkenly when he found her curled up reading in the cheery sitting room off the parlor.

"I have to take care of myself now that I'm carrying Cordell's child," she purred.

Addison sat down on the edge of the velvet chaise and leaned toward his daughter. Everything she was was his fault. He had neglected her upbringing. "Do you remember what I told you would happen if you didn't marry Chandler?" he asked in a voice void of emotion.

Katherine's heart began to pound with dread. If that twit was responsible for this, she'd make her pay. Katherine swallowed and forced herself to stare directly into her father's eyes. "Papa, why are we having this conversation?"

"I think you already know." He held out a silencing hand. "No. Don't try to deny it. I know the truth. I want you to know that Matilde—"

"That old—"

"Don't you *dare* say a word against the woman who's going to become your stepmother. I've neglected you for too long." He shook his head sadly. "How you've turned out is no one's fault but mine. So you needn't worry that I am going to disinherit you. Whatever you are, I've created. But tell me the truth: are you carrying a child, or was that a lie too?"

Katherine was shaking, she was so distraught. Never

before had her father accepted any responsibility for her behavior, and she found his confession strangely cathartic. So many layers of hatred seemed to melt away, and suddenly she felt vulnerable for the first time since childhood. Real tears brimmed her lids and she sobbed back a cry, turning her head away.

Addison brought her chin up until their eyes met and held. There was a silent plea in her dark eyes, a cry for love and understanding so long denied that Addison had to swallow his own sobs.

"Katherine. My God, I'm so sorry!"

"Oh, Papa, can you ever forgive me?" She threw her arms around his neck, wetting the front of his finely tailored suit. "I am going to have a baby," she sobbed.

"The gambler's?"

Katherine hung her head in true humility. "You know about him too?"

"Yes, and although he isn't exactly what I had in mind for a son-in-law, your child will need its father. I think the Rutcliff name and money will offer enough influence to see that the man's sentence is commuted."

"But Papa, he's—" She'd started to say Shelley was no good, but a voice in the back of her mind made her hold her tongue. Was it possible for people to change? Had she changed? Surely she felt different. The old drive for revenge, a heated vengeance against anyone who got in her way, had faded when she'd discovered her father did indeed love her and accepted her with all her faults. Could Shelley change? Would they have a chance? In her heart she knew the answer: only time and patience, a commodity she had never heretofore possessed, would tell.

They had used each other, she and Shelley, to get what they wanted. She almost wanted to laugh out loud. Shelley wasn't aware of it yet, but he was about to become a victor of sorts. He'd finally have the riches he'd wanted, with one qualification: his activities would

364

be closely monitored for the rest of his life. Her father would make a good husband and father out of Sheldon Sharpe, or break him trying.

"He'll be my son-in-law and the newest vice president of the Rutcliff empire. Who do you think will argue with that?"

"You'd really do that for me?"

"I'm willing to try if you are."

Life at the ranch continued to be tense for another three days. Katherine had had long discussions with her father and Matilde, and at last she'd resolved any residual conflicts she'd had over marrying the father of her child. Cordell and Libby listened, at first refusing to believe Addison's solution could bring anything but more grief. But acceptance was unanimous at last, if for no other reason than for Matilde's sake and her future with the man she loved.

There was a new place at the breakfast table. Addison and Matilde sat knee to knee, holding hands beneath the table. Katherine had a more relaxed pose, and even her hair signified a softening, the way it hung in a loose knot at the back of her head. Cordell and Libby sat at each end of the table for the first time host and hostess to their houseful of guests, while Murphy took up his duties plying his cooking expertise with gusto. Even Gulch sat with his boots under the table this morning.

Once the meal was over and everyone had had his fill of eggs, ham, muffins, and hash, Katherine came to her feet. "I have something to say to everyone." She looked at her father, who gave her his nod of support and encouragement. "Cordell and Libby, I want to say I'm sorry for all the grief I've caused. To you, Matilde, I want to say that I hope we can become friends, since you will become my Auntie Matilde after all."

At that everyone laughed and accepted Katherine's apologies. Libby, in particular, offered in return, "I know we had a difficult beginning. But in a way, it is I who should thank you." All eyes turned questioning gazes of disbelief on the beautiful black-haired young woman. "Because if you hadn't insisted I take your place, I never would have married Cordell."

"Then you truly forgive me?" Katherine blurted out, still learning that people could accept her and believe that she could build a new life.

"Of course we do," Libby said. "And after you and Mr. Sharpe—"

"Shelley. Call him Shelley," Katherine urged.

"All right, Shelley. After you and Shelley are settled and have your child, we intend to visit, don't we, Cordell?"

"If it makes you happy." Cordell sent Libby a look of doubt. He still wasn't as certain of Katherine as Libby was. But since his aunt was marrying a Rutcliff, the least he could do was make an effort.

"I hate to cut this reunion short," Addison announced. "But if we're going to travel to the capital and see to Sharpe's release, we'd better be leaving, Katherine. Are you sure you don't mind waiting here while I see to my future son-in-law, Mattie? I don't want to lose you again."

In he usual buoyant manner, Matilde gushed, "I've waited for over thirty-five years, haven't I? Another month won't hurt me. Besides, I want to stay and see my nephew officially wed before I leave the ranch. I couldn't think of living in St. Louis until I make sure Dell has a woman to keep him out of trouble," she pronounced. "And don't worry . . . there's no way you're going to lose me again."

Cordell smiled fondly at Libby. "I don't know how I ever got along before Libby came into my life and turned it upside down."

"Don't you mean inside out?" Libby added, feeling a little sheepish, thinking how she had tricked him into marrying her and then proceeded to keep him from divorcing her until he no longer wanted to.

"That too."

At that, Gulch raised his coffee cup and offered a toast. "Now that all your problems are settled, may two of my favorite folk," he motioned toward Cordell and Libby, "live happily ever after."

Everyone clinked mugs. But as Libby drank, she gazed over the top of the cup at Cordell, her heart yearning. For *happily forever* for them meant only until the reverend found her and crushed their happiness under the weight of his evil heel, as if it were no more than a dried leaf.

Chapter Fifty-four

Matilde was pleased at the preparations for a formal wedding between Cordell and Libby. She'd taken over all the planning, insisting she inform everyone it was *her* idea they celebrate their vows again, so she could be in attendance this time.

To Matilde's chagrin, Cordell intruded into her plans with the announcement that, "We're going to tell everyone Libby's rightful name."

"You can't! What will they say? What will *we* say?"

"I can't speak for the good people of this territory, except to say the majority will accept Libby, since many a person got a fresh start out here on the frontier. As for what we will say, I shall tell them that we fell in love at first sight and our silly fears created a mix-up we have since resolved."

"And what do I say?"

"You'll tell everyone that you were part of the resolution. Now quit worrying." He patted her shoulder. "We'll see you at dinner. I'm taking Libby out to the range with me today," he said with a gleam in his black eyes.

"Oh, Cordell," she hailed him back. "I almost forgot. All these papers were in my way," she added to herself, shuffling through the sheets. "Here it is. Gulch brought

368

this telegram out from town with him last night. Strange." She crinkled her white brow. "It's from the sheriff at Fort Benton."

Cordell took the cable and stuffed in into his pocket, then strode to the door.

"Aren't you going to open it?" Matilde cried, astounded, eager to open it herself.

"Don't have the time. Libby's waiting."

The vibrant shrill of Cordell's whistle as he left the house caught in Matilde's ears. "Ah, love." Humming merrily to herself, she laid pen to paper and scribbled Addison's name in her flowery script; around it she traced a heart and added her own name for good measure. It wouldn't be long before she'd join Addison. All her friends who had retired from life were wrong; it was never too late to begin to live again, to love, for love knew no age barriers. Love truly was eternal.

Libby stood in the sun, dressed in frothy lemon yellow with lace sleeves, an overflowing wicker basket in her white gloved hands. Topping her outfit was a wide-brimmed hat decorated with songbirds and banded with velvet ribbon.

"Are you sure we have time to spend the whole day on a picnic?" Libby shot him her most approving smile.

"I'll always have time for you." He bent to kiss her and promptly was poked in the eye by her hat. He slapped his palm over his eye. "I thought you gave up wearing those infernal contraptions."

Libby shrugged sheepishly. "I did . . . but when I saw this in the shop window in town, I just couldn't resist. It'll grow on you."

Cordell raised his brows. "Yes, I'm afraid it might."

Cordell helped her into the carriage and they rode out over the golden hills. Dust swirled up from behind the coach wheels, lending a trail of golden haze as the black stallion trotted toward a creek about five miles from the ranch. The passing breeze warmed Libby's shoulders and lent her face a natural blush.

Libby let her gaze wander. The land as far as she could see was dotted with steers, and the farther they traveled, the more understanding she had of the strength of his feelings.

Cordell reined the horse in alongside a shady grove of tall trees and hopped down. "Here we are, love." He reached up and helped her down.

Libby giggled, then seeing the abiding affection gleaming in his black eyes, she drew his head down to her and whispered against the softness of his lips. "This is the perfect spot for a very private picnic."

Cordell gave her a long, lingering kiss, savoring his wife. "Go find a place by the creek while I unload the blanket and lunch."

He watched his wife blow him a kiss and stroll among the tall grasses and wildflowers. As he crouched down to drag the basket from beneath the seat, the telegram Matilde had handed him fell out of his shirt pocket.

Absently he opened it and read, his passing interest changing to charged disbelief.

"Libby! Libby!"

"I'm over here," she sang back, completely unaware of the edge in his voice.

When he reached her she was perched on a flat rock, dangling her hand in the icy water. "I'm simply famished," she announced, and playfully splashed at him.

Cordell ignored her and spread out the checkered cloth. "Come and sit with me, Libby. We need to talk," he urged. He'd been afraid to press her about the reverend before because he feared the answer, but he could no longer put it off; the telegram had seen to that.

At the seriousness in his tone, Libby's smile faded and a foreboding crept inside of her throat. Something had changed since they'd started out this morning. Instinctively she knew that a picnic was no longer the only reason they'd come to this secluded spot. With feet

370

suddenly heavy as lead, Libby made her way over to her husband and gingerly settled in next to him.

When he took her hand, it was as cold as the hand of a man who knows he's doomed. "It's time you told me the whole truth about yourself, Libby."

She jerked her fingers out of his grasp. "I don't know what you mean."

"I think you do."

Frantically, she tried to read his eyes, but they were fathomless. She stiffened. She wasn't going to give in to the tears lurking behind her lids. She wasn't! "I've told you all about myself."

"You've told me you had a difficult childhood after your mother married some preacher. And I know you were accused of attacking the man. Libby, I haven't insisted that you tell me about it. But I received a telegram from Fort Benton this morning, and now I have to know."

"A telegram?"

"From the sheriff. Seems a Reverend Ardsworth paid him a visit and identified you as his attacker."

"Me? How can he be sure?"

"Libby," he grasped her shoulders, "the man had your photograph. The sheriff was kind enough to alert me that the man and his wife are on their way here to fetch you. Seems Ardsworth was insistent that you be returned to St. Louis."

"Why did he tell them where to find me? *Why?*" She was close to hysterics now.

Calmly Cordell offered, "The sheriff had to; it's his duty." He studied her frightened eyes. "You must tell me what happened."

Oh, dear Lord, this wasn't really happening . . . she had fought so long for this man. She'd managed to hold his love despite tricking him into marrying her and changing identities with Katherine; he'd accepted her when he'd learned her true identity, and even supported her when Katherine and Sheldon Sharpe had tried to tear apart their delicate match. But in spite of his faith in her, he was still a man, after all. And she had lied to him when she'd promised that she'd told him all about herself.

She raised her head and studied the sky, her eyes bleary with tears. "I told you I had a difficult childhood after Mother married Reverend Ardsworth . . . that was true. Once he found out that Mother was not married to my father when I was conceived, the reverend was furious." Cordell began to draw Libby to him, but she pushed his hands away. "Please . . . no."

He waited until she had calmed herself enough to continue. "He said I was the devil's own and set about to cleanse my soul. He told me that only by putting his . . . his hands . . . on me could my soul be redeemed . . ." Barely able to proceed, Libby spilled out the entire lurid tale, no longer attempting to hold anything back.

As her voice shattered, a deadly anger glinted into Cordell's eyes and his face turned murderous with rage.

"I—I'm sorry," Libby whispered.

"Oh, God, no." Emotion filled his voice, and he yanked her into his embrace and held her to him while she cried, stroking her hair and whispering words of comfort. "You have nothing to be sorry for," he muttered.

"But I *did* attack him. He made me kneel before him," she cried, unable to stop herself as the vile images of the reverend's abuse rose up in her mind, "and when he bent his head, I grabbed a crucifix from his desk and . . . and I . . . I struck him with it. Then I ran. I ran." She sobbed uncontrollably. Cordell held her tight. He had to manage to cut off the nightmare that had returned so vividly that she was now reliving it all over again.

"It's all right, my darling. It's all right now. That man will never harm you again. *Never,*" he said, the timbre in his voice hard as stone.

"But he has the law behind him."

"And you have me."

Libby searched his face. "You still want me?"

Tears threatened to engulf him and he had to swallow them back. "My, God—want you? I love you. You're my wife. And you'll always be my love."

"Are you sure you still want to marry me again?" she asked, disbelief and hope mirrored in her blue eyes.

"More than ever."

"But what about the reverend?"

"Don't worry. The ceremony will be over long before he gets anywhere near the ranch. Then I'll see to this Reverend Ardsworth. . . ."

Reverend Ardsworth stood purple-faced, his meaty hands clenched in rage. "What do you mean you won't have a hand in arresting her?" he demanded of the marshal who stood before him. "My wife and I have been forced to travel all the way from St. Louis to this godforsaken town called Helena, and now you tell me I'll have to go to some hick rancher and bring her back here myself!"

"I believe that's what I said." Marshal Hillard stood firm, his gaze darting to the nervous woman with fresh bruises on her face who was now wringing her hands in the doorway of his office.

"This is an outrage!" the reverend bellowed. "If you refuse to do anything, I'm sure there's someone in this city who will see that justice is done."

"This here is a law-abiding town, mister. And there's none better than Cordell Chandler. As I told you before, he's the one you'll have to see. There's nothing more I or anyone else here intend to do for you," the marshal said blandly, holding his ground. Dell was too well liked and influential. There wasn't a man around who would ride out to Chandler's ranch and try to take away the man's wife. Not in Helena, let alone Deer

Lodge.

The marshal watched the big preacher whirl around and stomp from his office. He knew something had been going on, the way Matilde had asked for his help with that gambler and the Rutcliff woman. He sat back on his chair and put his feet up on the worn desk. He sure wouldn't want to face Cordell Chandler from the business end of a gun. And he wondered how that sour preacher would fare when he did. To his mind, there was a unwritten code out here: a man didn't take another man's horse or wife without expecting to meet his maker. He wondered how that professed man of God planned to handle it.

Chapter Fifty-five

Libby parted the curtains and gazed out across the yard. She still couldn't believe all the people who had arrived from Deer Lodge, Helena, Fort Benton, and many faraway ranches. She had balked at first when Cordell had suggested the wedding ceremony. But now she was pleased he'd insisted on it.

The fence was laced with a variety of flowers bursting with color. Tables had been set up underneath the trees, and four sides of beef turned slowly on spits attended by Murphy and Gulch, who was standing awkwardly in his best suit. There were at least two hundred finely dressed guests clustered about.

Joy threatened to overwhelm her. Before Cordell had suddenly left to go into town last night, he'd gathered everyone together for a night of celebration, and with Libby at his side had told them plainly about her identity. She was amazed that after a few gasps everybody but the widow Spencer had accepted the explanation without question. Of course, dear Augusta Kohrs had added her support, which helped put to rest any concerns. Libby smiled to herself. Augusta had even managed to allay the widow Spencer's mutterings.

Libby wasn't so naive that she didn't know Cordell had enemies and they wouldn't hesitate to use the knowledge of who she was and how she'd tricked Cordell. But she wasn't going to let such thoughts mar her wedding day.

Matilde bustled into the room. "What are you frowning for? It's gorgeous outside, and you're about to marry the most wonderful man in the world, beside Addison, of course," she added girlishly. Dressed in an outlandish silver gown to rival Libby's hourglass confection of embroidered silk and lace, accented by pleated peplum and scalloped tiers, Matilde fussed with the veil. "Now, let me see you smile, girl. It's time for you to join your husband and repeat those sacred vows."

The instant Libby stepped into the sun, Cordell joined her. The guests had taken their seats and waited expectantly as the roughing-looking, robed minister took his place, a Bible clutched in his hands.

"Are you ready to try this again?" Cordell smiled down at her.

Libby looked around.

"What are you looking for?"

"The fainting couch."

Cordell chuckled. "You won't find one within a hundred miles. There's no way I'm going to let you even *think* about changing your mind."

"Me? I was afraid you might decide to use it this time."

"Never. Ready?"

"Whenever you are." She beamed up at him.

Cordell tucked her hand in his and held it as he ushered Libby down the aisle himself.

When the couple stood before him, the preacher proceeded with the ceremony. Shading his aging eyes from the brilliant sun, he asked, "You two sure everything's on the up and up this time around?"

"We're sure," Cordell answered easily, unperturbed by the levity of the preacher Matilde had obtained.

"And you, missy . . . is there anything you want to confess before I pronounce you two married this time?"

Libby stifled a smile, trying to honor this solemn occasion. But a grin bubbled to her lips. "No. Nothing, sir."

"Well, then, if there's no one to object to this marriage, and there better not be, since they already been married once before," the man improvised to the delight of the boisterous crowd, "by the power invested in me, I now pronounce you two lovebirds married—a second time."

Cordell gave Matilde a clandestine nod, which sent her scurrying from the celebration and toward the barn. He then lifted Libby's veil and cupped her upturned face. As he bent to kiss her, he whispered, "Now there'll never be any doubt that you'll always be mine."

Ignoring the spectators, Libby rasped with great emotion, "We'll always be together."

With all the hooting and hollering during and immediately after Cordell and Libby became man and wife, no one had noticed the late arrival of two uninvited guests. Pushing his way past the throng pressing to congratulate the couple, Reverend Elijah Ardsworth boomed in an arrogant voice, "I'm afraid that you won't always be together, since you, Elizabeth Marie Hollis, will be spending your days in a prison in St. Louis for brutally attacking a man of the cloth—me!"

With the swiftness of a lightning bolt, Cordell reacted. He pushed Libby behind him. "Then we'll both have to be arrested for attacking *a man of the cloth*." He drew back his fist and with a single blow sent the reverend sprawling in the dirt.

An instant silence fell over the celebration and a dark pall seemed to enshroud the guests. Regardless of the pain in his jaw, Elijah Ardsworth was not about to give up. He'd come too far not to claim what was rightfully his. Anger welled in his heart at the thought that the girl had lain with another man; he wanted to have her all to himself. But once he got her alone, he'd make her pay. He'd cleanse her evil soul and drive the devil from that luscious body of hers.

Elijah shot daggers of hatred at his wife, who was cowering off to the side; the last beating he'd given her had quashed any independent notions she'd had. Maybe he'd dispose of the used-up hag and take her daughter to his bed permanently. Holding his chin high, Elijah crawled to his feet and dusted off his clothes.

"How *dare* you strike a man of religion? I've come to save you." He pointed an accusing finger at Libby, who had rushed to her mother's side and stood with a protective arm around Marie's thin shoulders. "Those two spawns of the devil bring evil to all the lives they touch." As he continued to preach in his fiery manner, Elijah noticed he had the crowd's attention. He always could incite the pathetic dullards to his cause. He could feel the texture of doubt he'd woven, and he tasted his victory. Their apparent acquiescence only served to stir him on in his verbal attack.

Punctuating the reverend's ravings, Cordell jumped into the foray, launching his own attack. "I think you would be wise to stop your vicious lies before you're unable to continue." He stalked toward the big man, who held up a cross as if to ward the rancher off, but Gulch grabbed Cordell's arm.

Libby tightened her hold on her mother as the battle raged around them. "Come, let me help you into the house."

"You're not taking her anywhere. You're *both* coming back to St. Louis with me," Elijah sneered, directing his attention to the two women.

"Like hell." Cordell wrenched free of Gulch, jumped Elijah, and began pummeling the man, overturning chairs and sending tables crashing into the dust.

The ensuing fight was so intense that Marshal Hillard, in attendance for the joyous occasion, unholstered his gun and fired two shots into the air. "That'll be enough. I think it's 'bout time we get to the bottom of this," he hollered, moving to stand over the pair.

In spite of the lawman's efforts, it took four men to pull Cordell off Elijah and another two to hold the reverend back. "Arrest that man, marshal!" Elijah demanded.

"I think you'd best explain yourself," the marshal said none-too-kindly to the thickset man, although he'd already heard part of the tale back in Helena.

"This will speak for itself." Elijah unfolded the warrant he carried with him. With it he presented the *Wanted* poster. "Now, I expect you to do your duty."

The marshal's brows drew together while he studied the documents. " 'Fraid these *do* look to be official, Dell. I may be forced to arrest your wife—" he felt compelled to say, unable to forestall it any longer.

"And Chandler too," Elijah cut in. "I also intend to press charges against him."

"Why, you—" Cordell struggled.

"Dell!" A finely dressed woman whom Libby recognized from the crowd on the docks at Fort Benton stepped forward. "Do you want me to tell my story now?"

Cordell's men released him. "Yes, Josey, I think everyone will find what you have to say most informative."

Josey Mariner cleared her throat. "Well, after hearin' Dell's announcement 'bout his wife's runnin' for her life from a man who'd tried to hurt her in St. Louis, me and Birdie got ta puttin' our heads together. When Dell first fetched his wife after the steamer docked back in Fort Benton, we'd been talkin' 'bout a man I'd heard of in Toledo years before. He'd done nearly the same thing to some young girl—attacked her, I mean. Well, it seemed a strange coincidence, so I up and told Dell."

"Thanks, Josey," Cordell said.

Beginning to sweat, Reverend Ardsworth demanded,

379

"What does one woman's tale have to do with this? I recommend you do your duty, Marshal, without further delay!"

The marshal looked to Cordell. "Dell? Can you shed any light on this?"

"After talking to Josey, I went into town last night and did some checking. I think these posters I discovered are self-explanatory." He thrust the old *Wanted* flyers into the sheriff's hands.

"He looks much younger, but there's no mistaking him," the marshal said of a frowning Elijah Ardsworth. " 'Course, his name weren't Ardsworth then." The curious guests pressed forward. "It's all right, folks . . . these old, outstanding warrants bear out Josey's story. Seems that one's wanted for masquerading as a preacher and harming young girls in three separate towns before settling in St. Louis."

At Ardsworth's hiss of breath, Cordell's menacing tone silenced him. "You're all through ever trying to hurt anyone again."

"Even men in prison don't take kindly to what you done," yelled out one of the men, waving a fist. The man's anger was seconded with a "yeah, you'll get yours" from several others.

After the guests settled back down and Cordell brushed off the fine formal jacket he wore, the marshal scratched his head and quizzed, "Why didn't you show me these in the first place, Dell, and avoid all the fightin' and rough stuff on your weddin' day?"

"And deny myself the opportunity to beat the sh—ah, pardon me, ladies—*stuffing* out of that poor excuse for a human being when he showed up?" Cordell spat the words, his eyes boring into Ardsworth, who silently hung his head in defeat.

"See what you mean. All right, boys, take that yellow-tailed sack of dung away." The marshal turned to Libby and her mother. "You ladies don't ever need to worry yourselves 'bout that one, again. He'll be locked away in prison 'til his bones rot off his stinkin' carcass."

Chains were roughly clamped on Elijah's ankles and wrists, and a rope was strung around his neck at Cordell's direction. Just in case Ardsworth tried to escape, justice could be carried out swiftly at the base of the nearest tree.

"My, my . . . what was *that* all about?" Matilde questioned. She held a furry, squirming puppy. "Have I missed something?" She nodded in the direction of the four men roughly hauling a battered man off in chains.

"Nothing of any importance," Cordell answered and winked at Libby.

"In that case, who is this?" Matilde asked, still bemused at the overturned chairs and upset tables.

"This is my mother," Libby said proudly, "Marie *Hollis*.

"She'll be living with us," Cordell interjected as Libby's eyes filled with tears of gratitude.

"Thank you," Libby quickly whispered to her understanding husband. Libby finished the introductions. "Mother, this is Cordell's aunt, Matilde Chandler."

"Welcome to your new home," Matilde offered. "There isn't a better one nor better people to be found anywhere," she said with genuine sorrow; she would miss the young couple. "Since I'll be leaving, I'm happy they'll have someone to watch over them and keep them out of trouble," she rattled on an endless stream of praises. As if she had forgotten proper protocol she paused and said, "You'll forgive me, my dear, if I don't shake your hand. It seems," she shot Cordell a silent plea, "I have my hands full at the moment."

The timid woman, her face streaked with tears, nodded while Matilde noticed the way Gulch was hovering over her and seeing to her needs. They'd make a nice pair, Matilde decided. Perhaps she'd see to the match before she left to join Addison.

"If you aren't going to take this mangy mongrel off my hands, Dell, I'm just going to have to send it back to where you got it," she instructed. When he didn't take the animal immediately, she added, "Well, are you going to give your wife the gift you have for her or not?"

Libby's eyes shot to the puppy with the overgrown paws. "You mean it's mine?" she cried out and reached to take the floppy-eared pup in her arms.

The pup quieted, as if it knew where it belonged. It stretched out its tongue and slurped the tears of joy streaming down Libby's face. "How did you know?" Libby managed in between licks.

"Do you remember on the trail when you tried to adopt that coyote pup?"

"Of course I remember," she cried, recalling how he'd returned the young animal to its mother after stopping Binkley from killing it. "Oh, thank you . . . thank you. I couldn't have asked for a better gift."

She sniffled as Cordell enfolded her and the pup into his embrace and tried to kiss his wife, only to have the pup yelp and stick its head up between them so that Cordell ended up pressing his lips to the animal's muzzle instead.

Everyone roared with laughter while Libby set the insistent pup down. Then cheers went up as Cordell gave his wife a kiss that the territory would long talk about.

Matilde was beginning to blush at the length of their display of affection and finally interrupted them with two glasses of champagne in hand. "It's time for a toast."

"That it is." Cordell took the glasses and offered one to his bride. "To my wife. My love, my joy, my life.

With you by my side, there's nothing we can't do."

Matilde sipped the bubbly liquid, then turned a proud face to Cordell. "Didn't I tell you I'd pick the best woman for you?"

Cordell rolled his eyes and laughed, thinking about the wonderful old lady's matchmaking efforts. He winked at Libby, who returned a knowing smile. Then hugging her to him, he said, "That you did, Auntie dear. That you did."